My Single Friend

Jane Costello

**POCKET
BOOKS**

LONDON • SYDNEY • NEW YORK • TORONTO

First published in Great Britain by Pocket Books, 2010
An imprint of Simon & Schuster UK Ltd
A CBS COMPANY

11

Simon & Schuster UK Ltd
1st Floor
222 Gray's Inn Road
London WC1X 8HB

www.simonandschuster.co.uk

Simon & Schuster Australia
Sydney

A CIP catalogue record for this book
is available from the British Library

ISBN 978-1-84739-625-9

Typeset by M Rules
Printed and bound by CPI Group (UK) Ltd, Croydon, CR0 4YY

For my parents, with much love

Acknowledgements

My sincere thanks, as ever, to the brilliant people who've worked behind the scenes to make *My Single Friend* happen.

I'm indebted to my agent Darley Anderson for his invaluable advice and support and to his Angels – particularly Maddie, Zoe and Caroline.

It is a tremendous privilege to be working with the people at Simon and Schuster. I am especially grateful to Suzanne Baboneau and my editor Libby Yevtushenko, with whom I simply love working. You've helped make My Single Friend sparkle and, together with Joan Dietch, my eagle-eyed copy-editor, saved me from more clangers than I'd care to reveal.

Big thanks also to publisher Julie Wright, as well as the enthusiastic and talented people working in the sales, marketing and art departments.

Finally, a mention for my family: my parents Jean and Phil, my brother Stephen and soon-to-be sister-in-law Barbara and my children Otis and Lucas, both of whom are perfect in every way. Most of the time.

Chapter 1

Some might say I don't need another pair of glossy black shoes with a to-die-for heel. Particularly when, to the untrained eye, there are eight similar pairs fighting for space under my bed.

Others might point out that the success of a first date is rarely to do with the quality of the protagonists' footwear. That you're as likely to meet the love of your life in 99p flip-flops as in glorious sling-backs that cost . . . well, let's not dwell on the cost. Let's dwell instead on Sean, with whom I am going on a date this evening. The gorgeous, intelligent, chisel-jawed, tight-bummed Sean. That way, you'll understand about the shoes – and why, despite my strict rule that a first date will *never* result in sex, I have removed all trace of extraneous body hair so that my bikini area now resembles that of a Californian porn star. Just in case.

The dazzling shoes and enthusiastic depilation are but elements of a routine with which I've become extremely familiar in the last eight months. It was then that I was thrust back onto the dating scene with the eye-opening jolt of someone who'd spent the previous year in a relationship. A 'steady' relationship that turned out to be not as steady as I'd thought when I found out that my beloved was sleeping with his sister's best friend.

Still, being newly-single has its benefits, as my friend Dominique never tires of telling me – though admittedly, she's a nymphomaniac. 'Think of the fun you'll have looking for the next one,' she points out. 'And . . . think of the *shoes*!' I have to admit, the shoes always had their appeal.

Trouble is, after six and a half months of dating I'm starting to realize that I'm not very good at it. In fact, judging by how few first dates have resulted in *second* ones, I'm positively abysmal.

It's not that I can't get people to go out with me, it's what happens afterwards that's the problem – the date itself.

Dominique says I'm trying too hard. My other friend Erin insists I've just been unlucky. And Henry – my best friend for almost twenty years and flatmate for four – tells me I should be myself. Let them get to know *The Real Me*. Which is one of the reasons that I worry for him, because why would anyone want to go out with The Real Me?

The Real Me doesn't have a glass of sparkling water between every alcoholic drink, has never read anything by Chekhov, hardly ever washes her make-up brushes and doesn't help out at a centre for the homeless each weekend.

That, obviously, is not the Me on show tonight as I prepare to meet Sean, whom I encountered last week at a networking event in Liverpool, which is where I live and work. Even allowing for the fact that most of our conversation was about PR strategies for professional services, the chemistry was electrifying.

No, the Me on show tonight is the well-read, witty, charming Me, the one whose incredible shoes would make SJP look like Susan Boyle, pre-makeover. The me I want to be.

It's a mild evening for January and I have a good feeling about tonight.

My dark-blonde bob is satisfyingly bouncy (which it *should* be, given I put in heated rollers five hours ago) and, after a drastic post-Christmas diet, my size twelve Karen Millen dress just about fits. As long as I don't breathe out.

I see Sean the second I walk into the bar. It's one of my favourite venues – *Alma de Cuba*, a spectacular former church converted into the most stylish drinking hole imaginable.

It's dimly-lit and incredibly warm, so much so that I feel beads of sweat prick on my forehead almost immediately. I straighten my back and head towards him, imagining how Audrey Hepburn might enter a room. My feet stay firmly inside the new shoes instead of slipping up and down like they did before I followed a cunning trick I read in a magazine – to stick a blob of Blu-Tack under my heels. At least, it's an *adaptation* of the trick: I couldn't lay my hands on any Blu-Tack but I did find an old pack of bubblegum in the back of the kitchen drawer. After a few chews it stuck fast to the heels of my stockings and is working a treat. Note that the Me on show tonight is wearing stockings, as opposed to the more practical but considerably less sexy tights that The Real Me usually wears.

He looks up and smiles. It's a heart-stopping smile, a wide, sparkly-eyed, face-lit-up sort of smile. But I don't go to pieces, oh no. Instead, I allow the subtle trace of recognition to dance fleetingly across my face.

'Hello, Lucy. You look beautiful,' he says, kissing my cheek. 'Great shoes.'

I have to physically restrain myself from falling to my knees and declaring my undying love for this man and his exquisite taste in footwear.

Instead, I slide onto the stool and reveal a flicker of a smile. 'Thank you. You've obviously got good taste.' I suddenly realize how that sounds.

'I mean about the shoes,' I add hastily. 'Um, not about me. Looking beautiful, I mean. Although, obviously, that's not such a bad thing either. Clearly. But, you know . . . I'm not an ego-maniac or anything. Ha!'

He looks bemused. 'What can I get you to drink?' he asks, to my relief.

'White wine, please.' I regain my composure. 'A Chenin Blanc.'

'Coming up,' he smiles.

Feeling decidedly hot – a sensation exacerbated by the presence of the ravishing Sean – I slip off the backs of my shoes and place my heels on the footrest of my stool. There's no way I'm letting the over-zealous heating in this place make my feet puff up like they do anywhere more temperate than Blackpool.

As Sean turns to catch the attention of the barman I surreptitiously scrutinize his features. He is stunning. I am *so* punching above my weight.

'You still busy at work?' he asks.

'Oh yes,' I tell him brightly. 'But I can't complain about that.'

'Definitely not, when you've won all the best clients in Liverpool.'

Hee hee! He thinks I'm a high-flyer!

'I've been lucky,' I say modestly. 'But what about you? How's life at Stratton Bell?'

We spend the next half-hour engaged in a tantalizing

4

mixture of work-talk (which I don't mind as he seems to think I'm a PR genius) and lovely, flirty, pulse-quickening first-date talk. As he stands to whisk me to the restaurant across the road, I couldn't feel more optimistic if he'd started musing about venues for our first child's christening.

'Shall we?'

I take his hand and prepare to glide gracefully to his side. But as I go to stand, I suddenly realize that I'm not going anywhere. I realize that . . . *oh shit* . . . I'm stuck.

Clamping both heels on the footrest of my stool was not a good move – not when there's a big blob of bright pink gum on each.

I try to pull the right one away but it stretches and stretches and, despite my efforts to disengage, it continues stretching until it's flapping round my shins like a ridiculously-proportioned Hoover-belt.

'Ooh, um, sorry . . . give me a sec.' With blazing cheeks, I plonk my head between my knees and attempt to untangle myself.

'Are you all right?' he asks, peering down in bewilderment. 'Can I help?'

'No!' I cry, dementedly winding up reams of gunk and attempting to pick the remainder from my sole. 'Just a little, um . . . shoe issue. I'll have it sorted in no time.'

'Please, let me help,' he says gallantly, reaching down.

'No!' I snap, grabbing my left ankle and yanking it upwards as if wrenching a plunger out of the U-bend of a toilet.

'Really, if you'd just let me help, I—'

'No!' I shriek, rather louder than intended. 'I mean, look . . . I've got it now,' I declare triumphantly as I successfully unstick my foot and send the stool clattering to the floor.

I cough. 'Sorry about that.' I straighten myself out as my eyes dart around the floor, attempting to locate my right shoe.

'No problem,' he mutters, frowning as he bends down. He hands me my new Kurt Geiger with a disconcerting look.

'Ooh, and thanks for that too,' I smile weakly, seizing it from his hand and shoving it on my foot.

But there's something about his expression that tells me I've blown it again. That, new shoes or no new shoes, nothing will rescue me now.

Chapter 2

'It was a disaster of epic proportions,' I declare.

'I'm sure you're exaggerating,' says Henry.

'I'm not. By the end of the night, the look on his face was *exactly* the same as Dermot's.'

Henry looks at me blankly.

'The property developer from before Christmas,' I add.

'Which one was he again?'

'You know – the one who looked like a skinny Robbie Williams.'

Henry shakes his head, still baffled.

'The one whose arm I dislocated doing my "YMCA" routine,' I say reluctantly.

'Ah. Well, The Village People always have had a lot to answer for.'

Despite the quip, I can't help noticing Henry's sympathetic look. It is a look with which I am tragically familiar.

'Do you think you're going to see him again?' he ventures.

'Not unless he has a bout of amnesia and forgets what a moron he went out with.'

'It can't *just* have been the thing with the shoes, surely,'

Henry says. 'I mean, the thing with the shoes sounds quite bad, but . . . was that really it?'

'The thing with the shoes qualifies as a high point,' I reply. 'It went downhill after that. The moment I realized I'd drunk too much to calm my nerves was probably the worst part.'

'Why? What happened?'

'He told me I'd called him Shane all evening instead of Sean.'

Henry stifles a smile and reaches for the toaster. 'Would you like another bagel?'

'Why not?' I say despondently. 'I might as well be fat as well as miserable.'

Henry's in his brown and orange velour dressing-gown, the one his mother bought him for Christmas. I can't imagine where she found it, because I could shop the length and breadth of Britain and never stumble across anything so hideous.

I wish I could say it was a one-off, but unfortunately his mother still buys a lot of his clothes, despite him being twenty-eight. I've pointed out that this isn't normal, but to no avail. Besides, the few clothes he picks out himself are as bad, if not worse: polo shirts that should be illegal for under-fifties, jeans that were only *de rigueur* among balding uncles in the early 1980s.

Not that this is important. Henry is the best friend anyone could hope for. As a flatmate, he's excellent company, does more than his fair share of cleaning and always pays his rent on time (taking the pressure off me). More importantly, he's loyal, above-averagely witty and I've cried on his shoulder so often over the years it's a wonder he hasn't invested in a rain-coat.

Despite this, there is something about Henry that, no

matter how much I love him, is undeniable: he's a geek. A lovable, kind, couldn't-live-without-him geek, but a geek all the same.

He puts the toasted bagel on a plate, butters it and places it in front of me. I take a large bite.

'Haven't you got any eligible friends at work?' I ask, more in hope than expectation. 'Someone you could tip off about my tendency to embarrass myself – but convince that I'm worth persevering with?'

He thinks for a second. 'The only one who's single is William Leitch, but I don't think he's your type.'

'Why not?' I ask defensively.

'He's sixty-three.'

I roll my eyes.

Henry shrugs. 'Apart from that, there's only me.'

I look up and catch his eye. We both collapse into giggles.

Despite the fact that I love the film *When Harry Met Sally*, I know from personal experience that its premise – that a relationship between a man and a woman is never purely platonic – is a load of tosh. I mean, look at us: Henry and I have known each other for nineteen years and in that entire time there hasn't been a flicker of attraction between us.

Yet there isn't a person on earth I adore more. He's the intelligent, thoughtful, excellent-birthday-present-buying brother I always wanted – instead of Dave, who forgot for three years on the trot then made up for it with a hot-water bottle gift set. (I was born in July.) In short, I love Henry to bits. But I'd still never sleep with him, not if my life depended on it – and the feeling's mutual.

'I've already told you that I think you should just be yourself,' he says. 'You'd have more luck with men if you did. You need to relax and let them see The Real You.'

'Don't start on that again,' I groan.

'Think about Antony and Cleopatra and Mr Darcy and Elizabeth Bennet,' he continues. 'And don't forget Madame Bovary. Those women were loved passionately by their men – in spite of their flaws.'

This is a typical Henry comment. First, despite being a relatively short sentence, it contains not one but several literary references. Secondly, it betrays his idyllic, rose-tinted view of love – a view that's largely theoretical as his hands-on experience with the opposite sex isn't exactly extensive.

'Those women weren't real, Henry,' I say. 'They were fictional characters.'

'Antony and Cleopatra were perfectly real,' he replies, putting away the butter and loading my plate into the dishwasher.

'Well, I know that,' I mutter. 'The point is, you'll have to trust me on this one. These days, women are expected to outsmart Carol Vorderman, out-cook Nigella, and out-pout Penelope-bloody-Cruz – all at the same time.'

'Out-pout?' he smiles.

'You know what I mean. Men don't *really* want real women, Henry.' I'm on a roll. 'Not ones with unshaven legs, bags under their eyes and crusty, unpainted toenails.'

'First of all, can I point out that *I am a man*.'

'You're *Henry*.' I wave my hand dismissively.

'Secondly,' he continues, ignoring me, 'I'm not saying that men don't want women to look attractive. Obviously, that's not the case. I'm saying there's nothing wrong with not being perfect in every way.'

'I'd settle for not being *im*perfect in every way.'

He flashes me a look. 'Come off it, Lucy. You're not that bad.'

'Gee, thanks.'

'When am I going to convince you? You don't need to keep embellishing your personal CV.'

'I don't know what you mean,' I reply indignantly, knowing exactly what he means.

'Lucy – you're good enough as you are. There's no need to try to make yourself sound more exotic or accomplished.'

'I don't,' I say quietly.

'Right – so you didn't tell that chef a few months ago that you'd been a finalist on *Blockbusters* when you were in the sixth form?'

'You're always bringing that up,' I say resentfully. 'I did not *tell* him, he somehow . . . surmised it. I wasn't going to be the one to shatter any illusions.'

He raises an eyebrow.

'Until I sat on his soufflé, obviously.'

Chapter 3

The day I met Henry isn't one that I remember vividly. But Henry does, probably because he has a brain the size of Pluto, and I've heard his version of the event often.

He recalls the tiniest detail of our introduction, despite it having happened so long ago that every household in Britain owned a Rubik's cube at the time.

I was in my fourth year in Kingsfield Primary School and Henry was the new boy. His parents, who were both professors, had transferred from their jobs in London to Liverpool University and the family was new in the city.

Henry was wheeled into our class and forced to stand at the front of the room while Miss Jameson introduced him to the other pupils. He tells me that that moment – when he, a glasses-wearing swot with a funny posh accent and freaky hair, had to stand in front of thirty streetwise city kids – was the most traumatic four minutes of his childhood.

Whether primary-school children can be as tough as Henry remembers is up for discussion. But there's no doubt that he was immediately considered *different*. A stranger who was shy, sensitive, brainy and, worst of all, wore brown lace-ups that resembled under-cooked Cornish pasties – shoes no self-respecting nine-year-old should step out in. Not even after dark.

Henry says that after Miss Jameson's rambling introduction, she turned to the class and beamed: 'Now, children, who'll volunteer to look after Henry for the day?'

A silence descended that was so deafening you could have heard pins drop in Devon. In that terrible moment, one thing was clear to everybody. To Miss Jameson, to Henry, to those rotten kids whose only excuse was that they were at an age when tribal instincts kick in furiously: *nobody was going to put up their hand.*

Then somebody piped up from row three.

'Go on, Miss. I'll do it.'

Henry says my voice was the thick-accented squeak he'd heard. When he looked up, dizzy with relief and gratitude, there I was, wonky-fringed and defiant.

'You fancy him,' sneered Andy Smith.

'Shurrup or I'll tell our Dave,' I snapped. It was a threat I often issued, despite the fact that my brother reserved physical violence for just one person: me. Dave and I fought like rabid alley cats in those days – throwing each other downstairs, pulling hair, scratching and punching – so the prospect of him defending his little sister was as remote as a hamlet in the depths of the Amazon Basin.

'Now, now, children!' said Miss Jameson, clapping her hands. She didn't have what you'd call a commanding presence, even with a bunch of nine-year-olds. 'Well done, Lucy Tyler. Henry can take a seat next to you and you can show him the ropes at lunchtime.'

Henry shuffled to the desk and smiled. I frowned suspiciously.

13

'Thanks,' he said softly.

''S'all right,' I replied. 'Why'ja wear them soft glasses?'

The accent has been ironed out today. It hasn't gone completely, and I haven't tried to ditch it deliberately: I was brought up in a world where that would be the ultimate in pretentiousness. But after three years at St Andrew's University and nearly eight in PR, I've got a voice that has prompted certain members of my extended family to accuse me of 'going all posh'.

Anyway, despite not personally remembering the details of the day Henry and I met, I recall quickly feeling that he was somebody I both admired and wanted to protect.

Admired because, as well as turning out to be a great laugh, Henry knew the answers to *everything*. How many plates a Stegosaurus had, how volcanoes work, how to remember your times tables, plus a plethora of French swear words so choice they'd make a sailor blush.

There seemed to be no piece of knowledge Henry hadn't acquired in his short life. Which was liberating – because I wanted to know the answers to everything. I never had a particularly natural intellect, not as vast and effortless as Henry's, but I loved learning and knew that I wanted to do my best in life – to *be* the best I could. I was, and have always been, a tryer.

I'm digressing. Despite all this, Henry needed protecting from the Andy Smiths of this world, who entertained themselves by stealing his homework books and defacing his pencil case with Denise Gibbin's *My Little Pony* stickers (she was one of those girls you just knew would grow up to be a lap dancer).

Eventually, years later, Henry gained a degree of acceptance among our contemporaries. This was thanks entirely to the fact that one of the many things at which he excelled was sport – and, at our school, if you were good at sport, you can't have been all bad. So Henry got some positive attention for once, albeit as 'that weird kid who's shit-hot in midfield'.

What I knew that the others didn't was that he was also hilariously funny when he wanted to be. Frustratingly, if they could have seen that, they'd have loved him. But his shyness prevented that and the class geek he remained.

As we grew up, I was aware that my close association with Henry put me at permanent risk of a catastrophic downturn in kudos. But there was never any question of ditching our friendship to placate the in-crowd. Being Henry's friend felt as if I knew a secret nobody else did. I understood his magic and was luckier for it.

These days, Henry still gets the odd look that must take him back to that first day in Miss Jameson's class. It's not surprising. His glasses are abysmal. His dress sense wouldn't make it onto the fashion pages of *Railway Enthusiasts Weekly*. And his hair, to be frank, looks as if it's been attacked with a hedge-trimmer. But Henry doesn't care. So why on earth should I?

Chapter 4

'How do you think it went?' I am buzzing with adrenalin after one of my most important presentations ever.

'I can't believe you have to ask,' replies Dominique, perching on my desk. 'The panel couldn't have been more convinced if we'd bent down and given each of them a blow job.'

I suppress a smile and scan the notes I scribbled during the meeting. I've worked for weeks on this pitch but if we win the client – a massive property firm – it'll be worth it.

'You weren't thrown by the question about contacts in the north-east?' I fret.

'What's with the lack of self-belief, Lucy?' says Dominique, stuffing her dark-blonde hair into a clip. 'You're not Peaman-Brown's star performer for nothing.'

'Oh, give over,' I wince, though I can't help feeling a little pleased.

'Don't deny it,' she grins. 'I keep saying you'll be running this place in three years – and today confirmed it. The presentation was slick, our answers were textbook and, crucially, the MD had the hots for you.'

'Don't be ridiculous,' I say, hoping she might be right.

'Believe me,' she winks. 'It's in the bag.'

Dominique and I hit it off the minute we met. She's sassy, down to earth and a natural at this job – so much so, you'd never guess it wasn't her first career choice. Dominique had wanted to be an actress until she realized that, in her own words, she had the stage presence of a plank of MDF. She persevered for several years and won the odd bit-part, but nothing more. The crunch came on the day she was turned down for an audition to play a dead body in a British Gas training video. 'If *that* isn't a signal to get a proper job, I don't know what is,' she says.

Yet when you meet Dom it's impossible to believe she's experienced a single setback in life. I still remember her striding in here two years ago with her proud and plentiful curves, endless legs and admirable aura of confidence.

Dominique is one of the many reasons I love working for Peaman-Brown Public Relations. I've been with the company since university, yet what I do for a living still baffles most of my family. They can get their head around my brother being a salesman, but if anyone mentions that 'Lucy works in PR', they scrunch up their noses with a deep sense of bewilderment – and injustice that they're not paid to sit in a fancy office doing such a namby-pamby excuse for work.

What Peaman-Brown PR does for organizations is actually easy to understand, if not to do: we manage their image. On the one hand, this means unearthing positive stories and making sure the media knows about them. On the other, it means spotting negative news stories and making sure the media knows *nothing* about them. That's the theory anyway. The practice can be different, I'll admit.

'Remind me how much this contract is worth,' asks Dom.

I lift open the back page of my proposal and slide it over to her discreetly.

'Good God.' She shakes her head. 'We deserve the bonus to end all bonuses if we get this, Lucy. Seriously, I expect to retire to a yacht in the Caribbean. Just a small one, nothing fancy.'

'You'd be bored stiff.'

'I'd bring you to entertain me,' she grins. 'You and I would be good on the high seas.'

'It took me eight years to get my five hundred metres front crawl badge.'

'I'll buy you a pair of armbands,' she promises.

'You two are very full of yourselves this morning.' The voice from the desk opposite belongs to Drew. He's good-looking, well-bred and a charmer – when he chooses to be. It's a quality he uses when he needs to divert attention from his professional ability (which is shaky at best) or when there's an attractive female around – preferably wearing a skirt the size of a tea cosy. Such treatment is never directed at me; he prefers to wind me up instead. I'm sorry to say he's often successful.

'Of course we're full of ourselves,' grins Dominique. 'We did brilliantly.'

Drew smiles back. 'Glad to hear it, ladies. One of my pub quiz friends works for Webster Black PR and they're going after that contract too, apparently.'

'One of your pub quiz friends?' repeats Dominique.

'Yep. Did I mention I've been on the winning team of the north-west heats of Pub Quiz of the Year for three years?'

'Only every day since we met you, Drew,' she teases. Her phone rings on the other side of the office and she goes to answer it.

'Well, I hope you're right, Lucy,' continues Drew, as he examines his nails. 'I thought I'd let you know because Tim's certain they've won the contract. Webster Black are experts in the field. I'd hate you to get your hopes up.'

He leans back in his chair and subconsciously rubs his crotch. Drew is one of those men whose hand is never far from their nether regions, as if permanently drawing attention to what they consider to be the most magnificent package bestowed on a human male.

'I presume you were asked for a second interview?' he adds.

'I'm sure we'll get through to the second round,' I reply, filing away my documents. 'I hope so anyway.'

'Good. Glad to hear it.' He smiles. 'Apparently, they invited Webster Black back while they were still at the meeting.'

I look up.

'They told Tim they were making a shortlist of three and Webster Black's on it,' he continues.

I know full well he's trying to agitate me but refuse to rise to it. 'They might have said something like that to Dominique on the way out,' I reply breezily.

'Oh, that's good. Because it'd be awful not to reach the final three. That'd ruin your lucky run.'

'There's nothing *lucky* about our run, Drew,' I point out.

Before he can respond, Little Lynette, the office administrator, appears at our desk sporting new hair extensions.

'Morning, Lucy. Four letters today.'

'Cheers, Lynette,' I reply, putting them in my in-tray. 'Nice hair.'

Little Lynette has been known as such since she started on work experience aged sixteen. She's now five foot nine and twenty-three but the tag is unshakeable.

'Ooh, do you like it, Luce?' she beams, twiddling with the raven-coloured ends of her hair. 'It's taken a bit of getting used to. The glue hasn't half made it go crusty.'

'Your hair's lovely,' I reassure her.

'Not a bit knotty?' She scrunches up her face.

'If you need anyone to run their fingers through it, let me know, won't you?' Drew jumps in.

I catch Lynette's eye and tut. 'Drew's rehearsing for the role of office sex pest,' I tell her, but she's too busy whooping with delight to hear.

'Don't listen to her,' says Drew, winking. 'Lucy's irked because she'll be too old for men to lust after her soon.'

'I'm only twenty-eight—'

'Lust!' hoots Lynette. 'Ooh, I love a man with a big vocabulary.'

Drew doesn't miss a beat. 'That's not the only thing that's—'

'Oh God, Lynette,' I cry. 'How can a nice girl like you listen to this and not want to give him a slap?'

'Easy,' she giggles, and totters away.

When I open my in-box, seventeen new emails have arrived in the two and a half hours I've been out of the office. I skim the list and open one.

To: lucy.tyler@Peamanbrown.com
From: erin.price@circletheatre.com
Subject: Miscellaneous

Hi Lucy,
    A note from your favourite client to say we're over the moon with the opening-night coverage of *Fever* this

20

week. Danny must have watched himself on TV six
times since you set up those interviews. And the piece in
the *Guardian* . . . what can I say? Superb work as usual –
thanks so much.

On a separate and more important note, are you and
Dominique still in the market for a girls' night out this
weekend? My bank balance is begging for mercy but I
can't face another night of *Sex and the City* repeats.
Please say it's still on.

E xxx

Erin is the Marketing Manager of the Circle Theatre, one of
the accounts I manage, and if all those I worked with were
as nice as her, life would be significantly simpler. Erin isn't
just an easygoing client and a lovely person, she's a friend
too. A proper friend with whom I spend time outside work
because we genuinely get on – not because I'm 'building
client relationships', i.e. making sure we continue to get their
cash.

I hit reply.

To: erin.price@circletheatre.com
From: lucy.tyler@Peamanbrown.com
Cc: dominique.sampson@Peamanbrown.com
Subject: Re: Miscellaneous

Course it's still on. What do u take us for, lightweights?

L xx

As I go through my other emails, it's inevitable that not all are going to be as pleasant as Erin's. There's one from a small but demanding client – an insurance firm – suggesting I target *Hello!* with some two-month-old pictures of their staff drinks party.

Then there's the chain of DIY stores whose Marketing Manager has emailed with another set of amendments – the sixth – to a press release he officially signed off two days ago and which I sent out to the world's media this morning.

Finally, there's a note from a potential client saying he needs to cancel our dinner date tonight and rearrange for a week on Tuesday – when I'm going to *Cirque du Soleil*.

A response from Erin pops up.

To: lucy.tyler@Peamanbrown.com
From: erin.price@circletheatre.com
Cc: dominique.sampson@Peamanbrown.com
Subject: Re, re: Miscellaneous

Fab. Where shall we meet? Hear that new place in Dale Street is good.

Erin x
p.s. Your pitch with that property firm must have gone well because their Marketing Manager phoned me for a reference. Obviously told him u were the best PR company in the world and he said they're putting you on the shortlist.

To: lucy.tyler@Peamanbrown.com
To: erin.price@circletheatre.com
From: dominique.sampson@Peamanbrown.com
Subject: Re, re, re: Miscellaneous

I *knew* it!

   Lucy – will you break this to Drew? While you're at it, ask him to remove his hands from his groin. He has been rummaging there for half an hour and has completely put me off my prawn sandwich.

Dom x

Chapter 5

My love-life will never get off the ground unless I endeavour to become thinner.

Henry looked at me as if I was clinically insane when I shared this conclusion with him. I then explained that there *is* some logic behind the theory and I am not simply some *Heat* magazine-reading idiot who is obsessed with the size of her thighs, at which he pointed out that I love *Heat* magazine and spend more time contemplating the circumference of my legs than most people do inhaling oxygen.

My argument is this: first, had I the bum of a seventeen-year-old trampolining champion and a washboard stomach that made Cameron Diaz look like a pork-pie addict, I would radiate a level of self-assurance that would be irresistibly attractive. Secondly, were I possessed of such qualities, I would simply *be* irresistibly attractive.

Henry snorted at these suggestions in a manner I didn't appreciate, and I told him as much, before dusting off my old Diet World welcome pack and 'Nootrient' point calculator.

Worse, he's now looking at me with an air of amused disbelief as I walk around the supermarket calculating the Diet World '*nootrient*' value of our foodstuff before it goes into the trolley.

24

We currently have one artichoke (0 *nootrients*), a large bag of bean-sprouts (ditto), a box of ice cream (4 per serving – I've got to have a treat occasionally), a piece of Brie (5, ditto), two bottles of Pinot Grigio (24 *nootrients* in total – I have a stressful job), and a tub of margarine (1 per teaspoon – to be used sparingly).

Henry looks at his watch.

'Lucy, we've been here an hour and there are seven items in our trolley. At this rate it'll take until two weeks on Tuesday to buy enough ingredients for a stir-fry.'

'Eight items,' I correct him. 'The margarine came with a free fridge magnet.'

'You told me you hated Diet World.'

'I did not,' I protest.

'You called the leader Mussolini.'

'Only because she was going bald. And, okay, she was a bit of a bully, but it doesn't matter because I'm not going to the classes anyway. I've got enough willpower to do it by myself. I'm just following the diet, which I know from experience works a treat.'

'If it works a treat, why are you having to do it again?' he asks.

I tut, hiding the fact that I'm stumped for an answer.

'Is this allowed?' he asks, picking up a family-sized chocolate trifle that could keep a killer whale going through the winter months.

'God, no!' I leap back in horror. 'There must be . . . let me calculate this . . . SEVENTEEN *nootrients* per portion.'

'I don't know what seventeen *nootrients* means, but from your reaction I'm guessing it's potentially fatal.'

'Might as well be,' I tell him haughtily. 'It's out of bounds.'

'*You* don't have to have it,' he says innocently. 'I can hide it in the fridge drawer for myself.'

I glare at him. 'You're seriously going to keep a chocolate trifle the size of Centre Court at Wimbledon in our fridge – next to my measly bag of bean-sprouts?'

'Come on, Lucy, you're not going to inflict this nonsense on me, are you?'

Henry is one of those people who never gives a second thought to his diet. He can happily buy a mammoth chocolate trifle without a smidgen of guilt and, worse, can eat as much as he likes without putting on an ounce.

I, on the other hand, can't even look at a chocolate trifle – nay, *think* about one – without disintegrating into a car crash of complex body and food issues, of greed, lust and frustration.

The difference is knowledge. This is the only example I can think of in which mine exceeds Henry's. My expertise in the field of calories, fat and, latterly, GI is so pre-eminent that if I went on *Mastermind* I'd make televisual history.

Despite this, it hasn't done me a great deal of good over the years, and I've almost come to the conclusion that I'd be better off living in ignorance. Look at previous generations: my gran had a twenty-four-inch waist until she was in her late fifties. She was a skinny little thing and, like Henry, was as familiar with what constituted a kilo-calorie as the lyrics to Kanye West's back catalogue.

She'd think nothing about whipping up dinner for four using a pound of lard, a few cups of dripping and several ambiguous hunks of solid red meat. Yet she stayed the size of a malnourished sparrow. I can only put this down to the fact that – unlike my generation – she did not obsess about every item she put in her mouth for sixteen hours a day.

Clearly, I'm not going to let Henry know this.

'It is not nonsense,' I tell him, 'but if you want to be unsupportive, then fine. I thought you were more sensitive than that.'

'Lucy, as ever, I'm prepared to bow to your every need. But I'm not prepared to live on bean-sprouts for the week.'

I scowl at him.

'Besides,' he says, putting the trifle in the trolley, 'it'll test your strength of character.'

'I don't want strength of character, I want a pert bum,' I protest.

For the sake of time, I agree to use a less rigid method of determining the *nootrient* value, i.e. instead of using the special *Nootrient Calculator*, I simply guess.

I conclude that a tin of baked beans and sausages will be okay (approx one *nootrient* per tin, I'd say), as will a jar of pesto sauce (half a *nootrient* per serving) and some pro-biotic drink things in titchy plastic bottles (zero *nootrients*, surely?). I graciously allow Henry to throw in a big bag of gourmet crisps because they're olive oil flavour, which everyone knows is good for you.

When we get to the till, Henry pauses and picks up the trifle. 'Okay, you win. I feel bad. I'm taking this back.'

'Don't be daft,' I laugh. 'You're right. It's my diet, not yours. Leave it in.'

'Honestly, I don't mind,' he insists.

'Neither do I.'

'No really, I—'

'Henry!' I snap, like an armed response officer. 'Put – the – trifle – back – in – the – trolley.'

'But—'

'I might want a bit after dinner,' I mumble.

'What about your diet?'

'Everything in moderation is acceptable,' I tell him, thinking back to what Mussolini used to say. 'I can have a modest, tablespoon-sized taste. That couldn't have more than half a *nootrient* or so, I'm sure.'

'Okay, good,' he smiles. 'Great.'

A weird thing happens at the till, as I pack away our food and Henry takes out his wallet. The checkout girl smiles at him. *Really* smiles at him. She's not exactly a stunner – more Denise Royle than Denise Richards – but she's got a nice enough face and a cleavage I'd kill for.

'They're lovely, them chocolate trifles,' she sighs, carefully putting it in a bag and looking up at Henry. 'Me and me sister had one the other night with loads of that squirty cream all over it. God, it was gorgeous!'

If this were any other red-blooded male, being chatted to by an attractive young woman – particularly about her sister and squirty cream – would be a positive thing. An opportunity to engage in a friendly, potentially flirtatious conversation.

If Henry sees it thus, he doesn't show it. Instead, he mutters something under his breath, shoves his debit card into his wallet and, with his head bowed, scuttles away with the trolley. The poor girl must wonder whether she's got halitosis.

I almost challenge this behaviour in the car park, but stop myself. I know what it's about and torturing Henry by bringing it up will only make things worse. When it comes to women, he's desperately, dysfunctionally shy – and always will be.

So, when we get into the car, I don't say anything. Nothing at all. Instead, I calculate the *nootrient* value of the crisps which, it emerges to my disbelief, will put me over my weekly quota in one go.

Chapter 6

You know those apartments in *Elle Decoration* with elegant soft-furnishings, hand-cut flowers and room schemes that juxtapose striking colour with clean lines? Well, our apartment is nothing like those.

I'd like it to be. It's just never worked out like that, despite my considerable efforts. When we moved in, fired up with creative zeal, I attempted in earnest to recreate such a look.

Only, when I painted the hall 'Ochre', it looked brown. So I painted over it with 'Sienna' and that looked brown too. I followed with a 'Wheat', a 'Fallow' and an 'Ecru', but the most appealing shade I ever managed just looked like the unwashed shorts of a grubby Boy Scout. When Henry pointed out that the walls mightn't withstand much more, I went for broke and painted it 'Duck Egg'. Every time I walk in now, I feel as if I'm being committed to a prison cell. Still, we've learned to live with it.

The other reason our apartment is some way off those in *Elle Decoration* is that it isn't exactly clutter-free, and for that Henry is as much to blame as me. Every room boasts floor-to-ceiling shelves straining under the weight of his books; they're piled high on side tables, the bureau in the hall and the piano in the living room – his piano, not mine, in case you're wondering. And this isn't even his complete collection: the majority is at his parents' house.

These are just his favourites. I don't know why anyone needs four editions of Darwin's *Voyage of the Beagle*, or three of *Genetic and Evolutionary Aspects of Malaria and Other Blood Parasites* (they're classics apparently). But then, Henry doesn't see being a scientist as just a job; it defines him.

Henry – or *Dr* Henry Fox, to give him his full title – works at the Tropical Medicine Research Centre with a team of boffins (a word I can't resist using, despite knowing how much he hates it) studying malaria and ways of preventing its spread across Africa. It's the noblest profession I can think of and makes me feel rather humble when constructing press releases about half-price bathroom sales.

Anyway, Henry doesn't just read books about science. He has more first editions of classic and contemporary fiction than Russell Brand has split ends. All of which means our flat has some way to go before it features on *Grand Designs*.

'Have you opened the chocolate trifle yet?' I ask casually, curling up on the sofa.

Henry looks up from his paperback. 'I don't fancy it tonight.'

Panic registers in my brain, but I allow him to return to his book.

'Why not?' I laugh lightly. 'It looks lovely.'

He scrutinizes my expression.

'If I wasn't on a diet, and didn't have a date in three days' time, I'd definitely want to eat it,' I continue.

'Who do you have a date with?'

I can't help smiling. 'He's called Jake. I met him at the

31

opening night of the new play at the Circle. He's gorgeous. Which is why I couldn't possibly have any trifle. Though I'd scoff the lot under normal circumstances.'

He shrugs. 'I might have some later.'

'At what time?' I ask.

'At what time?' he repeats.

'Yes, at what time do you think you'll get round to opening it? I'm only after an estimate. You know, eight thirty-two . . . eight thirty-three . . .'

'Given that it is eight thirty-one, I'm guessing you'd like to open it now?'

'Well, if you *were* opening it now . . .'

'Like I said,' he continues, 'I don't fancy it at the moment – but you're welcome to open it.'

'*I'm* obviously not going to open it,' I tell him, exasperated. 'Not when I'm on a diet.'

'What difference does it make who opens it?'

'Oh Henry,' I sigh. 'Will you go and open it so I can pinch some and not feel guilty?'

He stops and smiles. 'Of course.'

He goes to the kitchen to get the trifle, returning with two dessert spoons, one for each of us. He sits next to me on the sofa and we dig in as I switch over the television.

'What are we watching?' he asks.

'Reality TV at its best. It's right up your street,' I tell him ironically, because this isn't Henry's kind of show at all.

He raises an eyebrow.

'Live a little, Henry. You might like it.'

'What's it about?' he asks.

'Some poor person who's never been lucky in love volunteers for a full makeover. By that, I don't just mean a new wardrobe. They get lessons in how to flirt and how to behave on a date. They get a new hairdo, facials, teeth whitening—'

'Is there anything left of them by the time they're finished?' Henry interrupts.

'The good bits stay,' I reply. 'Though admittedly, good bits are sometimes in short supply.'

As I tuck into the trifle looking not very like someone on day one of a diet, I'm gripped. This week's subject is a thirty-eight-year-old virgin called Brian who works in IT and has teeth like a Cheltenham Gold Cup winner.

'I thought *I* was in trouble,' Henry says.

'Just wait,' I reply confidently.

Fifty minutes later, Brian looks like a Levi's 501 model with more chicks at his feet than The Fonz.

'I admit it,' says Henry as the credits roll. 'That's impressive.'

'Told you. Oh dear.'

'What?' he asks.

'The trifle's gone.'

'So it has.'

'You must have eaten it all,' I tell him.

'I don't think so.'

'Henry, you *must* have,' I say. 'I can't possibly have devoured half a chocolate trifle – I barely noticed it. Tell me I didn't.'

He smirks. 'Course you didn't, Lucy. I scoffed the lot. Apart from one or two modest spoonfuls for you.'

'I thought so,' I say, taking out my *Diet World Nootrient Tracker* and marking down two and a half points – a reasonable estimate, I think.

When I put it down, Henry is gazing into space.

'What's up?' I ask him.

He shakes his head, snapping out of it. 'Nothing.'

'Come on, Henry. I've known you long enough to recognize when something's up.'

'Nothing's up.'

'*Henry . . .*'

He frowns. 'It's nothing really. Just . . .'

'Just *what?*'

He pauses and stares at his hands. 'You know the way I am with women?'

I look at him, taken aback. 'You mean . . . shy?'

He nods. 'It's a pain in the arse.'

I let out a little laugh, see his expression and stop. 'Sorry. You were saying?'

'Oh, forget it, honestly,' he replies, waving his hand.

'No, Henry – I'm sorry. Tell me what you were about to say.'

He frowns for a second and takes a deep breath. 'I'd like to have a girlfriend at some point.' He squirms with embarrassment.

Henry has had a relationship before, about five years ago. It was a kind of office romance – except he works in a laboratory, rather than an office. The point is, he spent ten months with Sharon from the Accounts Department before they drifted apart and she went to work in Cardiff.

There was absolutely nothing wrong with Sharon. She was quiet, unassuming, plain but not unattractive. But, at the risk of sounding like an over-protective friend, she wasn't good enough for him.

I wanted to like her when we first met, to get to know her hidden depths. Unfortunately, and this will sound awful, I never found any. Sharon, God bless her, was as dull as they come.

'I'm sure you'll find someone one day, Henry,' I tell him.

'I'm not,' he replies. 'I'm a glass-half-full sort of person, but I'm also a realist. I'm starting to think it's never going to happen.'

I go to protest then stop, not wanting to interrupt him.

'I'm hopeless with the opposite sex,' he continues. 'I don't know why, but I am. Utterly hopeless.'

I bite my lip. 'Why do you think you find it so difficult to talk to women?'

'I don't know,' he replies, looking genuinely bewildered.

'I mean, *I'm* a woman, and you're not nervous with me.'

'You're *Lucy*,' he tells me. 'There's a difference.'

'*Touché.*'

'Maybe I'm aware I'm not much of a catch,' he goes on. 'I don't look like any of those blokes in your magazines – Orlando Broom, or whatever his name is.'

'*Bloom*, Henry. Orlando *Bloom*.'

'Yes – him. I know I don't look like him. But then I already know that from a biological point of view, not everyone *can* look like him. Even accounting for evolutionary theories and survival of the fittest, the human race couldn't exist if only a select few were to successfully procreate. In fact, every multi-celled organism, particularly mammals, has the capacity to find a mate.'

'Which means?'

He looks up at me. 'Even duffers like me can get a girl-friend. In theory, at least.'

'There you have it,' I declare. 'That's your problem.'

'What is?'

'You think you're a duffer, when you're not.'

'Your loyalty's touching, Lucy, but the facts would indicate that I'm right.'

I am about to protest again when I focus on Henry. His hair. His clothes. His glasses. He could be modelling on the front of a 1950s knitting pattern. I wonder how to put this.

'Look, I stand by my view fundamentally, but . . .' My voice trails off.

'But what?' he asks.

'You could do with a makeover.'

'Really?' Henry looks shocked. Which shocks me. Although this is a conversation we've never had before, I can't believe he hasn't noticed that nobody else dresses like him. 'There's no way I'm going on television.'

'No, of course not. You don't need to. *I* could give you a makeover.'

How have I never thought of this before? I smile at my idea, at its brilliant simplicity, then I catch sight of Henry. He doesn't look convinced.

'Believe me,' I continue, 'as someone who has spent most of her adult life studying attractive men in detail, I'd know how to sort you out in the clothes department. And hair and skin – you'd benefit from a bit of microdermabrasion.'

'Isn't that how they remove corrosion from car panels?'

'Hang on a minute,' I tell him, 'let's do this properly.'

'What do you mean?'

Inspired, I look him in the eyes. 'This can be a project,' I declare. '*Project Henry!*'

'Oh God.'

'I mean it. Dominique could help. What she doesn't know about flirting isn't worth knowing.'

'Is that what you call it? I've seen Dominique flirting and it's like a lioness pouncing.'

'It works,' I argue. '*And* Erin used to be a personal shopper before she did her current job. She'll have you looking like Brad Pitt in no time.'

I stop and take stock. Henry looks terrible.

'Sorry,' I say, deflating. 'I didn't mean to get carried away.'

There's silence for a second. 'You didn't, Lucy,' he says to my surprise. 'And you're right.'

'Really?'

'Really. I don't want to spend a lifetime as a loser, as your terminally single friend. I mean, you're not going to be around for ever.'

'What do you mean?' I ask.

'Sooner or later, you'll settle down and have a family with someone. It might even be whatsisname – Jack.'

I frown.

'The guy you've a date with on Friday.'

'Jake,' I say.

'Whoever. The point is, that at some point in the not too distant future, I'll be your sad bachelor friend who no longer has anyone to butter bagels for.'

'You'll always be my best friend, Henry. Always.'

'Well, good. But I'd still like to get laid.'

I laugh. 'You say that like you're a virgin. What about your relationship with Sharon? And what was that girl's name at uni?'

'Karen Allagreen.'

'That's her.'

He looks at me. 'One fleeting relationship and a single drunken fumble in ten years. Casanova would be crapping himself.'

'Point taken. So is this reinvention a goer?'

He takes a deep breath. 'Yes. I suppose it is.'

'Great,' I say coolly, picking up the trifle bowl and heading for the kitchen.

When I get there, I have to bite my fist to stop myself squealing with glee. If you'd told me yesterday that Henry would agree to a makeover, I wouldn't have believed it. This could be the best thing that's ever happened to him. Scrap that: I'm going to make sure it's the best thing that's ever happened to him. I'm going to make sure that my single friend isn't single for very much longer.

Chapter 7

I'm so excited about *Project Henry*, I was almost tempted to bring proceedings forward and rearrange my date with Jake tonight.

But Dominique's out anyway, with a wealthy older man she's been seeing recently, and Erin and her boyfriend Gary have gone to the cinema. Besides, we couldn't have done it properly on a Friday night. Instead, we have the whole of tomorrow in which to hit the shops and begin Henry's reinvention.

Consequently, I have stuck to Plan A and arrived at the shabby-but-trendy bar where Jake and I arranged to meet. Judging by how sexy he looks when he walks in, it was a sound decision.

'Lucy, how are you?' He smiles as he approaches me at the bar.

Jake is a lecturer in Theatrical Studies, so as well as having a bum I could keep under observation all day, he's a renaissance man too. He's wearing slouchy jeans, vintage trainers and a T-shirt showing off biceps that could have been inflated with a tyre pump.

I've dressed in what could be the first thing to fall out of my wardrobe – skinny jeans with an Indian cotton shirt and biker boots. *Could be* because I spent three lunchtimes scouring every retail outlet in the city for them – not that he needs to know that.

We met last week while I was handling the media for the Circle Theatre's new play. He was on a field trip with his students. And I am *so* glad.

'My tutorial group enjoyed the play the other night,' he tells me, taking a sip of red wine. 'I thought it had hidden depths. Despite the garish disco theme. Perhaps because of it.'

Personally, I wasn't a fan of the play. If I'm honest I have no idea what it's supposed to be about, even though I've sat through it three times.

'I couldn't agree more,' I tell him, trying to recall one of my press-release quotes. 'I think the writer aimed to describe the "new reality" in which he's living. Where all communication with the outside is through the telephone or the internet.'

I sit back and scrutinize his expression. Okay, so my artistic impression is entirely off the shelf, but I'm quietly pleased with myself. And he looks impressed.

'You are *so* right,' he nods. 'That really came across. That and the boundless tragedy of human disconnection and how that has somehow mutated into the twenty-four-hour world.'

'Hmmm,' I say earnestly.

'Of course, the whole thing was so kitsch,' he laughs. 'You couldn't fail to walk away with a grim sense of the inexorable, phony electro-fun you get in places where all the joy has to be imported. This was electronic masturbation for the soul – in its most glorious, disgusting configuration. Don't you think?'

'Definitely,' I add, hoping he'll change the subject.

'That isn't to say the kaleidoscopic nature of the play wasn't one of the most moving elements of it. Even the most hardened of nay-sayers couldn't dispute *that*.'

'I wouldn't worry about them. Excuse me – I'm just going to the loo.'

After a touch-up of mascara, I return to the table, where Jake's on his mobile.

'No, I . . . I can't have this conversation now. Honestly, Mother, I've got to go.' He puts his mobile on the table and looks at me sheepishly. 'That was my mum.'

'Oh, right. Everything okay?'

'Yeah, yeah,' he says. 'Everything's fine. She's a little clingy sometimes. You know how mums are.'

In fact, my mum couldn't be less clingy if she was made of Teflon but I nod for the sake of politeness.

'Where were we?' he continues. 'Oh, yeah, the kaleido-scope effect of the writer's—'

But he's cut off when his phone rings again. 'Sorry about this. It's easier if I take it now.'

'Of course. Go ahead.'

He answers the phone and begins the conversation at the table, but when the voice at the other end becomes more agitated, stands up and gestures that he's taking it outside. I sit at the window, nursing my glass of wine and watching Jake pace up and down, waving his arms so much it looks as if he's trying to take flight.

After six or seven minutes, he ends the conversation, takes a deep breath and returns inside. '*So* sorry about that.'

'Really, it's not a problem,' I smile.

'Did I hear you saying you were a fan of avant-garde theatre the other night?'

Shit. Did I say that? I think I might have. 'Oh, I like it as much as the next person.'

He looks disappointed.

'At least, the next person who's seen every one of Samuel Becket's plays five times over,' I chuckle.

He brightens up. 'Wow. You and I have so much in common.'

'Haven't we?' I lean forward and hold his gaze.

'You're an amazing woman, Lucy,' he says dreamily.

'Oh, I don't know about that,' I reply modestly.

'I've never met anyone else with such a passion for theatre. Britain would be a better place if everyone was like you. We wouldn't need Arts Council subsidies and the independent theatres would be thriving.'

I smile at him in wonder at how well this is going. Okay, I might have to swot up between now and our second date, but that's no big deal. I managed to cram into my head everything there is to know about John Donne the week before English Lit A-level – so I'm sure I can manage this.

'You know, there's a play on in Manchester in a couple of weeks called *Translations into Spirituality* – oh, excuse me . . .'

His phone is ringing again. Shaking his head apologetically, he answers with a resigned look.

'Hi, Mum,' he says despondently, listening as she talks. And talks. And keeps on talking.

Eventually, he pauses and sighs. 'Okay, Mum, okay. Hang on a sec.'

He puts his hand over the phone and looks into my eyes. 'Um, Lucy . . . sorry about this. I won't be long, promise.'

Two hours later, Jake's mum has phoned eight more times and, with no one to talk to, I've taken solace in alcohol. I am now pissed out of my head. This would be bad enough, except it's made Jake's already challenging conversational manner near incomprehensible. He's banging on about some play he went to see in Barcelona now. It's like listening to the incessant crackle of a broken radio.

'The thing I love about Covas is his unique ability to assimilate so many layers of the physical versus the fantasy. It's not half as coy as it sounds, Lucy, believe me.'

A trickle of red wine escapes from the side of my mouth. 'It doesn't sound coy, Jake.'

'Good,' he grins. 'Because the collaborative effect of synthetically-generated visual and aural materials can be joyous beyond imagination – like the inhalation and exhalation of a revelatory journey.'

'Jake,' I whisper.

'The easeful death of the characters in that play, Lucy – well, what can I say? It represented a noisy montage of repetition and sensuality, a—'

'Jake,' I repeat.

'– harrowing version of childlessness that writhed in and out of focus. A diagonal representation of terror and—

'JAKE!' I slam down my glass.

He looks stunned. Suddenly I don't know what to say. So I stand up.

'What's the matter?' he asks.

I down my drink, grab my bag and sling it over my shoulder.

'I'm terribly sorry about this,' I slur, 'but I've got to go.'

He frowns. 'Go?'

I nod. 'It's been lovely, Jake, but unfortunately, I'm feeling a bit . . .' I can't think of anything appropriate.

'Ill?' he suggests.

I click my fingers and point at him. 'Ill. That's it. Ill. That's exssactly what I am.'

He stands to pull out my chair and the wounded look on his face makes me feel a surge of guilt. I am about to apologize and try to start again, when his phone rings.

He lets go of the chair and turns his back to me as he answers. 'Hi, Mum,' he says, and I head for the door with firm conviction but distinctly wobbly legs.

Chapter 8

Dominique looks as if she's bitten a jellyfish and washed it down with lighter fluid. 'That's *beyond* weird.'

She, Erin and I have hit the shops with Henry to begin his reinvention.

'I mean it,' continues Dominique, frenziedly rifling through a rail of sweaters. 'One phone call from his mother would have been suspicious. You deserve a medal to have lasted as long as you did.'

I shrug. 'I won't be seeing him again, that's for sure.'

'It seems so unfair,' sighs Erin.

'It wasn't just the thing with his mother,' I complain. 'I couldn't understand a bloody word he was saying. And that was when he was talking about the plays I've *seen*. When he got onto Roger Vitrac and *Power to the Children* he could have been speaking Cantonese.'

'Oh dear,' says Erin, concerned. 'Don't worry, Lucy. I'm sure you've just been unlucky.'

This is what she says after all my dates, but I don't point it out. Besides, unfettered optimism must come easily when you've got a love-life like Erin's. She and The Lovely Gary have been together for eight months and they're so smitten that she can't ask him to pass the milk without sounding like a Valentine card verse.

The Lovely Gary has been referred to as such since the evening Dom and I met him at a new bar opening, shortly after he and Erin got together. Erin had spent three weeks repeating how 'lovely' he was, until Dominique attempted to bring her back to earth, saying: 'Erin, sweetheart – no one's *that* lovely.'

Then he carried Dom into a taxi after an incident involving a snapped high heel and one too many Jackhammers, and she was forced to concede the point. Ever since, it hasn't sounded right calling him just 'Gary'.

There is no doubt The Lovely Gary has been good for Erin; you only have to look at her to see that. Today, with her beaming smile and glossy strawberry-blonde waves, she looks stunning. Her clothes are gorgeous too: Erin dresses in a way that's bohemian and fashionable at the same time – a look I've never been able to master. When I try to do bohemian I look as if I've slept rough.

'Oh well, there are plenty more fish in the sea.' I smile unconvincingly.

'Absolutely,' agrees Erin. 'You'll find someone soon, Lucy, I've no doubt.'

'I'm not desperate or anything,' I say for the record.

'Of course not!' replies Erin.

'Onwards and upwards.' I wonder if it's obvious that I'm hiding my lack of conviction with a string of clichés. The truth is that I am getting a bit depressed about my love-life. Dating has been fun, but . . . what am I talking about? It hasn't been remotely fun. I've enjoyed the anticipation of going out with new people, but am sick to death of it inevitably ending in disaster.

It's not that I'm not over my ex, Tom. But I'll admit that I miss the intimacy. I miss curling up together on a rainy Sunday afternoon and talking about nothing and everything, between kisses. I miss fingers winding round mine as we snuggle up at the cinema. And I'll admit this too: I miss sex.

I haven't had anything approaching amorous relations for months. Well, amorous relations with a human being. Dominique bought me a vibrator for my birthday and while it is undoubtedly effective it's also rather mechanical for my tastes; lacking in personality. There's no flirting with that bugger – no eye-contact or first kiss. Just a lot of vibrating. Still, it's got three settings, which makes it better-rounded than some of the blokes I've been out with. Oh God, I've become a cynic as well.

'Where's our hunk-to-be?' asks Dominique. 'It feels like hours since he went into that changing room.'

Henry wasn't bursting with enthusiasm when we arrived. In fact, while we scoured the shop, he hovered about looking so uncomfortable you'd think his underpants were a size too small. Unperturbed, we picked out an array of super-stylish ensembles and dispatched him to the changing room while we waited for him to emerge, transformed and triumphant. Except he's taking a very long time.

'Er, Henry,' I call, feeling awkward loitering next to the men's changing rooms. 'Are you nearly ready?'

When there's no answer, Dominique whips back the curtain. 'Henry, I'm coming in.'

'No.' He pokes his head round the door of his cubicle as semi-naked men run for cover.

'Hurry up then,' she replies. 'Your hair appointment's in a

couple of hours and we haven't achieved anything.' Then she joins us on the sofa, crossing her legs and leaning on the arm.

'You're not the only one who didn't have a great night last night,' she tells us. 'I finished with Robert.'

'Is he your older man?' asks Erin, wide-eyed. 'The one with the Porsche?'

'*Was* my older man. He's a nice guy, but I started to become obsessed with his bingo wings. Does that make me shallow?'

'Probably,' I say.

'Oh well, never mind. Besides, I'm starting to wonder if it might be time to settle down.'

'What?' Erin and I reply in unison.

Dominique looks indignant. 'Why is that so surprising? I'm not a complete freak, am I?'

'Not a freak,' I reply, 'but if you'd said you were joining the next Hubble space mission I'd have been less shocked. No offence, Dominique, but you've never shown the slightest interest in settling down.'

'I know,' she muses, 'but I'm starting to think I should.'

'Why?' asks Erin, agog.

She pauses. 'My Cousin Angie got engaged last week. She's so miserable normally. Honestly, she's spent most of her adult life in a sulk. Except last week she had a smile on her face. It was incredible. And it made me think that maybe I should give commitment a go. I've tried everything else.'

There is a rustle of the curtain and Henry pops his head out of the changing room. 'I'm not sure this is me.'

'*Doctor* Henry,' says Dominique, 'of *course* it's you. The clothes are gorgeous and you're going to look like dynamite. Now let me see. Come on!'

Dominique is relishing her self-appointed role as Henry's chief stylist and her approach is somewhere between Trinny and Susannah and a Soviet interrogator. Henry reluctantly drops the curtain and steps forward. The three of us are stunned into silence.

'What do you think?'

Until now, we were under the impression that we couldn't go wrong with these outfits. But this one *has* gone wrong. Very wrong.

'How did he do that?' mutters Dominique.

'What?' I whisper.

'Make those beautiful clothes look like . . . *that.*'

After ten minutes of close inspection, a number of problems become clear. First, a phone call to his mum confirms that the sizes he gave us were completely wrong, which explains why his trousers make him look like a nineteenth-century chimney sweep.

Secondly, despite the simplest of instructions, Henry managed to mix up the outfits, pairing the posh evening shirt with stone trousers meant for casual daywear. For someone so bright, he can be very dim sometimes.

Thirdly, Henry had attempted to accessorize his new gear with his old gear, and I'm afraid Giorgio Armani himself couldn't have worked with that tank top.

Henry is marched back to the changing rooms with a new set of correctly-proportioned items and strict instructions.

'What's that?' I ask, as Dominique stuffs something into her bag.

'Henry's tank top,' she replies.

I flash her a look. 'He really likes that thing, Dom.'

'I know,' she replies. 'Which is why, for his sake, I'm going to take it home and burn it.'

'I'm getting into the swing of this,' says Henry, picking up the most hideous shirt I've ever set eyes on. We're in the same shop, hunting for clothes, before we send Henry back into that changing room in the hope of more success.

'Good,' I reply, gently removing it from his hand and placing it back on the rail.

He looks at me quizzically. 'What? No good?'

I shake my head.

'It is a bit bright,' he concedes. 'If I joined the mountain rescue service and had to stand out in zero visibility conditions it'd be ideal.'

'But for becoming irresistible to the opposite sex, I'd recommend this instead.' I hold up a stripy Paul Smith shirt, the sort I'd buy for a boyfriend, if I ever managed to get one.

'Isn't it a bit dull? I thought the idea was to give my wardrobe lots of *pizzazz*,' he smirks.

'Are you taking the pissazz, Henry?' I ask sternly.

Dominique appears with an armful of clothes. 'Here's another selection to try – and this time I'm coming with you. There's a private cubicle over there.'

'Christ,' mutters Henry.

'There's no need for that,' she replies authoritatively, leading the way. 'You can keep your underwear on.'

'That's very decent of you, Dominique,' he says.

'This is for your own good, Henry,' she fires back. 'I'm only coming in because I need to ascertain your body shape.'

'My body shape is relevant because . . .?'

Dominique looks exasperated. 'Let me hand you over to my friend, the former personal shopper.'

Erin smiles sympathetically. 'The thing is, Henry, body shape is as crucial to helping men dress their best as it is for women. Men with short legs, for example, should wear one colour to elongate their body.'

'I don't think that applies,' I say. Henry towers over most of the men in the room.

'Of course,' agrees Erin. 'It's different for everyone, that's the point. Another example is men who are, you know, *heavy on top*.'

'Fat,' says Dominique, in case it wasn't clear.

'Yes. Such men,' continues Erin, 'should avoid double-breasted jackets or a lighter top than bottom.'

'I never realized it was so complicated,' grumbles Henry.

'Which is why you need me,' replies Dominique, grabbing him by the arm.

Ten minutes later, Dominique emerges from the changing room with a strange look on her face.

'What's up?' I ask.

She sits down and says, 'I'm sorry, I'm almost speechless.'

'What is it?' Erin asks.

'Henry's body.' She shakes her head. 'It's . . . unexpected.'

'What do you mean "unexpected"?' I ask, frowning. 'Is there something wrong with him? Has he got an extra nipple?'

'No, Lucy. It's great.'

'What – Henry's body?' I ask in disbelief. 'You're saying *Henry's* body is great?'

'*Bloody* great.'

'That can't be right,' I scoff.

'I'm telling you: he has a torso Michael Phelps would be proud of. His legs are amazing, and,' she leans in closer, 'he's got the package of a well-hung stallion.'

'Euooow, Dominique!' I am appalled. 'Do you mind? This is my best friend you're talking about. I don't want to know about his package.'

'You would if you saw it.'

I sit back and fold my arms. 'What did you say his torso was like?'

'Michael Phelps's,' she says.

'No way.'

'Maybe that's a slight exaggeration, but I'm telling you: his bod is *hot*.'

'He does play a lot of sport,' I muse.

'There you go.'

'But I can't believe he can have a body that is "bloody great" and that I've never noticed.'

'Neither can I. If a bum like that had been wandering round my flat for years I'd have had to be blind not to notice. Have you never seen him getting out of the shower?'

'He's got an ensuite.' I bite my thumbnail, thoroughly unsettled. 'Anyway, he wears this horrendous dressing-gown thingy so he's always covered up. As for the daytime, I mean – you've seen his clothes. There's no way you'd guess he had a decent physique hiding under those polo shirts.'

'They *are* distracting – but no more! Wait till you see how he's scrubbed up. How're you doing, Henry?' she yells.

He pokes out his head. 'I'm still not sure about this.'

'Come and show us,' Dominique instructs.

'The thing is, these trousers are incredibly tight around my . . . well, *buttock* area. It can't be good for the circulation.'

'Henry, I bet you look great,' says Erin encouragingly.

'And the T-shirt – I'd usually get a size bigger and—'

'Henry,' I interrupt. 'Why don't you let us see? What's the worst that could happen?'

He nods, still looking unsure. Then he drops the curtain and walks towards us slowly, eventually giving us a reluctant twirl.

He's wearing jeans which fit snugly around what I would have to concede is an impressive bum. A bum that has apparently been in hiding. Or at least one I've never looked at before – which is ironic because all three of us are struggling to tear our eyes away now.

On top is a plain white T-shirt, skimming a six-pack that couldn't be more in-your-face if it was on offer at Threshers.

Then I look up and see the world's worst glasses and a hairdo that makes him appear to share a stylist with the stars of *Fraggle Rock*. I'm not disheartened. I suddenly feel as if my flatmate could be on the cover of *GQ*. From the neck down, at least.

Chapter 9

Henry isn't the sort of customer the award-winning and terrifyingly trendy salon *Cut* is used to. Even I feel intimidated and, unlike Henry, I haven't got hair that could be home to several species of wild bird eggs. Everyone else looks so perfect they must get up at 4 a.m. to style themselves.

I'm in the place for two and a half seconds before I dig out my woolly hat and pull it on my head, tucking in stray strands so no one can see them. It isn't even that cold outside, despite being mid-January, and is even warmer in here. But without it on, I have a sudden fear I may be mistaken for a mop head.

After a morning's shopping, Erin and Dominique have left Henry in my capable hands for this part of the process, before we regroup this evening. We're shown to two seats at the back of the salon, where we wait obediently.

'No point trying to hide it . . . I saw those roots when you came in,' sing-songs a voice as my hat is whipped off and a pair of hands starts rummaging around as if examining my scalp for nits.

'What have we here? Light-blonde highlights with a touch of caramel . . . hmm, I think we need to take you a shade or two lighter. Never be afraid to add a dash of drama to your hair. And, dear God, you need those ends seeing to. *Who* cut this last?'

I look in the mirror at my assessor. He's slightly-built with a pinched nose, pouty lips and a fringe bearing about a ton and a half of Elnet.

'You did it, actually. Why, is it crap?' is what I *want* to say. Only I haven't the guts to carry off the lie, particularly as I hacked at my fringe with nail scissors when it was getting into my eyes a couple of weeks ago and I'd never pass it off as professional.

'Actually, I'm not your customer,' I whimper instead. 'He is.'

The stylist looks at Henry and gasps.

Henry smiles, unfazed. 'Hi.'

'Dear God, help me,' the stylist replies, picking up a copy of *Tatler* and fanning his face. 'Hi. I'm Anton.'

The name isn't entirely convincing, given the Norris Green accent, but I'm not going to argue.

'Our friend Dominique recommended you,' I tell him, deciding to namedrop to distract him from Henry's head.

'Dominique?' he smiles. 'The woman whose libido makes me look like Mother Teresa.'

I consider jumping to Dom's defence but decide she'd probably agree anyway. 'She sent us because we're giving Henry a makeover and she says you're the only man for the job. According to Dominique, you're the best in the business.'

He rolls his eyes and smiles. 'I don't like to blow my own trumpet . . .'

A stylist walking past sniggers.

'Ignore her,' continues Anton. 'Right, *Enrico*, let's have a look.' He takes a step back and studies Henry's hair with intense concentration. 'I think we need something slightly *avant garde* . . .'

'Great!' says Henry, as alarm bells go off in my head.

'I'm not sure *avant garde* is quite what we're after,' I add hastily.

Anton fires me a withering look. 'Oh. *Quite* what are you after?'

'Something sexy. And simple. Something that will make him instantly fanciable.'

Anton's face softens. 'Okay. I can do instantly fanciable. Right, dear: tell me what products you're currently using.'

I can't help but snigger.

'*Products?*' asks Henry.

'You know: gels, mousses, serums?'

'Nothing,' says Henry.

'Hmmm. I should have guessed that. Well, from now on you *will* be using them. We'll have you looking like Josh Hartnett in no time.'

'I rather liked Orlando Broom's hair,' says Henry.

'Bloom,' I hiss, wondering if he does this deliberately.

Henry is ushered to the sinks to get his hair washed by a sixteen-year-old with an approach to shampooing like a WWE wrestler. After pummelling his head for five minutes she proceeds to give him an 'Indian head massage', using slow, rhythmic movements with a semi-pornographic expression on her face.

Henry's escorted to the mirror and Anton begins his work. It takes half an hour and some of the most flamboyant scissor action I've ever seen, but the results are impressive.

It's short, but not too short. Shiny, but not too shiny. The style, in Anton's words, is a 'sexy-messy, just-showered, natural look that shouldn't take more than ten minutes to achieve'.

Henry is shocked. '*How* long?'

'All you have to do,' says Anton patiently, 'is avoid combing your hair when you step out of the shower –'

'I can do that,' says Henry proudly.

'– and instead, apply the gel and moderately mess up your hair. You know you've got it right if it looks like your lover has run their hands through it.'

Henry flashes me a look. I smile encouragingly.

'Don't worry,' I say confidently. 'It won't be long before you're very familiar with that.'

Chapter 10

Next stop is the optician.

'I feel a bit funny, looking like this,' Henry confesses as we walk across the city centre.

'Good funny, I hope.'

'I don't know. I think so. But I feel weird in these clothes. Don't you think I look weird?'

'No.'

'Not even a bit?'

I look up at him. 'Henry, can I tell you something?'

'What?'

'You looked weird *before*. You don't look weird now.'

'Really?' He stops for a second. 'I looked that bad?'

I feel a twinge of guilt. The last thing I want is to hurt Henry's feelings. 'Not bad exactly.'

'But weird?'

'Well . . . yes.'

'Why didn't you tell me?'

'I didn't think it bothered you.'

'It didn't bother me because I never knew.'

I bite my lip. 'Maybe I should never have started this.'

'No, no,' he insists. 'Lucy, I'm glad this is happening. I'm grateful to you and Erin and Dominique. Slightly terrified of Dominique, I'll admit, but grateful all the same.'

'She can be a bit full-on sometimes, can't she?' I grin.

'She's fine,' he smiles. 'Though I wished she'd kept her hands off my trousers in the changing room. I felt molested.'

I giggle and push open the door to the shop.

'Remind me what's happening tonight?' he asks.

'Dominique, Erin and I will be helping you take your first tentative steps towards being a master of seduction.'

He raises an eyebrow. 'I like the sound of that.'

'Good. Because we need you to be one hundred per cent on board.'

'I am.'

'Good.'

'One hundred and ten per cent,' he adds.

'I hope you're not teasing,' I say.

'Not at all,' he replies innocently.

'How about these?' I hold up some designer glasses similar to the pair sported by a male model on the arty, black and white promotional picture in front of us. In it, he is wearing the specs, a sultry look and the impossibly-toned thighs of a lithe, fresh-faced female model. And not a lot else.

'If that's the effect they have, I'll take three,' says Henry, trying them on. I scrutinize his face and wait to be bowled over by the transformation. Except it doesn't happen. The new glasses are undeniably a better model (well, it wouldn't be difficult) but somehow he doesn't look right.

'You don't look overly impressed, Lucy,' he notices. 'In fact, I've seen you look more impressed at dogs that have pissed in our front garden.'

'Don't worry,' I tell him brightly. 'They're only the first pair we've tried.'

Henry and I spend the next hour going through all the frames before deciding that not a single pair of glasses here suits him. We decamp to another optician's on the other side of the city centre. Only this one has exactly the same makes and models of glasses, none of which make Henry look anything like the glorious embodiments of male prowess in the adverts – and not just because he isn't naked with Kate Moss's sultrier sister dribbling on his pecs.

'How can this be so hard?' I ask despairingly. 'There must be five hundred pairs of glasses in this shop – why do absolutely none suit you?'

'Maybe I've got a funny face,' Henry offers.

'You have *not* got a funny face,' I say. 'There is absolutely nothing wrong with your face. In fact, I wonder . . .'

I stop and look at Henry.

'Hang on.' I reach over and remove his glasses. Putting my hand on his chin, I move it to the side to get a better look. Then I move it to the other side to examine that too.

'What is it?'

'It's obvious.'

'Is it?'

'Henry, you've got a lovely face,' I decide. 'It shouldn't be hiding behind glasses at all.'

I cannot believe this hasn't occurred to me until now. Haven't I seen what happens when Miss Moneypenny removes her goggles in the Bond films? Not just that, but it's absolutely true about Henry's face. He has the potential to be very good-looking: dark blue eyes, a lovely full mouth and a jaw that's as chiselled as any belonging to the models on the posters.

As I look into his eyes again, I find him looking back at me. 'Oh God, I've embarrassed you, haven't I?'

'No, Lucy, you haven't,' he reassures me, squeezing my hand. Henry has lovely hands – big, comforting and smooth-skinned, the direct opposite of some men's hands, which can be such a disappointment. I dated a bloke a few months ago called Simon and, for once, things weren't going too badly until he decided to hold hands as we walked home. It was like clutching a leaky hot-water bottle – wet and warm and distinctly not nice. Admittedly, I've lowered my standards since then.

'Well, I think we should ditch the glasses altogether and go for contact lenses.'

'Really?' He puts his hands in his pockets defensively. 'I'm not sure. I've always worn glasses. I feel more comfortable in them.'

'What has comfort got to do with anything?' I ask sternly.

'Oh yes, I forgot: your high heels cause so many blisters you almost qualify for a disabled badge.'

'Exactly,' I reply.

'Okay. I'll give them a try.'

This turns out to be one of the best decisions I've made all week. Not only does Henry immediately look better without glasses, but the optician who has given him his eye-test and taken his details is *extremely* attractive. Not as conventionally good-looking as Sean or Jake, but between his sparkly brown eyes and winning smile there is definitely something about him. He emerges back into the reception with Henry and heads to the main desk, flashing me a smile.

'So,' muses Sexy Optician as he scribbles a final note on Henry's file, and hands my friend a receipt, 'did I hear you say you're in PR?'

'No, medical research,' replies Henry.

'Excuse me, Mr Fox,' Sexy Optician says smoothly. 'I was talking to your friend.'

Henry doesn't respond.

'Um, yes,' I smile, gazing at Sexy Optician. There's something very appealing about a man in a white coat, I decide. 'I work for Peaman-Brown in Castle Street.'

'I've heard of them,' he says, flashing me a flirty smile. 'So if you had to transform the media image of this company, what would you do?'

'What, this place?'

'Yeah,' he grins. 'That too hard? Are we too boring?'

'Oh, God, no,' I say hastily. 'Not at all. Well, I'd begin by getting to know the business and its key personnel . . .'

'Hmmm.' He raises his eyebrows.

'And . . . probing you for potential stories.'

'*Probing?*' he repeats. 'I think I'd enjoy that.' He taps something into the computer on the reception desk.

'Is this going to take long?' interrupts Henry.

Sexy Optician smiles. 'Not too long, no.' He turns to me again. 'What do you do when you're not probing for potential stories?'

'Oh, you know,' I smile. 'This and that.'

He holds my gaze and I can't resist smiling back, despite my neck starting to feel very hot. 'This and that sounds enjoyable too.'

'Right,' says Henry, clearing his throat. 'How long before these contacts are ready?'

Sexy Optician drags his eyes away from me. 'Two to three days, then you'll need to come back. We'll give you a ring.'

'Good. Well, if that's everything, we need to be going.' He takes my arm. 'Come on, Lucy.'

'So soon?' smiles Sexy Optician, looking into my eyes again.

'Yes,' says Henry decisively.

'Before you go,' SO adds, 'do you think you'd be able to leave your business card? I'd be interested in talking to Peaman-Brown about some opportunities that might be mutually appealing. My name's Paul.'

'I'm Lucy,' I reply, grinning like an idiot. I fumble in my bag before handing over my card.

He looks at it briefly, puts it into his top pocket and pats it protectively. 'I'll be in touch.' He opens the door for us.

When we get into daylight I have a spring in my step. 'Blimey, he was nice, don't you think?'

'Hmmm,' replies Henry non-committally.

'Lovely eyes,' I muse. 'I hope he phones.'

'They sound like a boring company, if you ask me,' Henry says. 'Surely you'd struggle to get PR out of that place. I mean, how would you manage to get an optician on the telly?'

'If there's a way, then I'll do it,' I tell him indignantly. 'I'm quite good at my job, you know.'

'I don't dispute that,' he replies. 'But surely even you can't make a poxy optician shop sound thrilling.'

'They're exactly the type of organization that needs us,' I huff. 'Anyway, it's not just the business. I think Paul might have been . . . interested in me.'

'You don't say.'

'You don't sound very pleased. I mean, bloody hell, it's not like I've had much luck with my love-life. You could be a bit more supportive when I get a break like this.'

'Sorry. You're right. I hope you and Paul have a wonderful life together.'

'He hasn't even phoned yet!'

Henry smiles.

'Oh, you're joking. Right, I—'

I'm interrupted because my mobile is ringing.

'Hello, Lucy Tyler.'

'*Hi, Lucy. It's Paul.*'

My eyes widen.

'*I meant what I said about setting up a meeting to discuss PR. How about over a drink next week?*'

Chapter 11

It never ceases to amaze me how little my mum and dad's house has changed over the years. Mum might have replaced her nets with bamboo blinds from Ikea and the three-bar fire is now a 'living flame', but the house still boasts trinkets from the past that, to my bafflement, have never been thrown out. There's the limited edition soap-on-a-rope in the shape of Kevin Keegan holding up the FA Cup (it's never been used so the poodle perm is as lustrous as in 1974) and the 'Green Lady' picture bequeathed by Great-Auntie Lil – though that's in the spare room now. There's also an array of not-very-tasteful ornaments – wedding gifts largely – that Dad took to the *Antiques Roadshow* last year and discovered that, collectively, they were only slightly more valuable than a used teabag.

'If it isn't the family spin doctor,' says Mum, as I enter the living room. I've popped over to say hello as it's been longer than usual since I last saw my parents.

As ever, Mum's on her feet, dusting surfaces that are already so pristine an asthmatic could eat their dinner off them. 'What have you been up to?' she asks. 'We haven't seen you for weeks.'

'I've been mad-busy at work,' I tell her, slumping into the squashy chair in the bay window. 'Ohmygod, what's that?'

The question is rhetorical as it's perfectly clear that they have a new television in their ten foot by twelve sitting room. It's bigger than Screen One at our local multiplex.

'Good, eh?' grins Dad, glancing up from his remote control. 'Absolutely state-of-the-art.'

'So I see,' I reply. 'Isn't it a bit big?'

'It was a good buy,' he insists – confirmation that it fell off the back of a lorry.

'*How* was it a good buy?' frowns Mum. 'It cost an arm and a leg.'

'It should have been four times the price, Carolyn,' he fires back.

Mum shakes her head. 'Your father mustn't have noticed that we're permanently skint, Lucy – or he'd stop filling the house with more technology than the *Starship Enterprise*.'

My mum is the most sarcastic person I know. If there were qualifications in irony, she'd be an Emeritus Professor by now. This, however, is either lost on Dad or he chooses to ignore her.

Not that her comment isn't justified. While most dads have hobbies such as golf, football or train-spotting, my dad's only hobby is collecting. Collecting crap, to be precise. At least, that's what Mum thinks of it. Dad considers his trinkets as 'life-enhancing'. If true, then between the baromic weather forecaster, the roulette table, the elliptical cross-trainer and the octagonal party gazebo with pop-up sides, their lives must be so enhanced they're having a permanently spiritual experience.

'I can't complain,' continues Mum, polishing the coffee-table. 'It's not as if I don't get my fair share. The weekends to

Paris, flowers twice a week, Cristal champagne to wash my knickers with . . .'

Dad ignores her.

'Living with your father is like having my own Milk Tray Man,' she says. 'Do you want a cuppa?'

Mum and I adjourn to the kitchen and she sets about busying herself again, and not just making tea. She sprays, wipes, polishes and buffs the surfaces of the kitchen with such a vast array of cleaning products I wonder if she's being sponsored by Johnson & Johnson.

'Are you working hard?' she asks, pouring the kettle with one hand and polishing the hob with the other.

'Of course,' I tell her. 'You know I love my job.'

'Only you don't want to take things for granted on a salary like yours. A young woman like you, earning what you earn . . . it was unheard of in my day.'

'It sounds as if you're talking about the nineteenth century, not the eighties. You're only fifty-two.'

'Fifty-one, actually,' she grimaces. 'I'm just saying, you're lucky having a job like that. Not all of us get the opportunities you've had.'

I roll my eyes.

'I mean it. There's no company car and associated benefits when you've got a job scrubbing toilet seats.'

I frown, feeling guilty. 'I know. But you could work somewhere better than that cleaning company – I've already told you.'

She stops and smiles. 'It'll be my Ph.D from Cambridge that makes you think that, will it?'

Mum adores Dave and me. She'd do anything for us, and our childhood memories are littered with examples of this –

from my eighteenth-birthday present (a battered but lovely Mini she did extra shifts to pay for), to her trip with Dave to the Reading Festival (when he was twelve and desperate to see Nirvana). But does that mean we're spared from her biting sarcasm? Not a chance.

'Look,' I continue, 'you don't necessarily need qualifications to—'

'Or is it all those languages I've got?' she interrupts. 'Or my stint as head of the sixth-form debating society . . .'

'Now you mention it, I don't know anyone who can beat you in an argument,' I jump in. 'There are better jobs than the one you've got. Just because you've been cleaning for the last twenty years—'

'Twenty-one.'

'Whatever. It doesn't mean you have to do it for ever. That you're not capable of something else. There are other jobs out there and you should go for them.'

'Lucy, I'm fine with my lot,' she says unconvincingly. 'All I meant was that you've done well for yourself, and that's brilliant. But don't ever stop trying your best. Don't end up like me.'

'There's nothing wrong with you.'

'If you ended up cleaning floors for a living I'd wring your neck, Lucy Tyler.'

'Well, you can relax because it's unlikely.'

'Good.'

'I don't even clean the floor in my own house. Henry does it.'

She laughs and finally sits down at the table, taking a sip of her tea. 'How is our Henry?'

'Fine. I'm giving him a makeover.'

'A what?'

'A makeover.'

'I hope you're joking.'

'No, I'm not,' I say. 'What makes you say that?'

'You're so bossy with him, Lucy. Leave him as he is. He's happy that way.'

'As a matter of fact, it was his idea.'

'Oh yeah?' She's clearly not convinced.

'*Really.*'

She raises an eyebrow.

'Sort of.'

'Well, I like Henry as he is.'

'So do I,' I say truthfully. 'Though he looks a hell of a lot better now he's had his hair cut. And you should see him in his new clothes. He's transformed.'

'How transformed?' My mum narrows her eyes.

'Completely. At least, he will be when he's got his new contact lenses. And Dom says he's got a body like a stallion.'

'*What?*'

'I mean . . . something like that.'

She pauses for a second as an idea creeps into her head. 'Does he look good enough for *you* to get together with him?'

'Eh?' I reply, horrified. 'Mum, I'm *never* going to get together with Henry. Full stop.'

'Why not? He's a lovely bloke – better than some of the no-marks you've brought home.'

'Thanks for the vote of confidence.'

She puts an arm around me and grins. 'Oh, never mind, Lucy. If you're a really lucky girl and play your cards right, maybe you'll end up with someone as romantic as your father.'

Chapter 12

'What time are they coming?' Henry shouts from the hall.

'In about fifteen minutes.' I remove a bottle of wine from the fridge and pour a glass, before marking another *nootrient* on the Diet World chart. I know that, technically, my *Nootrient Calculator* gadget said each glass of wine had two points, but I've decided to let commonsense prevail and over-rule it. I mean, this is *liquid*. Liquid can't possibly contain two points when you can get a Milky Way for that. It's illogical.

'Aren't you ready yet?' I shout back at him. 'You don't need to go to too much trouble with your appearance tonight. You're only *practising* at being a love god.'

'I know.' He comes to the kitchen door. 'You're not letting me loose on members of the public yet. But it'd be nice to demonstrate that I've made some progress.'

'That's the spirit,' I begin, spinning round to face him. 'Oh.'

'What's the matter?'

'What have you done with your hair?'

Instead of the 'sexy-messy, just-showered, natural look', Henry has styled his hair with what appears to be several litres of chip fat.

'Anton said I was supposed to experiment. This stuff is quite the thing, apparently.' He holds up a tub of wax.

I groan quietly.

'That wasn't the reaction I was hoping for,' he says.

I grab him by the arm and pull him in the direction of his bedroom.

'Do me a favour and get it right first time before you start experimenting. Give me that.' I snatch the wax. 'You're only meant to use a blob the size of a five-pence piece.'

'Oh, that explains it. I didn't think such a little tub seemed good value.'

'Oh God,' I say, exasperated.

'I'm definitely sensing you're not bowled over by this look, Lucy.'

'That's very perceptive of you. And also . . .'

'What now?'

'I know your contacts aren't ready yet, but why don't you give Dom and Erin a surprise and do without your glasses?'

'Because I can't see.'

'You're exaggerating,' I say dismissively.

'Lucy, I'm almost blind. If I try to do anything meaningful without my glasses I risk injury or death to anyone within a twenty-five-yard radius.'

'Don't be ridiculous. Now,' I continue, straightening his shirt, 'at least you've dressed okay, that's one thing.'

'Thank God for that.' He looks secretly pleased.

'Don't get too carried away.' I spin him round. 'Now get your head under the shower and wash off that gunk.'

'Aye aye, sir.'

'Then do exactly as Anton showed you.'

'Yes, boss.'

'Remember – like your lover has run her hands through your hair.'

'I'm not sure I'd like to meet this lover,' he says. 'Her hair obsession sounds a bit disconcerting.'

'Hurry up, Henry!' I giggle, as he closes his door behind him.

Dominique and Erin arrive twenty minutes later.

'I found this woman loitering outside,' says Dominique, nodding at Erin.

'I was having a cigarette before I came in,' Erin replies. 'I don't like to smoke in other people's houses.'

'I thought you'd given up,' I say.

'I have. Well, *had*. Not very successfully, as you can see.'

'What does The Lovely Gary think about it?' asks Dominique.

Erin cringes. 'Don't ask. You know what a Nazi he is about smokers. Oh, I *have* to give up.'

'Yes, you do,' I agree. 'Though I'm sure he loves you despite your faults.'

'Yeah, I think he does.' She smiles happily.

As Dominique and Erin go into the living room, I pour everyone a glass of wine, put some pizzas in the oven, go through to join them and put the iPod on shuffle.

'How did it go after we left today?' asks Dominique keenly. 'I'm dying to see Henry's hair.'

'And his new glasses,' adds Erin.

'Are you going to have a stream of women battering down your door?' grins Dominique.

I pause and wonder how to break this to them gently. 'This might not be as easy as we thought.'

Dominique narrows her eyes. 'Why? What went wrong?'

'Nothing went wrong as such,' I reply. 'It's just . . . this sort of thing doesn't come naturally to Henry.'

'Tell us something we don't know.'

'I think he needs coaxing out of his shell.'

'What are you trying to say, Lucy?' asks Erin.

I sigh. 'Look, it's obvious Henry doesn't feel comfortable with his new look yet.'

'Didn't Anton do a good job?' asks Dominique.

'Yes, he did,' I stress. 'Though I suspect Henry's interpretation of his instructions weren't what Anton had in mind. The annoying thing is he didn't need to touch his hair after today.'

'What about the glasses?' asks Erin.

'There are no glasses. None suited him.'

'None?'

I shake my head. 'But it's not all bad news – he's having contacts.'

'Oh.' Dominique perks up. 'Well, that could be good. The Clark Kent effect.'

'Perhaps.' I bite my lip. 'But don't expect too much tonight. Seriously. If you're hoping for Daniel Craig to walk in, you'll be disappointed.'

'We get the message,' says Dominique. 'Keep our expectations low. Story of my life.'

'Good evening, ladies. Anyone care for a top-up?'

As we spin round, Henry is at the door with a bottle of chilled Chablis. The iPod shuffles to the opening bars of 'Love Machine' and I do a double-take.

'Bloody *hell*!' exclaims Dominique. Erin holds her hand over her mouth.

Henry has sorted out his hair – it now looks better than

when he walked out of the salon – and ditched his glasses. This is the first time I've seen the whole combination. I've got to admit: he looks hot.

Henry heads to Dominique and pours wine into her glass, pretending not to notice that her jaw is skimming the floorboards.

'You look lovely tonight – both of you,' he grins. I snigger.

'Henry, *you* look amazing. Daniel Craig?' Dominique turns to me. 'He should be coming to *us* for lessons.'

'That's very nice of you, Dominique,' replies Henry. I know he'll be thrilled with the compliment, but he maintains such an air of cool composure, you'd think people told him this every other day.

'I'm sorry, I've got to see this.' She plonks her glass on the table and stands up. She walks round Henry slowly, scrutinizing his appearance in the sort of detail a forensic scientist might examine a corpse.

'The hair, the clothes, the bod. And look at you without glasses, sweetie.' She grabs him by the chin. 'Never mind finding a girlfriend . . . be mine, baby!'

'Dominique, you're making me nervous,' Henry deadpans.

'You look fantastic, Henry,' beams Erin. 'You must realize.'

'I'll take your word for it. I tried to look in the mirror, but without glasses it's like examining an Impressionist painting.'

'I can't wait to get to work on your flirting lessons.' Dominique claps her hands in glee.

'Okay,' he laughs. 'But first let me change this music.'

Henry wanders to the iPod and puts on 'Scouting for Girls'. I have no idea whether he knows it's 'Scouting for Girls' – if what he says about his eyesight is true then it may just be luck that he hasn't put on my *Teach Yourself Italian*.

'Now,' begins Dominique, 'the first lesson needs to be about disregarding your inhibitions, Henry. Unleashing your inner sexuality.'

'My what?'

'Your *inner sexuality*.' She says it so casually you'd think she was reading a shopping list.

Henry looks thoughtful. 'I must confess my inner sexuality hasn't had an airing lately.'

'Henry,' she breathes, leaning forward on the sofa, 'there is a deeply sensual being desperate to break free from within you – ready to be unleashed upon womankind.'

'Unleashed?' He raises his eyebrows.

She nods. 'And tonight is about helping you unleash it.'

'Er, right.'

'Don't look so worried,' she says. 'You're ready for this. I can see it – I can feel it. Goddamn it, I can *smell* it.'

'That'll be the pizza,' he says.

'No, it's not that. Do you know what I'd compare you with? You are like a raging volcano, Henry – moments before eruption.'

'What – several billion years old and full of gas?'

'Er – I'd better check on that pizza,' I say, and head for the kitchen before Dom catches me giggling.

Chapter 13

Henry was top of the class at everything when we were growing up. But he's not at Kingsfield Primary now, and tonight, as he perches on the sofa, his expression is confused. He's plainly not following what's going on.

'Flirting Rule Number One,' says Dominique, jabbing her biro onto the flip-chart we created from a stepladder and a roll of wallpaper, 'is to feel good about yourself. Do you feel good about yourself, Henry?'

He takes a gulp of wine. 'Fine.'

'Fine, Henry? Fine?' She could be auditioning for the part of the Drill Sergeant in *An Officer and a Gentleman*.

'We don't want you to feel *fine*. We want you to feel *on top of the world*. Feel good about yourself and others will feel good about you. Everyone loves being around a confident, charismatic person.'

'Okay. Yep.'

'You've got every reason to be confident, Henry – because you look wonderful,' adds Erin encouragingly. 'Keep reminding yourself how attractive you are. If you walk into a bar looking like this, you'll be more gorgeous than most of the men in there.'

'And better dressed,' I add.

'With a hairdo Edward Cullen would die for,' adds Dominique.

'God,' says Henry, taken aback. 'I look that good?'

'Yes!' we all reply.

'If I'm that irresistible, can't I go into a bar and wait for them to come to me?'

We laugh.

'What's so funny?' Henry frowns.

'You're not *that* irresistible,' I tell him.

'Oh,' he says dejectedly.

'No one's that irresistible,' clarifies Erin.

'Oh,' he says once more, perking up.

'The fact is, love,' Dominique continues, 'women need a little encouragement. In fact, a lot of encouragement. I don't know any woman who would hit on a bloke if he'd given absolutely no indication that he liked her.'

Erin and I look at her meaningfully and she shrugs, saying, 'Okay, *I* would hit on a guy without that. But I'm an exception. Besides, I'm not Henry's type.'

I detect a flash of relief in his eyes.

'The point is,' she continues, 'you have to *engage* with a woman. To smile at her and say: "I like you, I think you're hot. I want to talk to you, to get to know you better." And you have to say all this to her . . . *without saying anything at all*.'

'I have to pass her a note?'

I stifle a giggle.

'You say all this *with your eyes*,' says Dominique huskily.

'My eyes,' he repeats.

'Your eyes,' she breathes.

'It'll be a lot easier once your contacts are ready,' I add reassuringly.

Henry crosses his arms. 'Heathcliff might have been able to say it with his eyes. Or Lord Byron. Or Dirk Bogarde. But me? At the moment, I can't even rely on my eyes to stop me falling over.'

'Forget those dudes, Henry,' says Dominique firmly. 'We're talking about *you*. Besides, it's not just with your eyes. It's with your whole body language – your smile, the way you hold yourself.'

'The way I—'

'Don't worry,' interrupts Erin. 'We're going to show you.'

'Yes, we are,' adds Dominique. 'Lucy, where is that stool you used to have in the kitchen? We need to create a bar atmosphere.'

I go to the hall, dig out the stool from the cupboard and brush away enough cobwebs to knit an Aran jumper. When I return, Dominique is considering options for a stand-in bar. She takes the stool from me and places it in front of Henry's piano, next to the one that's already there.

'That works,' she says. 'Now, on you go, Lucy.'

'What?'

'On you go. I need you to sit at the bar with your wine.'

'Why?'

'So that Henry can try and seduce you.'

'You can't be serious.'

She doesn't blink. 'Come *on*. It's only for the purposes of the exercise.'

'Why doesn't Erin do it instead?'

'Oh no,' frowns Erin. 'I don't know Henry as well as you do. He'll relax more with you.'

'But—'

'Come on, no buts,' says Dominique, guiding me to the stool. I am soon propping up the piano, glass in hand – and feeling distinctly uncomfortable.

'I have always hated role-playing,' I mutter. 'Besides, look at me – I'd never sit at a bar like some desperate floozy primed to pounce on the first bloke that appears.'

'You make that sound like a bad thing,' says Dominique.

'Very funny,' I reply. 'I feel weird, Dom. Henry and I are *friends*. I don't want him staring into my eyes and giving me gooey body language.'

'Don't be ridiculous. All you're trying to do is help him.'

I sigh. 'I suppose so.'

Henry enters the room looking as if he's suffering the sort of stage fright that could expedite a beta-blocker addiction.

'Right, Henry.' Dominique claps her hands. 'Off you go.'

He nods and walks tentatively to my side. 'Um . . . do you mind if I join you?'

'Remember what I told you,' coaches Dominique. '*Smile with your eyes*. Think Travolta in *Saturday Night Fever*. Connery as 007. And remember: you're irresistible.'

'Oh God,' I groan. Henry frowns. 'Sorry,' I mutter. 'Um, no problem, take a seat.'

'Now,' Dominique puts her hands on his shoulders and pushes him onto the stool. 'Turn your body towards her, like that. Yes, that's lovely. She can see your fantastic biceps now.'

Henry pulls a face like he's just been served eyeball soup.

'Now, you need to think of an opening line to engage her in conversation.'

'Right.'

'But make sure it's not corny.'

'"Do you come here often" is out then?' he asks.

'Try to be yourself,' says Erin. 'You don't need to come up with something that feels alien. Say something that comes naturally to you.'

'That's good advice,' adds Dom.

'Ummm.' Henry chews the side of his mouth. 'Ummm.'

'You need to say it soon, though – before she gets up and disappears,' adds Dominique.

'Right, yes. Um . . .'

'Come on, Henry.'

'Um . . .'

'Anything!'

'Right!' He turns to me decisively. 'Do you know much about biochemical parasitology?'

I burst out laughing.

'Come on, I was only joking,' Henry grins at Dominique as she looks close to fainting.

'Nevertheless, I'm changing Flirting Rule Number One: no matter how tempted you are, *never* attempt a chat-up line about infectious diseases.'

By two-thirty in the morning, Erin is slurring her words, I'm almost asleep and Henry has performed more than a GCSE drama student. Dominique meanwhile has decided she's bored of teaching flirting and wants to move on to the fine art of *cunnilingus*.

'Woah! Aren't we getting ahead of ourselves here?' Henry asks. 'It's only three hours since we covered open-ended questions. Oral sex feels a bit ambitious.'

'Nonsense,' replies Dominique. 'Henry, look like you do

tonight and act as I've told you, and it'll be no time before you've got a good woman between the sheets.'

Henry flashes me a sceptical look.

'I mean it,' she insists. 'You don't want to get her there with your scintillating conversation and inviting smile only for her to discover you don't know what to do.'

'Who wants another drink?' I say, hoping they'll go home.

'Oh, I'm going to order a cab.' Erin attempts to stand up, but falls back into the chair.

'You're welcome to stay,' offers Henry. 'We can make up the sofa-bed for you.'

Erin looks up with a drunken smile. 'You'll make someone a great boyfriend some day.'

'I hope so, Erin,' he whispers. 'I really do.'

Chapter 14

I've never considered myself an expert on fashion, beauty and hair care, but relative to Henry I'm Stella McCartney, Max Factor and Vidal Sassoon all rolled into one. I certainly know enough to help improve his appearance. And, seeing as I can't count the number of times he's helped me with things he's good at, *Project Henry* is his payback.

I'm not saying I'd have flunked school without him. I was a bright enough child and, more importantly, determined to grow up and get a good job.

When I was five, I announced that I was going to be a physiotherapist. I didn't know what a physiotherapist did, except that there was a glam one in a repeat I'd seen of *The Young Doctors*. Over the years, I aspired to be a television news producer, an architect, a barrister, a property developer and a cardiac-surgeon – though the latter was a fleeting ambition, given that I've never been able to look at a piece of offal without feeling queasy.

The problem was, the only people I'd encountered with jobs like these were on the television. Dad ran three market stalls selling a variety of 'genuine Italian leather goods' – imported from a back street in Taiwan – and Mum was a cleaner. While I have nothing but respect for my parents, I never wanted to follow in their footsteps – and I didn't exactly have a steady stream of people giving me practical advice on exams. With one notable exception.

Whenever I think about how Henry's changed my life for the better, I think about GCSE maths. I should explain that I haven't got what you'd call a mathematical mind. I am to the Pythagorean Theorem what a hippopotamus is to ice dancing: not a natural.

Basically, I hated maths: I didn't *get* it. No matter how hard I tried, none of it made sense. At every lesson, I'd follow the first five minutes, then find myself lost, befuddled and entirely unable to pick up the thread – until the evening, when Henry would explain all.

Despite having his own GCSEs to worry about (though he never worried), Henry spent weeks tutoring me in the run-up to the maths exam. He found the equations easy, but for me, getting to grips with them felt like climbing Mount Kilimanjaro with nothing by way of equipment but a small brolly.

I remember the night before that exam vividly: Henry knocked on the door at about five-thirty as I was finishing my Findus crispy pancakes, beans and chips. That's what I had every night, apart from on Saturdays when Dad would get us a Chinese banquet from the chip shop. Knowing what I now know about dietary fibre, I'm surprised I wasn't constipated until the age of twenty-three.

'Hello, Henry, love,' Mum said, as she opened the door. 'Go through to the living room. She's stopped revising to have her tea.'

'Thanks, Mrs Tyler. How's she getting on?' asked Henry.

'Oh, giving Stephen Hawking a run for his money, I'm sure,' quipped Mum.

I looked up from my plate and there he was, laden with books. 'Fancy some last-minute revision?' he smiled.

'It's too late, Henry. I'm doomed. I'm not cut out for maths.'

'Don't be such a pessimist. Besides, if you want to get into university, you'll need a C at least.'

'Impossible.'

'Not impossible at all,' he beamed. 'You're nearly there. If we get in another couple of hours tonight, you'll do it.'

We headed to my bedroom and spent four hours going over the principles of trigonometry. The really amazing thing about Henry was not just that he was a whiz at these things; he was also a brilliant teacher – far better than the doddery Mr Carter, who spent as much time picking his beard as he did on long multiplication. Henry was patient and kind, clear and concise. He made everything make sense.

I went to bed with a feeling I'd almost describe as confidence.

Then I woke up a bag of nerves.

I recall filing into the exam room in silence, quivering in terror. It was one thing being able to understand things while I was with Henry; quite another on the day.

As I solemnly placed my bag at the front of the exam room, realization struck: I faced a lifetime of crap jobs. University was a pipe dream. There was only one possible outcome: I was going to fail. *OH GOD, I WAS GOING TO FAIL!*

As I took out my pencil case, I spotted the note – slipped in without me noticing – and opened it up.

Pull yourself together, Lucy: you will not fail. If I'm wrong I'll run naked down Church Street with my dad's pants on my head.

I let out a giggle as I turned it over.

Shit, it continued. *You won't muck it up will you?! xx*

I caught Henry's eye on the other side of the room and he winked. I shook my head and tried not to smile.

Fortunately for him, he was right. In fact, by some miracle, I got a B. So the world was spared the sight of Henry, his dad's pants and more flesh than should ever be exposed to the so-called British summer. I can't help thinking it was a victory all round.

Chapter 15

Normally I don't mind Monday mornings, but this one's a challenge even for me. The weather is atrocious as I battle the crowds to work; desperately cold with a howling wind intent on forcing my mascara to relocate to my chin. I push through the doors of Peaman-Brown's offices and plonk down in my seat.

'Heavy weekend?' asks Drew.

My colleague at the desk opposite is wearing a slick Italian suit and pale tie. The sharp scent of his male grooming products assaulted me at twenty-five yards this morning.

'No, why?' I start combing my hair but it is like trying to groom a pan scourer.

He leans back in his chair and studies my appearance. 'You look a bit . . . peaky.'

'Not at all,' I reply indignantly. 'I feel perfectly . . . perky.'

'Only showing friendly concern. Maybe it's just your hair.' He goes back to his paper.

'What's wrong with my hair?' I reply, then curse myself. I know my hair looks like crap, but that's my business.

'Nothing's wrong with it.'

'Good.'

'Nothing's wrong with it *exactly*. It just looks dry.'

'Dry,' I repeat flatly.

'Hmmm. Oh, what do I know about these things? Maybe you haven't washed it.'

'I've washed it,' I reply firmly.

I take my packed lunch box out of my bag and decide to discontinue the conversation in favour of more important matters. Like my diet.

Now I have a date with Paul on Friday, I have resumed it with absolute commitment. My inconsistency with the *Nootrient Calculator* has got me nowhere. In fact, it's got me worse than nowhere – I've put on a pound and a half. Not a huge amount, but given I'm aiming to drop two dress sizes by Friday, it's a pound and a half I can do without.

I have weighed and measured every item of food in my Tupperware box and calculated the *nootrient* value of everything in sight. There is not a grain of rice unaccounted for. So if I don't eat anything that hasn't come from the box by teatime, I'll have only consumed a saintly six and a half points. I haven't eaten so little since I had gastro-enteritis last year. God, I feel better already.

'Have you got the *Journal*?' I ask Drew, looking round for the local morning paper. 'They're using the interview I set up with Philip La Salle today.'

'Must have been a quiet news day.' He throws the paper on my desk.

'Wow – it's made page one. They'll be thrilled. I wonder if their Marketing Manager's seen it?'

'Are you sleeping with Graham Klein?'

'No, Drew, I am not sleeping with the News Editor of the *Journal*, or anyone else at the *Journal* for that matter.'

'It never ceases to amaze me what you persuade them to print.'

I decide to do the mature thing and ignore him. Then I change my mind.

'Several journalists better qualified to judge considered the interview not to be rubbish. Otherwise they wouldn't have put it on page one.'

'That's what I'm talking about. No offence, Lucy, but I'm surprised that interview made more than a single column.'

'Even if it was only worthy of a single column – *and I don't think it is* – that would simply be proof that we're good at what we do.'

'We all get lucky sometimes,' he smiles knowingly.

I grit my teeth. 'Have you had any *luck* in getting coverage for Ernst Sumner yet?'

I immediately regret bringing this up, conscious that I've allowed our spiky banter to get out of hand. While Ernst Sumner isn't a big client, their dissatisfaction with Drew as their account manager – and therefore Peaman-Brown as a whole – is serious. I heard on the grapevine that they think he's as effective as a claustrophobic lift boy and are close to firing us. Raising it was a cheap shot.

'As a matter of fact, I'm confident of securing a page one picture for them next week,' he says, as the vein in the side of his neck twitches.

'Good,' I reply genuinely, hoping this closes the subject. Since when did I become the sort of person to gloat about another's failures? Even if they are Drew's.

'I've been doing a lot of background work with them,' he continues, his neck reddening. 'In fact, I'm about to—'

'Hey, Lucy.' My boss, Roger Peaman, bounds towards his

office on the other side of the room. He is fifty-seven but has the energy of a two-million-watt light bulb. 'Checked your emails recently?'

'No, why?'

'Have a look at the one Barry Dixon from Hattons sent. I've forwarded it. He's so pleased with your press launch he wants to extend our contract. You're a star!'

'That's brilliant,' I grin. I spin round to my computer and catch a glimpse of Drew's expression. He looks momentarily crushed; this is the sort of conversation I doubt he's ever had with Roger. I try to think of something nice to say, but Little Lynette appears at the side of my desk with the mail before I have a chance.

'Thanks, Lynette,' I say, taking my letters. 'How are you?'

'Ooh, fab,' she says. 'I'm getting a new car so I'm all excited. Drew, you're into cars, aren't you?'

He brightens. 'Love 'em. What I don't know about cars isn't worth knowing. What are you getting?'

She scrunches up her face as if rummaging in the back of her mind. 'It'll come to me,' she says hazily. 'It's blue . . . with four doors . . . or maybe two . . .'

'No idea of the make and model?' His eyes are drawn to her cleavage.

'Got it!' She clicks her fingers. 'It's an Alberto V05.'

Drew smiles. 'Fantastic vehicle, Lynette – an excellent choice. Sporty, sexy and highly charged. Rather like me.'

'Ooh, you mucky bugger!' she squeals and skips away. I fear for the future of this company sometimes.

Dominique and I are in meetings for most of the day, but finally catch up late in the afternoon.

'How's Loverboy after this weekend?' she asks.

'I think he feels like you and I would if we'd tried to absorb the entire curriculum for a Chemistry A-level in one weekend.'

Dominique shrugs. 'That's how I prepared for all my A-levels.'

'He's overloaded with information, but that can only be a good thing. Some of it's got to sink in.'

'Absolutely. Besides, I've got a good feeling about this. Henry looks amazing.'

'He certainly looks better.'

'Come on, Lucy. I know you two have been friends for ever, but you must be able to see it.'

'Hmmm, I suppose so. It's weird thinking of Henry as some sort of . . .'

'Stud?'

I wince. 'Henry's never going to be a stud. At least, I hope not.'

'Don't be so sure,' she grins. 'Anyway, that isn't the only thing I came over to tell you.'

'Oh?'

'Guess who's been appointed as the official PR firm for one of the biggest property companies in the country?'

My eyes widen. 'Not us?'

'What do you mean, *not us*?' she whoops. 'Of course us! I told you we had it in the bag, didn't I? They tried to phone you ten minutes ago to let you know, but you were in with Roger so the call came to me.'

Dominique and I spend five minutes jumping up and down and hugging each other. When we finally stop, Drew has his coat on.

'Congratulations, ladies,' he smiles insincerely.

'Thank you, Drew,' I reply. 'It's a great win for the company.'

'Well deserved, I'm sure. Anyway, I'm off to a meeting. Oh, and Lucy – you'd better phone Joe at the *Gazette*. I meant to tell you he rang this morning.'

'Right. What's it about?'

'The same thing he phoned for on Friday – the quote they need from Abrams Smith. He was pissed off you hadn't returned his calls and said if you don't get back to him in five minutes they're running a negative piece – with a "no comment".'

'What? But he never left any messages! There's no way I'd ignore something like that over the weekend.'

'Come on, he *did* leave a message.'

I frown. 'Not that I got.'

'Oh.' He picks up a Post-it note from his desk. 'Sorry, Lucy. My mistake.' He passes me the note and grabs his bag, before heading to the door.

Dom looks at my expression and frowns. 'He can't have done that on purpose . . . can he?'

'God knows,' I huff. Though the truth is, I suspect Drew is about as trustworthy as General Pinochet.

Chapter 16

Dominique was right about The Lovely Gary. He wasn't that lovely. At least, he wasn't lovely enough to stick with Erin. I could tell she'd been dumped the second she turned up at the flat with the red eyes and swollen features distinctive of a newly-offloaded girlfriend.

Fortunately, Henry's at rugby practice, so there's only me to console her, which I can't help thinking is a good thing. Henry might only be Henry, but he's still a man – and no one wants a man around at a time like this.

'I can't believe it,' she sniffs, taking a shaky gulp of wine as we sit at the kitchen table, conducting a post mortem. 'I honestly thought he was . . .' Her voice trails off.

'The one?' I offer limply. Poor Erin has told me four times this evening that she honestly thought he was the one.

Her face crumples as she blows into her tissue with the force of an industrial dryer.

'Do you know what he said to me, Lucy? He said I wasn't exciting enough. What does that mean, *not exciting enough*? Am I supposed to start paragliding every weekend?'

This is the fifth time Erin's told me the 'not exciting enough' line, though I'm obviously not going to point that out either. Instead, I shake my head tepidly and tut, carefully composing my next sentence.

'Sometimes men don't know when they've got a good thing,' I tell her, putting my hand on her arm. 'You see it all the time – great relationships thrown away for no better reason than itchy feet.'

I'm careful to refer to 'men', rather than specifically Gary. I've learned over the years that, when comforting newly-single friends, you shouldn't go overboard in slagging off the bloke in question, conniving scoundrel or not. This is largely because of the possibility that they might get back together, though admittedly in this case that sounds unlikely.

But there's also something else: Erin remains, very clearly, head over heels in love with The Lovely Gary. Perverse as it is, any criticism of him would be taken as criticism of *her*. So I'm treading a cautious line.

'Lucy, promise not to think I'm an idiot, but can I ask you something?' She takes out a tissue from her fifth 'handy pack' and wipes her salty cheeks. 'Do you think I could do anything to make him take me back?'

'Short of begging?' I smile softly, obviously not being serious.

'I've already done that,' she whimpers. 'I actually got down on my hands and knees. Can you believe that? I'm a twenty-seven-year-old woman. I own my own house. I have an influential job and responsibility for an annual budget of tens of thousands of pounds. Yet I've been reduced to going down on my hands and knees and begging a man to take me back. What's that about?'

'Oh Erin.' I put my arm around her and feel her shoulders heave up and down.

'I'm pathetic, aren't I?' she sobs.

'Of course you're not pathetic. You've been dumped, that's all. You're reacting exactly as people do when they've been dumped. It's a law of nature.'

'If that's true, I hate the laws of nature.'

'Of course you do. The laws of nature put men on earth who wouldn't appreciate a good woman if she came with a free BMW and a money-back guarantee.'

She smiles half-heartedly.

'The thing is, Erin, he might change his mind, bu—'

'Do you really think so?' she leaps in.

'He *might* change his mind,' I continue, 'but he might not. Hard as it is, the sooner you assume that he won't and – to use a horrible phrase – *move on*, the better.'

'I'm not sure I can,' she sniffs.

'I know it doesn't feel like it, but believe me, you can.'

Her lip starts wobbling.

'Listen,' I continue gently, 'nobody could blame you for wanting to curl up and feel sorry for yourself. In fact, indulging yourself is exactly what you should do.'

Erin is about to say something, when the door slams.

'Hi, honey, I'm home!' yells Henry. It'd be funny at any other time. I flash Erin a look as he appears at the kitchen door.

'Erin – is something the matter?' he asks.

She sniffs and looks embarrassed. 'I'd better be going.' She stands up.

'You don't have to,' I say.

'Don't go because of me,' Henry leaps in. 'Really, I'll get out of your way if you want. I'm good at that, aren't I, Lucy?'

'He is,' I agree.

'But I'm also not a bad shoulder to cry on,' he offers.

'That's also true,' I admit. 'When Tom dumped me, I spent three weeks chained to this table, with a glass of wine on one side and Henry on the other.'

'You see?' he says. 'I'm a world-class listener. I have to be, with Lucy's love-life.'

I purse my lips.

Erin tries to smile again. 'I'm not sure you'd understand.'

'Try me.' Henry sits down and pulls out the chair next to him. Erin sinks into it and I put her wine back in her hand.

'Gary split up with me.'

'Oh dear.'

I frown. He might look appropriately sympathetic but he'll have to do better than that.

'It's not only that.' Erin takes out her sixth handy pack of tissues and opens it with trembling hands. 'Do you know what he said?'

'What?' asks Henry.

'He said I wasn't exciting enough. Can you believe that?'

Henry looks appalled. 'Does he want you to start snowboarding every weekend?'

'That's *exactly* what I said!' Erin slams her hand down on the table and almost makes her wine glass topple over. I grab it immediately, mopping up the slops with a tea-towel. 'Well, I said paragliding, but I meant the same.'

'He sounds like a prat if you ask me,' says Henry in disgust, abandoning the cautious tone I've carefully deployed for last two hours. If he notices my warning look, he chooses to ignore it.

'What sort of insensitive idiot would say a thing like that when they're splitting up with someone?' he rants. 'Who does he think he is – God's gift to womankind? Erin, I know you were in love with him, but he doesn't deserve you.'

I scowl at Henry to indicate that if he doesn't shut up I'll gag him with my tea-towel.

'Sorry,' he shrugs defiantly. 'I think he's a prat. Simple as that.'

I glance tentatively at Erin. She looks shell-shocked.

'Henry, let's not get carried away,' I say, hoping to rescue the situation. 'Gary isn't a pra—'

But before I can finish my sentence, I realize to my astonishment that Erin has started to giggle.

'You know,' she manages, 'I think you might be right. He *is* a prat, isn't he?'

'A prat to end all prats,' Henry says with a rousing thump of his fist. Erin shakes her head, laughing.

'The Crown Prince of Prats.' She looks close to hysterical now.

He pauses and smiles. 'That's the spirit, Erin.' She gazes at him gratefully.

'Henry, you're right,' she says, lifting her glass. 'Here's to a future without Gary. A future without prats.'

Chapter 17

I'm sure my contribution to Erin's emotional recovery was crucial. To the untrained eye, it might have appeared that Henry waltzed in and transformed her from a gibbering wreck to a triumphant feminist. But I'm sure I laid the foundations.

'How's Erin?' asks Henry, after he returns from his morning run and fills a pint glass from the tap.

'Still fragile.' I take a bite of 'slimming bread' toast. It has the culinary appeal of the sweepings from a stable-floor. 'I think it'll be a long time before she turns a corner on Gary.'

'Really?' Henry wipes the sweat from his brow and downs half the glass. 'That's a shame. I hope she picks herself up soon.'

'Hmmm,' I say non-committally as I take a gulp of coffee. If I'm honest, I've been stunned by Erin's apparent buoyancy since the break-up. I wouldn't say she's 100 per cent rehabilitated. But while I expected her to spend all week sobbing relentlessly, she's been over here twice since it happened and hasn't cried once – except to shed tears of laughter at Henry's jokes. Even the crap ones. I can only put it down to her emotional turmoil.

After my years of psychotherapy training, courtesy of the

problem pages of *Jackie*, *Cosmo* and, latterly, Mariella Frostrup in the *Observer*, part of me wonders if I'm losing my touch. If I'd known all it would take was a couple of minor insults, I'd have done that at the start. It's not as if I can't come up with insults. After sitting opposite Drew for the last two years, I've become rather good at them.

'I'd better make a move.' I put my packed lunch box into my bag, relieved that this is the last one of the week. I can't stomach another brown rice, alfalfa seed and red pepper salad, particularly since, as it's Friday, I've run out of everything but brown rice.

Still, it will have been worth it. I've stuck to my diet religiously for four days. If, after this, the jeans I've bought for my date with Paul don't make my bum look like I've spent five years wired up to a Slendertone, I'll be asking Diet World for my money back. At least, I would be if I'd renewed my membership in the last eighteen months.

'Hopefully some of us will have more luck in the love-life department this weekend,' I smile, putting my bag over my shoulder. 'I'm out with Paul tonight, then you're searching for Ms Right tomorrow. Exciting, hey?'

'Oh, yes – I'd forgotten about that.'

'You'd forgotten you were going out to pick someone up for the first time in your life? Are you mad, Henry?'

He looks at me and smiles. 'Have a good day at work.'

'You too,' I call, shutting the door behind me.

Eleven hours later, I shut the same door and head to Paul's local where we've arranged to meet. The second I step inside, my heart beating wildly, I see him next to the bar. He looks up and smiles. It's that broad, twinkly-eyed expression I saw in the optician's a week ago, and it makes my knees turn to Angel Delight.

'She came,' he grins, pulling out a stool. 'It's always good not to be stood up on a first date.'

'What made you think I'd stand you up?'

'Oh, I don't know. You never know with beautiful women. They change their mind at the drop of a hat.'

'Not me. Besides,' I say, 'I thought we were here to talk about PR. You never mentioned a date.'

'Ah. Does that change things?'

I shrug. 'I suppose if I'm here we might as well make the most of it.'

'Good. Then what would you like to drink?'

Before long, Paul and I are deep in conversation, swapping anecdotes about our jobs and childhoods, discussing our favourite films and – to my deep enjoyment – indulging in some of the most outrageous flirting you'd find outside a French massage parlour. It also turns out we've got loads in common.

'Isn't it amazing that we're both such outdoors fanatics?' muses Paul. 'Did I tell you about my climb up Ben Nevis last year?'

Okay, so it's not strictly true that I'm an outdoors fanatic. In fact, I barely know a crampon from a tampon – but I can't let him know that.

'Oh, I've never done that one,' I reply, as if I've only missed it out because I've been training for K2 for three years.

'You should,' he says. 'The views are fantastic.'

After several hours and several glasses of wine, I can't help but hope that – for once – this date is going to result in something longer-lasting than the others. For a start, I'm having more fun. Paul's entertaining, funny, sexy and, even better, he hasn't come to the conclusion that I'm a lunatic. Not yet, at least.

'So what's the deal with you and the guy you were with the other day? What was his name? Harry?'

'Henry.'

'Is there something going on between you two?'

'Me and Henry?' I suppress a grin. 'Sorry, I . . . no. There's nothing going on between me and Henry.'

'Are you related?'

'No, though he sometimes feels like my brother. He's an old friend. My best friend. But there's nothing more to it than that. Never has been.'

'I don't know,' he replies, raising an eyebrow. 'I get a sense that he would if he could.'

'Would if he could what?'

'You know,' winks Paul. 'But then, who wouldn't, with you.'

I shake my head vehemently. 'You're wrong. Honestly.'

'Okay. Then, good.'

'Good?' I smile.

'That way, I haven't got competition.'

Paul has moved closer to me and, with our faces inches apart, he smiles. It's a smile that says: I'm about to kiss you. And you're going to love it.

Only, he doesn't move. After what feels like ten minutes, but is probably less than ten seconds, I feel distinctly awkward.

'Soooo,' I muse, 'exactly how long have you been an opti—'

I'm interrupted by Paul's lips, which are suddenly on mine, kissing me confidently, roughly. A wave of desire rushes through me as I breathe in his smell: sultry aftershave, mints and red wine. As I kiss him back, my unquenched libido goes into overdrive. I don't care that people in the bar can see us. He moves his mouth to my ear and brushes away my hair.

'The bar's closing soon,' he whispers. 'Come back to my place.'

Adrenalin courses through my body. 'I . . . I don't know. I should get back.'

He stops, leans back on his stool and shrugs. 'Okay.'

I am hit by a wave of disappointment. I could kiss, I tell myself – just to continue our chat. *Talking* to him won't break the first date rule. We could continue kissing, but nothing else. That'd be all right, surely?

'Maybe I could consider it,' I whisper, meeting his lips again. He returns my kiss as my pulse goes wild. He pulls away, stands up, grabs my coat and then my hand.

'Follow me,' he says, as I feel a flash of relief that I attended to my bikini line this afternoon.

Chapter 18

I don't end up sleeping with Paul. I always knew I wouldn't, but sometimes I surprise myself by how old-fashioned I am.

Instead, when we get back to his house, the two blokes he shares it with are competing with their girlfriends at SingStar. Never missing an opportunity to crucify an Abba track, I join in with gusto. We sing and drink until 3 a.m. At least, *I* sing; Paul abstains coolly, which would make me feel self-conscious if I was sober. When the others disappear to bed, things get steamy again on the sofa. Look, I never said I was a complete angel.

I reluctantly call a halt to proceedings at five-thirty, determined to leave him wanting. This requires every bit of willpower I can muster – a challenge, given that my willpower is largely obliterated, along with my ability to walk or talk properly. I sometimes wonder how I'd have coped in the nineteenth century, when you had to wait until your wedding night before reaching the inner sanctum of your beloved's trousers. Still, they didn't have tequila slammers in the nineteenth century, so that probably helped.

As I stagger out of my taxi and weave up our path and into bed, my mind is swirling with a combination of booze and excitement. I've been on a date *and it went well! Really well! Unbelievable!*

I have a long lie-in the next morning and am woken by the sound of Henry's piano music meandering through the flat. Henry's a fantastic pianist – he plays everything from Beethoven to Black-Eyed Peas – but we have a rule in the flat that at the weekends he's not allowed to touch it before midday. It therefore means I've slept in rather a long time. When I finally get up, Henry's in the kitchen having clearly had a more industrious morning than me.

'It went *really* well last night,' I announce. I'm so hungover I could sand the floorboards with my tongue, but I still manage to dance round the kitchen.

'I gathered. You haven't been home that late since you accidentally got on the night bus to Blackpool. Do you want some coffee?'

'Yeah, go on. God, Paul's nice. And I really think he likes me.'

Henry flicks on the kettle and spoons coffee into the cafetière. 'That's fantastic, Lucy.'

'Isn't it. Hey, are you okay?'

'Of course. A bit anxious about tonight.'

'You've got nothing to be anxious about. You know the theory now. All we've got to do is put it into practice.'

'I suspect the practice will be rather more challenging than the theory. Dominique and her flip-chart won't be much use tonight.'

'True. But she's right when she says it's about attitude.' I sit at the kitchen table and do battle with the plastic bag containing the newspaper supplements. 'Go in there thinking you're the hottest thing on two legs and people will believe it.

You walk in thinking you're a saddo who's never going to get a girlfriend and people will believe that too. It's a self-fulfilling prophecy.'

He nods.

'Besides,' I continue, opening the listings magazine, 'I'll be there the whole time – and Erin and Dominique.'

'That's partly what I'm worried about.' He pours the boiling water into his cafetière. 'I could do without the audience.'

'*Support team*,' I correct him. 'No one expects you to be perfect first time. In fact, it'd be odd if you were. But flirting and body language are practical-based subjects, Henry. Just like tropical medicine.'

He raises an eyebrow.

'We could sit around all year studying the theory,' I lecture him, 'but until you get out there and have a go, we'll never get anywhere.'

'I can't help thinking that epidemiology is simpler.'

'Look, in a few months' time, when you've snogged a handful of girls, been out on a couple of dates and possibly become intimately acquainted with someone's inner thighs, you'll be wondering what you were worrying about.'

'When did you stop worrying about the opposite sex?'

I reach over and take a bite of his sandwich, stumped for an answer again.

Erin is having a wobble – and I'm quite relieved. It's not normal to be as stoic as she was when you've been dumped.

'I'm not sure I'm coming out tonight after all,' she announces despondently when we speak on the phone at three in the afternoon. 'I don't feel up to it, Lucy.'

'The worst thing you could do is stay in and mope about

Gary. You need to get out. You'll feel better being with your friends than sitting in front of *Last Choir Standing*.'

'*Strictly Come Dancing*, actually. But I take your point.'

'Besides,' I tell her, 'Henry needs all the immoral support he can get.'

'I know. But what if I see Gary? I don't think I could cope.'

'If we do, we deal with it. You can't spend the rest of your life hiding, on the offchance you'll bump into him.'

There's a pause. 'You're right. Of course you're right. Thanks, Lucy. Pick me up at seven-thirty?'

By eight o'clock, *Team Henry* is in a taxi on the way to the city centre and I get a sense that my words of encouragement earlier didn't entirely dispel his malaise. He's hiding it well, but I can tell Henry finds this experience about as enjoyable as having his chest hair waxed by a chimpanzee.

Dominique, however, is full of confidence. 'Henry – you look gorgeous. If I saw someone looking like you walk into a bar, I wouldn't hesitate to make a move.'

Henry smirks.

'Of course, it would depend on the competition,' she clarifies. 'I mean, if Matthew McConaughy walked in behind, I'd have to think twice. Or Johnny Depp. Al Pacino in his *Godfather* days. Ditto De Niro. But, all things being equal, I wouldn't hesitate. Really.'

'That's very reassuring,' Henry says politely.

'How are you finding your new contacts?' asks Erin, applying lip gloss. 'You look so much better without glasses.'

It's nice to see Erin glammed up. I was starting to worry about her this afternoon, but I'm sure tonight is what she needs. She certainly looks the part. Tousled hair, Missoni top, cowboy boots . . . If The Lovely Gary could see her now, I'm sure he'd reassess how exciting he found her.

'The contacts are fine,' replies Henry. 'They took a bit of getting used to, but so did the clothes and hair. I'm not sure I've got the hang of everything yet.'

'If it seems unnatural, don't worry,' says Dominique. 'In time, it'll be second nature. Now, let me clear something up: is this the first time you've tried to pick someone up?'

Henry frowns. 'Yes, Dominique. Until I met you I was a lonely recluse who rarely emerged from my dungeon.'

'It was only a question,' she says innocently.

He smiles. 'I've had plenty of nights out with the rugby squad after matches. But if you mean, is this the first time I've circulated with the express intention of leaving on the arm of a female, I'd have to say yes. It's not as if I haven't *wanted* to do so before, it's just—'

'Let me get this straight: you go out with a rugby team regularly and you've never misbehaved?'

'And as you know,' he continues, ignoring her, 'Lucy and I also go out together a lot.'

'Perhaps that's why you haven't had much action,' she replies. 'Rule number – what are we up to? – don't stick like glue to another female. Anyway, here we are.'

The taxi pulls into the Albert Dock and we step onto the cobblestones. The dock looks beautiful at this time of night, the lights from the bars and restaurants shimmering on the water as they start to come alive.

The bar we choose is far busier than usual, though I have no idea why. It also seems to have attracted so many glamorous women you'd think Paris Fashion Week had relocated here.

I try to read Henry's expression and find myself taking in his appearance. Dominique was right. He does look hot. Which is amazing. Unfeasible. Odd, if the truth be told.

His old features are still there – blue eyes, full mouth, tiny scar from the football stud that impaled his chin when he was a teenager. But perhaps that's why it's so difficult to compute how drastically different he looks with a few simple tweaks.

I'd hoped when we embarked on this makeover that we'd be able to turn my old, lovable Henry into something approaching passable. But he's beyond passable.

'What are you smiling at?' asks Henry.

'Me? Oh nothing.' I snap out of my daze. 'Who'd like a drink?'

Chapter 19

Dominique's attention to *Project Henry* dwindles within twenty minutes. Not through any lack of commitment, she's keen to point out, but because a six-foot-three-inch Johnny Depp lookalike walks in and – well, we can't say she didn't warn us.

Instructing Henry to 'watch and learn', she sashays across the room in her skyscraper heels and touches Johnny D on the elbow in a way that couldn't be sexier if she had an NVQ from the Moulin Rouge.

Dominique cares not that he is ensconced in conversation with a group of eight. She cares not that, as she tosses her hair bewitchingly, she almost knocks someone's gin and tonic out of their hand. She cares even less that, as she introduces herself, the women around him glare at her so intensely you can almost see daggers.

Within seconds, she's deep in conversation with the best-looking man in the room – and he's lapping her up.

Henry shakes his head in amazement. 'If that's the standard I'm working to, I might as well give up now.'

'There are lap dancers who've yet to reach Dominique's standard of brazenness,' I reassure him. 'Let's take one thing at a time. Is there anyone you like the look of?'

Henry leans back on the bar, surveying the room. 'There are lots of attractive women, there's no doubt about that.'

'Who do you fancy?'

'It's difficult to say. Surely fancying someone is about so much more than what they look like.'

'You've got to start somewhere.'

'I know. Only, what if I choose someone who's physically attractive then spend the next half-hour talking to them, only to discover they're dull? Or stupid? Or a white supremacist?'

'Welcome to my world. You'll never find anyone unless you give them a try. Now, who do you think is good-looking?'

'Ummm . . . her?' He points to a woman with soft brown curls and a plunging top.

'She is,' agrees Erin. 'But I heard her saying in the ladies that she's here on a hen night – she's the bride.'

'Even Dominique might agree that's ambitious,' Henry says.

'What about her?' I point to a stylish redhead at the bar.

'Isn't she out of my league?' he frowns.

'No,' I reply truthfully. 'But if you want to try someone else, how about *her*?'

'She looks . . . loud.'

I am about to object, when the woman in question roars with laughter and slaps her friend on the back as if trying to dislodge something from her windpipe.

'What about over there?' Erin points. 'She's with a friend. I'm sure they won't mind you going over to chat.'

'Perfect,' I decide. 'What do you think, Henry?'

The reality of what he's about to do hits him and colour drains from his face.

'Are you all right?'

'Hmmm?' he says distractedly.

'Do you need to sit down?' asks Erin.

'I . . . um . . . er . . .'

'How about some water?' I'm getting concerned now.

'I'm fine,' Henry insists, taking a deep breath. 'And I'm going to do this.' He knocks back his bottle of beer, slams it on the bar and strides off decisively.

Then he stops and turns round, heading back to us. 'But I need another beer first.'

Erin and I nod. 'Fair enough,' she says.

Henry buys his beer, rolls back his shoulders and finally looks ready for action.

'Before I do this,' he turns to me, 'can I ask you something?'

'Anything.'

'Could you two go somewhere else?'

Erin and I exchange looks.

'And *not watch?*' he spells out.

My heart sinks. 'Don't you want us to assess your technique? I think it might help to have our feedba—'

'No, Lucy,' he tells me. 'I don't want you to assess my technique. As grateful as I am for everything you've done, having you assess my technique is about as appealing as watching my parents have sex.'

'You feel quite strongly, then.'

'I do.'

'Of course we won't watch,' says Erin decisively. 'We'll tuck ourselves away in one of the booths. Henry, you don't have to worry about a thing.'

'Good,' he nods. 'Well, here goes.'

'Great!' I say, waiting for him to move.

'There's a free booth over there,' he tells us.

'Okay, we'll head for that one,' I grin, still waiting for him to move.

'Go on then,' he says.

'You go on then!' I reply.

'Oh, Lucy . . . just bugger off, will you? I can't do this with you watching.'

'Fine, fine,' I mutter, as Erin and I head for the free booth. 'God, he's a spoilsport sometimes.'

Chapter 20

'This is killing me,' I say. 'We can't hide here all night. Go to the toilet again – go on.'

'I've been twice in the last hour and each time was a nightmare,' replies Erin. 'Why is it so busy in here? It's normally quite civilized.'

'I've no idea. Maybe it's pay day. Oh, come on, Erin. Do it for Henry.'

She frowns. 'If I go again, people will think I've got a bladder complaint.'

'Do you think I'd get away with going again?' I ask.

'I doubt it, if Henry spotted you the last three times, like you suspect. We should let nature take its course. He's still over there, so he must be doing something right.'

'We *think* he's still over there,' I clarify. 'He could have gone anywhere in the last three minutes.'

'Pop up your head again, if you must.'

'Okay,' I nod.

I clamber onto my hands and knees and spin round on my seat in preparation for my latest reconnaissance mission. I have this down to a fine art now. Pop up head; identify subject; zoom in to establish latest state of play; pop head down.

From start to finish it takes about one and a half seconds. If I haven't managed to get a proper look I repeat the exercise.

I like to think that I look like a Bond girl, preferably one of those sexy Russian double agents. Except of course I'm not from Vladivostock, or in the box of an Austrian opera house trying to assassinate someone. Instead, I'm on my hands and knees on the seat of a pub, trying to clock how successful my friend's chat-up lines are. Apart from that, the similarities are uncanny.

I count to three and pop up my head, scanning the room stealthily, before popping it down again.

'Did you get a look?' asks Erin.

'No, I think he's moved, the crafty devil. Let me try again.'

My head emerges from behind the booth, I survey the scene from left to right, then dip again.

'Definitely moved,' I huff. 'That should be against the rules.'

'Is everything all right, madam?' asks a voice.

I scramble round, fixing my top, until I am upright and staring at someone who appears quite cross.

'I'm the manager,' he announces. 'Our staff have noticed you've been behaving oddly for the last hour or so.'

'Oddly?' I repeat indignantly, as my face turns crimson. 'Not at all. I was looking out for my friend.'

'I'm sure,' he smiles, clearly unconvinced. 'Only, Mr McAfee is a long-standing celebrity client of ours, and when he's here, we like to make life as comfortable for him as possible.'

I scrunch up my nose. 'Who's Mr McAfee?'

He raises an eyebrow in irritation. 'I think we both know, madam, that you're very aware of who Tom McAfee is.'

I think for a second. Tom McAfee, the Australian

Supermodel, has been seen in the city several times in the last couple of days in advance of a big football match this weekend. As a well-known Liverpool Football Club supporter, it's not the first time he's been here, but he's so unfeasibly glamorous that he attracts attention everywhere he goes.

'Tom McAfee's *here*?' I scrunch up my nose.

He throws me a look as if to say I must think he was born yesterday. 'Over there, madam.' He indicates a booth right in front of where Henry was standing.

'Bloody hell,' says Erin, getting out her lipstick. 'I wondered why it was so busy.'

'Only, for your information, we don't tolerate stalkers in this establishment,' continues the manager.

'Stalkers?' I yelp.

'We work hard at making well-known figures feel as relaxed as possible.'

'I, well, I . . .' I bluster, outraged. 'That must be very nice for them. But I promise you I'm not a stalker.'

He purses his lips.

'The only celebrity I've even been within three feet of was Björn Borg – and that was to get his autograph for my mum's birthday,' I tell him furiously.

'I see.' He doesn't appear to be buying this.

'That in itself was enough to put me off stalking anyone. I explained to his bodyguard that I didn't trip up the woman in front on purpose – she fell. After queuing for forty minutes, what was I supposed to do? Personally drive her to Casualty? Or take advantage of the situation and ask Björn to scribble on my napkin? The only thing—'

'Is everything all right, Lucy?' Henry is standing next to the manager, looking perplexed.

'Henry!' I leap out of my seat. 'This is my friend,' I say to the manager, 'the one I was looking for.' I fling my arm around Henry possessively with a triumphant grin. 'The one I mentioned.'

He turns to Henry and looks him up and down. 'I see.'

'Can I help you with anything?' asks Henry coolly.

'No,' says the manager cautiously. 'No, everything's fine. Enjoy your evening.' He throws me a look and marches away.

'What was all that about?' asks Henry.

'No idea,' I say innocently. 'It's no wonder people complain about civil liberties, honestly.'

'Where's Dominique?' he says.

'Still chatting to Johnny Depp over there,' I reply. 'Now, spill the beans: did you get that girl's number?'

Henry shifts in his seat. 'Not exactly.'

'What do you mean, not exactly?'

'I mean . . . no.'

'Did you not get on?' asks Erin.

'We got on very well,' he tells us. 'Fantastically well. Norah was a lovely woman, absolutely lovely. And Tracy, her friend, was lovely too.'

'Well, if Norah wouldn't do, couldn't you have got Tracy's number instead?' I ask.

'No,' Henry tells me decisively.

'Why not?' I demand.

'Look, it was good practice. I enjoyed talking to them. They were interesting people. Norah recently returned from Canada and—'

'Henry, I don't care if she recently returned from another galaxy. If you got on so well, why didn't you ask for her number? She could have been your first date.'

'She couldn't,' he argues.

'But, she could!'

'No, she couldn't.'

'Why?'

'Because they were gay.'

'Gay?' Erin and I exchange looks.

'Henry,' I frown, 'you're telling me that on the first night we take you to try out your flirting techniques, on the night we unleash you onto the female population of this city with the express intention of getting you together with one of them . . . you spend half of the evening chatting up a lesbian couple.'

'Not chatting up. Well, I started off trying to chat them up, but when they told me their circumstances, it became less of a *chatting up* and more of a . . . *chat*.'

'Why didn't you leave so we could find someone heterosexual?' I feel exasperated.

'It would have been rude. And they were nice.'

Erin sees the funny side and starts laughing. 'Oh Henry. What on earth are we going to do with you?'

I roll my eyes and Henry spots me.

'I had a feeling you wouldn't be impressed,' he says.

Chapter 21

Henry's next seduction attempts aren't a great deal more successful. And although Erin and I aren't supposed to be monitoring him, in the event it's a good thing we do. Everything – and I mean *everything* – he learned in our practice sessions is forgotten when he's within ten feet of a real, live female.

The main problem is how unsettled he looks. Every time he approaches someone, his worried eyes make them glare at him suspiciously, as if wondering whether they might have to use their rape alarm on him.

When he finally engages with a woman at the bar, she's so drunk she can barely stand up, let alone focus on him. After five minutes of 'conversation' – which on Henry's part means blathering away at 210 words a minute and on her part involves a lot of dribbling – she slips off her chair and onto the floor.

Henry rushes to her aid and is grabbed by the shoulders by a seventeen-stone bloke with a face like a querulous bulldog. He turns out to be her brother. Henry tries to placate him, but Erin and I step in before things get messy and instruct him to leave.

'This isn't going well,' says Henry as we decamp to the other side of the bar. 'Maybe I'm not cut out for it.'

'Nonsense,' I tell him, thrusting another bottle of beer in his hand. 'You just need to relax. Seriously.'

'I don't think relaxation is the issue, Lucy. I'd have taken up aromatherapy ages ago if it was.'

'No, Henry – I'm with Lucy on this one,' asserts Erin. 'Remember what we told you. Remember how good you look. You've as much right to be chatting up a woman as anyone else here.'

'How's it going?' asks Dominique, appearing from nowhere with a smile on her face.

'So-so,' I say diplomatically.

'Oh? How many phone numbers have you got, Henry?'

'Don't ask,' he replies. 'Look, I'm sorry if I've let you all down, but it's not working. It was totally different in our living room.'

Dominique takes him by the hand.

'Where are we going?' He looks as if he's been apprehended for breaking a bail condition.

'You're coming with me,' she says, and they march across the room together.

'God help him,' I mutter.

Erin smirks and starts peeling the label off her bottle of Sol. 'Have I told you that Darren, James and Amanda are going travelling?' she asks.

These are Erin's old friends from college. Unlike me, who is terrible at keeping up with old friends (Henry aside), Erin religiously stays in touch with almost everyone, even the kids at her primary school, with whom she now has nothing in common, apart from a similar portfolio of milk-bottle-top collages.

'Didn't you once have a crush on Darren?' I ask.

'Oh, that was ages ago,' she smiles. 'I fancied him like mad at university but nothing came of it. We did lots of flirting but either he was seeing someone else or I was.'

'Where are they travelling to?'

'All over the place. Europe first, then the Far East. The aim is to see as many countries as possible before ending up in Australia after a year.'

'Wow. Aren't they a bit old for a gap year? What about their jobs?'

Erin shrugs. 'Amanda's been freelancing for ages and is sure she'll pick up work on her trip. The others have been saving up and will work when they need to.'

'I'm not sure that appeals to me any more. Henry and I did three months round Europe in a VW campervan after university and that was fantastic, but I'm too used to my creature comforts to do it now.'

'I know what you mean. I must admit I'm a bit envious though.'

'Really?'

She nods. 'Part of me wonders whether, now Gary and I have split up, I shouldn't consider something like that.'

'But what about your house, your job?'

'Mad, isn't it? That's part of the appeal.'

'Well, it could be good for you,' I admit. 'Just don't go doing something like that because you don't want to bump into Gary here, okay? *You've* done nothing wrong, remember – it's not for you to go running away.'

'I know.' She's clearly grateful for my concern. 'And I don't want you to think after our conversation this afternoon that I'm not getting over him. Most of the time I feel okay about it. I just have relapses. This afternoon was one of them.'

Dominique reappears and flops into the seat next to Erin.

'Mission accomplished,' she declares, looking at her watch. 'There might be only ten minutes before this place shuts, but I have finally left Henry chatting someone up.'

'How did you manage that?' I ask.

'I walked over to those girls in the corner and got talking to one of them about her Kate Moss at Topshop dress – I'd spot one a mile away. Then I introduced Henry.'

'And?' asks Erin.

'And he was on his way.' She looks rather pleased with herself. 'At least, I think he was. Justin, that's the gorgeous guy I was with before, was leaving because he's got to catch a plane tomorrow morning so I had to go out to give him a farewell kiss.'

I narrow my eyes. 'So you think Henry's doing okay with those women?'

'I couldn't have set him up better, that's for sure,' she replies. 'All he had to do was . . .'

Dominique's sentence trails off as Henry approaches our table – alone.

'What happened?' I ask.

'Well,' he shrugs. 'I'm not sure.'

'What do you mean you're not sure?' asks Dominique, exasperated. 'Did you get her number or what?'

Henry looks away.

'Henry!'

'No.'

'Why not?' demands Dominique.

'It seemed so corny. And . . . not me.'

120

'That's the point,' she says, frustrated. 'Getting dates *isn't* you – that's exactly what we're trying to change, remember?'

'I know you're right, Dominique. But I don't think she found me attractive.'

'How do you know?' I ask.

'I just got that feeling,' he says.

'Right, you lot,' says a doorman, approaching our table. 'Time to go home now.'

We reluctantly make our way out.

'Don't worry, Henry,' I tell him. 'This was only your first attempt. It'll get easier, believe me.'

I hold open the door for Erin, hoping no one can see that I'm crossing my fingers.

Chapter 22

'What's new?' I ask Mum, biting into my second Bourbon biscuit. I didn't particularly enjoy the first one but there's something annoyingly compulsive about them. Especially since there's only half a Diet World *nootrient* in each. At least, I estimate that there is.

'Oh, you know,' she sighs, polishing the picture-frames on the mantelpiece. 'Your father's been reciting love poetry and I've been on a big spending spree down Bond Street. You can't beat them Chanel knickers.'

'Not a lot then.' I take a sip of tea. 'Oh well, Mum, you never know – when I'm the boss of a big PR company I'll buy you as many Chanel knickers as you want.'

'I'm sure they're over-rated.' She finally relinquishes her duster and picks up her tea. 'Your father certainly wouldn't notice the difference between them and Aldi's finest.'

'That's men for you, Mum,' I tell her.

'They're not all like that, are they?' she mutters.

I lean back on the sofa as my brother Dave walks in. It's February and struggling to touch four degrees, but his Saturday-afternoon uniform is the same even when there's ice on the ground: North Face vest (in a pectoral-enhancing size too small), Quiksilver flip-flops (displaying feet that are mysteriously still tanned, despite his return from Ibiza seven months ago) and designer 'lounge pants' (tracksuit bottoms, to you and me). The latter item is Dave's favourite type of trouser – he owns enough pairs to clothe a small nation state. His evening attire is another matter. When Dave and his mates are due to hit the town, the staff at Ted Baker undergo such a major surge in activity they sometimes have to call in reinforcements.

'All right, sis?' he says, ruffling my hair. It now looks as if I've been backcombing all morning. He collapses onto the sofa and sends my tea flying.

'Oh, for God's sake,' I complain.

'What?'

'You've nearly given me third-degree burns.'

He looks at my tea-splattered top. 'Shouldn't be so clumsy.'

I narrow my eyes. 'It was my fault your fat bum caused a tidal wave in my drink, was it?'

He lets out a strange snorting sound, like an asthmatic bison dislodging mucus from its nasal passages. 'You can talk. I've seen less cellulite on the arse of a Sumo wrestler.'

'Dave, you're such a—'

'Takes one to know one,' he interrupts.

Deep down, I love my brother but this is still a depressing conversation. We are twenty-eight and thirty respectively and it is still impossible not to communicate like we did aged eight and ten.

'How's Cheryl?' I ask, maturely deciding to be nice.

'What?' He grabs the remote control and starts scrolling through the sports channels.

'Cheryl. Your girlfriend,' I remind him.

'Oh . . . fine.' He switches the channel to Sky Sports 14.

I'm using the term 'girlfriend' loosely, even though Cheryl and Dave must have been together for several months. In her world, this time-frame means they're on the brink of a proposal; in his, he simply has guaranteed sex with a part-time underwear model (that's what she tells us those photos are for, anyway) when no one else is available.

Not that that's often the case. Dave has women falling at his feet, although how and why is as mysterious a phenomenon as the Northern Lights. Personally, I don't think he's that good-looking, though I appear to be in a consensus of one. When I look at Dave, all I see is a strange cross-breed of boy band member and professional bodybuilder, an explosion of unfeasible muscles and hair gel. Yet, women love him.

'I was born with the Lynx Effect, simple as that,' is how he explains it.

'Yes – you're anyone's for about £1.99,' tends to be my response. But, as I say, today I'm going to be nice.

'How long have you been going out together?' I ask.

'Huh? Dunno. A couple of months,' he replies, switching the channel again.

I frown. 'Dave, she was at Baby Nicola's christening. So you must have known her for at least *six* months.'

'If you knew the answer, why did you ask?'

I roll my eyes. 'God help Cheryl, honestly.'

'She's just bought him some new aftershave,' Mum interjects. 'So he must be doing something right.'

'That's what it is,' I say, sniffing the air. 'I thought you'd had the Brasso out.'

In fact, Dave's aftershave is perfectly nice, but it would be against the rules to admit it. 'What is it?' I ask.

'Dunno,' he replies unconvincingly.

Mum smirks. 'David Beckham's new one. Cheryl's got the Victoria version.'

I stifle a smile.

'I don't know what you think is so funny,' he says. 'There's no danger of anyone buying you a his and hers set, is there?'

I am constructing my stinging riposte when Mum jumps in. 'Give it a rest, you two.'

'*He* started it,' I tell her, only partly being ironic.

'Bollocks.'

I stand and pick up my bag, deciding this is a good time to leave before I really want to throttle him. 'I'm off, Mum.'

'All right, love,' she says, coming out with me.

When we get to the hall, she opens the front door. 'How's Henry getting on with his makeover?' she asks. 'Is he Liverpool's answer to Burt Reynolds yet?'

I pull a face. 'If by that you mean *has he improved*, then yes. Henry looks great. You can't argue with how great he looks.'

'So?'

'Unfortunately, he remains as close to finding a girlfriend as I am to finding a new solar system. It appears that seduction isn't his forte.'

'Well, I'm sure seduction's over-rated too. That's what your father tells me, anyway.'

I chuckle.

'Seriously,' she continues, 'some blokes aren't cut out for all that chatting-up stuff – I think Henry's one of them. He's more honest than that. He's no bullshitter, Henry, is he?'

'True. But not being a bullshitter has got him nowhere with the opposite sex.'

'Oh dear.' She picks up some mail from the side table and

starts idly leafing through it. 'By the way, have I told you what Denise is up to?'

'No, what?'

She looks up from her letters. 'Salsa dancing.' She announces this with a tone that indicates salsa dancing is the most outrageously exotic pastime she's ever heard of.

'Great,' I reply.

She snorts. 'Well, good luck to her if she's hoping to find any Latin Lotharios to grind her hips against around here.'

'You don't go to salsa to find a man,' I chide. 'It's a hobby – a good way to keep fit. People love it. One of my clients does it every week and swears by it.'

'If you say so.'

I shake my head. 'You're so unadventurous sometimes, Mum.'

'Unadventurous? You know how it is, love. I once thought about going down the Lara Croft route and becoming an international antiquities dealer, but decided to become a cleaning lady instead. I thought it'd expand my horizons more.'

I can't help feeling a little annoyed with her.

'Just because you're a cleaning lady doesn't mean you can't have a life,' I point out.

She stops and spins around.

'I mean it,' I stress. 'Why don't *you* go to salsa dancing instead of complaining all the time?'

She looks hurt. 'I'm not complaining. Christ, when did you lose your sense of irony?'

'I didn't. But you're still young, Mum. Think of all the things you could be doing instead of endless housework here.'

'I quite enjoy housework,' she says, then pauses. 'Okay, perhaps "enjoy" is the wrong word. It's more of a reflex action.'

'Come on,' I challenge. 'Tell me why you can't go to salsa dancing with Denise?'

'I don't want to go to salsa dancing with Denise,' she says, exasperated.

'Why not? You might enjoy it.'

'I won't,' she says firmly. 'I'll feel like a dickhead dressed like one of those crap Spanish dolls you get in the airport.'

'It's not *flamenco* dancing!' I cry. 'It's *salsa*. You don't wear costumes.'

'I don't care.'

I pause for a second and look at her. 'You're scared,' I say accusingly.

She pulls a face. 'Listen to you with the dramatic lines. Have you been watching *Steel Magnolias* again?'

'You *are* scared,' I repeat.

'Don't be stupid.'

'Well, what else is it?'

'I just don't fancy it!'

'Whatever you say.' I go to step out of the door. When I turn back to look at her, her lips are so tightly pursed she looks poised to suck snake venom out of someone's leg.

'What is it?' I ask.

'Fine, I'll go,' she replies.

'Really?' I ask, genuinely surprised.

'Let me clarify: I'll go *once*. But the first sign of a pair of maracas and I'm outta there.'

Chapter 23

I am trying my best to look cool and confident. Unfortunately, my neck has come out in blotches again and my hands are sweating like a wrestler's.

The momentousness of being on *date number two* with Paul the optician is too much to bear. Logic tells me that I should feel nothing but positive about the occasion. The fact that he liked me enough to ask for a second date should help me muster some confidence. The problem is, logic isn't something I've got a grip on at the moment. And things haven't been helped by his choice of venue.

When Paul suggested a day trip to the Lake District, I had visions of a romantic lunch overlooking Ullswater, a relaxing stroll round the lake or, if we were feeling adventurous, a scenic ride in a steam boat.

I hadn't imagined – until we spoke on the phone yesterday – a day's 'fell walking' up Crinkle Crags, somewhere I'd never heard of but, frankly, didn't like the sound of one bit. And that was *before* I read the Lake District Walkers Forum website, which says – and I quote: *From the Langdale Valley, the route climbs by Red Tarn to traverse the Crinkle Crags, a craggy ridge with several summits, the highest being Long Top. Rating:* DIFFICULT.

I've no one to blame but myself. But I was worried that I'd never progress to a second date if he found out that the closest I usually get to fresh air is sitting next to the window at work. Besides, the picture I painted wasn't entirely fictional: I *did* go camping with a group of friends in the Yorkshire Dales. Okay, I was fourteen at the time and with the Girl Guides, but let's not split hairs.

Anyway, how hard can it be? I'm physically fit – thanks to the Pilates classes I've been doing four times a week for the last, um, week. But crucially, I now have another factor sure to help me on the road to success.

I own *all the gear*.

Having convinced Paul I made Ranulph Fiennes look like Homer Simpson, there was no way I could turn up on a day's fell-walking without the appropriate attire. I therefore took the afternoon off work yesterday and did ten circuits of Black's store with a shopping trolley, wondering how I'd never seen the attraction of climbing mountains before.

I was overwhelmed with images of beautiful, fit-looking men and women in trendy high-performance outdoor clothing and looking as if all they required to achieve a state of inner bliss was a two-man tent and a portable gas stove.

I have turned up bright and early this morning wearing my new 'durable, quick-drying interactive fleece' (though I've yet to work out what the interactive element is), a pair of 'super-lite chameleon' walking boots – the most expensive in the shop – a chic 'Patagonia half-zip sweatshirt' and a pair of socks so thick you could insulate your loft with them.

I worried last night that everything looked suspiciously new, so I smeared soil from one of Henry's spider plants onto the boots. They now look like I've done a tour of duty in Iraq in them.

'Where's your jacket?' asks Paul, as he slams shut the door of his Land Rover, looking delicious in a capable, rugged sort of way.

'Here,' I grin, pointing proudly to my new fleece.

'No, *your jacket*. I presume you're wearing a jacket as well as your fleece?'

'Um . . . I wasn't going to,' I begin, fearing I've made a faux pas already. 'This fleece is *interactive*.'

'Interactive,' he repeats flatly, as if even he, a veritable outdoor sports expert, doesn't know what interactivity has to do with anything.

'Oh yes,' I say, sticking to my guns.

'It's February, Lucy. It still doesn't look like it'll keep you warm enough at the top.' He looks genuinely concerned.

'Oh, in my experience, jackets weigh you down. Honestly, I prefer just my fleece. Anyway, I've got plenty of layers underneath.'

'How many?'

The answer is one. One and a half, if you include my Wonderbra.

'Oh . . . *several*. I've lost count.'

'Well, it's forecast to be cold today and you know as well as I do how much colder it gets at the top of that mountain. You've got a hat and gloves though, right?'

I glance round and register with alarm that not only are the other climbers in the car park wearing the sort of jackets sported by Eskimos during a chilly spell, but half of them also have walking sticks. All – without fail – are wearing hats and gloves.

I briefly considered such accessories during my shopping trip, but all the hats made me look ridiculous. I came to the conclusion that I'd prefer to be cold than look like a wally.

'It looks like I forgot my hat – and gloves – and, um, coat. I'm sure we'll be okay if we get up some speed though,' I smile.

He frowns. 'Lucy, I know you're an experienced walker, so don't take this the wrong way, but I'd worry about going up there with you without a jacket and gloves – and a hat. I've got spares in the boot. You're welcome to use those.'

Relief floods through me. Dying of exposure at the top of a mountain wouldn't be a successful conclusion to a second date by anyone's standards.

Paul pulls out the spare clothes from his boot and hands them to me one by one. I look at them and my heart sinks. The jacket is a man's and three times too big for me. As I put it on, all my efforts to look sexy in figure-hugging trendy gear are destroyed in one swoop. I look about as svelte as the Yeti.

While the bright red gloves are passable, the hat – a 'beanie' with green vertical stripes on the sides – seems to shrink my head to the size of a dehydrated *petit pois*.

'You ready?' grins Paul, as I am forced to stop scrutinizing my appearance in his wing-mirror.

'Absolutely!' I clap my gloves together enthusiastically.

We set off towards the mountain with patches of fluffy snow on the ground and the sun shining on our backs.

'Don't you love days like this?' says Paul. I swell with pride that I've managed to bag a second date with someone so sporty and dreamy.

'Fabulous,' I agree, breathing in the clear air and striding alongside.

'It's so nice to meet someone who's into this. You'd be

amazed at the number of women who do nothing but the odd yoga class to get their exercise. They don't know what they're missing, do they?'

'Tsk, no. Can't think of anything worse.'

I gaze across the valley and take in the view. Stunning scenery, a beautiful day and a gorgeous man at my side.

Perhaps I'll enjoy this after all.

Chapter 24

'Er . . . Paul, when do you think we might get to the top?' I say, barely able to breathe.

He pauses and turns to speak to me. 'Normally it's four hours up and two and a half down.'

I stop and put my foot on a rock, my chest heaving as I try to catch my breath. I push my glove back to look at my watch.

'I'm sure we've been longer than four hours,' I wheeze.

'Yes. We have,' he replies, and it strikes me that unless I think of something soon, my game's up.

I am going as fast as I can to keep up with him, but the muscles in my thighs feel as if they're on fire, my lungs are ready to collapse and – despite wearing more outdoor clothing than the average Everest climber – I am *absolutely bloody freezing*. I know without having looked in a mirror that my lips are blue. I can't feel the end of my nose, the tips of my fingers or any of my toes.

More than anything else, I am utterly exhausted.

The first signs of the gaping void between Paul's ability and mine came in the first ten minutes when he went striding ahead and I desperately puffed behind, trying to keep up. Which, of course, I couldn't. Paul had to keep stopping and waiting for me. By the time I caught up with him, I was desperate for a rest, but having waited for at least three minutes, he wanted to get going again, meaning I was too tired to catch up with him . . . and so the vicious cycle continued. *Continues.*

'Are you okay, love?' asks a concerned voice as I pause for a rest.

I look up and see a climber. He looks about seventy-five.

'Me? Oh, yes!' I pant, feeling as if my chest is about to spontaneously combust.

'Take it easy, won't you?' he adds with a worried smile. 'You're coming to the ridges now. It's quite hard going, even for those of us who've done it for years.'

'Oh, it's no problem. I'm with my . . . my . . . I'm with someone who knows what he's doing.'

I look up and Paul is nowhere to be seen.

'Okay. Well, good luck.'

As he strides off, I take a deep breath and remove my bottle of water from my rucksack. The water is freezing as it hits my throat but I'm so thirsty I don't care. What I really want is the coffee Paul has in his backpack but he says we're not allowed that until we get to the top.

The sun stopped shining long ago and the lovely fluffy snow at the bottom of the mountain has iced over up here. Which means that as well as being exhausted and freezing I've slipped over and almost broken my leg at least twelve times now. I'm starting to regret not actually doing so – at least then I'd have an excuse to be airlifted down.

I put back my bottle into the rucksack and try to summon some strength.

'*Lucy!* Are you coming?' shouts Paul, who has descended the mountain again to find out where I am.

'Er, yes, I . . . I've injured myself,' I tell him, as if I'm bravely battling against adversity.

'Oh, God.' He looks guilty. He scrambles down the mountain and pauses on the rock above. 'What have you done? Let me see.'

'It's my foot,' I improvise. 'I think I've sprained it. I don't think it's serious, but it is making me slower than usual.'

He looks at it and frowns. 'It's not swollen.'

'These things can be deceptive,' I reply.

'Right. Well, we're nearly at the top so it'd be a shame to turn back now, don't you think?'

'Well, of course, but—'

'Come on, I'll go a bit slower.' He hoists me up.

I can't help feeling annoyed. My injury might be entirely fabricated but he could be more sympathetic. Sulkily, I follow him up the mountain, which gets ever more slippery, treacherous, dark and unenjoyable.

'Here's the first of the steps on the ridges,' he announces. 'I love going across this. Such a challenge. Come on!'

I look across at the gaping chasm, with a sheer drop below. It would be a challenge for Indiana Jones, never mind me.

'Oh, er, I'm not sure this is a good idea with my injury,' I tell him.

'You'll be all right.' I'm sure he thinks his expression is reassuring. 'You've done it before, right?'

'Um . . . not for a long time.'

'Here, follow me.'

Paul proceeds to scale the rocks as if he could do it in his sleep, then turns round. 'Come on, Lucy – you can do it!'

He clenches his fist and punches the air. Fanciable or not, he's starting to get on my nerves.

'Go, Lucy, go!'

I shuffle to the base of the rock wall and look down. My heart freezes in terror and, despite the cold, sweat pricks on my forehead. I want to cry.

'Come *on*, Lucy! You can *do* this!'

I tentatively put out my foot but my leg isn't long enough to reach. Shaking, I try to put my hand on the top of another piece of rock to steady myself, but it slips off the ice. The only way I'm going to make it across this gap is to jump. The thought makes me positively ill.

'LUCY!' shouts Paul.

I take a deep breath, close my eyes and tell myself to find some courage from somewhere. Then I leap.

Instead of landing neatly at the other side like Paul, my foot wobbles and I stumble forward onto my outstretched hands. They're shaking so much they utterly fail to stop my cheek smashing against the rockface with a painful crunch.

'You okay?' He helps me up.

My heart is racing wildly as I take off my glove and hold my hand to my face. 'Am I bleeding?' I ask in shock.

'Only a little. Come on, we need to keep going before it gets dark.'

By the time we get to the bottom of the mountain, it has gone four-thirty and I feel like one of those *Titanic* passengers rescued after fourteen hours on a raft with their legs in freezing water.

My limbs could be made of lead. I'm convinced from the squelching in my boots that I'm developing trench foot. And my body is battered from the number of slips on our frantic journey down the mountain, desperate to beat the fading light.

I trudge into the Old Dungeon Ghyll pub and go straight to the toilet, something I've wanted to do for two and a quarter hours. My legs are so chapped as I peel down my trousers it feels as if they're taking three layers of skin with them.

When I emerge from the cubicle to wash my hands, I'm confronted in the mirror by the face of a banshee and hair that could have been washed in the sewers of turn-of-the-century London. The really weird thing is, I couldn't care less.

I pull out my tube of lip balm and smear its dregs onto my mouth before returning to the bar like I'm in a remake of Michael Jackson's *Thriller* video.

'A pint of bitter and a bowl of soup,' smiles Paul, inviting me to sit down next to him. 'You can't beat it.'

He bends down to his spoon and takes a hearty slurp. In contrast to me, he looks energized, rosy-cheeked and content. Like one of those blokes on the posters in Black's. The bastards.

I pick up my spoon and take a slurp. I have to admit it's good. But then, I could consume a bowl of dishwater at the moment and it'd taste like something Michael Roux had rustled up.

'Tell me, Lucy,' says Paul, leaning back in his seat, 'is it really only recently that you climbed Scafell Pike with a group of advanced walkers?'

I'd blush if I wasn't so numb.

'I haven't been walking for a while,' I mutter. 'But this foot was the main problem. It was playing up from the beginning – that's why I was so slow. I didn't want to say anything.'

'Poor you,' he says.

I look up to see if he's being sarcastic. He doesn't appear to be. Instead, he's smiling.

137

'I wouldn't mind taking a look at it later for you,' he winks.

I suddenly remember what it was that made me fancy him so much. The flirtatiousness. Those sparkly eyes. That winning smile.

'What do you think?' he adds mischievously.

'I don't go around letting *any* blokes examine my foot, you know,' I reply.

'I should hope not,' he adds. 'Only it was rather more than your foot I was hoping to examine.'

Suddenly, the soup is warming me up.

'We should have booked a room here for the night,' he says. 'Driving back is the last thing I feel like doing right now.'

'What sort of girl would I be if I agreed to stay the night with someone on our second date?'

'Does that mean you won't let me seduce you? I was hoping you might.'

'That'll be because I look so gorgeous, is it?' I say ironically, brushing a ratty-ended piece of hair out of my face.

'I'm sure it won't take long before you reclaim your gorgeous self,' he grins, taking a gulp from his pint. 'Your clean clothes are on the back seat of the car. Personally, I think you've got an earthy charm.'

'An earthy charm?' I repeat, appalled. 'Christ, where are those car keys?'

Chapter 25

'Oh Henry, he is lovely,' I enthuse, lowering myself onto a seat at the kitchen table with legs that are still trembling with pain. 'We've got loads in common, did I tell you?'

By the next day, I've forgotten all the horrible parts of my date with Paul and am finding it impossible to think about anything other than how gorgeous he is. This simmering sexual tension is no doubt fuelled by the fact that we still haven't consummated the relationship. I'm determined to leave it a little while with this one: Paul has boyfriend potential – I can feel it. The last thing I want is to give in to temptation and get it on with him too easily, leaving him with any doubts about my *girlfriend* potential. So, after our drive back to Liverpool, we had an old-fashioned smooch on the doorstep and said goodnight. I'm bloody proud of myself. Though how long I can resist, I don't know.

Henry looks up from his papers and smiles. 'You did.'

'It's amazing, he's so into *24* – just like me. And we're both Leos.'

'I thought you didn't believe in all that stuff.'

'I don't, I just thought it was a coincidence,' I tell him. 'How come you're working?'

'I'm going through this report about a new malaria vaccine that's being tried out,' he says. 'Things are at a pretty exciting stage.'

'Do you think malaria will ever be wiped out?'

'There's going to be a long, expensive battle before that happens, but yes, I do. It's got to be. Forget terrorism, Lucy – in terms of threats to the world's population, nothing beats malaria. It kills as many people per day as Al-Qaeda did in New York on September 11.'

'That's one of the things I admire so much about you, Henry. You're doing a job that will save lives.'

'Not enough lives at the moment.' He flicks through another paper.

'Do you think there's so little awareness about it because it mainly affects the third world?'

He considers for a second. 'I do. That's despite the fact that the majority of the victims are under the age of five. They're just babies.'

I feel a wave of pride at what my best friend is doing and it makes me feel slightly choked.

'Anyway,' he says, putting his papers to one side, 'I didn't intend to change the subject. Does this mean you've got another date with Paul?'

I sit up and smile. 'It does. *A third date* – can you believe it? It's been like the Holy Grail for six months and now, bang, I've got a boyfriend. I'm not a complete dead loss, after all.'

'Course you're not a dead loss. Though do me a favour and try not to come back with any more injuries. I'm no expert, but I'm sure that's not the usual turn of events.'

Henry is referring to my bloodied cheek, which is still as vivid after yesterday's battering. Fortunately, I'm not going out with Paul until next week so I have a couple of days to let it settle down. It is then that he's agreed to be my date at the North-west Business Awards, an important black-tie dinner I go to every year through work, and one at which I can't wait to show him off.

'How did *your* night out go?' I ask. Henry, instructed by Dominique to get as much practice as possible, joined the rest of his rugby team on their post-match night out.

'Not bad,' he shrugs. 'I got chatting to a couple of women. No phone numbers though.'

'Don't worry, Henry. It'll happen. I promise you it'll happen,' I tell him.

But neither of us suspects how soon.

Chapter 26

Despite the unpromising title, the North-west Business Awards in the first week of March is always a good night out. I have attended for the last three years, either as a guest of a client or on my company's table. The main purpose of my presence is to schmooze around the room, picking up as much business as possible.

I admit, it doesn't sound exciting. But because the award ceremony isn't exactly succinct, by the time the 'networking opportunities' begin, people are usually so inebriated they struggle to stand upright, let alone try to win their next big contract. It usually makes for a lot of fun.

In one now infamous year, some stockbrokers from one of the city's most traditional companies joined forces with the runner-up of the Best Fledgling Business Award – the boss of an online jewellery company specializing in pretty tasteless, but apparently profitable, earrings – and together, they persuaded half of the room to decamp to a karaoke emporium across the road after the bar had closed. The sight of Rathclays' Chief Executive – a man usually straighter than his golf club tie – singing 'Summer Lovin'' with the diamanté-clad co-owner of *earear.com* has to be one of the enduring images of that year's corporate calendar.

I have more reason than ever to look forward to it this time: Paul is my date. The only downside is that, having spent my entire overdraft on outdoor-wear, I couldn't afford a new outfit. Not without the bank reclaiming all my credit cards and setting fire to them.

So I am being forced to wear one of my wardrobe staples – a slinky strapless dress in deep scarlet.

'What time are you going out?' Henry shouts from the living room.

'I've got to be there for six-thirty,' I say, popping my head round the door.

'Did you want a lift?'

'Do you mind?'

'Not at all . . . oh, nice look.'

I'm sporting a headful of bendy rollers that make me look like a great, pink, re-incarnation of Medusa.

'I've always thought this headgear was under-rated,' I say, touching the rollers. 'Oh, is that my phone?'

I have a permanent mental block over where I've left my mobile and have often thought about attaching it to the end of a piece of string then threading it through my coat-sleeves like Mum used to do with my mittens. Someone should patent the idea. Put something like that on *Dragon's Den* and they'd be chomping at the bit.

'Oh God, what have I done with it?' I ask, throwing cushions and magazines on the floor in a desperate attempt to locate the ringing. 'Hang on, it sounds as if it's in the hall-way.'

'Kitchen,' says Henry.

'Are you sure?' I scuttle out. 'There must be something funny going on with the acoustics in this place because I could have sworn—'

I spot the mobile in the kitchen, next to the kettle, and dive to answer it, but it rings off before I do. I look down and see Paul's number marked *missed call*.

I press redial, but first he's engaged, then the phone goes onto messages. After three attempts, my phone rings again. It's my voicemail.

Hi, Lucy, it's Paul. Sorry to have to do this so late but something's come up and I can't make it tonight. Unavoidable, I'm afraid. Hope it doesn't cause too much of a problem. Speak soon. Bye.

'Oh God,' I groan. 'What am I supposed to do now?'

'Something the matter?' Henry squeezes past me to flick on the kettle.

'I . . . um . . . yes. I've been stood up.'

'Aren't you supposed to be leaving in an hour?'

I look at my watch. 'Forty-five minutes. Oh *God*.'

'What happened to your date?'

'It was unavoidable,' I tell him. '*Really* unavoidable. Family business. Paul didn't go into detail, but it sounded serious. And he was so apologetic. I mean, *really* apologetic.'

Henry continues to frown.

'I'm going to look like an idiot turning up without a date. And Roger will be furious at paying a hundred odd quid for a place that's now going to sit empty. This is a nightmare.'

'Could Dominique go with you?' asks Henry.

'She's already going – on someone else's table.'

'What about Erin?'

144

'At her grandma's seventy-fourth birthday party,' I continue. 'Anyone would do at this stage. *Anyone*.'

Henry pauses. 'I'm not doing anything.'

I think for a second. 'You're right. You're not, are you? Okay, Henry, let's see how you look in a tuxedo.'

Chapter 27

It turns out that Henry looks rather good in a tuxedo. *Really* rather good. I was surprised – and relieved – to hear that he owned such an item, but then I remembered him buying it last year after being nominated for some science award at a ceremony in London.

I never saw him at the time, so can't make comparisons. But tonight, his skin is cleanshaven and smells of an alluring aftershave, the tux gives his already substantial frame more stature, and his hair has been carefully ruffled in a way that would do Anton proud.

As our taxi pulls up outside St George's Hall, Henry steps out to open the door for me and it strikes me how he looks – to use my mother's phrase – 'the part'.

I've been to loads of events here since the hall was restored, but it never ceases to take my breath away. From its Corinthian columns to its imposing steps, the never-ending fluted pillars to the colossal bronze statues, there's nothing understated about this place. In fact, it's as flashy as they come – nineteenth-century style.

We head into the main hall, which is the epitome of Victorian opulence, all chandeliers and friezes, Minton tiles and Arabesques. The event organizers hardly have to try to decorate this place: nothing more than the crispest white linen and elegant fresh flowers are required.

'You seem more relaxed tonight than you were at that bar the other week,' I tell him. 'What's your secret?'

'No secret,' he laughs, picking up two flutes of champagne and handing me one. 'It's nice to be out without the pressure to get someone's phone number. Without having to perform.'

'You never know, you might meet someone tonight who—'

'*No*, Lucy,' he interrupts. 'Tonight, I'm having a break. Being myself.'

'That's all anyone wanted you to be,' I tell him.

I feel a hand on my elbow and turn around to see Roger Peaman, my boss. He's trimmed his beard tonight and looks rather dapper.

'Lucy, how're things?' He kisses me on the cheek.

'Great, Roger. Have you met Henry?'

'Lovely to meet you.' Roger shakes Henry's hand. 'You're the optician, right?'

'Oh no, Roger, that's Paul. He couldn't make it.'

'I believe you're in the running for an award,' Henry says, removing the need for Roger to feel awkward.

'Best Marketing, PR or Advertising Agency,' Roger beams. The award has been on his mind for weeks. He tries to pretend he's not bothered but is about as good at nonchalance as a four-year-old on Christmas Eve.

'Of course, there's a lot of competition. About twenty firms are in the running. Still, it's nice to hear people say we stand a chance.'

'Of course we stand a chance, Roger – we're the best,' I say.

My boss chuckles and nods to Henry. 'I dread to think what she says behind my back.'

Roger is soon off working the room and we're joined by Tom Mathews, a young design company entrepreneur, and a glamorous brunette called Rachel, who I assume is his latest squeeze.

Tom's company is one of Dominique's clients. She's managed to foster an extremely positive client-agency relationship, despite (or perhaps because of) flings with Tom, his Marketing Director *and* his Creative Director.

'How are things, Tom?' I kiss him on the cheek. 'Is Dominique keeping you satisfied these days?'

As the words escape from my mouth I realize how inappropriate they are in the presence of his girlfriend, and blush. Tom doesn't seem to mind.

'You know Dominique,' he replies with a cheeky smile. 'She takes a personal interest in keeping us all satisfied. What line of business are you in, Henry?'

'Nothing like anyone here, I'm sure,' says Henry, clearly self-conscious. 'I work for the Tropical Medicine Research Centre.'

'Really? How *fascinating*,' gasps Rachel. 'I used to live next door to one of the senior people there – Professor Stevens?'

'I know him well.' Henry's eyes light up. 'I'd consider him a mentor. Fantastic guy. He's retired now.'

'I know,' she replies. 'It's years since I lived next to him, but I tell you . . . some of the work you do there – I take my hat off to you, honestly.'

Henry's self-consciousness starts to melt away.

'Henry's working on a cure for malaria,' I add proudly.

'Really?' sighs Rachel. 'That's *amazing*. You make what anyone else in this room does feel trivial.'

'Oh, I don't know about that,' laughs Henry, flashing a look at Tom.

'Don't worry,' grins Tom. 'She's right. Besides, I never argue with my little sister.'

'Oh, you're sister and brother?' I ask.

'I'm afraid so,' she jokes. 'Ooh, I must go and catch up with Nick Dickinson. Henry – I *have* to sit next to you at dinner. I'm dying to hear more about what you do.'

When Tom and Rachel are out of earshot, I turn to Henry. 'You've won a fan.'

'I know.' Henry widens his eyes in astonishment. 'I don't know how that happened.'

We are soon mingling among the guests and I detect a change in Henry. It might be slight, but it's there all right. Instead of the nervy chap we dragged to the bar the other week, tonight's Henry is distinctly self-assured. Not too much, though: he has the right balance of confidence and self-deprecation, of assertiveness and niceness. Deciding he's not here to pick someone up has done wonders.

'How's Loverboy?' says Dominique, as she marches over and slaps him playfully on the bum.

Henry shakes his head in amusement. 'If that slap was the other way round, you could have me arrested for sexual assault.'

'I'd never do that to you, Henry. You can smack my arse whenever the mood takes you. What are you doing here, anyway? I wasn't expecting to see you tonight.'

'Paul had some urgent family business,' I mutter. 'He couldn't make it at the last minute.'

'Hope you're going to make him pay for that.'

'Oh, I'm certain it was genuine,' I leap in, 'and he was really apologetic.'

'Good,' she says. 'Though, looking at Henry tonight, I think you've ended up with a better date anyway.'

Chapter 28

Political correctness gets a lot of stick these days. But when you come across men like David Carruthers, you're reminded why it was invented.

With facial hair like an Old English Sheepdog and a semi-permanent dribble, Carruthers is the conspicuously wealthy owner of various manufacturing businesses – two of which Peaman-Brown represent. He is also the sleaziest man you could meet, someone who, given the choice, I wouldn't sit within a mile of, never mind *next* to.

I hadn't realized men like him existed until I attended a similar event a couple of years ago and spotted him groping the backside of Savilles' Head of Finance.

She responded by spinning round and slapping him across the face in a move that could win her a part in *Kung Fu Panda*. Unfortunately, this only encouraged him. After twenty minutes of fighting him off, she gave up and left, leaving the other guests – male and female – appalled. Yet no one wanted to step in. Somehow, he got away with it. I don't know how, but he did.

'Lucky old me, next to the prettiest girl in the room,' he slobbers, invading so much of my personal space someone should call NATO.

I smile uneasily and inch my chair closer to Henry's.

'Here – would you like a menu?' I thrust the cardboard at Carruthers, hoping its presence between us will send him a clear message. Instead, he grabs it and discards it, before thrusting his elbows on the table and leaning towards me. When I find out who arranged this seating-plan I'm going to throttle them.

'You're one of those lovely PR girlies at Peaman-Brown, are you?' He pulls a handkerchief from his pocket and wipes sweat from his beetrooty brow.

'I work in PR, but have never classed myself as a "girlie",' I reply with a ball-breaking glare. I can't help myself, despite him being one of our clients.

'Are you a secretary?' he asks.

'Apart from Roger Peaman himself, I'm the most senior member of staff here.'

'Hahahahahahhaha! We've got a feisty one here!' He winks at Bob McIntyre, the boss of a shipping company, on his left. 'Dontcha love 'em?'

I glance in desperation at Henry, who is seated on my right. But with Rachel, his one-woman fan club, to *his* right it's clear he isn't in a position to talk. Carruthers grabs a bottle of red wine and splashes it haphazardly into my glass, before starting on his own.

'Come on, let's get plastered,' he snorts, nudging me in the ribs.

'I don't drink red,' I say flatly.

'What?' he bellows. 'You should. It's been scientifically proven to give women stronger orgasms.'

'Is that right?' I say coldly, as Bob McIntyre shifts uncomfortably. He's obviously toying with the idea of rescuing me, but hasn't worked out how without making a scene.

'Not that any woman needs to worry about that with me around. Hahahhahhahahha!' He slaps his hand on the table, delighted at his own wit, as I inch even closer to Henry.

'White wine, madam?' asks a waiter.

'Please,' I nod, taking a large sip as soon as he's filled my glass.

I'm about to get up and excuse myself to go to the ladies, when everyone is asked to take their seats, if they haven't already.

'Greeeaat! Just what everyone needs,' Carruthers scoffs. 'Five hours of speeches from a load of boring businessmen. We need to make our own entertainment,' he adds, leaning towards me and winking again.

I shift my chair so violently I almost cause a four-person pile-up involving Henry, Rachel and the two guests to her right. 'Sorry,' I whisper, but Rachel doesn't look as if she minds.

The awards are longer and duller than previous years. That at least means Carruthers doesn't have the opportunity to open his mouth much – except to make juvenile comments about 'women on top' when any of the award-winners are female.

As the night wears on, my thoughts drift to Paul's message. At first I'd taken it at face value, that something important had come up. Now I'm starting to wonder. Has he gone off me because I was crap at walking up mountains? He obviously didn't believe I'd done Snowdon last month. Or, worse, perhaps he thought my injury wasn't as bad as I said. Maybe he's got me down as a hypochondriac. Hang on a minute: what a *cheek*! Who's he to make judgements about my injuries? He's not a qualified medic. I feel a flash of indignation, before reminding myself that my foot couldn't have been healthier if it belonged to an Olympic sprinter.

A thought strikes me. *I should text him.* To say something subtle and easygoing – but caring at the same time, in case the emergency is as important as I told everyone.

I slip out my phone and start texting.

Hope everything's ok. Shame u couldn't come – is a gr8 nite!

I switch it on to silent and place the phone next to my side plate, flashing Roger a look as if I'm expecting a crucial call from *The Times* newsdesk. Clearly, the only thing on his mind is his award nomination, as it barely registers.

I wait patiently for a response, drifting in and out of a daze between awards. But an hour later, I am forced to accept: Paul is not going to respond.

Chapter 29

The awards drag so much I'm almost catatonic by the time that the 'Best PR, Marketing or Advertising Agency' is about to be announced. I glance in Roger's direction to give him a supportive thumbs-up. Except his seat is empty.

'Where's Roger?' I mouth.

The woman to his right, a retail park chief executive, gives a bewildered shrug. Whispers are exchanged across the table. People start to look agitated. The strongest theory is that Roger stepped outside to take a phone call a couple of minutes ago, but hasn't been seen since.

'Choosing the winner of Best PR, Marketing or Advertising Agency was a particularly difficult task for our judges,' says the presenter, a cheerful, prematurely-balding building society executive. 'The competition in this sector has become stiff in recent years, with an aggressive rate of new business start-ups making it a particularly buoyant – but demanding – industry.'

'What if we win?' I hiss to no one in particular. 'Who'll collect the award?'

'Looks like that'll be you! Hahahhhhha!' laughs Carruthers, tucking into a plate piled high with booty from the cheeseboard.

'But I can't.' My stomach goes into freefall. 'I hate speeches. I can't do them. I just can't.'

'The agency chosen demonstrated all the factors critical to success in this sector: impressive profit growth, a good spread of customers from different sectors and a high level of creative expertise that ensures every one of its clients is promoted to the full.'

I spin round, seeking help. My mouth is suddenly so dry it feels as if I've been gargling with sand.

'Don't worry,' whispers Henry, sensing my panic, 'there are twenty agencies up for this award.'

'And the winner is . . .'

The presenter opens his gold envelope and I bite my fist so hard I almost take a chunk out.

'Relax, Lucy,' continues Henry. 'You probably won't—'

'Peaman-Brown PR!'

A spotlight swirls across the room as 600 guests begin a lacklustre but somehow still deafening applause. I squint as the light shines in my eyes and hold my hand over my forehead. Every guest on the table is looking at me.

'Lucy,' Henry murmurs, 'I think you're going to have to go up.'

'No way,' I reply numbly. 'I can't move.'

This is no exaggeration. Despite nine pairs of eyes imploring me to stand and walk to the stage, my legs couldn't be less inclined to service me if I'd had an epidural.

As the applause dies down, there's a bewildered hush across the room. The only sound that can be heard is my heartbeat, which thunders in my ears like I've spent the weekend next to the speakers at a hardcore dance festival.

'Er . . . Peaman-Brown, are you out there?' laughs the presenter nervously. The audience titters.

'Come on, girlie! I thought you were the most senior person here!' Carruthers guffaws, spraying semi-chewed Stilton and Digestive biscuit.

'Lucy, you're going to have to do this,' Henry tells me. I look at him in desperation. He smiles supportively. 'You'll be *fine.*'

'Can't you go?' I whimper.

He pauses. 'Do you want me to?'

I am about to say yes. I know Henry will do it for me, without a shadow of a doubt.

Then I realize how ridiculous that would be: my flatmate collecting a gong on behalf of *my* company, a company he has nothing to do with. I owe it to myself, to Peaman-Brown, and to my mentor, Roger Peaman himself, to do this. Despite the fact that I could happily kick him for disappearing.

'Don't worry, I'm going.' I rise to my feet.

The spotlight swirls and lands on me decisively. Music belts out in what's clearly the sound engineer's attempt to whip up the audience again. Sure enough, they start clapping.

I stumble forwards, my high heels wobbling as I clatter between tables. I reach the stage and begin to negotiate the four steps up to the podium as if conducting a high-wire act. Miraculously, I reach the top in one piece, snatch the award from the presenter, kiss him on the cheek and scuttle behind the lectern, which I grip for dear life in an attempt to halt my cardiac-fit style trembling. I can hear my teeth chattering and pray that the mike won't pick it up.

I gaze across the sea of expectant faces and vow that I *will not* freeze. I *cannot* freeze. I can't let my company, Roger, or indeed myself down.

Yet have I ever stood before such a terrifying sight? I don't think so.

'Would you like to say a few words, Miss . . .?' asks the presenter, clearly wishing I'd get on with it.

'Um, yes.' I clear my throat.

I try to think of something to say. Something strong, memorable, witty – something that will make everyone in the room want to hire Peaman-Brown immediately. Yet I can't think of anything. God Almighty, why can't I think of anything?

Then I get a surge of inspiration: I'll do that old trick and imagine everyone in the room naked. *Yes!*

I close my eyes and take a deep breath. When I open them, *everyone* is starkers – every last one. It's not a pretty sight. In fact, it's a bloody awful sight. But it works . . . *it really works!*

'This is a huge honour for a company such as ours,' I tell the audience, surprising myself at how convincing I sound. 'We've achieved a great deal of success in recent years – winning some of the best clients in the region and recruiting the most talented staff. This prestigious award is recognition of the immense hard work carried out by a brilliant team of people.'

This is going quite well.

I ponder my next sentence and smile at a woman in the front row. Like the others, she is completely nude, and has such pendulous boobs you'd think she'd spent the last seventy years breastfeeding.

'There is, however, another person who should be accepting this award. Someone who wasn't able to come up here tonight – and has instead rather landed me in it.'

The audience chuckles, to my relief and satisfaction. A

man a few tables to the left who's had too much to drink continues laughing after everyone else. I'd find it intimidating if he was wearing anything more than a dickie bow and Mr Men socks.

'The person who should be here is the driving force behind Peaman-Brown's success. A man who's great to work with and a truly inspirational boss . . .'

I'm building to the crescendo of announcing Roger's name, when the guy with the Mr Men socks uncrosses his legs, leaving me with an unpleasant eyeful of his tackle.

'My Managing Director . . .'

I desperately try to shake the image of sock Man's willy, but for some reason I am mesmerized by it.

'Roger . . .'

The only thing I can concentrate on is his . . .

'. . . *Penis.*'

I wait for the next round of applause but, bafflingly, the room is silent. Then people start laughing. Laughing uncontrollably. And not a single one of the buggers is clapping.

Deciding to make a sharp exit, I sprint across the stage and stumble down the steps as my face burns so wildly I'm surprised I don't set off an alarm. When I return to my seat, everyone on the table looks stunned, including Henry.

'Why was that so funny?' I feel tears prick in my eyes.

Henry looks surprised.

'Don't you realize what you said?' He looks as if he's about to break the news of a bereavement.

'What?'

He shifts in his seat and leans over to say something quietly.

'Lucy, you called your boss Roger *Penis.*'

'Roger Peaman,' I repeat.

'Not Peaman, *Penis*,' he hisses.

'Peaman,' I repeat. 'I called him Roger Peaman. That's his name.'

'No, Lucy. You didn't. You called him Roger *Penis*.'

I start shaking my head, but I'm so numb I can barely feel it. 'No,' I croak. 'I couldn't have. I couldn't.'

Henry puts a kindly hand on my arm and I look up and see that Roger has returned. Holding up the award, I smile at him in a weak attempt to look triumphant. But the expression on his face would indicate that my boss is not in a jubilant mood.

Chapter 30

'Roger, I'm sorry. I'm so sorry. I don't know what else to say. I really am desperately sorry.'

Roger takes another gulp of wine.

'Let's forget it, Lucy, shall we?' His tone doesn't reveal whether he's planning to forgive me or kill me and bury my remains under the company stationery cupboard. 'We'll talk about it at work tomorrow.'

'You're not going to sack me, are you? Oh God, Roger, please don't sack me. I beg of you. I love this job. I love the company. I love *you*, Roger. I'd do anything to—'

'Lucy, stop it. Please.'

I think I'm about to cry. Again.

It turns out that Roger had stepped out to take a phone call from his mother's nursing home. She's had a spate of funny turns recently and he won't take any chances – even if, like this time, she's just phoning to request he brings over a new M&S nightie.

'I'm not going to sack you,' Roger sighs. 'Fortunately for you, your clients would object too much. Of course, how impressed they'll continue to be after their PR company's MD has been called a bloody great cock, I don't know.'

'Oh God, Roger, I'm so sorry,' I wail, throwing my head onto the table.

Henry appears at my side.

'Take her home, will you?' Roger says to him. 'Please, just get her out of here.'

Henry hoists me up.

'It's probably time we left,' Henry says softly. 'Dominique said she'd see you in the morning. One of her clients insisted they go on to a club, but she said not to worry. Shall we go and get a cab?'

I nod miserably. 'I need the loo first.'

I reach the ladies and hover in the toilet forlornly, almost too ashamed to emerge afterwards. When I finally do, Rachel is at the mirror reapplying her make-up.

'You okay?' She sucks in her cheeks as if entering a decompression chamber and swirls blusher on each side.

I nod. 'Still hoping I'm not going to be sacked, but fine apart from that.'

'Oh, I wouldn't worry about it,' she tells me, picking up her mascara. 'Everyone's had so much to drink they'll barely remember it.'

'Well, thanks,' I force a smile. 'But I suspect they might. All I want to do is go home and curl up under my bed. Until next Christmas, preferably.'

Rachel pauses mid-swipe of her mascara wand and looks at me in alarm. 'You're not going, are you?'

'Well . . . yes.'

'Right,' she nods, trying to look casual but failing miserably. 'Is Henry going too?'

'Yes, we're about to flag down a cab, but . . . why?'

'Oh, you know,' she replies, looking at me meaningfully.

I'm stumped. 'No – what?'

Now she frowns. 'You and he aren't an item, are you? He told me you were just friends and I assumed—'

'No, we *are* just friends. Hang on – you don't *like* Henry, by any chance, do you?'

Rachel goes into meltdown. '*Like* him? God, how could anyone not like him? He's *gorgeous*. I don't know how you can live with somebody who looks like that and keep your hands off him. He's *so* good-looking – and intelligent too. I didn't think they made men like that. Not in real life. Not the *whole package* like he is.' This panegyric is delivered with barely a breath between each word.

'The whole package?' I ask, astonished.

'He *is* single, isn't he? He told me he was.'

'Well, yes.'

'God, what are the chances of that!' Rachel nearly collapses with joy. 'Tell me, do you think I should ask him out? You know him better than I do. Would he think that was brazen?'

I stand back and look at Rachel. At her glossy chestnut hair, glowing skin, luscious lips, impeccable dress sense. I shake my head. 'No, I don't think he'd consider it brazen. I think he'd be delighted.'

'Do you really think so? Oh God, thanks! Do I look all right?'

'You look fabulous,' I reply, thinking how much better Henry's night is turning out to be than mine.

Chapter 31

'Would you really have rescued me?' I sniff in the taxi. 'You know – gone up and collected the award in my place?'

Henry shrugs. 'Yes. Of course.'

'But you don't know the first thing about PR. What would you have said?'

'Oh, I don't know,' he muses. 'Something vague like "Every organization needs PR as much as . . . ER . . . or R and R".'

I burst out laughing. 'You'd have fitted in well. There was a lot of bullshit in those speeches.'

'I enjoyed myself,' he confesses.

'I bet you did. Got Rachel's number, did you?'

He smiles self-consciously. 'Hard to believe, isn't it?'

'Not at all. You need to buy into your own hype, Henry.'

He lowers his eyes. 'Yes, well . . . let's see if she phones.'

'She'll phone.' I've never felt more confident of anything in my life. 'But to go back to my original point, I wish I'd *let* you rescue me. If had, I wouldn't have made the worst acceptance speech since someone thanked their chiropodist at the Oscars.'

He suppresses a smile.

'Except, I can't let you rescue me all the time, can I?' I moan. 'I need to stand on my own two feet.'

'It's not as though you've never rescued me,' he replies.

'Have I?' I stare at him, puzzled. 'I don't remember rescuing you from anything.'

'Course you have. Let me think . . . Colomendy, 1994. There's a good example.'

I grope around in my long-term memory for Colomendy, 1994, before the penny eventually drops. 'I'd forgotten about that.'

Colomendy was an outdoor activity camp in North Wales that played host to 'city kids' like us at least once during our school career – twice if we were unlucky. No, 'unlucky' isn't fair – it wasn't that bad. But it is fair to say that memories of the first trip away from Mum and Dad are bittersweet for most of us.

There was some good stuff: midnight feasts, country walks and missing school for three days. On the flipside though were the kids from the tougher schools, the putrid dinners and more mud than you'd find in the Dead Sea.

For eleven-year-old Henry, there was also Andy Smith. I'd like to say that Andy had matured into a charming, sensitive boy since the days when he used to steal Henry's homework books. Sadly, as we discovered the day of the obligatory cross-country race, the opposite was true.

'Who's signing up for the big race?' called Mr Rogers, the Geography teacher. Mr Rogers was one of those trendy teachers, fancied by all sixth-formers because he wore hooded sweatshirts and was oft-spotted in HMV on a Saturday.

'Go on, Henry.' I nudged him as we sat on a wall sharing a

bag of cola bottles large enough to prompt a diabetes out-
break.

'Hmmm . . . maybe.'

'What do you mean, maybe? I've seen you run and it's like
watching someone with a firework up their bum. You've got
to be in with a chance of winning.'

'I'm happy here,' he shrugged.

'Don't be daft. Our school's hardly got any decent runners.
We'll look like a bunch of losers if you don't.'

It was obvious from the look on Mr Rogers' face that he
didn't consider Henry a potential winner. Although I knew
he could run like the proverbial off a shovel, he kept his skills
to himself and had never signed up for the running club. He
never would, as long as Andy Smith was Captain of our year.

'I'll cheer you on,' I added encouragingly.

He hesitated and stepped down from the wall. 'I'd better
get my shorts on then.'

'Yeah, give us all a laugh, mate,' jeered Andy, when Mr
Rogers was out of earshot. 'Are they the ones with the stripes?
You are *so* uncool.'

By the time Henry was at the startline, the competition
was more intense. Not only had Andy signed up; so, it
appeared, had every hard-knock in the north of England. I
was looking at Fagin's gang in Diadora tracksuits.

'Come on, Henry!' I shouted from the sidelines as he disappeared into the woods with throngs of other competitors to
complete four circuits – about two miles – before emerging
and heading for home. I waited at the finish with the other
too-lazy or too-slow kids, and it seemed to go on for ever. Or
perhaps that was a reflection of how tense I was, desperate for
Henry to prove himself.

When the front-runners finally appeared, it sent the crowd into a frenzy. Four were way ahead of the others: two kids at the front from St Peter's – a rival school – Andy in third place and Henry right behind him.

'Come on, Henry, you can do it!' I squealed.

As the final four approached the finish line, Henry looked up and got a surge of energy. He whizzed past Andy, past the hard kid in second and, after a nailbiting few moments when he was neck-and-neck with the leader, sailed across the finish line as if he'd barely broken a sweat.

The best part was the cheering: scores of kids yelling Henry's name.

'You're a hero!' I screeched excitedly.

'Give over, Lucy.' He blushed, but he knew it was true. God, I was happy for him.

After the race, everyone was supposed to head for the canteen for dinner but I'd forgotten something from my bunk and left Henry being congratulated by teachers and pupils alike. I can't remember what it was – just that the diversion made me late. As I headed to the canteen, hoping to slip in unnoticed, I saw something that immediately raised my suspicions.

I hid behind one of the sheds as Andy emerged from the shower block and sprinted across the grass, carrying what looked like a bundle of washing. He threw the clothes over the fence just into the muddy, cowpat-ridden field next to him, then picked up a stick and jabbed it through, smearing his bundle until it was nicely coated in the recently discharged contents of a bovine bowel. He chucked the stick to the ground and left.

As I approached the spot, I could tell almost immediately

who the clothes belonged to, since nobody else would own a shirt in that shade of green unless they were colour blind.

Under normal circumstances, I'd have picked up the clothes and returned them to the block. Unfortunately, they were covered in enough cow dung to keep a field of leeks fertilized through the year. I was furious; my first instinct was to storm to the food hall and confront Andy myself. Then I remembered Henry. I ran to the shower block.

'Hello?' I called out tentatively.

'Lucy!' His head appeared from one of the windows. 'Oh, thank God. This is really embarrassing, but—'

'Someone pinched your clothes,' I finished for him. 'It was Andy Smith, the nasty little sod. Clearly couldn't cope with being beaten. He's got a problem. Do you know, I ought to—'

'Lucy?'

'Yes?'

'Could you get me some clothes?'

'Oh. Course I can.'

Fortunately, as everyone was at dinner, I was able to sneak to the boys' dormitory and get Henry some clean clothes from his bag. But by the time we walked into the canteen twenty minutes late, Andy had shared the details of his little act with his clique. We sat at the end of a bench with our sloppy mashed potato, limp green beans and leather boot soles (or 'roast beef', as the dinner ladies claimed, though they didn't fool us), as their snide laughter catapulted through the room. Henry put on a brave face but I know it took the shine off his victory. How could it not have?

I'm happy to say that Henry didn't have to put up with the bullying for much longer. The following term, Andy's parents moved him to a private school – something he spent weeks boasting about before he went – and that was the last we saw of him. Life became a lot easier as a result.

Of course, Henry was never going to be Mr Popular overnight – he was still too shy, still too weird. But his social leprosy became less acute after his triumph at Colomendy. So I suppose this is what he means when he says I rescued him, though I'm certain it can't be attributed to me.

I'm also certain of something else: that I'm going to feel like total crap tomorrow morning.

Chapter 32

I know I've hit rock bottom at work when I find myself wondering whether staying at home watching Jeremy Kyle would be a better alternative.

My hangover is nothing compared with the burning, shameful memory of last night. Or the fact that Roger has refused to look at me all morning. Or that my speech is reported – word for word – in the business gossip section of one newspaper (picture caption: *All present and erect . . . Lucy Tyler, who paid tribute to Peaman-Brown owner 'Roger Penis'*).

On top of this, a problem has emerged: two TV stations have finally agreed to a 'behind the scenes' piece with one of my clients, a hospital. I've been pitching the idea for weeks so, under normal circumstances, I'd be delighted. The problem is, they want to go today, to coincide with the publication of an NHS report – at exactly the time I'm running a major product launch for another client. Both are too important to delegate, yet I can't be in two places at once. My only option is to raise it with Roger.

I take a deep breath as I knock on his open door and smile nervously. Roger looks up from his computer and visibly stiffens. He looks as cheerful as a battery hen.

'Got a minute, Rog?'

'Come in,' he replies as I enter the room and shut the door behind me. 'If this is about last night . . .'

'It's not,' I say, and immediately wonder if it ought to be. 'Well, that's obviously *one* of the things I wanted to talk to you about, but—'

'Let's not dwell on it.' He has a weary look on his face, as if he's trying to forgive me, but it's causing him physical pain to do so.

'No, of course. But I *am* sorry, Roger. Honestly. I'm absolutely gutted. In fact—'

'Lucy, I said let's leave it,' he interrupts. 'Consider the matter closed.'

I take another deep breath. 'Thanks, Roger. You're a great boss.'

He rolls his eyes in a way I'm not at all comfortable with. Normally, Roger and I are as close as an employer and employee can get – in a purely above board way, obviously. I've always worked my socks off for him and, from the moment I started work here, Roger and I just clicked.

This morning, for the first time, I feel as though the bond between mentor and student is shattered. I am now the office dunce, the weakest link. It's a sensation I dislike intensely.

'You said there was something else?' he says, interrupting my thoughts.

'Oh, yes. I've got a bit of an issue today.'

As I explain the problem, I analyse his demeanour and become even more paranoid. His body language couldn't be more negative if he was blowing raspberries.

'So basically I need someone to act as back-up on one of the clients,' I conclude. 'The only question is – who?'

'You'll have to keep the games one,' he replies decisively. 'That's the bigger client and there'll be national media to look after.'

'The games one' is the UK launch of a new video game developed here in Liverpool. It's been adopted by one of the world's best-known gaming companies and will eventually be rolled out across the globe. As the city was chosen for the first phase of the launch, they needed an organization with local connections to help pull it together.

'I understand what you're saying but my worry is that the hospital is one of our biggest and longest-standing clients,' I reply. 'They're also desperate to raise the profile of their new Chief Exec, so it's vital the TV crews are persuaded to interview her. Plus, with a new boss in place, we've *got* to underline our worth as their lead agency.'

'But that job's more straightforward.'

I nod reluctantly – not convinced, but with no alternative. Whoever inherits the hospital job had better be good.

'Give the NHS one to Drew,' Roger says, turning back to his computer.

I hear a sharp intake of breath and realize it came from me. 'Pardon?'

He looks up again. 'Come on, Lucy. Drew's an account manager. He should be more than capable.'

I bite my lip and nod. He *should* be more than capable. But if his performance on the Ernst Sumner account is anything to go by, he *isn't*.

I've never been able to work out why Roger can't see Drew's limitations. No, actually, I have: Roger's a great boss in many ways but hasn't exactly got his ear to the ground. As long as the company hits its targets, he's happy. Which is fine usually, but at times like this I can't help feeling resentful. Roger is entirely unaware that Ernst Sumner are on the verge of firing us because of Drew's abysmal performance – and while part of me wants him to know for the sake of the company, I'd feel as if I was telling tales if I mentioned it. Besides, people in glass houses shouldn't throw stones and after last night's performance, my glass house must dwarf the Louvre.

'Okay,' I say reluctantly. 'Drew it is.'

He nods and looks away, leaving me analysing his body language again.

'If that's all, Lucy, I've got a lot to do today,' he says grumpily.

'Of course, Rog,' I reply, backing out of the door. 'Um . . . how about when this is over we arrange that lunch we've been meaning to do?'

He shifts in his seat. 'Maybe. I've got a lot on at the moment.'

As I skulk across the office, I can't help wondering if my relationship with my boss will ever be the same again.

Chapter 33

Every time my mobile beeps this morning, I nearly leap out of my seat like it's wired up to an electric current. This time, I rustle around my bag, praying – again – that Paul has texted me and I'll have something to cheer me up.

When I open it, it's only from Henry. I feel a stab of disappointment.

Hope u r feeling betr, and don't 4get: at least yr speech was memorable. H xxx

Despite everything, I smile. I'm torn between gratitude that I have a friend in Henry and despair that I evidently *haven't* got a boyfriend in Paul.

'I hear I'm being drafted in to save the day,' announces Drew, sliding into his chair and manoeuvring his hand to its permanent resting-place between his legs. 'Couldn't cope on your own?'

'My multi-tasking doesn't stretch to being in two places at the same time.' Then I rein myself in, reminding myself that he is helping me. 'Look, thanks for stepping in. The hospital's an important client, so I appreciate your help.'

'Fine,' he shrugs. 'Oh, I heard about your speech last night. Shame I couldn't be there. Your bit sounded like the highlight.'

The temperature of my blood starts to rise, settling just below the melting point of lithium.

'How did you get along with David Carruthers?' he continues. 'He's one of my favourite clients.'

I shiver. 'Really? Did you meet at the same charm school?'

'I suggested Lynette put you next to him on the seating-plan,' he grins. 'I thought you two would get along like a house on fire.'

'Oh, did you?' I try to keep my mouth shut but it requires so much effort I get toothache.

'Hiya all! Hardly any post today, I'm afraid.'

I look up and see that Little Lynette has had her spray tan topped up and is the colour of a well-soaked conker.

'You're looking very healthy, Lynette,' says Drew, as he puts his hands behind his head and looks her up and down appreciatively.

She giggles. 'I'd never get away with saying I've been to Barbados, would I? I've been for my Fake Bake,' she whispers to me. 'J'ya know, Lucy, I'd recommend that salon in Whitechapel – they do it lovely and deep. Not like the last place I went to. I came back looking like Wednesday bloody Addams!'

In fact, in the seven years I've known her, Little Lynette has never been a shade paler than chestnut.

'It suits you,' grins Drew. 'But then, I can't think of anything that wouldn't suit you.' She collapses into more giggles of delight.

'You know,' he continues, 'it struck me the other day that I never see you in the Dog and Whistle after work, Lynette. How am I going to chat you up if you never come for a drink?'

'The Dog and Whistle isn't really my style,' she says apologetically, referring to the fact that if you asked for a Cosmopolitan in the office local they'd send you to the newsagent's.

'Really?' he says. 'Not even on pub quiz night? Come on my team, Lynette, and I'll show you what it's like to be one of life's winners. Have I told you I've been on the winning team of the North-west Pub Quiz of the Year competition for three years running?'

'Not in the last ten minutes,' I mutter.

'You did mention it,' says Lynette, looking impressed. 'I'd love to be dead clever like that.'

'I went to a good school,' says Drew in an uncharacteristic attack of modesty.

'Aren't you lucky?' she says dreamily. 'I was never academic, I've got to be honest.'

'Nothing wrong with that, Lynette.' He gazes down her top. 'You've got many other attributes, of that there's no doubt.'

The rest of the day is spent pulling together the final pieces of the gaming launch and setting things up before the TV crews go to the hospital. Given that Drew is supposed to be looking after this client today, you might think this was his job. Instead, it is left to me to frantically get everything sorted: arrange times and places, brief personnel and beg my contact at the news station to interview Lena Williams, the hospital's Chief Exec.

Drew meanwhile twiddles with a press release not due until a week on Thursday and, to my disbelief, makes *one* call all afternoon – to the *Journal* business desk, asking again about the Ernst Sumner story that is yet to make it into the paper.

By the time I leave for the launch I feel like a juggling octopus. But the preparation for both jobs is done and I am satisfied that all Drew has to do is turn up and babysit.

It doesn't stop me feeling twitchy – and not just because he's as trustworthy as General Pinochet. TV crews are forever pulling out at the last minute to dash off to a breaking news story. Until their footage is in the bag, I'm not taking anything for granted.

The launch is a whirlwind of activity: of harassed marketing people, nervous commercial directors, bemused technical people and tons of media. Which means that it goes off without a hitch. Because tons of media means tons of coverage – and a job well done.

I get into my car with the Operations Director's glowing words of thanks swirling round my head, but there is no way I can relax until I've reached Drew. I've been texting him for reassurance for the past hour and a half – with no response. As I reverse out of the car park, I put my phone on hands-free, dial his number and feel a swell of relief when he picks up.

'How did it go?' I ask hastily.

'What kind of a greeting is that?'

'Come on, Drew, tell me. Did the crews turn up?'

'There's no need to be so aggressive, Lucy.'

'Drew, *for God's sake*. Please tell me what happened this afternoon.'

'Sorry, Lucy, I'm about to go into the tunnel. I'm going to lose you . . .'

The phone goes dead. I spend twenty minutes trying and failing to get hold of him before I start to fear the worst. I try to reassure myself that I did *everything* I could; I planned it to the last detail. All he had to do was turn up. Surely even Drew can't have buggered that up . . .

Then I remember we're talking about Drew. Roger may believe he's brimming with potential, but as far as I'm concerned he's brimming with something else altogether.

I hit redial, but for the umpteenth time it goes to voicemail.

'Drew, listen . . . can you *please* phone back and let me know how it went? You know how important this client is to me. Come on, put me out of my misery!'

I still haven't heard from him by the time I swerve into our road, pull my car into the kerb and leap out of it. Our front gate is shut and, in a rash attempt to emulate Cagney and Lacey, I leap over it, stub my toe and hobble upstairs with a stoop like Mrs Overall.

'Christ!' exclaims Henry as I burst into the living room.

'I'm in a rush, I'll explain later,' I tell him, snatching the remote and flicking on the television as the title music for the regional news starts.

Chapter 34

I needn't have worried. The item is on fifteen minutes into the programme and it's perfect. The crews turned up, produced a three-and-a-half-minute package (a marathon in TV news terms) and even interviewed Lena Williams, exactly as I'd pleaded with the producer to do.

When the item is over, I lean back and close my eyes in relief.

Then something strikes me: I ought to say thank you to Drew. Little of this was a result of anything he did, but he was the one on the ground today and not to say something feels petty.

I pick up my BlackBerry and start typing. *Drew – saw the piece and it was great. Thx again.*

I'm about to press send, when the BlackBerry flashes, showing that an email has arrived. When I open it, it's from Roger to Drew. I am cc'ed.

Drew, I watched the news and wanted to congratulate you on an excellent piece of work. This is particularly the case given it wasn't your client. I understand it was important that their Chief Executive was interviewed – so to get her on screen for so long was a masterstroke. Your star is rising rapidly in this company. Many thanks, Roger.

'Bloody hell,' I splutter. 'Bloody, bloody hell.'

'Something the matter?' asks Henry.

'Don't ask.'

He doesn't say anything.

'Okay, *do* ask.' I've got to get this off my chest. I am halfway through the story, when the BlackBerry flashes again and I open it up. It is Drew's response.

Thanks, Roger, glad to know my efforts haven't gone unnoticed! The client also seemed delighted with what I'd arranged! It makes all the hard work worthwhile! Drew.

The addition of three cheery exclamation marks makes me want to drive to his house and take a bread-knife to his tyres.

'What is it now?' asks Henry, concerned.

I sigh. 'I think tonight might be a chocolate trifle night.'

He smiles. 'Fine. I'm celebrating anyway.'

'Oh?'

'Rachel called. I've got a date.'

Chapter 35

It is more than a week since I heard from Paul and abundantly clear that another promising relationship is nestling miserably in my emotional wheelie-bin, awaiting collection.

It's so demoralizing. When did I become so unattractive? I'm sure I never used to be. What's ironic is that my diet, with the exception of the chocolate trifle, has been going splendidly. If I stand in a certain position on the scales – on one foot and leaning slightly to the left – I've lost at least five and a half pounds, often more after I've been to the loo.

'Lucy, you are *not* unattractive. On the contrary, you are gorgeous,' Dominique tells me on the phone on the way home from work. I've been with her all day but this isn't a conversation to be had in the presence of your colleagues. 'Some men wouldn't know a good thing if it hit them in the face.'

'I haven't tried hitting them in the face.'

'I wouldn't recommend it,' she laughs. 'Seriously though, you mustn't blame yourself for this. I mean, you played it cool this time, didn't you?'

'Ummm . . .'

'What do you mean, "ummm . . ."'

'I mean, yes,' I say decisively. 'I was an ice maiden.'

'So you didn't phone him?'

'Ummm . . .'

'*Lucy!* How many times?'

'Twelve,' I reply sheepishly. 'Thirteen maybe. I've lost count.'

'Good God,' she says, taken aback. 'I hope you did 1571 to make sure your number didn't show up?'

'Of course. I might be desperate but I'm not stupid.'

'You are NOT desperate,' she howls.

'No, you're right.' I bang my fist on my steering-wheel. 'Oh God, I *hope* you're right. I don't want to be desperate, honestly I don't. It sounds so pathetic. But I'd be lying if I said I wasn't getting worried. How can I not be? At this rate I can pencil in my next snog at about the time I'm starting the menopause.'

'Here's my advice, Lucy: forget about Paul. If he can't see you as the fabulous, intelligent woman you are, then he needs a new pair of his own specs.'

I nod, determined to feel determined again. 'You're right. If a man stands you up on a date and then doesn't bother to phone you for more than a week afterwards . . .'

'Then he's a prize-winning prick,' she finishes my sentence.

'Quite right,' I agree. 'Even if he *begged* me to go out with him after this, I wouldn't.'

'Good girl,' says Dominique, as if toilet-training a puppy.

'Right – thanks. So, where are you and your hot date off to tonight?'

Since meeting Justin, Dominique has been unusually absent. If I didn't know any better I'd say she was looking dangerously like someone in the early stages of a proper relationship – a concept as alien to my friend as facial depilation to Father Christmas.

'We thought we'd stay in and chill in front of the TV,' she says casually.

I pause to check I've heard her right. 'That's not like you.'

'I know,' she whispers, as if she can hardly believe it herself.

Usually, Dominique's idea of a date involves an expensive dinner *à deux*, a wild night on the tiles and then rampant carnal relations at least until dawn the next day and often the day after.

'Is everything all right?' I ask.

'Yeah.' She sounds weird. 'Yeah, it is.'

I narrow my eyes. 'So how are things with Justin?'

'You know, hon, good. Really good. He's . . . I don't know what to say. He's lovely.'

I almost swerve across the road in shock. I've never heard Dominique describe a man as 'lovely'. It's not in her vocabulary. 'Well-hung', yes. 'Loaded', no problem. But 'lovely'? Something's going on.

'You really like him, don't you?'

There's a silence.

'I'd better dash – someone's at the door,' replies Dominique. 'Don't worry about your love-life, Lucy. You never know what's round the corner.'

When I arrive home, I throw my keys on the side table, then stop and smile. Classical music is melting through the apartment like warm caramel: Henry is playing the piano.

As I quietly push open the living-room door, he is completely absorbed. I stand watching him, fondness sweeping through me. Sensing my presence, he stops and turns. 'Hey, Luce – I didn't see you there.'

'Don't stop on my behalf. What are you playing?'

'Debussy. *Clair de Lune.*' He starts up again. 'Do you like it?'

I throw myself on the sofa. 'It's gorgeous.'

He stops again. 'How about a newer one?'

'Feel free.' He launches into another piece.

'Justin Timberlake? Henry, you're such a smartarse. Nobody's meant to be as good at as many things as you are.'

'Not everything,' he corrects. He doesn't have to spell out what he's referring to.

'Well, all that's about to change. Are you excited about your first date?'

'Yeah,' he replies. 'I am.'

For some reason I can't quite put my finger on, I feel a stab of something I can only describe as – and I hate myself for this – *jealousy*. Jealousy that Henry, like Dominique, is about to go out with someone he really likes when I've been dumped again and will be stuck all by myself at home.

I force myself to smile. He smiles back and returns to his piano, resuming his Debussy. I drag myself off the sofa and head to my bedroom to get changed out of my work clothes, appalled at this nagging feeling.

I can't really be jealous of Henry, can I? How *the hell* can I be jealous of Henry? My lovely, wonderful friend who's finally found a woman who fancies the pants off him? Can I really be such a selfish, horrible person that I can't feel 100 per cent happy for Henry – just because nobody wants me? Dear God, don't make me so desperate for a man to like me that I resent—

My mobile is ringing.

'Lucy Tyler,' I say.

'Lucy, it's Paul. How're things?'

Chapter 36

I know what I said I'd do if Paul asked me out again. But that was before he did. Besides, the prospect of being alone on Saturday night while everyone else is out was about as appealing as an Ann Summers party at my grandma's house. So I agreed to another date, probably too easily.

I would have liked him to come up with a brilliant excuse for his no-show at the business awards. Sudden death in the family, accidental amputation of a limb, major earthquake causing widespread structural damage to his property – all would have been acceptable. That and a grovelling apology for not phoning for more than a week.

In the event, he never mentioned the issue and I'm ashamed to say that I didn't press him. It was a betrayal of every post-feminist bone in my body but, desperate that he didn't change his mind, I took the easy option and kept my mouth shut. My self-respect is in tatters but at least I don't have to sit in watching *Britain's Got Talent*.

'Come on, Ivana Trump, show us what you've bought,' says Mum.

Obviously, I also had to find a new outfit, just a modestly-priced one – nothing over the top. I might have known it'd be a mistake to stop at my parents' house when I'm carrying shopping bags, though. Particularly when there are six.

'None of it was expensive,' I tell her, wondering why I feel the need to justify myself.

'Oh yeah,' she says sarcastically, examining my Coast skirt. 'Looks just like it came from a charity shop.'

The kitchen door flies open and Dave walks in. He's carrying nine shopping bags.

'Good God!' exclaims Mum. 'We can safely say you two are getting through the global recession unscathed. You appear to have more disposable income than Elton John.'

'All right, Mum,' says Dave, plonking his bags at the table and heading for the fridge. 'Got anything to eat?'

Dave is permanently eating, and not especially healthily either. If he ever stopped weight training, he'd assume the Great Buddha look within weeks.

'There are a couple of things in there,' says Mum, 'but for God's sake don't touch the pork pie, your father'll go ballistic and—'

Dave spins round, revealing a mound of pastry in his mouth like a suckling pig. He takes a bite. 'Tell him I'll owe him one,' he says between mouthfuls.

Mum rolls her eyes. 'What have you bought? Come on, let's have a look.'

'None of it was expensive,' he says innocently.

'There's a Reiss bag there,' I point out.

He pulls a face. 'So what?'

I shrug. 'I'm just saying, it's hardly cheap in there.'

His eyes widen in exasperation. 'You've been to bloody Whistles. Bet there weren't any customers in there who'd come straight from the Job Centre.'

I frown. 'What does it matter?'

'Exactly my point, you dope.'

I've already donned my best grotty fifteen-year-old's face in preparation for my next comment, but Mum beats me to it. 'Give it a rest, you two. Are you still going to be like this when you're in your eighties?'

I stand and pick up my bags.

'I'm off now anyway, Mum,' I say. 'Thanks for the tea.'

When we reach the hall, I remember something. 'Oh, I haven't asked – how was your salsa class?'

She looks at her nails. 'It was a bit naff. I thought it would be.'

'Naff?'

'Well,' she sniffs, 'not really my thing.'

'What do you mean?' I ask.

'All those gyrating hips, everyone getting worked up, it was all a bit . . .'

'A bit what?'

'Over the top.'

'Right. So you didn't enjoy it?'

'Not especially.'

'So you're not going again?'

She shrugs. 'Well, I *wouldn't*, but Denise is absolutely insisting.'

'You enjoyed it,' I blurt out.

'I did not.' You'd think I'd accused her of GBH.

I am about to leap back in and reconfirm the fact of which I'm certain, but instead I content myself with a knowing smile.

Mum opens the door for me. 'I don't know what that funny face is all about. Cough and you'll get stuck like that.'

Chapter 37

I've been in a few 'brainstorms' in my time, but none like this.

'How about *chivalry*?' says Erin. 'Those little touches like opening doors for her, pulling out the restaurant chair – and simply being a perfect gentleman. That's really important.'

'Brilliant!' Dominique jabs her permanent marker in the air and spins round to add the word to her flip-chart. She's getting into her training co-ordinator role and today's tutorial is one of her favourite topics: how to behave on a date. 'That's a good one, Henry. Mind you, I reckon that'll come naturally to you. Let's recap.'

Henry is concentrating hard. Now that he's secured a date with Rachel he's determined not to blow it. As he sits on our sofa before a list of dating rules – the result of our 'blue sky thinking' – Dominique has his full attention.

'Number one: *listen* to her. Most men end up jabbering away about themselves and there's nothing more offputting. Ask about *her* for a change. Where she grew up. Her job. Her likes and dislikes. You get the picture.'

'Absolutely,' says Henry.

'Number two: act confident. You might feel anything but,

Henry – that's only natural. But don't give it away. Relax your shoulders. Make sure you smile. Don't twiddle your thumbs.'

'I feel as if this is a job interview,' says Henry.

'It is, Henry,' I tell him. 'The vacant position is "boyfriend".'

'Number three,' continues Dominique, 'is flirt. We've been through this in detail. Lightly touch her arm. Make eye-contact. Hold her gaze.'

'Yup,' says Henry. 'I've got it.'

'Good,' says Dominique. 'Because there's a final rule. One we've not discussed until now. It's crucial that you don't forget it.'

'Another one?' Henry looks worried.

Dominique nods. 'Enjoy yourself.'

Chapter 38

Tonight, something new and exciting is happening in our household: Henry and I are *both* getting ready for dates.

We dash around ironing clothes (Henry), retrieving lost hair curlers from under the sofa (me), and checking mobiles in case of a change of heart (both). By the time we're ready for the off, we've generated enough nervous energy to fuel a light aircraft.

Henry takes a deep breath. 'You look gorgeous.'

'So do you,' I reply, feeling strangely self-conscious.

I catch his eye and am unable to control myself. 'Oh, Henry – come here and give me a hug!' I throw my arms around him. 'This is so exciting.'

He hesitates and squeezes me back. I wonder for a second if I can detect something wrong, but he unravels from my clutch and smiles. 'I know.'

'You nervous?' I ask.

'I'd feel more relaxed doing a tandem parachute jump with a suicide bomber.'

'You've got no reason to be anything other than confident,' I tell him, brushing fluff from his shoulder. I stand back to examine him and am struck by how true my words are.

He is stunning tonight. It's not just the new pale blue shirt and flattering jeans. His skin is glowing, his eyes sparkling. 'Rachel thinks you're the hottest thing on two legs.'

'She must need her head examined,' he grins as he opens the front door.

The city-centre bar is already packed when I meet Paul. I'm relieved that I glammed up as the place is WAG-Central. Not all the women are real WAGs, of course, though there are one or two genuine ones, with legs as long as their hair extensions and micro-dresses as short as their attention span. But there are lots of girls who look the part – a bling-tastic bevy of beautiful women who appear to have spent three weeks French-manicuring their nails. I can't hope to compete and not least because, next to theirs, my nails look as if they've been filed with a chisel.

'Lucy!' Paul spots me approaching the bar and beckons me over. I take a deep breath and head towards him, trying to hide my nerves.

'Hi,' I grin. He throws an arm around my waist and pulls me in, kissing me hard on the mouth. The kiss only lasts for a second but when he releases me, I can feel myself blush, somewhat stunned.

'How's it going?'

'Oh, um, fine,' I reply breathlessly. I pull back and look into his eyes, reminding myself how gorgeous he is.

He removes his arm from my waist and grabs me by the hand. 'Come and meet some of the guys.'

I shake my head, wondering if I've misheard him. 'The guys? What guys?' *Did I say that out loud?*

'A few mates are hitting the town tonight so I thought we'd join them for a couple. You don't mind, do you?'

191

Before I get a chance to lie – *of course* I don't mind! – I am standing in front of three blokes clutching designer bottles of beer and laughing uproariously. When they sense our presence, the laughter dies down and they turn to look. I feel like a museum exhibit.

'This is Jimmy, Brian and Chas,' announces Paul.

'Hi. Lovely to meet you,' I beam. Their expressions are so surly I'm half-expecting to be issued with a parking ticket. 'I'm Lucy. Lovely to meet you.' *You already said that, you idiot.* 'Um . . . do you know each other through work?'

I look directly at Jimmy, then Brian, then Chas. My aim is to detect a flicker of warmth from one so I can engage in conversation and begin bonding. If my relationship with Paul is to work out, I *must* demonstrate what a fantastic, convivial and all-round nice girl their friend is going out with.

Sadly none of them answers.

'We go way back,' says Paul, downing the last quarter of his bottle in a demonstrative gulp. 'Drink?'

It doesn't take long to realize that Jimmy, Brian and Chas, who clearly resent the intrusion of a female on their lads' night out, are going to be hard work. In fact, calling them hard work underestimates it. I feel like a dancing monkey before a Roman Emperor more used to seeing virgins' heads ripped off by marauding lions. My attempts to engage in small talk are greeted with one-syllable grunts – if I'm lucky – and it soon becomes clear that they think Paul was insane to bring me along tonight. Which is about the only thing on which we agree.

If Paul notices this dynamic, he doesn't show it. Instead, he joins in as they leap from topics of conversation which include (in no particular order): Keeley Hawes's tits; last night's *Top Gear*; whether it is acceptable form to fart on a first date (apparently this is not simply okay, but to be encouraged). For two hours – despite the peals of laughter – I struggle to detect a single genuinely witty remark among this poor excuse for schoolboy humour. Yet the last thing I want is to be dismissed as having no sense of fun, so I stand redundantly with a smile fixed to my face. This sounds easy, but it's anything but. Unlike Paul, who has tears rolling down his cheeks, I find his friends about as hilarious as dysentery.

'God, they're funny!' laughs Paul. He turns to the bar and I have a rare opportunity to talk to him alone. 'Don't you think? Brian's like the next Billy Connolly – everyone says so.'

Comparing Brian with Billy Connolly is akin to calling a cack-handed painting-by-numbers enthusiast the next Vincent Van Gogh. He might have an extensive repertoire of jokes, but you'd have to be lobotomized to find any of them amusing.

'He certainly knows a joke or two,' I force myself to say. Then: 'Are we going somewhere else soon?'

'Oh, dunno. Maybe,' shrugs Paul, handing over a twenty-pound note to the bartender. 'We'll see what the boys are doing.'

My heart sinks. 'Oh, weren't they going somewhere else?'

'They'd planned to but, well, we're all having a laugh here, aren't we?'

I look at him blankly, unable to think of something to say. We're interrupted by Jimmy.

'Paul! Wait till you hear this cracker Brian's got about a nun with a boob job . . .'

Chapter 39

We finally get rid of Jimmy, Brian and Chas at 2.15 a.m. when, having bar-crawled round the city centre, Jimmy throws up under a table and we are politely asked to leave. On the way out, Brian and Chas bump into two women from a call centre where Chas's brother Darren used to work. Mercifully, we manage to lose them.

'So, you've been initiated,' grins Paul, putting his arm round me as we wander up Castle Street looking for a taxi. 'I get the feeling my friends like you.'

I get the feeling Paul must be out of his mind, but decide not to say anything.

He squeezes my waist and leans down to kiss my hair. My pulse quickens and it suddenly makes me forget to be irritated that he's put me through one of the worst nights of my life. Instead I feel a rush of lust.

'Shame we didn't get much chance by ourselves though,' he continues.

'True,' I shrug.

He stops and turns to me, cupping my face in his hands as the light from the Town Hall lamps flickers in his eyes.

'God, you're sexy, Lucy,' he breathes. I can feel his hips

gently pressing against me and gulp. He leans in and brushes his lips against mine. Fireworks explode inside my new underwear – underwear I strangely found myself purchasing despite swearing that sex was off the agenda until I could trust Paul again after the North-west Business Awards.

I wrap my arms around him and feel a bulge against my leg. I don't know how long we kiss in the street for, but it's long enough for me to know that when he suggests getting a taxi to his place, I'm not going to hesitate. We kiss the whole way home and, as the taxi trundles along, I feel myself getting more turned on.

By the time it stops outside his house, I am breathless with desire and anticipation, so much so that I can't bring myself to stop his hand as it moves underneath my top. We stumble into his flat, still kissing, and I know as the door slams that my rules are about to go out of the window.

Before I know it, I'm in my bra in his hallway with his lips on my neck. I'm stumbling up the stairs as his shirt comes off. We're collapsing through his bedroom door as my skirt is discarded. I'm panting with desire as his trousers are thrown to one side and the condom packet in his wallet is decisively ripped open.

Writhing on his bed, my eyes close as I submit to the pleasure of the moment, to the sheer exhilaration I feel in the knowledge that the rest of the night is going to be the most sensual experience I've had in a very long time.

I am staring at the ceiling of Paul's bedroom as his snores ripple across the room. Pulling up his duvet over my chest, I wonder if I ought to go home.

There is clearly no way he's going to be roused from his

slumber to continue this liaison. Besides, I don't think I could work myself up again if I wanted to. Paul falling asleep on the job – in fact, *before* the job – is the mood-breaker to end all others.

I wonder if it would have been good sex? Probably not, judging by how quickly he dropped off. Knowing my luck, it would have been over faster than you could soft-boil an egg.

I sigh, nudge Paul to the other side of the bed and start retrieving my clothes before realizing that I've left my top draped on the bottom of the stairs and my bra outside the bathroom.

I open his door and peer out. When I'm confident nobody else is in the house, I creep downstairs, grabbing my top from the banister and galloping back towards his bedroom, scooping up the bra on the way.

'Hiya.'

I am so startled by this voice I almost drop my top again, but fortunately manage to clutch it defensively to my chest.

The source of this greeting turns out to be one of Paul's flatmates.

'Good night?' he says.

'Oh, great,' I reply, wondering whether he's noticed the fact that I am standing at the top of his stairs, bare-breasted and, therefore, not in the mood to chat.

'Where'd you go?' he asks.

'The Loft.' I clutch my top tighter around my chest.

'Right,' he nods. 'Can't stand it in there.'

'Really? Never mind. Must go.'

'No problem,' he says. 'Catch you soon. Janice, isn't it?'

'Lucy,' I correct him, hovering behind Paul's door.

'Right,' he nods. 'Catch you soon, Darcy.'

'Yeah,' I smile, as I close the door behind him decisively.

Paul has shifted onto his front when I return, his athletic back on full view, his buttocks barely covered by his quilt. I crouch down close to his face as it presses against his pillow. His soft mouth is slightly open, his flickering eyelids revealing busy dreams. He looks vulnerable, almost childlike, and it makes me smile. I lean down and kiss him on the head.

'Not quite what I was hoping for,' I whisper, brushing away a hair from his face. 'Shame I still fancy you so much.'

Chapter 40

When I wake the next morning in my own bed, I don't feel good. The fact that I almost had sex with someone so soon after meeting him has made me feel cheap. I could live with this puritanical disappointment in myself if it had been steamy and sensational; that it was short and not especially sweet is the real killer. Then I close my eyes and picture Paul's face, laughing, and feel a swell of affection regardless.

My phone beeps. I pick it up from the side of my bed and see that a text has arrived. It's from Paul.

Sorry about my performance last night. Was a blip – honestly. Feel horrendous. Can we try again? xx

I close the text and phone Dominique.

'Jesus. How bad was it?'

'It wasn't great,' is all I'm prepared to say. 'But sex isn't everything, is it? I'd be pretty shallow if I let this put me off, wouldn't I?'

Dominique hesitates and I realize I'm asking the wrong person. 'So, everything else went well until that point?'

'N-yes.'

'Here's what I think: part of me admires the guy for admitting he screwed up. That takes balls. Certainly enough to risk seeing him again. *If* you really like him, that is. I think you should give him a chance to redeem himself.'

I am satisfied with this answer. So the date wasn't the stuff of a Cary Grant and Doris Day movie, but something still makes me want to give it a go with Paul, if only to prove I'm capable of being part of a couple.

'What about Loverboy?' she continues. 'Did he have any more luck?'

'I don't know yet,' I reply, then hear a pan clang in the kitchen. 'Ooh, I think he's up. I'll let you know.'

I grab my dressing-gown and pull it over my pyjamas as I step over my clothes, shoes and used make-up wipes from the night before. After Dominique's pep talk and Paul's confession, I am no longer too depressed about the fact that the night ended with me in my M&S nightwear with a fully-cleansed face, rather than being made breakfast in bed after a long and fulfilling night of passion.

'Morning.' I scan Henry's features for a clue to the success – or otherwise – of last night.

'Hey, Luce,' he says, like every morning. 'Do you want a bagel?'

'No, I won't.'

I ought to stick to my diet if I'm going to persevere with Paul, so head for my slimming bread in the freezer. I attempt to take out a piece but it's stuck solid, even when I remove the whole loaf and go at it with a butter-knife as if I'm sculpting a piece of marble. I finally manage to chip off half a slice and put it in the toaster. It would look unappetizing to a starving sewer rat, but can't contain more than twenty calories.

'How'd it go last night?'

'Fine,' he replies.

'Fine?'

He shrugs. 'Fine.'

I shake my head. 'Henry, this was your first proper date in twenty-eight years. If you think you're going to get away with "fine", you're horribly wrong.'

He grins and looks at the toaster, from which a thin stream of black smoke is pouring. The bread has been in there for seconds but already appears to have fossilized.

'Do you want something more substantial?'

I examine the charred remains of my toast. 'Possibly.'

'Well, we've run out of bagels,' he replies. 'Get dressed and I'll buy you breakfast.'

It's ages since Henry and I ate out for breakfast and it feels like a real treat.

As always, we order a Full English – mine veggie, Henry's with enough meat to give a rapacious caveman indigestion – and wait for them over newspapers and steaming cups of strong coffee. A couple of years ago, a Sunday morning wasn't a Sunday morning unless we began the day at our local café. Then I struggled to get my jeans past my upper thighs without the aid of a crowbar and decided to make it an occasion only indulged in every couple of months.

'If you're trying to keep me in suspense, I'd prefer to go home and read a Lynda La Plante novel,' I tell Henry.

He glances up from the *Sunday Times*. 'She's nice,' he replies, then returns to his newspaper.

I snatch the paper from him, fold it up and pointedly slap it onto the bench next to me, out of his reach. 'Elaborate, please.'

He squirms. 'What do you want me to say? She's pleasant, extremely attractive. It went well.'

'Are you seeing her again?'

He pauses. 'She asked me to go to the theatre this week. *King Lear* is on at the Royal.'

'You love *King Lear*.'

'Yes,' he agrees with a distinct lack of exultation.

'Henry,' I begin, frustrated. 'Can you talk to me about this? Or do you really not want to?'

'I . . . it's like I said, she's nice. Really nice. Attractive, intelligent, fun. She's wonderful.' He sighs.

Now we're getting somewhere. 'So?'

He frowns, trying to work out the issues before he speaks. Then he shakes his head as if there's only one way to put this.

'I don't fancy her.'

My eyes widen, stunned.

'I see,' I manage finally.

'I know it sounds ridiculous for someone like me to say that. I mean, I'm Henry. *Henry who hasn't had a date in twenty-eight years*. Who am *I* to not fancy *her*? It's not right, is it?'

I think about this for a second. 'If you don't fancy someone, you don't fancy someone. There's not a lot you can do about it.'

'I know, but it's *why* I don't fancy her that's the problem.'

A waitress arrives with our breakfasts and, after a reorganization of the table, finds space to put them in front of us. I pick up a knife and fork and begin cutting a Quorn sausage. Then I glance up at Henry. He is looking at me.

'What is it?' I put down my knife and fork.

He reaches across the table and holds my hand.

'Lucy – perhaps I should be more honest with you.'

I squeeze his hand. 'You're always honest with me, aren't you?'

He meets my eyes again. 'Not entirely.'

'Really?'

'Lucy, I . . . Oh God, it's no good.' He looks frustrated.

Then something strikes me. 'Are you gay?' I whisper.

He lets go of my hand and laughs out loud. 'No, Lucy, I'm not gay.'

I didn't think this was the case, but thought I'd ask in case I've been labouring under the false assumption that my friend is heterosexual for the last nineteen years when, in fact, he harboured desires for half of my boyfriends.

'Then what is it?'

He picks up his fork, stabbing it into a piece of bacon. 'Nothing, sorry. Pretend I didn't mention it.'

'As if,' I bluster.

'Honestly, Luce, it's fine. You're right. I'll go out with Rachel again – I'd be stupid not to.'

I am about to point out that I didn't say he should go out with Rachel again, when I stop myself. Of course he should go out with Rachel. She's lovely. So lovely that it's only a matter of time before he *does* fancy her.

I prod my fork into a mushroom, and dip it into my fried egg – but for some reason, my Full English isn't as appetizing as it was earlier.

Chapter 41

Every April, one of the most spectacular sporting events in the world takes place ten miles from where I live. Much of the UK, half of Ireland, and a few from elsewhere in the world descend on the city. At least, it feels like it.

The Grand National Festival at Aintree Racecourse is the ultimate day out, no matter which of the three days you attend. But today – Saturday – is when the big race itself is run and you can feel excitement buzzing in the air. I know as much about horse racing as I do about particle science, but that's irrelevant. To me, the event is about white wine on sunny spring afternoons, girls dressed to the nines, and more fun than you'd find outside the walls of a Bouncy Castle.

It is compulsory to attend with a group of friends, the law of averages dictating that at least one will win enough, either on the Grand National itself, or the races before it, to treat the losers to a curry at the end of the day.

We are here en masse on what is, miraculously, the warmest day of the year so far: Henry and Rachel, Dominique and Justin, Erin and a guy she works with called Carl. And Paul and I.

He arrived to pick me up at eleven-thirty on the dot this morning and when I answered the door he was every bit as attractive as when we first met.

He's been the perfect gentleman all morning, holding open doors, bestowing compliments on me and lavishing attention on my friends. I can tell Dominique is impressed by the way she keeps winking at me when his back is turned.

'You ladies look absolutely amazing,' says Paul, as we head to the racecourse gates. He's right. Erin is beautiful in her printed dress and a wide brimmed hat. Dominique is stunning in figure-hugging pink and heels so high it'll be a miracle if she's not in traction by the end of the day. And Rachel is more gorgeous than ever in a tailored trouser suit with plunging scarlet top and a red rose in her hair.

As for me: well, my outfit took me three months to unearth – which I know is probably longer than Howard Carter took to find Tutankhamun's tomb, but believe me is worth it. My yellow dress is a dead ringer for Liz Hurley's Roberto Cavalli number but was a fraction of the cost.

'Let's do this properly,' says Paul, producing his wallet outside the Princess Royal stand. 'Who's for champagne?'

'I like your style,' Dominique tells him, and I feel a stab of pride.

'Are you sure?' asks Erin. 'I bet it won't be cheap.'

Paul grins. 'It's a special occasion. Besides, I backed a couple of winners yesterday when I was here for Ladies' Day with my friends.'

A shiver runs down my spine at the mention of his friends but I keep smiling to maintain the illusion I'm as big a fan as him. Paul heads to the bar and returns with a bottle of Moët & Chandon and eight glasses on a tray. He opens the bottle with a rambunctious pop and fills our glasses, champagne fizzing over the tops. By the time he gets to Henry's glass, the bottle is empty.

'Oh, sorry,' says Paul. Something about the way he says it makes me do a double-take. The apology sounds genuine enough, but I'm not entirely convinced by his expression. Maybe I'm imagining it. Either way, Henry doesn't seem concerned.

'Here, have mine.' Rachel thrusts her glass at Henry.

'No, it's fine,' replies Henry cheerfully. 'I'll get a drink from the bar.'

'Really, Henry,' insists Erin, 'we've all got too much. We'll top yours up a bit. Here . . .'

'It's fine,' he repeats, but despite the protestations, Erin and Rachel lead a reorganization of the contents of the champagne glasses, filling his from the others, until it is distributed equitably.

'Who's for a flutter?' asks Paul. 'Do you know much about horses, Lucy?'

I briefly consider passing off today's *Guardian* racing tip as my own, then remember I'm surrounded by friends who'd spot my blatant fibbing a mile off. 'Not a lot, I must admit.'

'I have a scientific method of selecting my horse,' announces Dominique. 'It never lets me down.'

'Oh?' asks Erin.

'I look up their birthdays and only pick horses that are Sagittarians.'

'Why Sagittarians?' asks Henry.

'Sagittarians are dynamic, natural athletes and big thinkers. If that isn't the definition of a winning horse I don't know what is. Look: here's one – *Alabama Rain*. Perfect. A surefire winner.'

'It's five hundred to one,' I point out.

'Don't care,' she insists. 'It'll have character – you watch.'

Justin grins and puts an affectionate arm around her. 'Anything else you're an expert at?' he teases.

'Oh yes,' she says. 'But you already know about that.' She smiles her usual flirtatious smile but I swear I can see the hint of a blush round her neck. Justin kisses her gently on the lips. When they pull apart, she puts on a show of being cool that fools everyone but Erin and me.

It's hard not to warm to Justin and not only because of the effect he's having on our friend. As a trainee restaurant manager who grew up on the wrong side of the tracks, he's a far cry from Dominique's usual type – particularly given that he's six years younger than her. But he is warm, charming and apparently impossible for my friend to resist.

'How about you, Henry?' asks Rachel eagerly. 'Are you any good on the horses?'

Henry and Rachel's date the other night clearly went well from her point of view. I'd thought it impossible for her to gaze at him more dreamily than at the business awards. But today she appears so infatuated I'm starting to think she suffers from separation anxiety.

'I can't say I bet regularly,' he replies, 'but I'm going to give it a go. And if I don't win I'm sure Lucy'll stump up for this month's rent.'

'Don't hold your breath. I can barely afford my own rent after buying these shoes.'

'Well, I'm going to go and study the odds down at the

fenceline,' Paul announces, putting his arm round my waist. 'You coming, Lucy?'

I smile contentedly as warmth spreads through my body. How *nice* it is to have a boyfriend again.

Chapter 42

Having been pleased at the prospect of time on my own with Paul, I soon feel less enthusiastic.

Instead of a romantic stroll past the winning-post, Paul marches up and down the side of the course, debating with bookies in flat caps and dragging me to the parade ring so he can examine the horses' ears. Why is he looking at the horses' ears? Because, Paul maintains, the perkiness of the equine auricle is the key to its success. Personally, I found Dominique's reliance on the signs of the zodiac more convincing, but he's absolutely determined.

We head for the Tattersalls enclosure to watch the first three races because, although we're in possession of more expensive tickets, Paul claims that the atmosphere here is far superior. It's certainly louder, rowdier and more full of drunk people.

I don't want to give the impression I'm not enjoying myself. But, having come here with my best friends, I'd now like to *be* with my best friends – particularly since Paul obviously hasn't steered us away to whisper sweet nothings in my ear. He's more interested in the horses' ears than mine.

On the plus side, he does well on the races. By the third he is two hundred pounds up and in buoyant mood, while I am more than forty pounds down – but as my expectations are about as low as the land around the Rhine Delta, I'm not overly worried.

'Two hundred quid and we haven't even had the big race yet.' Paul's eyes are sparkling with glee. 'Not bad, eh?'

'You were obviously right about those ears,' I smile.

He winks. 'Told you, didn't I?'

'Do you fancy going back to the others yet?' I ask, more in hope than expectation.

'Why not? Let's see if any of them have done better than me.'

By the time we reach the others, it's apparent that the bottle of champagne was a mere apéritif. There's been plenty to celebrate in our absence.

'Lucy!' cries Rachel, her eyes almost popping out of her head. 'You won't believe this.'

'What is it?' I ask.

'Henry's *brilliant* at this,' she gushes. 'He's backed two winners and had another placed.'

'You're kidding? That's fantastic, Henry. Have you won much?'

'Well, a bit,' he shrugs. 'I won't be retiring to Bora Bora because I didn't put on much in the first place. I'm only doing this for fun.'

'Oh, yeah,' I say sceptically.

He grins. 'Admittedly, it's more fun when you're winning.'

'Right, Henry,' says Dominique, her arm still so tightly around Justin's waist I'm convinced she hasn't moved it in the two hours since I last saw her. 'What are you backing for the big race? Because whatever you're backing, I'm backing.'

'Oh God, the pressure,' he laughs.

'You want to go for *Mister Misery*,' says Paul. 'There's no such thing as a dead cert in the National – but it's the closest thing to it.'

'Great horse,' agrees Henry.

'Is that what you're going for?' asks Dominique.

'No, I'm going for *River Runs Thru It*.'

'Is that a good one?' I ask.

'Well, statistically, it's got everything going for it: it apparently loves dry conditions like today *and* the weights have been favourable. Plus, I can't resist the literary reference. I love Norman Maclean.'

'I have no idea who Norman Maclean is,' shrugs Dominique, 'but you seem to know what you're doing, so it's good enough for me.'

'Bollocks,' says Paul. 'I saw it in the parade ring earlier and it was so laid back it looked like it'd been smoking pot all morning.'

Henry chuckles. 'Well, I'm not going to bet my car on it in case you're right.'

'I'm telling you, *Mister Misery* – that's the winner,' insists Paul.

In the event, we all back at least two horses: I go for *Ebony and Ivory* for no other reason than I used to like the old song. I also quietly put five pounds on *River Runs Thru It*.

By the start of the race, the atmosphere is electric. You can feel anticipation charging through the air as 70,000 people gather round the course and in the stands to watch the horses get ready for the off. This is a race that – like millions of others – I've watched on TV for as long as I can remember. But being next to the finish line is an altogether different experience. You can smell the adrenalin, feel the excitement and, as the sun streams across the course, you can almost hear everybody's heart beat faster.

Paul puts his arm round me and flicks his sunglasses onto his face. Then the starter's gun fires, the horses pound away and the crowd lets out an almighty roar.

I don't know how long the four-and-a-half-mile race takes, but it seems to go very quickly. Horses fall and groans of disappointment echo through the crowd. Others drop back, their hopes of greatness over for this year at least. As the remaining horses reach the final stretch, the entire crowd seems to hold its breath.

To my amazement – for the first time *ever* – both of my horses appear to be serious contenders. *River Runs Thru It* is giving a steady run in fourth place, while *Ebony and Ivory* is fighting for a place at the front with *Mister Misery*.

The voice of the BBC commentator becomes so animated he sounds as if he's been inhaling helium, and as the horses belt to the finishing line, it is almost too much to bear. The crowd is roaring and jumping, and as the horses battle each other with literally metres to go, I have to remind myself to breathe. With seconds before the finish, *Mister Misery* looks certain to win; only a miracle would change the outcome now.

But in the last few seconds, a miracle does occur. *River Runs Thru It* summons a surge of energy so impressive it's as if someone has injected him with Red Bull.

He belts towards the finish, past *Ebony and Ivory* and nose-to-nose with *Mister Misery*. As the two of them cross the line, there is a hum in the crowd as everyone looks round, bewildered. Who won?

'The winner is . . . *River Runs Thru It*,' confirms the commentator as an earsplitting cheer surges through the racecourse. 'Followed by *Mister Misery* in second, *Ebony and Ivory* in third and *Forrest Rule* in fourth.'

'Bastard,' mutters Paul, shaking his head.

It's not clear if he's referring to his horse or Henry.

Chapter 43

The rest of the afternoon is as close to the definition of pure enjoyment as you can get. We laugh, drink and cheer our way through the final two races before stepping on a packed but merry train to the city centre. No one cares when their toes are pulverized by wobbly stilettos or their hat falls off and ends up looking as if it's been through a car wash. We ought to stop drinking and go home to a cup of cocoa, but the city's nightlife is too seductive.

As the train pulls into a station to let a couple off, I glance at Dominique and Justin. Their arms are wrapped round a pole – and each other – with their eyes locked in mutual adoration. Dominique catches me looking at her. 'You okay?' she mouths.

I nod and smile. As Justin pulls her tighter, I know I don't have to ask her the same.

Rachel, meanwhile, is resting her head drunkenly on Henry's shoulder two seats away from where Paul and I are sitting, holding hands. I can't see Henry's face as a woman wearing a hat the size of a Notting Hill Carnival headdress is blocking his way. But from Rachel's expression, I'd say her pheromones were doing overtime.

'What's the plan when we get to Liverpool?' asks Carl, resting his arm on the back of the seat behind Erin. It is clear that Carl is keener on Erin than she is on him, only she's too nice to give anything but the subtlest brush-off. As she registers his arm, she bends forward to pick up her bag, rustling round in it then checking her mobile for non-existent messages.

'Everywhere will be packed,' I say.

'Let's go to Mathew Street,' suggests Paul.

I'm sceptical. 'Have you seen how mobbed Mathew Street is after the Grand National? Last time I tried it I spent a week dreaming I was being transported to France for slaughter.'

'Everywhere will be mobbed,' Paul states.

'Yes, but Lucy's right,' says Dominique. 'Mathew Street's in another league on nights like tonight.'

'How about that piano bar off Victoria Street?' Henry says suddenly. 'Dominique, don't you know the owners?'

'Brilliant!' exclaims Erin.

'I can't stand it in there,' mutters Paul.

I smile at him uncertainly. 'At least we know we'll get in.'

Before he has a chance to protest, Dominique is on her mobile, organizing the rest of the night.

An hour later, we've bypassed the queue, thanks to Dominique's efforts. The place is almost unrecognizable: what's normally a low-key piano bar is heaving with people fresh from the races – though given that the party started for most of them before noon, perhaps 'fresh' isn't the right word.

As Henry takes my wine and passes it to me, I am struck by the look on the barmaid's face. It's remarkably similar to Rachel's. She fancies Henry – it couldn't be clearer.

'Take one for yourself,' he smiles, as he hands over a couple of notes.

Her hand lingers and her eyes, flashing and flirtatious, meet his. She's gorgeous. Dressed in a black wraparound shirt and with long, caramel-coloured hair against creamy skin, she is the sort of woman whose sole experience of zits is to walk past the tubes of Clearasil in Boots.

Yet, here she is, making blatant eyes at Henry. *Unbelievable*.

As she returns with his change and hands it back with an amorous smile, something else strikes me that's also unbelievable. Henry's smiling back, holding her gaze.

Christ, he's flirting.

After what feels like an age, he turns to me. 'Have you had a good day?'

I snap out of my trance. 'I have. Though not as good as you. When did you become such an expert at horse racing?'

'Never,' he assures me. 'It's pure luck.'

'Well, Lady Luck was obviously looking at you with generous eyes today. Although I don't think that's the only lady looking at you at the moment.'

'What? Oh, let me get that for you . . .'

A passing race-goer has dropped her handbag. Henry bends down to pick it up. As she takes the bag, she registers his face and pauses.

'Oh, thanks.' She smiles coyly.

'A pleasure.' Henry smiles back.

The woman flicks back her chestnut curls with an enticing pout.

'Thanks for the drink, Henry,' interrupts a voice, which turns out to be Rachel's. With her eyes drilling into those of

Handbag Woman, whom she immediately recognizes as a pretender to her role, she flings her arm round his waist. She's trying her best to look casual – but I suspect she wishes that Henry could be electronically tagged.

Chapter 44

The evening passes so quickly, it's as if someone has pressed fast forward. Our day out began at eleven-thirty but, before I know it, it's one in the morning and we're still going strong. I've perked up since earlier in the evening when, before we ordered bar snacks to refuel, my body was begging for mercy. Now I have a second wind and feel as if I could carry on until dawn.

'Dominique talks a lot about you,' Justin tells me as he takes a slug of beer. Dominique and the others are chatting to one of her work contacts so it's the first time I've spoken to him alone. So far, we've talked horse racing, my (permanently-lapsed) gym membership and whether cocktails are only for girls (he thinks so, unless you're in the Bahamas).

'She talks a fair bit about you too,' I reply.

'She's a nice girl,' he says.

I scrutinize his expression. 'Nice' isn't quite the adjective I was looking for. Dominique is as close to being serious about this bloke as she's ever been, so I was expecting something more effusive. 'Devastatingly wonderful' would do. 'The woman of my dreams' at a push. 'Nice'? No.

'Of course, *you're* a nice girl, too,' he smirks.

I smile uneasily.

'Hello, Lover,' says Dominique, appearing from nowhere. He leans into her and kisses her slowly on the lips. When they part, she turns to me and grins. 'God, I'm a lucky girl, aren't I?'

Rachel has successfully kept Henry to herself for the last hour and when I catch up with them, she's in a giggly mood.

'Is Henry a good flatmate?' she grins.

'Oh, he's a nightmare,' I say. 'Don't let his easygoing charm deceive you, Rachel. He's very challenging when he wants to be.'

'Thank you, Lucy,' laughs Henry.

'I'm joking,' I add. 'He's great really. Ridiculously great. The closest Henry has come to anti-social behaviour is playing his piano too loud.'

Rachel goes into meltdown again. 'You play the piano? I *love* the piano.'

I'm starting to think that if I told Rachel that Henry unblocked drains in his spare time, she'd *love* that too. Still, I can't complain: this is the precise effect we'd hoped for with *Project Henry*. I just never expected it to be so successful.

'Are you any good? Oh, I bet you are,' she continues.

'I'm okay,' says Henry modestly. 'Relatively competent, no more than that.'

'Relatively competent?' I smirk. 'Relative to whom? Liberace?'

'Oh Henry, they've got a piano here,' gushes Rachel.

'Have they?' He suddenly looks nervous.

'Come on, why don't you give us a tune?' she beams.

'Oh, I c-couldn't,' Henry stutters. 'I mean, there's music playing already.'

Rachel looks disappointed. 'Are you sure I can't twist your arm?'

'Quite sure,' he says.

Rachel smiles but her disappointment is obvious – that wasn't the answer she was looking for. 'Will you excuse me while I go to the ladies?' she says.

As she disappears to the other side of the bar, Dominique appears from nowhere. 'Did I hear Rachel trying to persuade Henry to play the piano?'

'Yes,' says Henry, 'but I was about to tell her that doing something as geeky as that would do nothing for my—'

'There's nothing geeky about being able to play an instrument,' interrupts Dominique. 'Some of the least likely sex symbols in the world owe their appeal to music. Look at Mick Jagger. Liam Gallagher. Steven Tyler. If they were behind the counter at the Co-op, no one would give them a second look. On stage, it's a different matter.'

'Is it?' Henry starts scanning the emergency exits.

'Yes!' Dominique cries. 'If you think Rachel's impressed so far, wait till you see her reaction to your piano-playing. Come *on* – let's step up a gear on your reinvention. Don't let Lucy and me down.'

Henry looks at me and his shoulders sag. We both know he stands no chance of escape.

Henry and I glare at the piano as Dominique disappears to ask someone to turn off the music.

'What are you going to play?' I ask, feeling nervous for him.

Jane Costello

'Christ, I don't know,' he hisses. 'I can't see Vivaldi going down well here.'

'What about "Chasing Cars"? I love it when you play that – especially the plinky plonky bit in the middle. And you know all the words.'

'You want me to *sing*? Lucy, are you insane?'

'Well, you've got a lovely voice.' I read his expression. 'But, no, you're probably right.'

'Come on, Henry!' Dominique appears again and drags him up to the piano stool, before stepping down to rejoin Rachel and me.

Rachel and Dominique are clapping their hands in excitement, but the rest of the bar is oblivious. Reluctantly, he takes off his jacket and slings it on the piano, loosens his tie and rolls up his sleeves. I recognize a flash of the old Henry. The *real* old Henry, who would panic when a woman spoke to him, even if it was only to ask for directions.

He takes a deep breath, briefly closes his eyes and makes a convincing stab at composure. When he opens them, he looks at me and smiles. I smile back, hoping I look supportive, instead of paralysed with terror for him.

He puts his hands on the keys of the piano.

And he plays . . .

I recognize the opening bars of the Oasis song immediately, though the version most people know starts with crashing guitars. Henry's performance of 'She's Electric' is loud and proud, full of attitude. The bar is noisier than ever but he demands to be listened to. It's impossible to relegate it to background music. You have to stop and take it in. Take *him* in.

With increasing numbers noticing, Henry, immersed in the

music, does something that amazes me. He leans into the microphone and he sings.

'She's electric . . .'

I've heard Henry's voice hundreds of times. He sings when he's playing the piano at home. He sings in the shower. He sings when he's making toast in the morning. Yet, tonight, his voice is stunning – gloriously rough and rousing, a sublime accompaniment to the boldness of his piano. I can hardly take my eyes off him.

'. . . A family full of eccentrics . . .'

'I think I'm in love,' swoons Rachel, as her legs visibly go weak.

Dominique grabs me by the arm. 'This is un-bloody-believable!' she giggles.

'He's always been pretty good—'

'Lucy,' she interrupts. 'Look at everyone.' I scan the room. 'Check out the girls.'

It's a surreal sight. Henry is surrounded by men and women – okay, mainly women – dancing and clapping, lapping up his performance.

I push to the front to get a proper look. The man I see is one who's instantly familiar, yet not familiar at all. It's Henry, *my* Henry, but someone completely different at the same time.

He's relaxed now, thoroughly enjoying himself and aware of his effect on the crowd. My eyes absorb the contours of his face as he sings with intensity and pleasure. They follow the flex of his bicep as his fingers strike the keyboard, dominating it utterly. They skim over his sensuous neck, his smooth, tanned Adam's apple . . .

Oh God, what's going on? Why am I thinking weird things about Henry? *About Henry!*

I find my heart racing and blood rushing to my face. I'm only glad Paul isn't here to see it. That's a point – where *is* Paul? And do I care?

I lift up my head and feel my stomach lurch as my gaze lands on Henry's mouth. For a reason I can't fathom I find myself wondering what it must be like to kiss him. Not like before, like friends. But to run my tongue against his, to taste the wetness of his mouth, to gently bite his soft, full lips . . .

'Are you all right, Lucy?' asks Dominique, grabbing my elbow.

'No,' I reply.

'What's up?'

The song reaches a crescendo and the bar erupts into rapturous applause. Henry seeks out my face in the crowd. As his eyes meet mine, I feel my crotch flood with warmth and am assaulted by an image in my mind: of me unzipping Henry's trousers and frantically wrapping my legs around him as I groan with pleasure. It's one of those horrendous mucky dreams about someone totally inappropriate – except I'm awake.

I feel faint.

I turn to Dominique and say huskily, 'Nothing's up. Nothing except . . .'

'What?'

'Dom, I think I fancy Henry.'

Chapter 45

Dominique scrunches up her nose. 'What did you say you fancy? I couldn't hear you over the noise.'

I stare at her, unable to repeat the words, let alone believe them. 'I fancy . . .' My voice trails off.

She looks at me in bewilderment. 'What – a dance? A drink?'

I nod, snapping out of my daze. 'Yep. I fancy a drink.'

'Well, it's my round,' she says, pulling her purse from her bag. 'You'd better wait here in case people start throwing their knickers on stage.'

As Dominique heads for the bar, I find myself wandering away to look for Paul. I spend twenty minutes scouring the venue, desperate to reinstate order in my twisted mind.

I fancy Paul, not Henry. Paul, not Henry. Paul, not Henry.

The more I say it, the more convinced I am and the better I feel.

Unfortunately, the improvement in my psychological well-being is temporary. It becomes clear that Paul has gone the way of Captain Oates – he's abandoned us and disappeared to God knows where. I feel a flash of panic that he saw me watching Henry and somehow worked out that I was fantasizing about ripping off his clothes.

223

In a daze, I locate my coat and tell Dominique apologetically that I've decided against another drink and am going home, despite her protestations. By this time, Henry has done three more numbers and appears to have a fan base comparable to Westlife's.

I'm about to head for the door when, with applause still ringing through the bar, I feel a tap on the shoulder and spin round. It's Henry.

'Are you going, Lucy? Wait, I'll get my jacket.'

'You don't need to.' My words are cut short as Henry is leaped on by a stunning redhead. If her neckline plunged any lower it'd be subterranean.

'That was *amazing*,' she raves, her hand brushing the hairs on his arms. 'Where did you learn to—'

'Henry,' interrupts another voice. It's Rachel, clearly determined not to be gazumped by another glamorous pretender. But she's got more competition than she bargained for.

'Hey, I didn't catch your name, but I work here,' says a man. He's gorgeous, tanned and immaculately dressed. 'Can I give you my card?'

'Oh, I don't think I'd want to do this professionally,' laughs Henry, overwhelmed by the attention.

'That's not what I meant,' he purrs. 'I just thought you might like my number.'

Great. So now Henry's not just irresistible to women, he's a gay icon too. I've seen enough.

'I'm going. You've got a key, haven't you?' Before he has the chance to answer, I charge to the door and onto the street. After the heat of the bar, it's freezing. It is also entirely bereft of taxis.

Predictably, I'm still there twenty minutes later, bordering on hypothermia, when I finally manage to find one. I'm warmer by the time I get home, but still race to pull on my pyjamas and cocoon myself in bed, craving its cosy familiarity. I stare at the ceiling – my only option, given that when I close my eyes my head starts whirling so violently, it's as if my brain is on a spin cycle.

What the hell is going on?

I get flashbacks of Henry in the bar, the unrecognizable, unconscionably sexy Henry. The Henry that makes me think disturbingly rude, primal thoughts. The Henry I never knew existed until tonight.

I force my eyes closed, but it takes ages for me to drop off. Even then, sleep is fitful, with strange dreams barging in uninvited. Some of them are about Henry. I'd rather not repeat the details.

I wake suddenly to the slam of the front door and scramble around my bedside table to locate my alarm clock. I press its light and peer at the face. It is twelve minutes past three.

I pull the duvet over my shoulders and am about to drift off again when I hear someone's voice. It's Rachel. I can't make out what she's saying, but there is enough giggling and whooping to tell she's mightily happy.

Next, I hear the door to Henry's room open and shut and Rachel's giggling disappear as she – clearly – ends up in the place where she's wanted to be all day. Henry's bed.

I close my eyes again and take a deep breath.

So, he's done it. *Project Henry* is an unqualified success. He looks amazing. He got the girl. And he could have had at least ten others, judging by tonight.

I should be congratulating myself on a job well done.

So why do I feel like screaming into my pillow?

Chapter 46

Rachel stays all of Sunday and I spend the day bumping into her and Henry and exchanging awkward pleasantries. I keep expecting her to leave, but she doesn't. By Monday morning, I'm desperate to get out of the house so head off to work at seven-twenty. I have my bag over my shoulder and my hand on the door knob when Rachel emerges from Henry's room wearing one of his new T-shirts – and a flush on her neck.

'Hi again.' All of a sudden she looks shy, which is odd from someone who's had no compunction about her orgasmic groans reverberating through the walls for over twenty-four hours.

'Hi, Rachel,' I smile. 'Good weekend?'

She giggles. 'You could say that.'

I'm at my desk by eight and spend the first hour trying to sort through the mountain of emails I didn't manage to look at on Friday. At eight forty-five, I can hear Roger approaching the double doors from the corridor; I'd recognize his laugh anywhere. He's chatting to someone as the doors open.

'Hi, Roger!' I beam, as he steps into the office.

He stops laughing. 'Morning, Lucy.'

Drew glides in behind him with an obsequious grin. 'Catch

you later, Rog,' he says, touching his arm. 'Don't let that birdie go to your head, will you?'

Drew sits at his desk and continues grinning. His teeth are so white it hurts to look at them.

'And how was your weekend, Lucy?' he asks, firing up his computer.

'Wonderful, thank you. I had a fabulous time at the Grand National and—'

'I played golf with Roger,' he declares, and leans back to wait for a response.

I pause. 'Oh. That's nice. You had good weather for it.'

'It was great spending quality time with the boss. It's one thing getting on well at work, but sometimes you need to kick back and enjoy the company of your colleagues – don't you think? That's what Roger said when he suggested I joined him for a round.'

'Where did you play?'

'Roger's club. He's going to put me forward as a member. I feel quite honoured.'

I feel a stab of envy. Roger has never invited me to play golf. Okay, my experience of the game amounts to one round on an Ancient Rome-themed circuit one wet Easter holiday when I was seven, but that's not the point. Roger's supposed to be *my* mentor. How *could* he play golf with Drew? I feel like an abandoned wife.

Things have never been the same after the business awards. It's hard to put my finger on how; Roger hasn't done or said anything specific, but he's been cool and distant in a way that's entirely new to me. And I hate it.

A shadow descends on the desk and when I look up, it's Roger.

'I've got a cracking lead for a new client here,' he says, holding a pile of papers. 'A big firm of accountants is looking to outsource its PR. I need a brilliant proposal.'

I smile, relieved. I'm overflowing with work at the moment, but I'd relish winning a big new client to remind Roger what I can do. 'Hand them over,' I say, holding out my hand. 'Dominique and I will work our usual charms.'

Roger frowns. 'Actually, Lucy, I want Drew to handle this one. I think it fits his skill-set more.'

As Drew takes the papers, he catches my eye and winks. I suddenly feel so very depressed.

Chapter 47

The *Rachel Weekend* as it's become known by me, Dominique and Erin turns out to be just the start.

The new Henry has been unleashed.

The weekend after the *Rachel Weekend*, he has a date with a restaurant hostess called Jasmine. It lasts for several days. The Saturday after that, there's a date with a gym teacher called Diane. She only lasts one night, but then he's back with Rachel. But only on the Tuesday, Thursday and Friday. By Saturday, a financial analyst called Wendy pops up out of nowhere. She stays until Monday, when Rachel appears again. But only for one night, because he's back with Jasmine the following evening, while I'm left to fight off phone calls from all the others. And so it goes on.

In the three weeks or so after the Grand National, I hardly see Henry. When I do he's either off out with some woman or other, or coming back home with them, where they closet themselves in his bedroom, emerging hours – or, more often, days – later with the most nauseatingly dreamy expressions you've seen outside a 1980s Cadbury's Chocolate Flake advert.

By early May, I've come to the conclusion that Henry is

making up for a lifetime of being romantically unattached by shagging everything that moves.

I know, I know. I know this was the point of *Project Henry*, but I hadn't counted on turning my flatmate into Hugh Hefner.

Maybe I'm exaggerating. I have technically only seen him with four women – though that's quite enough, thank you. I feel distinctly uncomfortable with the idea of Henry's bedroom, once home only to a library of dull medical books, as a temple of seduction. I'm even more uncomfortable with the fact that I'm so uncomfortable with this. The reason is *not* that I fancy Henry – a shortlived aberration on Grand National Day that could happen to anyone after seven glasses of Pinot Grigio.

I must be jealous. While we were in the piano bar, Paul apparently disappeared off the face of the earth and I haven't heard from him since. It's not that I thought he was the love of my life, but can't *I* do the dumping for once? Worse still, I haven't been out on a single date since, not even an unsuccessful one. My love-life is like a desert – parched, arid, uninhabited. And my self-esteem is at rock bottom.

'Your mum called last night,' I say, as Henry wanders into the kitchen. It's Saturday morning and I'm at the table reading the papers and nibbling on a miniature saucer of compressed sawdust, otherwise known as slimming toast. Henry was out again last night, though God knows with whom.

'Oh, did she?' He idly flicks on the kettle. 'Did she keep you on for a while? She's buzzing from her Papua New Guinea trip.'

'About twenty-five minutes, but I don't mind. I love your mum – she can talk as much as she likes.'

'Well, the feeling's mutual – she loves you too. Though if you deny you switched off when she got to the bit about the freshwater swamp forests, I won't believe you.'

'I'm saying nothing,' I smile, looking up for the first time. He's wearing a pair of hastily thrown-on Levis with the buttons done up wrong. And no T-shirt. The sight of his torso, to which I'd never given a second thought until recently, makes my neck redden. I drop my eyes and pretend to be engrossed in a story about the over-breeding of Neapolitan mastiffs.

'What are you up to today?' I ask, too brightly. 'I'm meeting Dominique and Erin for lunch if you want to join us.'

'Oh no, it's all right,' he says, pouring hot water in his cafetière and opening the mug cupboard. 'I'm busy.'

I notice that he's holding two mugs and the penny drops. 'Oh, you've got company.' My neck gets hotter again.

'Yes,' he says awkwardly. 'It's Diane. You know, the gym teacher.'

'Oh, right,' I say, through a forced smile. Yes, I know Diane. Diane of the Porn Star Pout and Tennis Ace Arse. Can't say I'm a fan.

'Well . . . see you later,' he smiles, picking up his cafetière.

'Yep. See you.' Henry heads for his bedroom.

When I meet the girls for lunch two hours later and recount this episode, Dominique greets it with the unbridled joy you'd reserve for hearing that someone who's endured twenty years of IVF was finally expecting.

'This is *fantastic*!' she whoops. 'We ought to celebrate.'

'What are we celebrating?' I mutter.

'What are we celebrating?' She says it as if I've left my commonsense on the top deck of a bus. 'We're celebrating the phenomenal success of Henry's reinvention. We're celebrating our collective genius. We're celebrating the fact that Henry has managed to get his bloody leg over for once.'

'Not once,' I point out forlornly. 'He's always at it. It's his new hobby. He should put it on his CV next to reading and piano-playing.'

'He is incredibly attractive these days,' continues Erin blithely. 'Hard to believe the effect of little more than a few new clothes and a decent haircut.'

'It's all about confidence,' adds Dominique knowingly. 'I'm telling you, this is *not* just about the new gear Henry's going around in, it's not about his new haircut and the fact he's ditched those god-awful glasses. It's about the fact that he exudes self-assuredness. He's genuinely sexy. Don't you think, Lucy?'

'I suppose,' I shrug.

Actually, attempting to deny that Henry is sexy is like trying to deny that Fairy Liquid is green, but I feel uneasy discussing it.

'Anyway, enough about Henry,' I say to Dominique. 'What about you and Justin? How's it going with him at the moment?'

'It's going fabulously,' my friend replies, glowing like she's stepped out of a Ready Brek advert. 'We've been together for over three months – and he's still gorgeous.'

'Is it love?' winks Erin, grinning.

Dominique takes a sharp intake of breath. Then she hesitates. 'Do you know . . . I'll have to think about that one.'

Erin flashes me a look.

'What?' asks Dominique. 'What's with the conspiratorial looks?'

'Oh, nothing,' teases Erin. 'You'll come round to the idea, sooner or later.'

Dominique giggles and it strikes me that she's never looked happier. Which is brilliant, obviously. But there's something about Justin that bothers me. I just can't put my finger on what.

Chapter 48

As my only other single friend, I invite Erin over to share nachos and a bottle of wine.

There was a time when, if I didn't have a date on a Saturday night, I'd sit in with Henry watching something from the DVD shop round the corner. It was an exercise in compromise as this is the DVD shop that time forgot. If you want a mid- to late-nineties classic, this is your place. Anything approaching a new release and you have to wait another five years before Ajmail, the owner, contemplates getting it in.

Aside from that, Henry's idea of a great movie and mine aren't always the same thing. So we'd take it in turns. My choice one week (*Dirty Dancing*, *Maid in Manhattan*); his choice the next (*Jean de Florette*, *The Year of Living Dangerously*).

I took it for granted until now. I can no longer count on Henry to just be there. To listen as I whinge about my love-life. To hold my bag of Maltesers so I can pretend he's eaten them. To hand me the tissues when Johnny announces he's gonna do his kinda dancin' . . . with somebody who taught him about the kinda person he wants be. *Sigh*.

Still, I'm having a nice time with Erin, when I can stop my mind from wandering onto what Henry's up to.

'Do you get sick of being single, Lucy?' asks Erin, dipping a nacho into some guacamole.

I briefly consider denying it. 'Yeah,' I confess. 'You know the way recently divorced celebrities always say: "I'm enjoying being single"? Well, I wish I was, I really do. But it's either exhausting when you manage to get a date, or boring when you don't.'

'I know what you mean,' she agrees.

'This is going to sound sad . . . but I *want* a man.'

'There's nothing wrong with that.'

'I know. But I'm starting to get the feeling I'm never going to find one who I really fancy *and* really like. Oh, and who feels the same about me.'

'Yes, you will. I'm sure you will.'

'I'm not so certain. I want someone I really click with. Someone I can have fun with. Whose wavelength I'm on completely. I don't think he exists.'

'Of course he does – you have a relationship like that with Henry, don't you? All you need to do now is find someone exactly like Henry, but who you fancy as well.'

I blush again. I've started doing it all the time. I know as soon as it happens that Erin has seen me.

'Oh God. How stupid of me,' she says slowly.

'What?' I'm pillarbox-red by now.

'You don't think . . . you haven't considered, you know, you and Henry getting together.'

'Hhahhhahaaaa!' I blurt out. 'Of course not! Henry? And me? Hahahaaaa!'

Erin looks stunned at my verbal ejaculation. 'That's a no,' I add.

'Oh. What a shame. You'd be perfect together in so

many ways. You share this amazing history, you get on well, you—'

'But we don't fancy each other,' I interrupt. 'That tends to be a prerequisite.'

I know I'm not being remotely honest about my feelings for Henry. But how can I be? My thoughts about him lately have been *just wrong*. Under normal circumstances, when a man was playing on my mind, I'd want to analyse every element of the situation with my friends; to get their feedback and advice. But I can't discuss Henry with Erin and Dominique as if he falls into the same category as Jake or Sean or Paul. He's Henry. He's different. And he's their friend, as well as mine.

'What about you?' I ask, changing focus rapidly. 'How do you find being single?'

'I don't mind it,' she shrugs. 'I thought I would, but I don't. In some ways it's liberating. Do you remember I told you that Darren, James and Amanda were going travelling?'

'Oh yes. Have they gone yet?'

'Not until September,' she says. 'They've asked me to go with them.'

'Really? Erin . . . my God. Are you going?'

'I haven't decided. But I like that I could if I wanted. When I was with Gary I wouldn't have considered it. The fact that I can is almost as good as doing it.'

Our conversation is interrupted by the phone ringing. 'Excuse me a sec.' I pick it up.

'Hi, is that Lucy?'

'Yes, it is. Hi, Rachel. How are things?'

'Oh. Not bad.' She sounds as if she's spent the afternoon on a suicide self-help website. 'Is Henry in? I can't reach him on his mobile.'

I hesitate. 'Er, he's out, Rachel, I'm afraid. Can I take a message?'

'Oh. Tell him I called. Again. Thanks, Lucy. Bye.'

I put down the phone and can't help feeling rather sorry for her. And I come to a conclusion I've been building up to for some time now: it's time to have words with the Lothario I call my flatmate.

Chapter 49

Henry arrives home at ten the next morning and immediately dives into the shower. Twenty minutes later, he wanders into the kitchen as I am making my breakfast.

'Rachel called again last night,' I tell him, trying to unpurse my lips.

'Oh, did she?' He at least has the decency to look guilty about messing her around.

'Yes,' I reply haughtily.

Henry is wearing his combats and a plain dark T-shirt. Nothing special, yet he manages to look unfeasibly sexy. I haven't got my head around that idea yet. Henry being sexy, I mean. Henry looking half-decent used to be a difficult enough concept. Every morning I expect him to emerge looking like he used to: as if he's stepped out of a time-warp, all monstrous manmade fibres and mad hair.

Instead, his clothes enhance a physique to which I never paid a moment's attention until recently. One with sculpted biceps, a tight stomach, a broad, muscular back and perfectly-formed buttocks. It's hard to believe that's always been there, unnoticed and unloved.

As he walks past me to grab a bottle of milk from the fridge

I get a waft of his smell – of shower gel and sunshine. My heart begins to flutter. I knock over my coffee.

'Oh . . . shit,' I mutter, scooping it up.

'Everything all right, Lucy?' Henry grabs a dishcloth, just in time for the liquid to seep into it.

'Yes. No. Yes.'

Jesus Christ. I sound like Vicky Pollard. My love-life must be bad. Has it really got to the point where a sniff of whatever Henry's washed his armpits with makes me feel fruitier than a packet of Starburst?

He looks at me with a concerned expression.

'Anyway,' I continue hastily, 'about Rachel . . . don't you think you ought to tell her straight that you and she are no longer an item?'

He nods earnestly then pauses, thinking. 'Hmmm. I'm not sure I don't want us to be an item.'

'Henry,' I begin sternly, 'you've slept with three other women since you met Rachel. As far as I'm concerned, that makes you *no longer an item*.'

'I didn't sleep with all of them,' he protests.

'You ended up in bed with them,' I reply disapprovingly.

'I know, but in not every case did I—'

'PLEASE! I do not want to know the finer details of what you did or did not do with those women once you got them horizontal,' I say furiously.

He takes a swig from the milk bottle, finishing it off. 'Look, I never told Rachel I was going to marry her. I never even said we were serious.'

'So dump her.'

'I like her.'

I roll my eyes.

'I just like the others too,' he adds.

'Oh God!' I slump into my chair and put my head in my hands.

'What?' he asks innocently.

'You've turned into a . . . a . . .'

'A what?'

'A man! A typical bloody man!' I whine.

'I was always a man,' he says, looking quite bewildered.

'No!' I yell, thumping the table-top. 'You weren't like this. You were *nice*.'

'I'm still nice.' He looks hurt.

'No, you're *not*,' I tell him with conviction. 'You've gone from being the nicest person I know to being – officially – A Right Bastard.'

'I am *not* A Right Bastard.'

'Deny it if you like.' I sniff and look out of the window.

'Really, Lucy, I'm not,' he maintains. 'At least, I don't think I am. I certainly don't mean to be.'

'That's no defence. What about poor Rachel?' I huff. I don't know when Rachel became 'Poor Rachel'. I was never massively fond of the girl and, to be perfectly honest, her fawning over Henry was starting to make me feel queasy. But I feel the need to stick up for her.

Henry pulls out a chair and sits down next to me, forlorn.

'You're right,' he says. 'I ought to tell her I don't want to see her again. Draw a line under it, for everyone's sake. It's just . . . well, she is very attractive, as you said. And nice.'

'Then stop seeing anybody else and stick with her,' I tell him.

'Yes,' he decides. 'Though I was supposed to be going out with Wendy tonight.'

I stand and thrust my chair under the table in disgust. 'I give up!'

'Lucy – come back. Let's talk about this.'

I stop at the doorway, cross my arms and spin round, snapping, 'Okay. What?'

'You're absolutely right about Rachel, I accept that. And I'll do something about it this afternoon.'

'Good.'

'But, as for the other people I've been seeing . . . have I been doing anything so wrong? All I've done is gone out on a few dates with one or two nice people. I haven't proposed to anyone; I haven't deceived anyone – I've been enjoying myself. Surely that was the point?'

I try to think of an answer, but can't.

'What's so awful about that, Lucy?'

I look into his eyes, my heart pounding.

'Forget it, Henry. You wouldn't understand.' I spin on my heels and head for the door. I'm well aware of my hypocrisy – because part of me doesn't understand either.

Chapter 50

The following weekend, things are looking up: I have a date.

I know that some people might not see this as a reason to celebrate, given my success rate. But, as I have discovered only too well, it's better than sitting at home watching *Pretty Woman* again and listening to the groans of ecstasy coming through Henry's wall.

Besides, I have a good feeling about this one. Call me blindly optimistic, but Will – whom I met at a Chamber of Commerce lunch – seems a gentleman, unlike some of the blokes I've been out with. He's also slightly less, how can I put this . . . *obvious* in the looks department. A bit shorter. Thinner. Pointy-nosed. Oh, that makes him sound awful and he's not. He's quite good-looking. Certainly passable. Which will do for me because what makes a man sexy and nice – and all the other things I'm looking for – has nothing to do with how he looks. I've learned that much.

I'm also convinced that Will has the potential to be more tolerant than all the others if I do something inappropriate. Not that I'm planning to – but then, I never do plan these things.

Will is a quantity surveyor who recently relocated from

Bristol. His dress sense is slightly conservative. In fact, Will as a whole is slightly conservative.

In the light of this, I considered forfeiting my subtle application of St Tropez, new choppy bob from Toni & Guy, outfit from Karen Millen and shoes from Kurt Geiger. Only they had a sale on in the Metquarter and I couldn't resist. Plus, Dominique was getting her nails done at a place where there was a two-for-one offer and I couldn't resist that either.

I've never had acrylic nails before and I can't believe what I've been missing. What a slattern I must have looked before two o'clock this afternoon, with the unpolished and woefully stubby efforts at the end of my fingers.

Now, as I rest my hands gently on top of my new clutch bag, I feel a surge of self-confidence. God, they're glam. Dominique tried to advise me to go for a shorter look, given I was an Acrylic Virgin. But, in for a penny in for a pound. Now, they're so luscious and long that at a distance I must look like Edward Scissorhands's big sister. Just joking. Kind of.

The only downside to these magnificent talons is that, while they look the part, they make doing just about everything – from putting a key in the door to applying make-up – tantamount to embarking on an obstacle course. I had particular fun trying to get the lid off my shaving foam before doing my legs. Not only did I dislodge one edge of a nail (which is still hanging precariously despite some emergency DIY), I also ended up flinging the can across the bathroom and almost taking out a window. Thankfully, we're double-glazed.

It's a balmy early summer evening as I sashay into the restaurant's bar and see Will perched on a stool. He has a gin and tonic and is typing away on his BlackBerry as I approach. When he looks up, his expression relaxes me immediately.

'Wow,' he says, putting his phone away as he stands and kisses me on the cheek. 'You look amazing, Lucy.'

'Thanks,' I smile as I sit next to him. 'I hope I haven't kept you waiting.'

'Not at all.' He's clearly fibbing as he's almost finished his gin and tonic. 'Can I get you a drink?'

The conversation feels stilted at first, but after a couple of drinks we loosen up. Admittedly I have to be flexible with the truth when he asks about my qualification in yoga (I don't even remember telling him that) and being president of my local chess club – particularly since the last board game I played was *Buckaroo*. But by the time we sit down to eat and order our food, I'm confident the evening is going well.

'Is your relocation a permanent one?' I ask.

'Who knows? I'm here because of the job, but I could end up settling here. It'd be a bit strange, I suppose, given that my friends and family are in the south. But you make new friends, don't you?'

'I'll look after you, if you like,' I offer flirtatiously. When he doesn't answer immediately I panic. Maybe my efforts to bring him out of his shell have been misjudged.

Then his face cracks into a wide smile. 'That's settled it. I'm staying.'

Chapter 51

The restaurant is busy and service relatively slow, but that's fine because it means that I get to learn all about Will. I decide I like him. I like him a lot. I can't say we've a great deal in common, given that he grew up in a seven-bedroom house in Bedfordshire and I didn't.

Nevertheless, he is one of life's good guys and therefore exactly what I need. By the time our food arrives I'm determined to impress him.

'What did you go for?' he asks, looking at my plate.

'Tempura of king prawns with chilli and lime jam. I love seafood.'

'Mmm, me too,' he says. 'But I also love a good soup and this one sounded lovely. Vine tomato and basil.'

'Nice,' I nod, picking up my fork delicately and wondering how to negotiate the dish without exposing my nails to further trauma.

'Did you always want to go into PR?' he asks.

'Not exactly. I was interested in the media – read a lot of newspapers and that kind of thing. I toyed with being a journalist, but everyone wants to do that when they're at university, don't they?'

'A lot of people seem to,' he smiles.

'I never really knew what I wanted to do. Then a friend did work experience at a PR agency in Manchester and loved it. I liked the sound of it, so decided to give it a go.'

'Did you start at the bottom?'

'I was a graduate trainee, which involved making as many cups of tea as it did writing press releases. But I loved it. I still do.'

This remains just about true, despite recent events – not only the awards ceremony fiasco, about which I still have nightmares, almost two months later, but also the fact that Drew seems to have been unofficially crowned God's Gift to the PR Industry since.

'You're lucky to have found a job you enjoy so much,' Will says.

'I suppose I am.'

'I don't know how you fit it all in, what with your extra-curricular activities. What was it you were telling me the other night . . . you can fence?'

I feel my neck getting hotter, even though this is, in fact, true. Well, perhaps *true* is pushing it a bit. But I did get chosen to take part in a demonstration by a retired fencing champion at school when I was thirteen – and he said I was a natural. Under the circumstances, I feel I can hold my head high.

'I don't do it as much as I used to,' I say. 'In fact, I'm a bit rusty.'

'I'm sure it'd be like riding a bicycle. I've always fancied fencing myself. How about showing me the ropes next weekend?'

'Er . . .'

'Unless you think I'd hold you back.'

'It's not that.'

'Then it's a date!' He takes a spoonful of soup.

'I'm busy next weekend,' I blurt out. Clearly, it comes out more forcefully than I'd hoped as he sits up in shock.

'Oh. Oh . . . I see.'

No, you *don't* see. Oh, now I've gone and made him think I don't like him. What am I going to do?

He continues to eat his soup silently as I solemnly make my way through my prawns, wondering how things have gone so awry.

Will looks out of the window. 'I hadn't realized how magnificent the architecture was in this city.' It is a random comment, but I'm so grateful at his attempt to get the conversation back on track that I nearly lean over and kiss him.

'Oh yes,' I smile instead. 'There are more Grade One listed buildings here than anywhere outside London.'

I put down my fork to pick up my wine. But as I go to grab the glass, I catch my hand against a large pot of black pepper and hear a ping, as pain tears through my finger.

I suck air through my teeth and briefly contemplate the source of my agony. Then I catch sight of it: my false nail. Rocketing across the table like a heat-seeking missile.

My eyes widen in panic and I hear a squeak escape from my lips. Shit! My false nail is airborne. And it's heading . . . directly for my date's soup.

My heart stops as the nail lands with a small splash, pauses momentarily on the surface, then capsizes into the deep like a tiny version of the *Titanic*.

Oh my God. Oh my –

'I particularly like the Cunard building,' Will continues, apparently oblivious to the synthetic nail I've catapulted into his starter. 'Terribly grand, all that Italian Renaissance-influenced stuff. Over the top almost – but I still can't resist it.'

He waits for a response.

'Um . . . no,' I grin weakly, my heart pulverizing my ribcage. 'Me neither.'

Barely able to catch my breath I stare, incredulous, as he dips his spoon into his soup and lifts it to his mouth. I pause, while he sips, apparently successfully, before resting the spoon back in the bowl. I breathe a momentary sigh of relief.

'Tell you what,' I begin, trying to sound casual, 'I'm in a bit of a hurry. Why don't we send back these starters and move onto the next course?'

He looks at me, clearly wondering if I'm demented.

'Waiter!' I shout, beckoning over one of the blokes serving the table next to us.

The waiter turns and frowns.

'Over here, please!'

'I'm serving this lady and gentleman,' he responds sniffily. 'But I'll be right with you, madam.'

I turn back to Will, my face burning.

'Actually, I'd like to finish this soup,' he tells me with a worried look. 'It's nice.'

He lifts his spoon up to his mouth once more and I hold my breath again. As the liquid seeps between his lips, without incident, I nearly pass out with relief. It's shortlived.

'Why are you in a hurry?' he asks, dipping his spoon into the soup again.

'I just . . . I . . .' I am unable to think of a response.

The spoon lingers as a disappointed look settles on his face. 'You don't want to be on this date, do you?'

'No, I do!' I cry.

'You don't like me very much, I can tell.'

'I do! Honestly I do! It's just—'

I consider cutting my losses and confessing about the stray nail. But just then, our waiter arrives.

'Now, madam,' he says with a stiff smile. 'What can I do for you?'

I glance at Will as he slurps another spoonful of soup, then at his bowl – and can see the white edges of my nail poking out. Sweat breaks out on my forehead.

Regardless of Will's desire to finish his starter, I turn to instruct the waiter to remove the offending bowl, when I catch sight of Will out of the corner of my eye slurping another spoonful. I glance down at the bowl again and – *arrgh!* – the nail is gone.

I look at Will and gulp. He looks at me and smiles. But his smile lasts less than a second. Soon he's frowning. Soon his expression becomes very strange. His face very . . . red.

'Cchhrrr!'

'Are you all right?' Panic sweeps over me.

'Chhrr!' He grabs his oesophagus.

Paralysed, I watch as Will coughs and splutters, his cheeks an alarming shade of purple. He stands up and starts gesticulating wildly to the lower part of his throat, as guests on the next tables wonder what's going on.

'Oh God!' I shrill, leaping up and knocking over my wine.

'He's got something stuck in his throat,' yells the waiter, perceptively.

'Do something!' I cry.

'Chhhecrrhrhrhh!!' says Will.

249

'I know the Heimlich manoeuvre!' A large, middle-aged woman from the next table barges forward.

She lifts Will up, grabs him from behind and wraps her arms round his ribcage. She then starts thrusting backwards and forwards, tightening her arms around his body as his face turns even brighter and he wheezes like a burst bag-pipe.

The woman pauses to gather her forces, before putting every last bit of might into another thrust. Will's head flies forward and my nail shoots from his mouth as if powered by a jet engine.

She releases him and he slumps down into his chair.

'God, Will . . . are you all right?' I kneel to look at him, praying that he's come through this unscathed. He's panting like an asthmatic greyhound and tears are pouring down his face, but he manages to nod.

'What *the hell* was that?' asks the waiter.

Diners and staff start scrambling on the floor to try to work out what almost killed a man. I look at Will and see that he's recovering rapidly. I seize him by the elbow and murmur. 'I think we should go.'

'W-what?' he wheezes. 'Well, yes but . . . give me a minute.'

I look at the door, biting my lip.

'Ready now?' I ask, hoping I don't sound unsympathetic. I mean, I *am* sympathetic – honestly, I feel terrible. But I only have one chance of escape.

Will is wiping his face with a napkin, pouring out some water.

'It's a nail!' shrieks someone from the next table. 'It's one of them bloody fake nails! Was that in his food? This place should be shut down.'

My Single Friend

I catch Will staring through bloodshot eyes at my middle finger – the only one with a short, stubby nail, covered in half-set glue – and I know I've been busted.

Again.

Chapter 52

I pray Henry's around when I arrive home after ten. I'm desperate to talk about what happened tonight and he is the only person who'll do. Aside from the fact that Dominique and Erin are out, they're not as good at listening as Henry. No disrespect to them, but no one is. And after tonight's shenanigans, I need someone to do some *serious* listening.

I remind myself, however, that it's Saturday night and Henry hasn't been around on a Saturday night since dinosaurs roamed the plains of east Africa. At least it feels like it. The point is, I'm not holding out much hope.

As I put my key in the door and push it open I spot Henry's coat on the rack in the hallway, hanging next to mine. The sight makes my heart skip with happiness. Henry's home and I know I'm going to be all right.

His keys are on the side table, next to his mobile phone. I pick it up and look at the screensaver, a daft shot of him and me taken on the beach last summer. I can't help smiling, though I've seen it a thousand times. *Thank God I've got Henry.*

I head for the living room, assuming he's watching telly, and push open the door. I couldn't be less impressed with the sight before me if I tried.

Mercifully, they're fully clothed. Yet, the position of Henry and this woman – whoever she is – is so intimate, she might as well be fellating him.

Henry is lying on his back, biceps resplendent with a hand behind his head, as this She-Devil with glossy black ringlets and a skirt up to her crotch is leaning on his chest, impossibly toned legs entwined around his. She's gazing at him, her expression oozing awe and lust. In his hand is a battered paperback entitled *Love Poetry of the Eighteenth Century*.

'My poor expecting Heart beats for thy Breast,' Henry murmurs with a tongue-in-cheek smile, 'in ev'ry Pulse, and will not let me rest. A thousand dear Desires are waking there . . .'

He stops and looks up. 'Oh Lucy, hi. I didn't see you there.'

The siren scrambles up and pulls down her skirt. Thankfully, I no longer have an eyeful of her lacy black knickers (cheap-looking, I couldn't help but notice).

'Hi! Sorry to interrupt. I'm Lucy. Lovely to meet you.' Beaming, I march over and hold out my hand to the woman, determined not to make my resentment apparent.

'Hi!' she replies brightly, sitting up and straightening her top. 'I'm Davina. Henry's told me a lot about you.'

She's pretty, with a winsome smile, a stick-thin body and breasts that could double for space hoppers.

'All good, I hope.' I breathe in and subtly stick out my chest.

'Of *course*,' he says smoothly.

Then we all stare at each other, smiling politely.

'Well, you've got a lovely place here,' says Davina awkwardly.

'Oh, this?' I reply. 'We've been here a while, haven't we, Henry?'

'Four years.'

We carry on staring at each other, grinning.

'You're home early,' Henry says. 'Everything all right?'

'Oh.' I look at my watch and pretend I hadn't noticed the time. 'Oh, yeah. Fine.'

'Did you have a date?'

'Hmmm? A date? Well, yeah, kind of. Not really. I was out with people from work. It was dull, to be honest.'

'How come you're home at this time?'

'I wasn't feeling well.' I trot out another lie.

'Oh?' asks Henry.

'A bit . . . queasy,' I improvise. 'Quite a lot queasy actually. Can't imagine what it could be.'

'Oh God,' breathes Davina, 'my flatmate came home early last Saturday feeling queasy and she's discovered she's pregnant.'

I glare at her.

'It's spooky,' she continues. 'She said exactly the same as you: that she felt queasy but couldn't imagine what it could be. Found out three days later she's expecting.'

'I'm not pregnant,' I say flatly.

'Are you *sure?*' asks Davina, looking genuinely concerned. 'Are you retaining water?'

'No,' I reply firmly.

'You know, my friend was the last person I'd ever suspect would get pregnant, yet she has. I'd double-check if I were you.'

'Really, I'm not pregnant.' I laugh, as lightly as possible.

'You can get the tests from the supermarket these days – they're less than a tenner, which is worth it for the peace of mind.'

'I don't need peace of mind – I'm not pregnant,' I tell her.

Davina looks at me pityingly. 'Only, if you are then they say it's best facing up to things early on. That way, you can keep your options open. Being in denial is the worst thing for it – that's what they say.'

'Honestly,' I insist, feeling rather frustrated now. 'I'm one hundred per cent certain I'm not pregnant.'

'Well, that's what Lucinda thought, but—'

'Look,' I shriek, throwing my arms up, 'I've had about as much sex lately as the founder member of a pro-chastity group, so unless there's been an immaculate conception I AM NOT PREGNANT!'

The room falls silent. Davina is dumbfounded. Henry shifts uncomfortably.

'Perhaps we should get out of your way.' He stands and takes Davina by the hand. 'I was planning to show Davina my . . .'

Henry stops speaking as it dawns on him that I may not want to know what he's about to show Davina.

'No. *I'll* get out of *your* way.' I back out of the room. 'Sorry, I . . . I'm sorry.'

As I get to my bedroom and throw myself onto the bed, I look at a crack in the ceiling, feeling thoroughly depressed. A minute later, there's a knock on the door.

'Come in,' I say, sitting up.

Henry walks in and shuts the door behind him.

'Haven't you got a guest to entertain?' I ask as he sits at the end of the bed.

'She'll be okay for two minutes. Did something happen tonight?'

'Oh Henry, don't ask,' I say, then regret it immediately

because I'm desperate to talk. 'I had another crap date. The worst. I nearly killed someone.'

'Are you serious?' His eyes widen. 'What did you do?'

I fill him in on all the gory detail and he sits, listening as patiently and sympathetically as ever. 'The worst thing is,' I say, 'it was going so well before the false nail disaster. He'd even asked me to go fencing with him . . .' My voice trails off.

He frowns. 'Fencing? That's an odd choice of date.'

'Hmmm . . . yes,' I say sheepishly.

A look of recognition flashes on his face. 'You told him you could fence.'

'I . . .' I am about to protest but realize immediately that there's no point.

'Lucy, can I make a suggestion?' he asks.

'Why not?' I shrug.

'The thing with the nail was unfortunate, but sometimes things happen that are beyond your control – and there's no point worrying about them. It's the things that *are* in your control that you need to think about.'

'What do you mean?'

He looks me in the eyes. 'You've got to stop lying to these people, Lucy.'

The bluntness of the statement punches me in the stomach. I suddenly feel embarrassed – and defensive.

'I don't lie, Henry,' I protest. 'I just . . . just . . . okay, I admit I have been known to *exaggerate*. Slightly. But it's no more than that.'

He frowns. 'Are you sure about that?'

'Of course I'm—' Then I stop, mid-flow, and sniff. 'No,' I say meekly. 'I'm not sure. You're right, Henry.'

Tears well in my eyes and he leans over and holds my hand.

'I don't know what makes me do it,' I whimper. 'Desperation, I suppose. I just want one of these bloody dates to go well. For someone to think I'm special enough to want to see again.'

'Lucy, what have I been telling you?' Henry says. 'You're special enough *as you are*. Lying gets you nowhere – can't you see?'

'In the cold light of day, of course,' I mumble. I look down at his hand, squeezing mine, then back at his eyes. He lets go and stands up.

'I'd better get back to Davina.' He heads to the door. 'But think about it, won't you? Face up to what you're doing – and stop it.'

'Okay,' I sniff.

He looks into the hall, then back at me. 'Are you going to be all right?'

I nod. 'Course. Get back to your . . . to Davina.'

He smiles and leaves, shutting the door behind him.

I've never felt so desperate to continue talking. To analyse this ludicrous compulsion I have to tell giant porkies to everyone I go out with. And I'm desperate for Henry to tell me that, despite everything, he still loves me; that I'm still his best friend in the world.

But as the sound of Davina's giggling seeps through the cracks in my door, I pull my pillow over my head and curse myself for ever having thought up *Project Henry*.

Thanks to my bright idea, my one successful relationship with a bloke is slipping through my fingers. And I can't do a thing about it.

Chapter 53

Something strange is going on with my mother.

It's Monday lunchtime and I've nipped into John Lewis. I'm testing out a Clinique lipstick when I glance over and there she is. My mum. At Elizabeth Arden. With not one but *three* items in her hand.

I know most people wouldn't find this suspicious, but my mother does not frequent upmarket cosmetic counters at department stores. She buys her make-up from her mate Julie down the road and always has. Her idea of a luxury skin product is a bottle of Skin So Soft from Avon, which she's been buying since about 1961.

I *have* to know what's going on.

I march up to Mum and tap her on the shoulder. She almost drops a jar of anti-cellulite cream.

'What's up?' I say.

She gasps. 'Wha— Lucy, you nearly gave me a heart-attack!'

'You don't normally get your make-up from places like this, do you?'

'I was just having a look.' Her shoulders stiffen.

'You look like you're buying them.'

She frowns. 'So what if I am, Inspector bloody Clouseau?'

I uncross my arms. 'It's out of character, that's all. What would Julie say?'

'I've gone off Avon lately,' she says quietly, picking up a tube of eye-cream.

I am taken aback. 'She'll be distraught.'

'No, she won't. I hardly think me not buying a two-pack of talc every six months is going to put Julie out of business.'

'Don't get me wrong – it's nice to see you spending some money on yourself for a change.'

'Well, you'd never guess. All I've done is come in here for some bits and bobs and it's like being interrogated at Guantanamo Bay.'

'Sorry. I was just surprised to see you here.'

'Instead of chained to the kitchen sink, you mean?' Without waiting for an answer, she goes off to pay for her goodies. They come to more than sixty pounds and she hands over her Barclaycard without hesitation. I have to stop myself from doing a double-take.

'Have you had lunch?' I ask as we head outside.

'Not yet. I was going to grab something and eat it on the bus.'

'Have you time for a sandwich? My treat,' I tell her. 'I've only got half an hour though.'

The café is busy but Mum and I manage to get a table next to the door. I take a bite of my chicken and pesto wrap while she stirs four packets of sweetener into her tea. Mum has always had a sweet tooth. If someone hadn't invented Aspartame she'd be the size of an eight-berth motorhome by now.

'Have you had your hair done?' I ask, realizing that the new make-up isn't the only thing different about her.

Her neck reddens. 'Yeah. Trevor Sorbie himself came round to put my Nice 'n' Easy on. Can you tell?'

Despite the sarcasm, it's immediately obvious that Mum's new highlights are *not* the result of a home kit. They're too professional. But if she doesn't want to confess, I'm not going to force her.

'How did your date go on Saturday?' She takes a bite of her sandwich.

'Don't ask,' I tell her. She waits for me to elaborate. 'I mean it, really don't ask.'

She shrugs. 'Shame you're not having as much luck as Henry these days. Did I tell you our Dave saw him last week? He barely recognized him. But then, six months ago you'd never have guessed Henry'd be going out with some leggy blonde, would you?'

'He was with a blonde?' I didn't even know there was a blonde on the scene. I assumed brunettes were his speciality.

Mum looks at me and pauses. 'You're not jealous, are you?'

'Mother!' I shriek.

'Sorry. Calm down. I was only joking.'

'Well, good. For the record, no, I am not jealous. Of course I'm not jealous.'

'Fine. "Of course she's not jealous",' she mimics.

I take another bite and look out of the window. 'Is Denise still dragging you to salsa dancing, by the way?' I ask.

She nods, refusing to give anything away by her expression. I find myself smirking.

'That's about three months you've been going now,' I point out. 'Not bad going, considering it's "crap". That *was* what you said, wasn't it?'

She gives me another look – a warning one this time. 'It's *all right*. That's as far as I'm prepared to go.'

'I might come myself one night.'

'Don't you dare!' she leaps in. 'I mean it. I'm not having you turning up and taking the piss.'

'I wouldn't,' I protest. 'I'm genuinely interested, that's all.'

'Yeah? Well, stick to being genuinely interested somewhere else, if that's okay.'

'Fine,' I mutter.

'Oh, I meant to say,' she says, deliberately changing the subject, 'thanks for the anniversary card.'

'No problem. I'm guessing Dave didn't bother.'

'Dave? Your bloody father didn't bother, never mind your brother.'

I know this shouldn't surprise me – Dad has always been like this. Mum used to get anniversary cards from him, but we knew that Nana Hilda bought them, a fact confirmed when they dried up the year she died. While I know plenty of men are the same, part of me can't help feeling cross on her behalf.

'Doesn't it annoy you that Dad never buys you an anniversary card?'

'I knew when I married him I wasn't getting Omar Sharif,' she says.

'He should still send you a card,' I grumble. 'I'm going to tell him.'

She laughs. 'Don't waste your breath. It's not a big deal anyway.'

'But surely it—'

'Look, if there's one thing I've learned over the years it's that men never change. And if you attempt to change them, you're on a hiding to nothing.'

'I wish someone would tell Henry that. He's unrecognizable these days.'

'Yeah, well,' she says, 'he always has been a bit different, hasn't he?'

Chapter 54

I am starting to feel so frustrated about things between Henry and me that I decide it's time to take action. Only as I come home and find the flat empty again, I acknowledge that it's easier said than done. Throwing my keys on the hall table I wander through to the bathroom. With two empty bottles of conditioner lingering in the shower and toothpaste barnacles encrusted on the sink, it's more neglected than usual. The same thought strikes me in the kitchen as I wipe away the crumbs under the toaster and begin to wash the coffee cups abandoned in the sink.

Then I realize the difference: Henry. Our division of labour used to be perfectly clear cut though we'd never officially designated jobs to each other: I'd cook dinner – because I enjoyed it – and he'd look after the housework – because I didn't. He's got better things to do these days than mop up after me.

I grab my mobile and dial Henry's number. He answers straight away. 'Hello, Lucy, how's it going?'

'Fine. Where are you?'

'Driving. But it's okay, I'm on the hands-free. What's up?'

'Will you be home tonight?'

'Should be, but not until late. I've got a rugby match then I'll probably go for a couple of drinks with the guys. Why do you ask? Is everything okay?'

'Yeah. I just wondered . . .' There's a pause as I consider how to put this without turning it into a big deal.

'What is it?' Henry asks.

We might be living virtually separate lives these days but his instinctive ability to pick up on the nuances of my mood is as sharp as ever.

'I feel as if I hardly see you,' I confess. 'We've been friends for so long I'd hate it if . . . you know, things changed between us. It'd be nice to spend some time with you again, that's all.'

I feel like a saddo saying this, but I can't help myself. I cringe as soon as my sentence is over.

'I know what you're saying and I agree,' he replies. 'We've hardly seen each other lately – and we should do something to change it.'

'Good,' I say, comforted by his response.

'This is all your own doing, you know,' he tells me. 'I'd still be sat at home on my own if you hadn't devised *Project Henry*.'

'Yeah,' I chuckle.

'When do you want to do something?'

'How about Friday?' I suggest excitedly. 'I could cook, like the old days, then we could slob out in front of the television and talk rubbish like we used to and—'

'Friday could be difficult,' he interrupts.

'Oh, right. You've got a date.'

'Not a date exactly. Though I am going out with someone.'

'Sounds like a date to me.'

'I suppose so.'

'Anyone I know?'

'Hey, Lucy, stop quizzing me about my love-life,' he laughs. 'How about Saturday instead?'

'I'll have to check my diary.' Who am I trying to kid? My Saturday nights couldn't be less action-packed if I'd spent them in a padded cell. 'Though I'm pretty sure I'm not doing anything,' I add, before he changes his mind.

'Great. Saturday night it is, then. I'll look forward to it.'

Chapter 55

Every organization needs a good PR woman. But there are times when they need us more than others. For one of my biggest clients – *Peach Gear*, a fashion chain for twelve- to sixteen-year-olds – it's one of those times. With knobs on.

I knew it as soon as I saw the expression on the face of Janine Nixon, their Chief Executive, at the start of my meeting with her and her Marketing Director, Phil McEwan. The venue they chose is JD's dockside café, an establishment famed for its bacon sandwiches but not, judging by the peeling wallpaper, its interior design.

I take a sip of tea and am surprised to discover it tastes better here than in the coffee shop next to the office. What they lack here in baristas, they make up for in value – nothing on the menu costs more than it did in 1972.

Still, it's the last place you'd expect to find Janine and Phil. My *Peach Gear* meetings have always, until now, taken place in their swanky fourteenth-floor boardroom, where I've sipped Italian coffee from Villeroy & Boch cups and admired the view.

It can only mean one thing.

'We're in a spot of trouble,' says Janine, wiping off the egg yolk she's picked up on the sleeve of her Armani suit.

266

'Whatever it is, I'm your woman,' I reply confidently. I am hoping to impress Janine, whom I have only met once before. Until now, she's always left Phil to handle media matters. 'I've dealt with all manner of crisis situations in my years with Peaman-Brown.'

She takes a deep breath. 'This is certainly a crisis situation.'

'Right,' I say. 'Well, we'll go through the issues involved, draw up a plan, and you can count on me to implement it.'

Janine looks happier already. I smile. 'So – what's the problem?'

Phil and Janine exchange looks.

As I know, Phil says, *Peach Gear* has a long-standing and very public commitment to ethical trading.

At least, they *thought* they had a commitment to ethical trading. Three days ago, they discovered that a supplier had been hand-finishing sequinned vests, not in a strictly-regulated factory in Delhi like they thought, but a back street in Bangalore. Worse, they've been using children aged eleven, which is illegal, immoral and reprehensible by most standards. The team at *Peach Gear* are devastated, they tell me.

'So you had no inkling of this?' I ask the question as if this is part of the process, but I want to suss out whether they *really* knew nothing. While crisis management is often a dirty job, I won't defend the indefensible.

Janine looks me in the eyes. 'We knew nothing. You're right to ask, but we knew nothing.'

I study her expression. She doesn't look away.

'Okay,' I say finally, turning over a page of my notepad. 'That helps.'

She leans back, grateful. 'If it also helps, I can tell you what we've done since we found out.'

'Fill me in.'

Janine explains that they've contacted the Ethical Trade Alliance, whose representatives will travel to Bangalore with a contingent of senior *Peach Gear* staff next week. They'll do everything they can to fix things: namely, work with those involved to get the children into school – and make sure the work is carried out by the staff it was intended for.

'Although we've done everything right,' continues Phil, 'our worry is that it won't be presented like that if the press gets hold of it.'

'Does something make you think they will?'

Phil runs a nervous hand through his hair. 'A report is due to be read out in the House of Commons next month about this issue – and we're named in it. That's how we found out about it.'

'If it's discussed in the Commons it will definitely be picked up by the media,' I tell them. 'What we need to do therefore is announce it ourselves. *Before* the report comes out. That way, we retain control of the message – as much as we can, anyway. Leave it with me and I'll see what I can do.'

An hour later I am back in the office writing my strategy. I've spoken to the Ethical Trade Alliance myself and, if there was any lingering doubt that *Peach Gear* were genuinely in the dark about what their supplier was up to, that's quickly dispelled. According to their press office, they wished every company acted so responsibly.

Determined that handling a major issue like this is what I need to show Roger my worth, I pop in to see him when I've finished. I hand over one of only four copies of the confidential document – the others are for Janine, Phil and myself. It's short but, I hope, impressive; I even get Little Lynette to bind each one in a cover so they look the part.

'You okay?' asks Dominique when I bump into her in the corridor.

'Handling a crisis for one of my favourite clients.'

'Who?'

I look around to check that no one can hear. '*Peach Gear*,' I whisper, and fill her in as quickly as I can.

Roger flicks through my strategy document and looks worried. 'Here was I thinking this account only involved getting blouses into the fashion pages.'

I don't say anything. Getting anything on the fashion pages is clearly a damn sight harder than Roger appreciates.

'What are your recommendations?' he asks.

I perch on the edge of his desk. 'We need to go public before the report comes out. Otherwise, we're on the defensive and all hell will break loose.'

'Announcing this isn't going to be easy, whether they've done the right thing or not.'

'I know. But trying vainly to cover it up would be worse. My plan is to hold a series of briefings with trusted journalists in the days before it's read out in the Commons.'

'Do you need any back-up? It's a big job and I know Drew would love to—'

'No,' I say immediately. 'I should be fine by myself.'

Chapter 56

As Henry is out tonight, I decide to use the time constructively. I wax my legs, paint my toenails, administer fake tan and, inspired by a picture of Cheryl Cole in *Heat*, attempt to apply semi-permanent eyelash enhancers. I end up with three lashes successfully stuck to my lids and so much glue I look as if I've developed cataracts.

When I retire to bed, I'm satisfied with my extensive beautification and find myself thinking constantly about tomorrow night. I drift into a light sleep, waking just after two when Henry comes in. I use the opportunity to go to the loo and bump into him in the hall.

He's looking strikingly handsome in an end-of-the-night-type way. He's slightly dishevelled – his tie is loose and his tuxedo is flung over his arm – and he's unbuttoning the top of his shirt as we come face to face. My eyes are drawn to his Adam's apple.

'Nice night?' I ask.

'Better than I imagined.'

'Oh good. So your date lived up to expectations?'

He smiles sweetly at me but does not reply.

'Oh no, I forgot,' I tease. 'It wasn't a date, was it?'

He merely laughs.

'Only, you certainly smell like someone who's had a good old smooch with a member of the opposite sex,' I continue, sniffing.

'My compliments, Lucy. There are bloodhounds lacking your sense of smell.'

'Don't try and wriggle out of it.'

'I'm not. My date was delightful, thank you.'

'Good,' I reply. 'Does she know what a playboy you are these days?'

He makes a tutting sound. 'Go on – bugger off and have your wee,' he tells me, yawning. 'You can grill me about it tomorrow – if you must.'

One of the few things I'm better at than Henry is cooking. I don't pretend to be Nigella, having neither the enunciation nor the boobs for a start. But there are few things I enjoy more than rustling up a home-made curry or lamb casserole.

Tonight, after much deliberation, I have gone for a Caribbean monkfish stew, which I've made before but I know Henry adores. I get up early to buy the ingredients, making certain I get the best pickings in the fishmonger's before half of south Liverpool heads there for their dinner-party fayre.

I buy a couple of bottles of good wine, a bunch of peonies for the windowsill, and candles to replace the ones that melted down in 2005 and have since looked more like volcanic debris than home accessories.

Henry's out of the flat for most of the day and he texts me at lunchtime. *We still on 4 tonight?*

Yes, I respond. Y? *Have u had a better offer?*

It is fine. So he *did* have another option. *CU at 7.30?*

As the afternoon wears on, there's something about my preparations for the evening that feels strange. Henry and I have dined together for most of our adult lives and yet for some reason it feels like I'm getting ready for a date. There's a fluttery sensation in my stomach whenever I think about the evening. By the time I've showered, I'm ridiculously stressed about what to wear.

In the end, in an effort to make it clear that this *isn't* a date, I choose an old but favourite pair of jeans and my Diesel vest top. I'd usually wear it to look casual but sexy, though clearly, in this case, I'm not trying to look sexy. I just want to look casual, not scruffy.

I resist the temptation to go down the heated roller route and instead give my hair a better-than-average blow dry, before setting the table. I spread out the tablecloth I'd washed earlier and put my candles in the middle. I check the stew and am satisfied it's coming along nicely, then head to the living room with a glass of wine.

Henry arrives at seven-thirty on the dot, clearly having exerted himself to make it on time.

'Blimey. Are you in a rush?'

'I got caught up.' He's slightly out of breath as he runs his hand through his hair. 'Sorry. Am I late?'

'No – it's fine. Relax.'

'Have I got time for a shower?'

'Of course. I can keep the stew going for as long as you want.'

I relocate to the kitchen and when Henry emerges five minutes later, he's buttoning up his jeans. My eyes are drawn to his crotch. As his hands work their way upwards, I catch a glimpse of his flat, toned stomach and the hairs at the top of his trousers. A wave of heat spreads through my body. I turn my back and decisively stir my stew.

Chapter 57

Henry's praise for the dinner is so lavish you'd think he'd dined at Claridge's.

'Lucy, that was a triumph.'

I top up our glasses. 'Shucks, you'll embarrass me.'

'I doubt that. I have a suggestion though: instead of telling those blokes you go out with that you're a champion trapeze artist, or whatever it is you say, why don't you cook for them? They'd be more impressed.'

'For the record, I've never claimed to be a champion trapeze artist. Anyway, I'm turning over a new leaf. No more fibbing to impress men.'

'Really? What brought this on?'

'I thought about what you said the other night and I agree. Besides that, a *really* compelling reason has suddenly dawned on me.'

'Oh?'

'The fact that it never works.'

He laughs and stands to pick up my plate.

'Why don't you leave the dishes?' I suggest. 'We can go through to the living room and shut the door to pretend they don't exist. Until tomorrow, anyway.'

'If you insist.' He puts them in the sink. 'Though I'm conscious I haven't been pulling my weight in terms of the housework lately. I felt guilty when I saw you'd done the bathroom as well as the cooking.'

'Oh, don't.' I wave my hand. 'I've got years of doing sod-all to make up for.'

Henry and I adjourn to the living room, where he slumps on the sofa. I find myself studying his features. The full mouth. The defined jaw. The smooth, tanned skin. He opens his eyes and catches me looking at him.

I leap out of my seat towards the iPod. 'What music do you fancy?'

He walks over to join me. 'How about a blast from the past?' he suggests, choosing 'Praise You' by Fatboy Slim.

'God, we must have been in the fifth year when this was in the charts,' I work out.

'Ah yes, the fifth year. Those were the days,' he says with a faux-hazy look.

'What days?'

'Let me think . . . you were obsessed with Hugh Grant after watching *Four Weddings and a Funeral*.'

'But had to settle for Daniel Prosser in the sixth form instead,' I giggle.

'A bit of a compromise,' Henry grins. 'Though to be fair to Daniel, he had a spectacularly floppy fringe.'

We spend the next few hours drinking, laughing and singing to everything from Stevie Wonder to The Saturdays. When I finally remember to look at the clock it is a quarter to two. 'God, look at the time. I don't know where the evening has gone,' I say.

'It really is like the old days, then.'

'You're telling me you used to have this much fun every night living with me? I don't believe it.'

'Lucy, living with you is a permanent riot. Believe me.'

'I'll try to take that as a compliment. But, hey, you've got a better-rounded life these days, haven't you?'

'Thanks to you.'

I take a sip of my wine and realize I'm quite drunk. Not unpleasantly so. Far from it.

'Has *Project Henry* lived up to expectations?' I ask.

He pauses, thinking about it as if the answer wasn't obvious.

'Well, I should hope it has, Henry!' I laugh. 'Because if you were expecting to bed any more women than you have so far, then I can only conclude you were being greedy!'

'Oh, Lucy,' he squirms.

'It's true, isn't it? Your sex-life is so active it deserves a PE kit.'

He laughs. 'Not exactly.'

'Look, don't knock it. I'm jealous.'

He pauses for a second. 'I'd have to admit the sex has been . . . nice.'

'Nice?' I say, exasperated. 'The Southport Flower Show is *nice*. Baby bunnies are *nice*. Nice is not a word which is supposed to apply to your sex-life. Not if you're doing it right.'

'Maybe I'm not doing it right.'

'From what I've heard through your bedroom wall, Henry, you're doing it right.'

He sits up, alarmed. 'You haven't heard – you know . . .'

'Once or twice,' I shrug.

He looks distraught. 'That's awful.'

'Relax,' I tell him dismissively. 'I've stayed in halls of residence, remember. Listening to the second year Zoology

student above going at it was my backing track to three terms'
worth of revision.'

'But still . . . God, I'm sorry, Lucy.'

'Don't worry about it,' I reassure him. 'Anyway, what were
we saying . . . oh yes, *Project Henry*. Has it achieved everything you wanted?'

He thinks for a second. 'That's a tough one.'

'What does that mean? You're obviously not a hundred per
cent convinced.'

'Oh, it's definitely been a success,' he assures me. 'I mean,
I look better. So I feel better. I'm confident with women. And
they find me more attractive than before – which admittedly
wouldn't have been difficult.'

'I can feel a *but* coming on.'

'I don't want to appear ungrateful . . .'

'*But* . . .'

He pauses. 'You've always known that I'm an old-fashioned
sort of guy, Lucy.'

'Yes,' I concede.

'If I was being really picky I'd say that what I want out of
life is not to be some – what did you call me? – playboy.' He
gives an exaggerated shiver.

'I was only joking.'

'I know. The point is, I want to love someone. Preferably
someone who loves me back.'

I look into his eyes and, for some reason, feel a wave of
relief; of happiness at this confirmation that the Henry I knew
is the same as ever. Part of me always knew that my friend was
never interested in the poncy clothes and the expensive haircut. They were simply a means to an end – finding someone
to fall in love with.

'It'll happen, Henry,' I tell him softly. 'You'll find someone.'

He looks at his hands. 'I hope so. Because, all those women . . . I could never do *this* with them.'

'What?'

'Sit around getting drunk and singing shit songs.'

'No, it takes someone really special to do that with, doesn't it?' I laugh sarcastically.

I look up and realize he's not laughing. I study his expression, but it's difficult to make out. As I gaze at his parted lips and dark eyes, I feel my pulse quicken and a tidal wave of adrenalin rush through my body.

We look into each other's eyes for too long to be comfortable and my body temperature rises suddenly. I can hear nothing but my own heartbeat thundering through my head and time stands still.

Despite every bit of sanity urging me not to move, I find myself leaning in to him. My mouth is being drawn to his. I close my eyes and wonder drunkenly whether what I think is going to happen really will.

I know that Henry's my friend, not my lover, and that kissing him will change everything. But I can't stop myself. It's as if I'm being pulled by a force of nature. As our lips touch, he tenses. I respond by moving my body closer to his, kissing him more decisively. At first he doesn't move, as if he's in shock.

Then his shoulders relax, his body edges into mine and he reaches for the back of my neck. He does it with conviction, his strong hands fingering my hair without hesitation.

Our mouths delve into each other's, our tongues exploring as I feel weak with desire. At first it's soft and deliberate, then passionate and unrestrained. Kissing Henry is like nothing

I've experienced. My mind spins with pleasure as I revel in his taste, discovering a new and glorious part of this person with whom I'm so familiar – yet apparently not.

We kiss and we kiss. I look up and feel Henry's mouth on my neck. He caresses me with his tongue, making his way down to my collarbone. His fingers slide downwards across my bare shoulder and he slips them under the strap of my vest. I gasp as he pushes it gently down, leaving me exposed and breathless with desire.

He bends down and I watch the swell of his lips on my breast as I groan with pleasure. I arch my back, my body exploding with longing. When he finally lifts his head, it is to kiss me on the mouth. I hurtle towards an orgasmic dream-world, a haze of lust.

Then I open my eyes and see that he's moving away.

'What's the matter?' I whisper.

'Should we be doing this, Lucy?' he breathes. 'Should we really be doing this?'

My eyes ping wide open, scrutinizing his face. The answer is no, we shouldn't. Of course we bloody well shouldn't. We've got years of history together and we're jeopardizing it.

'I don't know,' I confess, my inner logic battling with my inner lust.

But that's all it takes. He pulls away, lifting my bra strap back into place. He swallows self-consciously.

'I want you, Lucy.' His eyes can't meet mine. 'I *really* want you. But this would make our friendship impossible.'

'Henry, it wouldn't—'

'Of course it would.' He forces himself to look into my eyes. 'You know it would.'

Now I swallow. Then I nod, vigorously, crossing my arms over my chest in embarrassment.

'Good decision,' I tell him. I cough, straighten my vest again, and stand, flustered. 'I'd better go to bed.'

He nods. 'Me too.'

I turn round and go to leave, when I hear his voice.

'Lucy,' he says urgently.

I spin round and look at him, but he clearly doesn't know what to say. By now, I am on the verge of tears and I want to get out of here.

'Goodnight,' I mumble, and flee for the safety of my room.

Chapter 58

I've had some bad mornings, but none have come close to this. It's horrible. I lie in bed for what feels like hours, listening to Henry move about the flat and praying that he leaves before I have to get up. Sadly, he doesn't. As I toss and turn, biting my nails and whipping myself into a nervous frenzy, I start to wish that four years ago, when we moved into this flat, I'd chosen the bedroom with the fire escape.

Eventually, I get up, get dressed and – when I hear Henry flick on the kettle and conclude he's in the kitchen – dive in the bathroom to wash my face and brush my teeth.

Even that part of my morning ritual is far from positive. As I reach the sink, I wonder for a second why our anti-bacterial bleach wipes – the ones I used yesterday to clean the seat of the loo – are sitting where I expected my make-up remover wipes to be.

I realize why, when I glance in the mirror and see my face: I look as if I've undergone a skin graft. *Oh God.*

Only I, Lucy Tyler, would encourage my best friend to nuzzle his face into my boobs *and* remove my make-up with household bleach in a single evening. How do I manage it?

I splash my face with water, wincing as it stings my skin.

Tears prick in my eyes and I force myself to look away from the mirror.

Come *on*, Lucy.

If there's any chance of salvaging things between me and Henry, I've got to march out there as if nothing has happened. Things would have been easier if nothing *had* happened . . . but there you go. I make a big effort to compose myself.

At least I'm not the only one in this boat. Henry's going to have to face me too.

The thought sends me into a wave of panic. What the hell is *Henry* thinking?

I hope he doesn't want to move out.

I hope he doesn't think I'm easy.

I *really* hope he doesn't think my boobs are too small . . .

'Lucy? Are you all right in there?'

I drop my electric toothbrush and it clatters to the floor, spraying toothpaste over the toilet pedestal and a leg of my jeans.

'Um . . . yep!' I cry.

I straighten my back and, before I've got a chance to think about it, I march to the bathroom door and open it decisively.

'Morning!'

I steam past Henry to the kitchen and put on the kettle.

He follows me. 'Good morning,' he replies, sounding thoroughly calm.

I don't look at him long enough to see his expression, even though I'm dying to. In fact, I don't look at him at all. I busy myself with rooting around in the kitchen cupboard for something. Anything.

'What are you after?' Henry asks eventually. 'There's plenty of tea in the caddy.'

'Hmmm?' I refuse to remove my head from the cupboard. 'I fancied a cup of Earl Grey.'

'I thought you hated Earl Grey.'

'Used to. Love it now.'

'Oh,' he says.

I eventually locate an old box of Earl Grey tea bags and set about rearranging the crockery cupboard.

'Fancy one?' I ask cheerily.

'Go on then,' says Henry. 'Though I'll have a PG Tips.'

'Okeydokey,' I reply. Oh *God*.

Henry sits at the table and waits for me to do the same. Instead, I bend down to the cupboard under the sink and start scrambling around in it, not knowing why exactly.

'Lucy . . .'

I grab a bottle of Cif and, flicking up the top purposefully, pour some on a cloth and begin polishing the kitchen tap.

'Lucy . . .'

'Hmmm?' I say, refusing to stop despite the muscles in my arm feeling as if they're about to ignite.

'Lucy . . . why don't you sit down?'

'Just a sec.' I'm getting a hot flush or something.

When my arm can take no more, I fling the cloth in the sink, splash some boiling water into our tea cups, followed by some milk, and plonk Henry's cup in front of him.

'Right.' I take a slurp of mine. 'Must dash.'

'Lucy – *wait*,' insists Henry. I stop in my tracks, my back still facing him. 'Come and sit down.'

Reluctantly I turn round, walk to the table and sink into the chair opposite him. My eyes are glued to my cup.

'The thing is . . .' He pauses. 'God, what's wrong with your skin?'

'Nothing,' I reply self-consciously. 'It's feeling sensitive, that's all.'

It's not the only one.

'The thing is,' Henry repeats, staring into his tea, 'I think we should talk about last night.'

'There's nothing to talk about,' I say, shifting in my seat.

'But there is.'

'Henry, really.' I force a smile. 'The worst possible thing would be for us to make a big deal out of it.'

'It *is* a big deal.'

'No, it's not,' I gulp.

'But—'

'Look, it was a mistake. A stupid mistake. Mistakes happen all the time, don't they?'

He looks at me, saying nothing. I refuse to meet his gaze.

'We need to accept that it was a ludicrous, ill-judged, drunken . . . thing . . . that never should have happened,' I ramble. 'And be thankful that it didn't go further. The sooner we can put it behind us, the better. That's the way I see it. Don't you?'

I finally look up. I can't make out his expression. His jaw is locked, his eyes intense. 'I think there's more to be said than that.'

Part of me is dying to know what else Henry has to say. But mainly, overwhelmingly, I can't bear to continue this discussion.

'Honestly, Henry, *I* don't. We both know that we'd never have done anything like that if we'd been sober. I know I wouldn't. God – the very idea of it. You and me. Ha!'

He frowns.

'Things will be back to normal in no time,' I gabble. 'What

am I talking about . . . they already are, aren't they? I mean, I don't fancy you in the *slightest* in the cold light of day. Not in the *slightest*. And I know the feeling's mutual. There – see? All back to normal.'

He looks at me strangely and sips his tea.

'Right,' I smile stiffly. 'I'm off shopping. Do you want anything?'

Chapter 59

It is hard to describe the atmosphere in the flat over the next two weeks. Things couldn't be weirder if Marilyn Manson had signed up as our cleaning lady.

At first Henry seems to be there every time I go home – which is hard to get used to, given that his presence had been so rare before. He makes repeated attempts to talk about what happened, but I cut him dead every time.

This defies everything I've learned from the lifetime of study I've devoted to problem pages – and I'm certain that Mariella Frostrup wouldn't approve. But I can't help it. I am mortally embarrassed. Terminally ashamed. Permanently wishing I lived somewhere else. Like Saturn.

I still haven't discussed what's going on with Dominique or Erin. And I definitely haven't told them what happened on the night of the Caribbean Monkfish Stew. I've thought about it, of course, but it's as though discussing my feelings for Henry makes them more real – and I'd rather pretend they weren't real, thanks very much. I'd rather they went away.

So my strategy is to pretend it never happened; to maintain a stiff upper lip. It's *sort of* working. At least, Henry eventually stops raising the issue, even if he still lingers in the flat, desperate to clear the air.

I should stress that I too want to clear the air, obviously – only it's easier said than done. My thoughts about Henry used to be blissfully straightforward. I loved him as a friend and nothing more. Now my head is a riot of confusion and emotions that are impossible to deconstruct.

In its simplest form, I mourn the way things were; our pure, platonic friendship that existed effortlessly, devoid of romantic stirrings. I miss the casual banter, the conversations that are only possible between two people who know each other inside out and always have. I cringe at the strain in our voices, the attempts to recreate our uncomplicated relationship faltering every time.

In short, I know that nothing will make things return to how they were, with the exception of time. Lots of it. The hope I am clinging to is that, if Henry and I pretend that nothing has changed, over time it'll become a self-fulfilling prophecy.

But there's a spanner in the works: I fancy him. I fancy him like mad.

How shallow must I be that all it takes to whip me into a girlish infatuation is for my flatmate to go on a shopping spree and get a half-decent haircut?

More importantly, *this is Henry we're talking about. Henry, for God's sake. I cannot fancy Henry.*

Yet, patently, I do.

Why else would I experience repeated flashbacks to our Caribbean Monkfish Stew night; ones that involve him slipping down my bra strap and . . . oh, you know what happened.

It's getting ridiculous. We can't be in the same room

together without my heart racing and blood rushing to my neck. When his hand brushes mine – though we jump away like there's a cattle prod in our backs – my knees go weak.

It was so bad at one point that I prayed he'd go out more. Then he did – and now I miss him again. I have no idea who Henry's seeing at the moment because I don't ask. It feels wrong to discuss his love-life. I prefer to stick to safer subjects. Such as the state of the economy. Or the refit at the pizza shop round the corner. Or the fact that the bathroom tiles need regrouting. No wonder he wants to get out of the house.

Despite how much I hate what's going on between us, there is one thing keeping me going. A memory. One that proves that we *will* get over our ill-judged moment of passion – no matter how messy it's made things.

You're probably wondering why I'm so confident. Well . . . how can I put this?

It's not the first time that it's happened.

Chapter 60

Henry and I had one previous *indiscretion* when we were four-teen, though to call it that makes it sound far more sophisticated than either of us were.

It was the summer of 1996. The Fugees were at number one, everyone was hoping England would win Euro 96 and I'd recently made friends with Simone Hemmings. Simone was the teenage daughter no parent wants: physically precocious (she'd been in a B-cup when I was still watching *Scooby Doo*) and obsessed with boys.

I sat next to her in French and one day, when we were sup-posed to be learning to complain about an over-priced train ticket, she passed me a note. I unfolded it under my desk and read it while trying to appear fascinated by a passage in my *Voila!* textbook.

What do you think of Ben Bachelor? I think he looks like Gary Barlow.

I pressed the paper on my leg and wrote: *More like Ken Barlow*, before passing it back to her stifled giggles.

In the following weeks, it became a ritual. Even when I swore I'd concentrate on lessons in the run-up to the exchange visit that summer, I was sucked into corresponding with Simone over everything, from who we thought would be the best kisser in the class, to Jake Roberts – a friend of Dave's – and his spectacularly cute bum. I'd secretly fancied Jake for three months, but hadn't told anyone except Henry, and now Simone.

At the end of each class, I would stuff the notes in my bag among pencil-case tins, a copy of *Just 17*, a Rimmel cover stick and two compasses. After seven weeks of French lessons I had enough stray paper to ignite a small forest fire.

I never dreamed anyone would find them – until one Tuesday night when I was in my room and I heard Dave and his mates laughing downstairs. I walked down tentatively and froze. They were reading a note Simone and I had written that day, in which she asked if I'd let Jake put his hand up my top. My response was unequivocal.

Definitely. But he'd find more of a handful on a Bernard Matthews turkey.

As six hysterical boys – including Jake himself – turned and looked at me, the author of this mortifying confession, I almost collapsed with shame. Brimming with tears and fury, I decided a low-key discussion was the best way of tackling Dave about it.

'I HATE YOU, DAVE, YOU HORRIBLE LITTLE SHIT!' I yelled and pushed past them as fast as I could.

My face burning with tears, I raced to the door and was almost outside when a sharp pain tore through my arm. Without stopping, I glanced down and realized I'd sliced my skin against the frame. Blood was seeping through the fabric of my school shirt but I didn't care. I needed to get to Henry.

His house was five times the size of ours and the first time I went there I remember feeling as if it was a parallel universe.

It wasn't only the books that made it different from our place, though their collection would rival that of the British Library. It was also the souvenirs of his parents' politically-active student days, the framed *Private Eye* covers, the joss sticks, the ethnic knick-knacks. This was the house of a sophisticated, educated family and, despite the peeling paint-work and damp in the bathroom, I was in awe.

When Henry answered the door that evening it was a second before he registered my distress. 'Lucy – what happened?'

'Can I come in?' I muttered.

His mum was working late and his dad was in the garden tending to his hellebores, something capable of distracting him for several days. Henry ushered me to his bedroom where Leftfield was on his CD-player, pushed a pile of textbooks off his bed, and urged me to tell him, between tears, what was going on.

Repeating what had happened ought to have been embarrassing. Henry was a boy, like Dave's friends – so why wasn't my immature bosom as mortifying in front of him? I don't know. I only knew what his response would be.

'If they can't recognize a great line in self-deprecating humour, they're denser than I thought,' he said, crossing his arms.

'They're pretty dense,' I sniffed gratefully.

'There,' he smiled. 'They're not worth giving a second thought to.'

I nodded unconvincingly. Then burst into tears again.

'Oh Lucy.' He looked troubled.

Then the most amazing thing happened. Henry stood up and grabbed his coat.

'Where are you going?' I asked.

'Over there. To your place.' His eyes were blazing. I'd never seen him like that before. I was impressed. What I wasn't, though, was stupid. Henry was fourteen years old. Dave and his cronies were two years older – and there were six of them. Confronting them was tremendously valiant, but we both knew he didn't stand a chance.

'Don't be ridiculous,' I whispered.

'It's not ridiculous. I've never seen you so upset.'

When I looked into his eyes, I saw how sincere he was. How he was prepared, against monstrous odds, to challenge six kids who were older, harder, and dangerously thicker.

I eventually persuaded him that I'd prefer to sit and talk. But I can't pretend that, privately, I wasn't as pleased about his reaction as I was surprised. And nor was it to be the only surprise of the evening.

As Henry and I talked, my troubles washed away. It was only when I went to go to the bathroom that I winced in pain.

'What's up?' Henry asked.

'Oh, nothing,' I said, peeling away my cardigan. The cut looked worse than it was: it wasn't deep, but *appeared* as though my arm had been lunch for a half-starved Rottweiler.

'It doesn't look like nothing.'

'I ran out of the house so quickly I scraped my arm on the doorframe,' I told him. 'It wasn't the dignified exit I was hoping for.'

'Let's have a look,' he said, gently rolling up my shirt-sleeve. 'Stay here a minute.' He disappeared downstairs and returned with a First Aid kit and a bowl of water.

Henry bathed the cut as I sat and gazed out of the window. The damp cotton wool melted into my skin and I submitted to its comforting warmth, closing my eyes as the events of the evening drifted out of my consciousness.

Then I felt something other than the cotton wool on my skin and opened my eyes. Henry's lips brushed against the bruises, so soft and gentle, his tenderness made my heart swell. He stopped and looked away self-consciously. 'Sorry.'

'It's okay,' I whispered – and it was. Tears of happiness pricked into my eyes and I felt a wave of love, proper love, for Henry.

Then I blew it.

I don't know what possessed me to do it, because it's clear that Henry's kiss was an innocent gesture solely intended to soothe my injury. It should have been left at that. Instead, I leaned forward and kissed him on the lips.

It wasn't a proper snog – I was yet to have my first of those with James Feathergill on a school trip to Alton Towers. This was like a kiss you see in old films, where both protagonists keep their lips firmly shut, without a hint of tongue.

I realized halfway through how wrong it was. How inappropriate and ridiculous. I pulled away.

'I'm sorry.' I held the back of my hand against my mouth.

'It's okay,' he mumbled. But it wasn't – I could tell.

It was months before things were back to normal, well after Dave's apology and his assurance that Jake Roberts was 'a bit of a dick anyway'. Months before Henry and I could look each other in the eye without me dissolving into a wreck of insecurity and remorse.

But things *did* get back to normal. It took a while, but they did.

Given that fourteen years have passed before Henry's lips touched mine again, I'm certain that things will get back to normal again. Sooner or later.

Chapter 61

A few days later on a glorious June morning, I switch on the radio as I drive to work and Dolly Parton is singing 'Nine to Five'. I only know the chorus but my vocal cords take the clobbering of their life. By the time I've reached the city centre, slapping my thigh at the traffic-lights, I am so fired up I'm almost line-dancing in my seat.

It's an important week – on Thursday, I'll be implementing the *Peach Gear* plan. It'll be the challenge of my career but one to which I'm determined to rise. *This* is the week I prove my worth to Roger.

My mobile rings. I reluctantly silence Dolly and put on my hands-free.

'Lucy, it's Phil McEwan.' He doesn't sound happy, but that's only to be expected, given the week ahead.

'Hi, Phil. What can I do for you?'

'It's out, Lucy. It's already out.' He sounds as if he's referring to an escaped tiger.

'What's out?'

'The news about the vest tops!' he hisses. 'The *scandal* about the vest tops, as the reporter I spoke to described it.

What else do you think I'd be phoning about at seven-fifteen in the morning?'

'Okay,' I reply slowly, hoping to appear a bastion of level-headedness, despite my hyperactive heart. 'Who's onto it?'

'I had a call from the *Gazette*. They're printing the story tomorrow. They know everything. Everything, that is, that was in *your* strategy document.'

I pause, taking in the implications of his statement, the tone of his voice. 'W-what?'

'That's right, Lucy. Your strategy document. The reporter virtually quoted it word for word.'

'I . . . but they can't have . . .' I pull over and attempt to compose myself. 'It was confidential. Nobody saw it.'

'Nobody did in *our* organization. Which leaves yours.'

'Phil,' I say insistently, 'it can't have come from within Peaman-Brown. Other than me, the only person who went near that report was the boss, and he's hardly going to stitch up one of his biggest clients and leak it to the press.'

I did, of course, tell Dominique about the issue, but I'm not bringing that up. There's no way she's behind this, and mentioning her name would raise doubts when there are none.

'I've always enjoyed working with you, Lucy, but Janine's reaction this morning . . .' It's as if he's not hearing me. 'I've never seen her like this. I've no choice.'

'What do you mean? You're not firing me?'

'I've been instructed to set up a meeting with Webster Black this morning.'

'You *are* firing me.'

'I'm afraid so. Look, I've got to go. We've some fire-fighting on our hands before the *Gazette*'s deadline.' The line goes dead.

I stare ahead, dumbstruck, as a splat lands in front of my eyes. It's so large I wonder for a second whether an incontinent ostrich has emptied its bowels on my windscreen.

'Thanks,' I mutter to the seagull responsible. 'Thanks a lot.'

I dread breaking the news to Roger but he's reasonably understanding.

'There's only one way to handle this and that's to be pragmatic.' He paces round his office. 'Get on the phone to the marketing guy – what's he called?'

'Phil.'

'Yeah, Phil. And persuade him to let you handle this.'

'That's easier said than—'

'*You're* the one who knows the issue and the company inside out. Otherwise, by the time they get Webster Black up to speed, the papers will be all over the story and it'll be too late. If they let us manage their press over the next forty-eight hours, they'll be more likely to emerge with a positive result. Once the drama's over, we can dissect what went wrong – but not before. Let's deal with it first.'

'Okay. I don't know what his reaction will be, but I'll try my best.'

'In the meantime, I'll get on the phone to – what's he called, the Chief Exec?'

'Janine.'

'Oh yeah, Janine, and try to smooth things over.'

'You know it wasn't me who leaked the story, don't you, Roger?'

He frowns. 'It doesn't make sense that you'd leak it. Only someone with a death wish would deliberately create bad press for their own client. Besides that, I trust you.'

I take a deep breath. 'Thank you, Roger. I wish they would.'

My boss and I spend the day on the phone and in meetings with the client and a reporter from the *Gazette*.

Mercifully, Roger manages to persuade Janine Nixon to stick with us until the crisis is over when, he promises, there will be a full enquiry. Heads will roll, he assures her. I'm hoping he doesn't mean mine.

As for the story, sadly there's no way we can prevent its publication by the *Gazette* – why should they hold back, with a clear public interest argument?

The objective is to make sure that two things are clear in the article: first, that *Peach Gear* knew nothing about the situation when they started working with the company in question. Secondly, as soon as they found out, they contacted the Ethical Trade Alliance (who, mercifully, have agreed to supply me with a glowing quote to use in my press release) and are now working with them to help the children involved. In short, they did everything right.

That won't be that, of course. Tomorrow's *Gazette* story will just be the start of a frenzy of media activity, local and national. Just thinking about it makes me want to lie down in a darkened room and not come out until a week on Wednesday.

'Looks like you're having a busy day,' remarks Drew. He takes a bottle of cologne from his desk drawer and sprays himself liberally enough to repel flies in the Congo.

'Yes,' I grunt, picking up my phone again.

'Anything I can help with?'

'No, thanks.'

'Only I've got a bit of time on my hands before my meeting with Ernst Sumner. They're pretty happy with us at the moment. Have you seen the piece I got in the business pages?'

Drew holds up the paper proudly. So he finally got his story about Ernst Sumner published. It's only taken about six months. I have to hand it to him though – it's a decent-sized piece for a subject that's as compelling as a set of lawnmower instructions.

'Well done,' I say.

He smiles. 'If you ever want any tips . . .'

'Drew, I've got work to do.'

'Oh yes. Heard you had a crisis on your plate.'

I dial half of Phil McEwan's mobile number for his twelfth update of the day but am again interrupted – this time by Little Lynette.

'Do you think I'm too young for Botox, Lucy?' She drops three letters on my desk.

'How old are you?' I ask distractedly.

'Twenty-three.'

'No.' I look up at her horrified face. 'I mean, yes. Yes, of course you're too young.'

'Only I was reading about how it was good to have it as a preventative . . . oh God, you're busy!' A look of understanding hits her face.

'Sorry, Lynette. It's not that I wasn't listening.' Patently, I wasn't listening. 'It's just—'

'You're up to your eyes, I know,' she interrupts. 'Don't worry, I'll catch you later.'

'Definitely. You can tell me all about your new man. You've been very secretive about him.'

'What?' says Drew in mock horror. 'Lynette's got a new man? What about me? Will I have to go on dreaming?'

'Drew Smith, what *are* you like!' Lynette giggles and totters to the photocopier, flashing him a flirtatious glance. I dial Phil's number for the third time, hoping the distraction might quell my nausea.

Chapter 62

When I get home at ten-thirty at night, Henry is still up. The lights in the living room are dimmed and he's at the piano, caressing the keys, as a melody melts through the room. He stops when I open the door. I'm so tired I almost forget to feel awkward.

'I didn't know you'd added Beyoncé to your repertoire.'

He smiles. 'It's Stravinsky.'

'Close,' I shrug. 'How's it going?'

'Not bad. God, you're late.'

'The day from hell.'

'At least it's over.'

'Tomorrow will be ten times worse.'

He pulls a face. 'That doesn't sound too optimistic. Anything I can help with?'

'I don't think so. I've got a bit of a crisis involving a client. Strike that: a great big crisis. The only thing that will get me through the next twenty-four hours is hard work, luck and perhaps the power of prayer.'

'Is that standard in the PR industry?'

'I'm starting to think it should be.' He smiles. 'Goodnight anyway.' I turn to go back through the door.

'Oh, Lucy?' I turn around again. 'When your crisis is over, do you fancy going for a drink?'

I raise an exhausted eyebrow. 'Yeah,' I nod. 'That'd be nice.'

'The night after tomorrow?'

'Deal. At the very least I'll want to drown my sorrows.'

When I get into my bedroom I lie on the bed with a nagging thought whirling through my mind. I pick up my phone and start texting Dominique.

Sorry 2 text so l8. U didn't tell anyone about peach gear, did u?

I fire it off and go to the bathroom to wash my face and brush my teeth. When I return to my room, I pick up the phone. She hasn't responded.

I am the luckiest woman alive, as jammy as a WI preserves and pickles contest.

The article in the *Gazette* turns out better than I, Roger, or anyone at *Peach Gear* could have hoped.

It's fair, balanced and, as well as highlighting their swift, positive action, even praises their determination to make amends in the editorial comment – alongside the quote I'd sourced from the Ethical Trade Alliance and an interview with one of their people I'd managed to set up.

The media coverage in the next twenty-four hours follows the same tack, taking on board the conversations that Roger and I had with producers of TV and radio stations, and news editors of papers. One bulletin even compares *Peach Gear* with another high-street clothing store who didn't act so responsibly. When I meet Phil McEwan for coffee – this time in a suitably trendy joint in the business district – I hold my head high.

'Lucy, you did a really good rescue job,' he tells me, stirring his cappuccino.

I smile, thoroughly relieved. 'Thanks, Phil. I—'

'That's the message I gave Janine.'

I pause to read his expression. He looks uncomfortable.

'Right,' I say cautiously. 'What's Janine's take on our performance?'

He unwraps a second cube of sugar slowly. 'The board still believes that we'd never have been in this situation if the story hadn't been leaked. They remain convinced it came from you.'

'Why would I do that to one of my own clients?' I blurt out furiously.

He picks up a spoon and stirs his cappuccino again. 'I hear what you're saying. I'm fighting your corner, Lucy, honestly. But the reporter from the *Gazette* knew virtually everything that you did. How do you explain that?'

I bite my lip. 'Maybe someone overheard us talking at the café when I met you and Janine.'

Phil looks at me pityingly.

I gaze out of the window to conjure up another explanation. Sadly, I can't.

Chapter 63

I read somewhere that wrongly-convicted Death Row prisoners have a higher than average chance of developing alcohol-related problems following their release. After today I can see why. Okay, my troubles aren't quite in their league, but, after being falsely accused of spilling the beans about *Peach Gear*, I race to the pub so fast I come dangerously close to beating Flo-Jo's world record in the 100 metres sprint.

'You're eager,' Henry says, as we turn the corner. 'They're not going to run out of booze, you know.'

'I've had a stressful few days. I'm not prepared to take the chance.'

At least something good has come from this week: my stiff upper lip has paid off and Henry and I are behaving almost as we used to. It'd be like old times – if he was dressed like Ned Flanders from *The Simpsons* and I were a stone and a half lighter, that is.

'I'm guessing from the bumper pack of bean-sprouts in the fridge that you're back on your diet,' he says, as if reading my thoughts.

'Yes, but not any old diet. This time I am supplementing it

with a super-duper herbal diet pill to boost my metabolism. I'm surprised I don't look like Paris Hilton already.'

He smiles and shakes his head.

'I've also started almost constant secret buttock squeezes to strengthen my gluteus maximus muscle,' I inform him.

'Really? Doesn't that get tedious, doing them almost constantly?'

'Not at all. It's multi-tasking. From now on, if I take a call from a journalist without simultaneously working out my bum, I'll be falling short.'

'Won't that make it hard to concentrate?'

'I don't think so. Though I almost crashed into a taxi this evening as I reached two hundred and twenty squeezes.'

'How many?' His eyes widen.

'The traffic was bad,' I explain, and we both burst out laughing.

Our local pub is a funny old establishment: a once-impressive building whose ornate grandeur is now a little faded, it's frequented by an eclectic mix of regulars – ageing bohemians, young professionals, the check-out girls from the local supermarket and members of the Liverpool Philosophy Association.

Henry goes to the bar and I dive into a recently-vacated space. He returns with our drinks and squeezes in next to me. As his arm touches mine, a flicker of electricity runs through my veins and I do my best to conceal my reaction.

So everything's not quite back to normal. Our banter's returned. Our conversations are as jocular as ever. But, if I'm honest, my feelings for Henry – my growing feelings – aren't just platonic. Not any more.

The challenge of having an attractive, athletic, stylish, charismatic bloke round the house is too much. Even if it is only Henry. I have succumbed to my hormones. Or pheromones. Or whatever it is that's making me contemplate his six-pack so much.

A question keeps popping up, over and over again. What should I do about it? Do I try to make Henry fancy me, like when I go out on a date? Do I flirt with him? Come on to him? Tell him I want to get inside his Levis?

I've considered all of the above, but the problem is twofold: first, I remain afraid of losing the friendship we've had for almost twenty years. Second, and more practically, I haven't the guts to act, particularly after his reaction on the Caribbean Monkfish Stew evening. I am, it appears, a wimp. *And* a hypocrite. I've been telling Henry that a faint heart never won a fair maiden, but it turns out that I'm as spineless as an over-anxious roundworm.

Perhaps I'm being harsh on myself. It's easy to be brazen with someone when, if it goes wrong, you never have to see him again. It's significantly harder when you share a roof: you can't go from full-on seduction attempt one minute to discussing your damp-proof course the next.

'You are not going to believe who I saw at the bar,' Henry tells me, taking a sip of his pint.

'Who?'

'Andy Smith.'

'The bloke who presents *Newsnight?*'

'No, that kid we used to go to school with.'

'Oh God . . . not the one who –'

'– stole my trousers at Colomendy,' he finishes.

'Little horror,' I tut. 'I don't think I'd recognize him.'

'He has a swanky suit and expensive haircut but it was definitely him – I'm sure of it.'

'Did you say anything?'

'Like what? "Have you stolen anybody's trousers recently?"'

I shrug. 'It's a fair question.'

He smiles and takes a mouthful of his beer. 'Anyway, I've got some good news for you. I've signed us up for the quiz.'

'Oh excellent. I'm good at quizzes, if I do say so myself.'

Henry says nothing.

'What?' I ask. 'That game of Trivial Pursuit at Christmas was an aberration. I wasn't well.'

'You had a verucca.'

'Yes,' I concede, 'but it was a very bad one.'

I stockpile a couple of glasses of wine before the quiz starts, certain I'll perform better if relaxed. Henry looks sceptical.

'Let me get this straight,' he says. 'You're saying you're only at the top of your game when half-pissed?'

'It's the same with pool,' I assure him, taking a large gulp. 'I can't hit anything unless I'm completely cross-eyed.'

The quiz master gives us a five-minute warning and I'm about to go to the loo when a shadow is cast on our table and I look up. It's Drew.

I'm about to say hello, but Henry speaks first.

'Hello, Andy. It is Andy, isn't it? Andy Smith?'

Chapter 64

I frown at Henry. So does Drew. 'Andy?' I repeat.

'I haven't got it wrong, have I?' asks Henry. 'Attended Calder Bank High School until about 1994?'

'This isn't Andy,' I tell him. I look up and notice that Drew's neck has turned a peculiar shade of red, a bit like a rancid sangria.

'And you are?' Drew glares at Henry.

'Henry Fox. You stole my trousers at Colomendy. Not that I'll hold it against you,' he laughs. 'It was a long time ago. What are you up to these days?'

I sit, agog, unable to shut my mouth.

'Hang on a minute,' I interrupt. 'Drew: you're Andy Smith? Is this true?'

'I haven't called myself Andy for years,' he says sulkily.

'Do you know each other?' asks Henry. 'I mean, apart from when we all went to school?'

'We work together,' I tell him, meaningfully. 'This, Henry, is Drew Smith.'

A look of realization flashes across Henry's face. 'Drew. Right . . . I've heard a lot about you.'

'All good, I'm sure. So you're Henry Fox? I remember you.

You were a freaky kid – I hope you don't mind me saying so.'
He laughs, to create some ambiguity about whether this is
good-natured joshing, as opposed to odious venom.

Henry doesn't rise to it.

'Did you realize you and I went to school together, Drew?'
I ask. 'Why on earth didn't you say anything?'

'It's hardly important.'

'Maybe not,' I say slowly, 'but it's odd that—'

'I see you're doing the pub quiz,' he interrupts.

'Yes,' I tell him.

'Better watch out,' he grins. 'My team's a force to be reck-
oned with.'

'How very modest of you, Drew.'

'Only telling it how it is. I've been on the winning team of
the north-west heats of Pub Quiz of the Year –'

'– for the last three years. I know,' I say.

When Drew or Andy or whoever he is disappears back to
his table, where he's sitting with three others, I turn to Henry.

'I can't *believe* I never recognized him,' I say, still stunned.
'I've worked with the guy for two years and it's never struck
me that Drew Smith and Andy Smith were the same
person.'

'I suppose he was eleven when you last saw him. Why do
you think he never said anything?' asks Henry.

'Because Drew Smith likes to give the impression he was
brought up with a silver spoon in his mouth. The idea that
he'd attended a school like ours wouldn't fit with his image.'

'How sad.' Henry pulls a face. 'As if it matters.'

I take a swig of my wine. 'Anyway, that's not my priority
tonight.'

'Oh. What is?'

'Trouncing him and his mates in the pub quiz. Come on, it's about to start.'

It becomes apparent that I would only excel at the pub quiz if they had a specialist round entitled 'The greatest hits of Girls Aloud – 2002 to 2010'. Sadly, they don't. They only have one question about Girls Aloud – and everyone else in the pub knows the lyrics to 'Something Kinda Oooh' anyway.

Worse, it appears that Drew has been showing off with good reason. After four rounds, he and his loud and obnoxious friends are in the lead, followed closely by Henry and me. This isn't bad going – especially as I've only contributed three answers.

'Well,' I huff, 'what possible use is it, to be able to name the year in which Pablo Picasso died? I ask you . . .'

'Nineteen seventy-three,' whispers Henry, scribbling the answer.

'What?'

'That's the year Picasso died. It's geography next.'

Henry writes the answers to everything from the capital of the Caribbean island Grenada (St George's) to the country with the largest coastline (Canada) and the name of the dam on the Zambia–Zimbabwe border (Kariba).

He gallantly confers with me after each question, apparently not noticing that I don't disagree with a single suggestion.

'It's not a sign of proper intelligence, being able to win at these quizzes,' I inform Henry. 'Not that I'm knocking *you*, obviously – I know *you're* properly intelligent. It's just, some people go through quiz books memorizing the answers – where's the skill in that? At least in your case, Henry, you've answered these questions because you genuinely know all this, though Christ knows how. Half of this lot have spent too many nights ploughing through their *University Challenge* annual.'

I change my tune slightly when I manage to answer another question, a proper one too, naming James Harding as Editor of *The Times*.

'Not completely useless, then,' I say, pleased with myself.

Sadly, I let myself down when, a glass of wine later, I spontaneously shout out 'Ibiza' when asked which country's flag has the most colours. Apparently it is South Africa, though I bet the buggers sniggering on the next table didn't know that.

As the quiz continues, Drew and his friends become louder, drunker, more annoying and full of themselves. Worse than all of that, *they continue winning*.

Then, as if the gods are smiling on us, the next round is announced: classical music. After five questions, Henry puts down his pen.

'I wasn't sure about the *Dido and Aeneas* question,' he frets.

'Don't worry, Henry.' I pat his leg reassuringly. 'Neither was I.'

Chapter 65

In the event, we don't absolutely stuff Drew and his team mates – though, given their reaction, we might as well have. We beat them by two points: seventy-eight to seventy-six.

Drew is furious, flouncing out of his chair and straight to the gents. I'm ecstatic, leaping up and hugging Henry as if he's won the Monaco Grand Prix. Laughing, he prises himself away from my grasp and looks at me.

'You seem pleased to have won.'

'You're a master of understatement sometimes, Henry. Too right I'm pleased to have won.' Unable to control myself, I kiss him on the cheek, before pulling away in embarrassment. Henry looks awkward too.

'I'm starving,' he says, filling the gap.

'How about we head home and grab some toast before bed,' I suggest.

'You're a woman who knows how to live, Lucy,' he grins. 'Toast it is.'

Henry and I are at the door of the pub when Drew appears looking like one of those talking germs in a bleach advert.

'I suppose you're going to be as smug about this as everything else?' he spits drunkenly.

'I'm not smug,' I protest.

'Ha! It's your middle name. Every time you win a contract, or get a piece in the paper, or Roger asks you to look after a big client, you're as smug as a . . . very bloody smug thing.'

I narrow my eyes. 'Poetic as ever, Drew. *I mean Andy.*'

He narrows his eyes. 'You're such a bitch,' he mutters, almost falling on me.

'For God's sake!' I push him away furiously. 'It was only a quiz.'

'It was *only a quiz, only a quiz,*' he mimics, swaying from side to side. 'You have to win at *everything*, don't you, Lucy Tyler? Well, looks like you've come unstuck with that *Peach Gear* account, doesn't it?'

I don't say anything. 'Screwed up badly, didn't you?' he sneers. 'Come on, was it you who leaked the story?'

'Why would I leak the story, when all it's done is lose me a client?'

'Hmmm, good point,' he leers. 'Then perhaps you shared the information with someone you shouldn't – Dominique, perhaps? You seem to tell her everything, confidential or not.'

He registers my expression and smiles triumphantly. 'I'm right, aren't I? You did tell her. She can be a real blabber-mouth from what I hear, Lucy. I'd be careful in future.'

'Why are you so interested in what went on with *Peach Gear*?'

For a second I'm convinced Drew is behind the *Peach Gear* disaster. Then I realize he can't be. There's simply no way he could have known about the issue with the vest tops before it hit the press.

'It was nothing to do with me,' he chuckles. 'Sorry, Tyler, but you can't pin this one on me. So, how're you going to get out of it? Oh, I know – maybe you can sleep with the boss.

That should be right up your street, you slapper. I've never met anyone who's been through as many men as you have, Lucy.'

'I do not *go through men*, Drew.' I hate myself for rising to the bait. 'I just haven't found anyone to settle down with.'

'You'd rather sleep your way through them?'

My mind whirrs with cutting ripostes, none of which seem cutting enough, when Henry steps in.

'We've heard enough, Andy,' he says quietly, ushering me to the door.

'It's *Drew*,' he growls.

'Fine,' replies Henry calmly. 'Drew. The point is, Lucy doesn't want to stand here and listen to this. I don't either.'

Henry turns and guides me through the door.

'You *fucking freak!*' we hear.

Henry pauses. I glance up to see his reaction. Remaining completely calm, he simply says, 'Come on. Let's go home.'

'You always were a weirdo, weren't you, Fox?' Drew looks like a demented bulldog. 'I can't believe you and she have hooked up together. Ha! You deserve each other. The slapper and the fucking freak.'

Henry spins round and glares at him. 'What did you say?'

'You heard me, you fucking fruitcake.'

Henry shakes his head, with a look of pity on his face. It seems to infuriate Drew more. As Henry goes to walk away again, Drew dives on him. Literally dives on him. Punching and spitting, he goes at Henry with every ounce of fury running through his poisonous veins. I stand, stunned, with my hands over my mouth and my heart racing with panic. Then something happens that I'd never have imagined.

Henry lifts up his head resolutely, grabs Drew by the throat

314

and, with his body at arm's length, he punches him. Clean in the face.

Drew falls to the ground.

'Oh. My. God.' I gaze at the heap before me.

Henry sighs, straightens his shirt and crouches down next to Drew to examine the damage.

'Don't come near me,' he whimpers, attempting to crawl away.

Henry stands, running his fingers through his hair with frustration. 'I *didn't* want to do that,' he says. 'I really didn't want to do that.'

As we head for home, I struggle to keep up. Henry is striding quickly, working off his frustration. He stops to take my arm as the soft light from our porch falls on his troubled features.

'Honestly, Lucy, I didn't want to do that.'

'I know, Henry.' I squeeze his hand.

But *I* wanted you to.

Chapter 66

I can't get to sleep after that. It's not just that the events of the evening clatter round my brain, determined to keep me awake. It's not just the thrill I get, replaying Henry's eyes meeting mine. And it's certainly not the things Drew Smith said and did, even after Henry knocked his lights out.

I've come to a realization. One it's taken twenty years to work out.

I'm not only fond of Henry. He's not simply my friend. I don't even just fancy him, not any more.

I *love* him. With every ounce of my being, I love him. He's everything I ever wanted. And he's Henry. My Henry.

So I make a decision: no more *in*decision. No more wimping out. I'm telling my best friend I'm in love with him and that's that.

Chapter 67

The only question is when. The next day I am preoccupied by this thought – almost, but not quite, to the exclusion of the ongoing *Peach Gear* issue.

I return home in the evening with a tornado in my stomach and, when I see I've arrived before Henry, dive into the bathroom to tart myself up. Subtly, of course. He might have seen me tons of times with a head of Velcro rollers, or a hangover pallor the shade of an avocado. But today I am going to tell him I love him – and I refuse to look anything other than gorgeous for the occasion.

After half an hour in the bathroom, my skin buffed, moisturized and Touche Éclat-ed to oblivion, I hear Henry's keys clatter on the hall table.

I open the door as he races to the kitchen and follow him, my heart pounding.

'H-Henry,' I stammer as I reach the door.

'Oh hi, Lucy,' he says distractedly, rummaging in the cupboard under the sink.

'I was wondering if you had ten minutes?'

My veins are bursting with adrenalin. Henry grabs the iron and plugs it into a wall socket.

'Not really,' he says apologetically. 'I'm horribly late.'

'Oh.' My heart sinks. 'You've got a date.'

He picks up the ironing board and battles with it until it's upright. Then he flings his Hugo Boss shirt on it, the gorgeous dark one I picked out for him.

'I don't know whether it's a date,' he admits, frantically running the iron over the sleeve. I scrutinize his expression. Does he *want* it to be a date?

'Is this the same woman you've been out with a few times?' I ask nonchalantly. 'The one you deny you're dating?'

He nods. 'I've only denied we're dating because nothing's ever happened between us. I'm not sure it ever will. What do you think I should do?'

Two weeks ago I'd have instructed Henry to seize the initiative and make *sure* something happens. But now isn't two weeks ago. Things have changed.

'It must be nearly a month since you started seeing her, isn't it?' I chew my lip. 'To be honest, it sounds like a bit of a dead loss.'

He pauses momentarily and looks up, surprised. 'Really?'

I nod, feeling only slightly guilty. 'If there was any real chemistry, something would have happened by now.'

'Hmmm.' He mulls this over. 'Well, I'm seeing her again this evening. Perhaps if something doesn't happen tonight I'll call it a day. But if it does, I won't.'

I am rooted to the spot, as the iron hurtles over Henry's shirt. Do I say it now? Do I snatch the Morphy Richards from his hand and tell him to forget this other woman – forget *all* the other women – because I, LUCY TYLER, LOVE HIM?

'That sounds okay, doesn't it?' he asks.

'Well, I . . . maybe there's something I should tell you first.'

My heart thunders against my ribcage and is only just drowned out by the steam setting.

'Oh bugger.' He lifts up his shirt and examines it under the light. 'There's a stain on the collar. Where's that cloth?'

'Henry, I . . .' As he frantically rubs off the stain from his shirt, unplugs the iron and heads to the door, I know it's not going to happen.

'I've really got to run,' he says, then hesitates. 'Sorry, Lucy. Was it important? If it was I can always—'

'No, Henry,' I interrupt. 'It'll wait.'

'Great,' he smiles. 'I'll catch you tomorrow.'

Ten minutes later, Henry dashes out of the house. I wander to the hall and breathe him in, the lingering scent of his after-shave igniting my senses.

With the flat empty of sound, I head for the living room and slump on the sofa where I flick through the channels, cursing the quality of television. Deep down, I know it's not the schedulers' fault. Nothing would distract me from the same thought, whirring through my head over and over again. A short prayer which, despite being an entirely improper subject to call upon the Lord Almighty for, I can't help saying: *Dear God, please don't let anything happen between Henry and his woman tonight. Please don't let anything happen . . .*

Chapter 68

When Henry doesn't come home I know that my prayers have gone unanswered. It's hardly surprising – even I'm appalled to have raised this with Our Maker when parts of the world are ravaged by war and famine. The fact that I tagged on a perfunctory note about world peace and cruelty to animals is hardly going to have satisfied Him.

It is now 10 a.m. and the only conclusion I can come to is that Henry officially has a new girlfriend.

I phone Dominique, trying not to whimper when she answers. 'I need some retail therapy,' I announce.

'Did you have a date last night?' she asks.

'What makes you say that?'

'You sound depressed.'

'Not this time. Are you around for a shopping session or what?'

'Sorry, hon. Justin and I are going away for the night,' she says apologetically. 'Nice little guest house in the Yorkshire Dales. The sort of place that used to be my idea of hell.'

'Oh. Well, have a great time, won't you?'

'What is it, anyway? Can't you fill me in over the phone?'

'I'm fine, honestly.'

'You're sure?'

'Of course.'

'How about we catch up over lunch next week?'

'Perfect,' I say, trying to sound upbeat. 'Have a brilliant weekend.'

'You too, hon,' she says.

I put down the phone and try Erin, but her mobile goes straight to messages.

'Hi, Erin,' I say. 'Hope you're okay. It's ages since we caught up and, well, I wondered if you fancied getting together today? You know where I am, so give me a ring. Bye.'

Erin doesn't phone back, but texts me at lunchtime instead. *Sorry Lucy, can't make it today. Will ring u l8r!*

Shopping alone is a vacuous experience. It's not that I don't shop by myself all the time, but today, its *raison d'être* was the company, not the purchases.

Still, I make up for the lack of company with an explosion of buying activity and, within an hour of my arrival in the city centre, I am carrying enough bags to launch my own clothing line. I might be miserable, but at least I'll be well dressed and miserable. I battle my way back to the car park before I risk complete bankruptcy, and am about to step into the lift when I see them.

Henry and Erin.

My Henry and *my* Erin. Together. Arm-in-arm, laughing.

All I want to do is cry.

Chapter 69

Henry returns at eight on Sunday night and the knot in the pit of my stomach tightens. It's been there since yesterday, constricting every time I replay the car-park scene with a nauseating clench.

'Hi!' I try to smile as I look up from my plate of bean-sprouts. They're even less appetizing than usual, every grim mouthful an affront to the word 'edible'.

'Hi,' he smiles, standing at the door. He looks slightly dishevelled, totally gorgeous – and utterly unobtainable.

'Did you have a nice weekend?' he asks.

'Very relaxing,' I lie.

'Oh good,' he replies, playing with the leather bracelet on his arm. 'Well – I'm going to have a shower.'

'Okay,' I say.

He nods and backs out of the door.

'Henry. I take it your date went well? *With Erin?*'

He freezes, taking in the last two words. His eyes dart across my face, checking out my expression. Only I'm ready for this. And when he sees the convincing look of goodwill I've plastered on it, he relaxes.

'Er . . . yes.'

'Good,' I reply coolly.

'You knew it was Erin, then?'

I nod, as if I'm almost surprised he had to ask the question.

'I saw you out shopping yesterday.' My tone is so deliberately casual it nearly dislocates my jaw. 'Hey, I'm really happy for you.'

He straightens his back. 'Are you?'

'Of course,' I reply brightly. 'Why wouldn't I be? You're two of my closest friends.'

'There wasn't anything going on until this weekend, you know,' he tells me. 'We weren't hiding anything or—'

'Henry, it's fine,' I interrupt. 'Really.'

'Well, that's great.' He is visibly relieved. 'I wondered if you might feel a bit funny about it – you know, with Erin being your friend.'

'What? No! Funny? Not at all!'

He smiles, looking genuinely touched. 'Thanks, Luce. That means a lot.'

Chapter 70

'I'm enjoying being in a couple,' announces Dominique, picking up an olive and popping it into her mouth. 'But I miss this: we three, having lunch and talking twaddle.'

'Twaddle?' laughs Erin. 'I thought we were having a deeply stimulating and important discussion.'

'About shoes,' I say.

'Not just shoes,' Dominique adds. 'Though I don't know why my love-life suddenly features so highly in every conversation.'

'Yes, you do,' says Erin. 'We never thought we'd see the day when you'd have a Significant Other.'

'*You* didn't?' Dominique cries. 'You should hear my mother.'

'*You told your mother?*' I ask. God, it must be serious.

'They haven't met yet. I haven't changed that much. But I thought I'd lay the foundations for . . .' Dominique's voice trails off.

'For what?'

Dominique pauses. 'Nothing – forget I said anything.'

'As if we could,' says Erin.

Dominique lowers her voice. 'Okay – but don't repeat this.'

Erin and I lean in.

'I think he's about to ask me to move in with him.'

'Ohmygod!' breathes Erin.

'Dominique, that's fantastic,' I tell her. And I mean it. *I think.* The more I hear from Dominique about her and Justin, the more I'm convinced that I was imagining something untoward about him. The guy is clearly as lovestruck as she is.

'Yeah, well, it hasn't happened yet.' She leans back. 'He's dropped a couple of hints and . . . just call it feminine intuition.'

I'm enjoying our lunch, but I'd be lying if I said things didn't feel strange after the revelations about Erin and Henry. I've tried not to let it affect me, but I can't help it.

'How's Henry?' asks Dominique, as if sensing my thoughts.

'Fine, I think. I haven't seen him a lot lately. You'd better ask Erin.' Erin blushes and I feel a stab of remorse.

'He's . . . fine,' she replies uncomfortably.

'Well, I'm so pleased for you,' says Dominique, sipping her drink. 'We were worried after your split from Gary, weren't we, Lucy?'

I conjure up a *Stepford Wives* smile. 'Yes.'

'And now you're with Henry. I can't think of a nicer couple, can you, Lucy?'

'No.'

'I think your prospects are pretty good, don't you, Lucy?'

'Yes.'

'And since his transformation, I—'

'*How come you never told me?*' The words erupt from my mouth entirely involuntarily. Dominique looks at me as if my body has been possessed.

Erin clears her throat awkwardly. 'About me and Henry, you mean?'

I nod.

She frowns. 'I don't know really. I thought there wasn't anything *to* tell at first. Nothing happened. Henry accompanied me to a couple of work events and, well, we acted like friends. We'd *always* been friends – so why would I bother telling anyone that?'

'But you're not just friends now, are you, hon?' hoots Dominique, giving her a nudge. 'From what I hear, you're *way* beyond friendship!'

Erin's blush deepens. 'It's early days. It was only this weekend that anything happened.'

'Anything?' laughs Dominique. 'Lucy nearly called a search-party – Henry didn't come home all weekend.'

From the depths of my being, I try to look happy. I suspect I look as chipper as a funeral director – but I *do* try. Erin glances at me nervously.

I get a grip on myself, saying, 'That's right. It's great, Erin. Really great.'

She smiles gratefully and I feel like such a fraud I'm expecting the Serious Organized Crime Agency to burst in. Two of my best friends have found love with each other and I have to *pretend* to be happy. What a horrible person I am.

'I'm only surprised it took you so long to make a move on him,' continues Dominique.

Erin swallows a piece of tomato. 'I thought about it a while ago. I realized how much I liked him soon after splitting up with Gary, but I worried about having a rebound fling with Henry. If it'd been anyone else, I wouldn't have thought twice. Then, eventually, I realized I liked him so much that I had two choices: sit around thinking about it for ever or take a chance and go for it.'

'Well, I for one am glad you chose the latter,' says Dominique, 'and I bet Henry is too.'

By the time lunch is over, despite the juicy olives and heavenly main course, I'm glad to be heading back to my desk. I need something to distract me from my feelings for Henry – and sitting here with the new woman in his life isn't it.

We split the bill and are on our way to the door. It's then that I see him. I gasp like an asthmatic hyena.

'What is it?' asks Erin, careering into my back. She freezes and I know she's seen him too.

'What are you two doing? Oh my God.'

I glance at Dominique. Even if I wanted to stop her from witnessing Justin using his tongue to excavate the ear of his blonde companion, I couldn't.

I can't work out whether she's going to cry. But she grits her teeth, thrusts her handbag in my arms and marches over. Justin stops smooching. As he glances up and sees Dominique, he might as well be facing Godzilla.

'Shit . . . Dominique. Look – I can explain.'

'Can you?'

He snatches his hand away from his companion. 'Um . . . um . . .'

'I think the word you're searching for is "no",' Dominique says.

It's clear she doesn't want explanations anyway. Instead, she turns to a waiter and taps him on the shoulder. 'Excuse me, is that the tiramisú?'

He studies his tray. 'Er, yes.'

'Who's it for?'

'The lady in the corner.'

'Madam?' Dominique hollers.

Justin, his blonde, and the rest of us wonder what she's doing.

'Madam, so sorry about this,' she continues politely. 'I need to borrow your tiramisú.'

She reaches over to the tray, dips her bare hand in the bowl and scoops out some of the contents. Mascarpone and brandy-soaked sponge drip down her arm. Now we know what she's doing. But there's a sublime artistry about the way she smears it over Justin's face, with the command of a Renaissance sculptor. When finished, she stands back and examines her work. Justin is entirely mute. His transformation is complete. He is *Trifle Man*.

She licks her finger. 'That could be the most satisfying dessert I've ever had.'

Chapter 71

Despite the performance, Dominique is distraught.

I can tell because, as I accompany her back to the office, she keeps threatening to kill people. Well, mainly Justin, but a couple of pedestrians who don't dive out of the way quickly enough too.

'Wanker!' she hisses under her breath, marching ahead as I struggle to keep up. 'Wanker, wanker, wanker.'

'He's definitely that,' I concede breathlessly.

'Did you see the slut he was with?' She spins round and takes me by surprise. I only stop just in time to avoid colliding into her, only to cause a three-person pile-up.

'I did.' I untangle myself from somebody else's iPod and hand it back apologetically. In fact, the woman Justin was with didn't look like a slut. She looked perfectly respectable – and as shocked as Dominique.

'Wanker!' she repeats, continuing along the street. 'Wanker, wank—'

'Dominique, *slow down*,' I insist eventually.

She stops and turns. Her lips are trembling, her eyes filled with tears.

'Come here,' I demand softly, putting my arms round her and drawing her into me.

'Oh God, Lucy, what am I going to do?' she sniffs.

I put my hand in my bag to find her a tissue. Unfortunately, the interior of my handbag is like a jumble sale in the Tardis. I can lay my hands on a concealer, a set of keys, a miniature bottle of Molton Brown shampoo, a box of Elastoplast, six nail files, four hair bands, twelve biros, a tube of athlete's foot cream, a shopping list from early 2008 and a travel alarm clock. But no tissues.

I rub her arm instead.

'I'm in love with him,' she whispers between tears. '*Was* in love with him. Oh, who am I kidding . . . *am* in love with him. What am I going to do?'

I spin her round and link her arm as we continue up Castle Street.

'What you're going to do, Dominique, is cry,' I tell her. 'You're going to call him a wanker. You're going to hate him and love him in equal measure. You're going to cry a bit more. Ultimately, you're going to realize that there are men more deserving of your love.'

'Oh God. Is that supposed to make me feel better? How depressing.'

'What did you expect?'

'I didn't expect to see what I saw in that restaurant. What an idiot I am.'

'You're not an idiot,' I say gently. 'You fell in love. There's nothing idiotic about that.'

'I fell in love with a two-timing . . . *wanker*.' Dominique's vocabulary on this issue is uncharacteristically minimalist. 'I'd say that was extremely idiotic. Clinically insane, in fact.'

'You weren't to know, Dom.'

'Well,' she straightens her back and wipes mascara from her

reddened eyes. It's an improvement, but she still looks as if she's had a makeover in a blackout. 'Never again.'

'You don't mean that.'

'Oh yes I do,' she says defiantly. 'Shagging about is far easier.'

But far less fulfilling. Only now isn't the time to tell her.

We turn into Victoria Street, not caring that we're forty-five minutes late after lunch.

It's then, when I think I've had enough drama for one day, that I spot my mother on the other side of the road. She looks different: her hair is curled for the first time since she tried to recreate Farrah Fawcett's do in the late seventies, she's wearing enough make-up to get a job as an air hostess, and she's in heels. The last time my mother wore heels in the daytime was for my Cousin Kerry's wedding three years ago, and she had to have her Scholl's surgically removed for the occasion.

If that wasn't suspicious enough, she's accompanied by . . . A MAN. A tall, chisel-jawed man, with a George Clooney crop and a fashionable three-quarter-length overcoat.

She's laughing and joking and . . . Oh. My. God. My mother is flirting. I don't believe it. My mother isn't *allowed* to flirt, not even with my dad. It's a breach of her job description.

I am rooted to the spot, my lungs drained of oxygen.

'Everybody's at it!' I glare at Mum. 'Every time I walk through this city centre, I spot somebody. *At it.*'

'At *what?*' asks Dominique, blowing her nose.

'First Henry and Erin, then Justin and that blonde, and now this! I can't believe it.'

'Who?'

'Look.' I point to the other side of the street where my

mother is behaving as though she's halfway through a third date.

Dominique squints through her bloodshot eyes. 'Is that your mum?'

'Apparently so.'

'She looks *amazing*. Who's the guy? He's gorgeous.'

'*Dominique*,' I hiss, 'that is my mother you're talking about. My mother who is married. TO MY FATHER.'

'Good point. I'm sure there's nothing in it. It'll be perfectly innocent.'

I watch Mum and this impostor make their way to the plush doorway of the Avalon Hotel, a place renowned for being chic, expensive and very romantic. He puts his hand on the small of her back and guides her to the door.

Perfectly innocent?

I am perfectly unconvinced.

Chapter 72

'DAVE, WAKE UP! COME ON, YOU LAZY GIT. WAKE UP, WILL YOU?'

I am standing outside my brother's terraced house, throwing stones at his bedroom window.

'DAVE! THIS IS IMPORTANT! LET ME IN!'

He surfaces like a narcoleptic diplodocus and emerges from behind the curtain. The neighbours are treated to a view of his naked torso, which is an alarming terracotta shade – a dead giveaway that he's fallen asleep on the sunbed again.

Fixing his boxer shorts, he opens his window and scowls down at me. 'Are you trying to get arrested?'

'Open the door,' I reply urgently. 'This is important.'

'It can't be more important than me getting some sleep.'

'It's six-fifteen p.m.,' I point out, exasperated. 'Who sleeps at six-fifteen p.m.?'

'I've just come back from a conference in Frankfurt, you idiot.'

I don't feel at all guilty about ruining the beauty sleep of someone who's been overdoing it on a company jolly, but it's easier not to say this.

'You'll understand when I tell you,' I call up.

'Come back later,' he instructs sleepily, closing his window.

'No!'

'Give me a shout in an hour an—'

'MUM'S HAVING AN AFFAIR!'

He looks at me as if I am loopier than a Red Arrows formation. 'You're off your head,' he mutters, starting to close the window again.

'Look, are you going to leave me on the street to shout the gory details, or are you going to let me in?'

He grunts and turns away.

When the front door opens a minute later, I barge past and go straight to the kitchen. Like the rest of Dave's home, the room is a cross between the *Big Brother* house and a permanently horny adolescent's bedroom, circa 1992.

Posters of semi-naked Zoo girls adorn the walls and his furniture is an unsettling combination of flat-pack hand-me-downs from Mum and Dad's place and tacky new items paid for in instalments (the electric blue plastic bubble chair in the living room is a favourite).

The feminine touches Cheryl has attempted make it even weirder. The dried flowers from Next Home are fighting a losing battle, I fear, on top of his collection of Street Fighter games.

'Right,' he says, appearing at the kitchen door in a short black dressing-gown and Quiksilver flip-flops. 'What the bollocks is this about?'

'It's Mum,' I sigh, putting my head in my hands. 'I think she's having an affair.'

He snorts. 'You've been reading too many of them Jilly Cooper books.' He marches to the fridge, sticks in his head and emerges with a carton of leftover curry.

I close my eyes in frustration. 'I haven't.'

'You have,' he grins. 'You'll be telling me she's a champion polo-player next.'

'I *saw* her,' I insist.

He wanders to the cutlery drawer, removes a fork and starts making his way through a chilled chicken jalfrezi that looks more like Pedigree Chum.

'Saw her doing what?'

I ponder for a second on how to articulate this. 'Carousing,' I tell him.

He frowns, taking this in. 'Why's she carol singing at this time of year?'

'Not carol singing,' I hiss. '*Carousing*. With a man.'

'What sort of man?'

'A good-looking one. A smartly-dressed one. One who looked distinctly like he was flirting with her. And she with him.'

He swallows his last mouthful and burps.

'Oh God,' I say in disgust.

'What?' he replies innocently. 'No point being overburdened with a sense of decorum.'

'No chance of that. Look, can we stick to the issue?'

'You must have got it wrong,' he says confidently.

'Listen to me: she's been buying loads of gorgeous make-up lately and going to salsa dancing and—'

'Wasn't it you who told her to go to salsa dancing?'

'Yes, but—'

'So if she is having an affair, it's your fault.'

'I never suggested she turn into a . . . a harlot.'

He rolls his eyes clearly still unconvinced, and returns to the fridge to see what else is available.

'Look, there's another thing I haven't told you.' I look at

my hands. 'When I saw her this afternoon, they were going into the lobby of a hotel.'

He stops in his tracks. 'A hotel?'

I nod.

'What's she going to a hotel for?'

'You tell me.' At last I feel as if I'm getting somewhere.

'With a bloke?'

'A bloke,' I nod.

Dave scratches his bum and considers this information. 'And you really think—'

'Dave, our mother is having an affair. I know it.'

Mum answers her mobile after three rings.

'Ma, where are you?' Dave demands. He's never been big on pleasantries.

'What do you mean, where am I?' she hisses. At least, I think this is what she hisses because Dave and I are sharing the handset and, frankly, his big head is taking up most of the available space.

'I *mean*, where are you?'

'I'm in town, if you must know,' she replies, bewildered. 'I'm having a drink—'

'Where?' he interrupts.

'What does it matter where?'

'Tell me where you are, Ma.'

'I'm in some bar.' She sounds flustered. 'I don't know what it's called. Schmooze or Booze or something.'

He cuts her off and turns to me. 'She's in Newz.'

'Right,' I reply. 'So what do we do?'

'We go there. Obviously.'

I pause as alarm bells start ringing in my head. 'I'm not sure that's a good idea.'

'Why not? If she's having an affair then there's one way to make sure it stops.'

'No. Dave, no. Really, no.'

He frowns. 'What did you tell me for, if you didn't want me to go and smack him?'

I'm starting to wonder myself. 'Moral support.'

'Moral support?' He gives a short laugh. 'Next time, try the Samaritans.'

Chapter 73

It never ceases to amaze me how many women are attracted to my brother. The car journey lasts ten minutes and in that time he's winked at, smiled at and swooned at so much it almost constitutes an epidemic.

The first time it happens, when we're next to a brunette in a VW Golf at traffic-lights, I do a double-take to check she isn't having a stroke.

'What do these women see in you?' I ask, incredulous.

'Oh, thanks. Boost my self-esteem, why don't you?'

'If I boosted your self-esteem it'd be propelled into orbit.'

'As a matter of fact . . .' he begins, then stops.

'What?'

He shakes his head. 'Nothing.'

'Come on. Since when have you been shy and retiring?'

He fixes his eyes on the road. 'You might as well know. Cheryl and I have split up.'

'What?' I am shocked. 'Why on earth did you split up with her? She was *great* for you. Honestly, you men have got so much to answer for. She showered you with presents, she was sweet, pretty . . . okay, she wasn't the brightest, but—'

338

It suddenly dawns on me. 'Oh my God. *She* dumped *you*, didn't she?'

His jaw tightens and a vein bulges in his neck. 'Apparently I took her for granted.'

'She's got a point,' I can't help saying, then regret it.

'I know,' he says solemnly, to my surprise.

'Have you tried to get her back?'

He nods. 'She's seeing someone else.'

'What? So soon? Dave, I can't believe it. I'm sorry.'

For the first time in my life I think I'm about to see my brother cry. Then he pulls in the car and I realize we're outside New Zealand House, home to Newz Bar. 'Come on. Let's go and sort this out.'

As expected for early on a Thursday evening, the place is busy, and locating Mum isn't easy.

There are ways and means of handling the issue of Mum's affair – and I'd prefer any of them to this. I tried to persuade him to let things lie so we can discuss it maturely with her at the weekend, but Dave is resolute.

'I don't think she's here.' I grab his arm and try to spin him round.

He shakes me off and points to the corner. 'There.'

I stand and stare. Sure enough, there's my mum. And there *he* is – The Impostor.

'Maybe I got this wrong.' I clutch at him again.

'Looks clear enough to me.' He frees himself and walks towards them.

I'm trailing behind when Mum's companion stands and heads for the bar. Dave goes to follow him, but I say hurriedly, 'Let's speak to Mum first.'

'I'd rather go and smack him.'

'You can do that after,' I tell him, buying time. He hesitates, then nods.

When we arrive at Mum's table she couldn't look more shocked if the Famous Five had turned up for a picnic. 'What the hell are you two doing here?' she whispers furiously.

'Who's this bloke you're with?' asks Dave. He's always had an ability to get straight to the point.

'*Bloke?*'

'Yes, *bloke*,' he replies accusingly. 'Don't try and deny it. We saw you. And Lucy saw you earlier *going into a hotel*.'

Mum glares at me and, as she's about to say something, The Impostor reappears with a cranberry juice and a glass of wine.

'Thanks, Jasper,' she says nervously, taking the juice.

The Impostor turns to Dave and me and gives us a friendly smile. I'm not fooled. 'Hi. Can I get you both a drink?'

'They're not stopping,' says Mum, before we can answer.

'Yes, we are,' replies Dave.

'No. You're not.' She smiles through gritted teeth.

We all stare at each other, wondering who'll speak next.

'I'm Jasper Paige.' The Impostor holds out his hand to Dave.

He eyes it suspiciously and doesn't move. 'Well, Jasper Paige, I wonder if you could explain something.'

'Jasper's my new boss,' Mum interrupts. She's still trying to smile but looks in such pain, she could be concealing the early stages of labour.

'Boss?' says Dave, screwing up his face. I realize I'm doing the same.

'Pleased to meet you both.' Jasper smiles and takes hold of my hand, shaking it with a self-assured grip.

He sits down and the cogs in my brain creak as I work out where I've heard the name. Jasper Paige. Jasper Paige. Jasper Pai—

'These are my kids,' Mum explains reluctantly.

'Ahh,' he says. 'Well, Carolyn's going to make a superb office manager for us. It's wonderful to have someone who feels as passionate as she does about what we do.'

'What you do?' echoes Dave.

'Hotels and restaurants,' Jasper replies.

Then I remember – and feel my throat constrict. Jasper Paige: entrepreneur extraordinaire and owner of half of the bars, restaurants and hotels in the north-west. He's famed for spotting shabby buildings and transforming them into places so hip you'd have to sell a kidney to get on the guest list.

Then I remember something else. *He's gay.*

'We spent the afternoon at Avalon,' he continues cheerfully. 'Your mum joined us for a meeting with the interior designers. She hasn't officially started yet, but it felt like a good opportunity to get to know the business.'

'Let me get this straight,' I say to Mum. 'You're going to work at the Paige Group? As . . . as office manager?'

There's an obvious question: how has she swung this one when her entire career so far has been as a cleaner for the Council's Planning Department? I know everyone embellishes their CV, but Mum must have gold-plated hers.

'That's right,' Jasper answers for her. 'Although your mum hasn't a lot of experience in this field, she's got all the key skills: she's a quick thinker, excellent at people management

341

and, above all, she is enthusiastic. My instincts are never wrong. I could see her potential the day we met.'

'Where *did* you meet?' asks Dave, uncrossing his arms.

'Salsa dancing,' they both reply.

Dave flashes me a look. And if looks could kill . . .

Chapter 74

Henry's at home tonight and it feels strange. Not just because he's so often at Erin's place these days, but also because I'm an emotional and physical wreck whenever he's near. I find myself talking like a Formula One commentator on speed, or barely able to talk at all. I'm filled with longing for him, desperate to reach out and touch his cheek, kiss his lips, feel his arms around me. I'm riddled with jealousy about him and Erin. And shame that I could feel like this about two of my best friends.

This episode has brought out a wicked witch side of me and frankly, I don't like her. She's a bitch. And a miserable bitch at that.

Henry wanders into the kitchen and takes out a chicken breast and some vegetables from the fridge as I'm preparing my dinner.

'That looks . . . appetizing,' Henry says.

I look at my bowl of breakfast cereal. Only a hundred and thirty-five calories, or two and a half Diet World *nootrients* per portion. I'd feel saintly if I hadn't devoured seven mini-quiches, four king-prawn skewers and six mini-cheesecakes at a lunchtime event.

'I'm not hungry anyway,' I lie. Canapés are the western equivalent of Chinese food: they fill you up initially but within three hours you're ravenous.

'I'm making a Thai curry. There's plenty here to share if you want to join me.'

I'm torn between the straightforward option of doing a runner and the more tempting option of staying to gaze into Henry's eyes and torture myself.

'Okay. Thanks.' I abandon my cereal. I never did have any willpower.

'How's your week been?' he asks, starting to chop a pepper.

'Oh, don't ask,' I sigh.

'Is Andy Smith bothering you again?'

'He's the least of my worries. I thought my mother was having an affair.'

Henry's eyes nearly pop out of his head.

'Don't worry, she's not,' I tell him. 'The bloke I saw her with was her new boss – her new *gay* boss. She's barely speaking to me now because, to cut a long story short, I told Dave and he marched into Newz to confront them.'

'Dave *is* noted for his tact and diplomacy,' Henry smirks.

'There's no need to rub it in.'

Henry and I cook and eat the curry, do the dishes together and continue chatting at the kitchen table afterwards. It strikes me how uncomfortably absent the subject of his new girlfriend is. Eventually I feel obliged to say something.

'How's Erin?' I make sure my expression betrays nothing.

'She's great,' he says, his eyes lighting up.

'Sooo . . . is it serious between you and her?'

'Who knows? I'm pretty sure I'm not in love with her.' I feel like cartwheeling across the kitchen. 'Not yet anyway – it's early days.' I feel like lying on the floor and weeping.

'There's no doubt that she's the closest I've come so far.' There is a flicker of shyness he's trying to hide. He has no idea how attractive it makes him. 'I think she's a wonderful person,' he adds.

'She is,' I agree.

'And beautiful.'

'Yes,' I agree again.

'She's also one of the most intelligent people I've ever met.'

'Yes,' I add, feeling nauseous.

'That's not to say kind. Gentle. And, you know, sexy in an understated way.'

'Understated. Yes.' I feel like jumping off a cliff. 'You're a lucky man,' I say faintly.

'So you know, Lucy – things are different now I'm with Erin. I'm seeing her and her alone.'

I try to look approving. 'Good.'

'Rachel and all the others were lovely, but there's no way I'd continue seeing any of them now I'm with Erin. I know you'd never forgive me if I messed a friend of yours around. But you've no need to worry: I'm a one-woman man now.'

'Glad to hear it.'

He nods. 'But what about you? Anyone taken your fancy recently?'

With adrenalin pumping through my body, I want to grab his shoulders, shake him and shout: *YOU! YOU – HENRY! YOU HAVE TAKEN MY FANCY. I ADORE YOU. I CAN'T LIVE WITHOUT YOU. AND I CAN'T KEEP UP THIS CHARADE ANY LONGER!*

Instead, I cough nervously. 'No one special. You know my love-life, Henry. Never simple.'

He reaches over and clutches my hand. It sends a shot of heat through my body.

'You'll find someone, Lucy,' he whispers. 'Someone handsome and kind. Someone who deserves you.'

I look into his eyes and my heart feels ready to explode.

I've already found him. And he hasn't got a clue.

Chapter 75

I know Dominique's in a bad way because she looks terrible. Usually Dominique looks so far from terrible, only Gisele Bündchen could stand beside her and not be intimidated.

When she turns up at the flat to drop off a document for work, her eyes are bloodshot, her complexion is grey and the bum of her sweatpants is so saggy it looks as though she's been shoplifting groceries in it.

'You don't have to say anything,' she says, as she hands me the folder. 'I know I look like shit.'

'No, you don't.' I try to sound convincing. 'A little more . . . *low key* than usual, but no way do you look like—'

'Lucy, I look like shit,' she interrupts. 'Don't worry. I can take it.' She marches through to the living room and plonks herself down on the sofa.

'Can I get you a cup of tea?' I ask.

She gives me a speaking look.

'Okay – wine it is.' I spin round and head to the kitchen.

When I return, she's gazing mournfully out of the window and I feel a stab of pity. Dominique is usually so upbeat you'd be forgiven for thinking she brushes her teeth with serotonin every morning. The Justin experience has clearly hit her hard.

'How are you feeling?' I ask, handing her a glass.

'Okay,' she says, attempting to appear bright.

I gaze at her sceptically.

She shrugs. 'I feel how I look . . . like shit.'

'Oh Dominique.' I walk over and put my arm around her.

'Why do people go around falling in love if they end up like this?' she asks dully.

'It doesn't always end like this,' I say gently.

'Doesn't it? I'll take your word for it, because I won't be trying to find out again. I'm having a break from men.'

This is like having Gordon Ramsay say he's having a break from swearing.

'What?' she says innocently, seeing my face.

'Nothing. Look, I know it's easy for me to say, but it'd be terrible if you tarred every man with the same brush as Justin and let one bad experience shape all your future relationships. Why deny yourself because of one bloke?'

She smiles in a sad way.

'You know, Lucy, one of the things I've always admired about you is your unfettered optimism.'

'Oh dear,' I groan.

'I'm serious. All those horrendous experiences you have with blokes – they've never put you off, have they?'

I can't help but laugh. 'I suppose that is a bit mad.'

'I think you've been around Henry too much. Because he's the most decent man this side of Mars, you assume they all are. The reality is different.'

I try to keep smiling. Try to pretend this comment hasn't stung me to the core. For once, Dominique is so wound up in her own issues, I get away with it.

'Speaking of Henry,' she continues, 'I had a long conversation with Erin on the phone yesterday.'

My heart skips a beat. 'Oh yes?'

She takes a sip of her wine. 'I reckon she's fallen for him.'

'What?'

'Hook, line and sinker.'

I gulp. 'Really?'

'I'm convinced.' She studies my reaction. 'Are you surprised?'

I phrase this carefully. 'I'm not sure I can see them as a couple *long-term*.' This is wishful thinking. 'Erin's still getting over Gary. I can't help thinking she might be on the rebound.'

'No way,' says Dominique, as if this is preposterous. 'This is the real thing, Lucy. Listening to Erin yesterday, I'm certain of it.'

Chapter 76

Dave and I have been summoned to Mum and Dad's house. Things couldn't look more serious if we were heading to court on charges of peeing in the magistrate's front garden.

When I arrive, Dave is in the kitchen with Mum. She is five foot one and has the legs of a bluebird; he's twelve stone with biceps like Popeye after a spinach smoothie. He looks terrified.

'It was Lucy's idea,' he protests. 'She said she'd seen you at a hotel with some bloke and *just knew* you were having an affair.'

Mum looks up. 'Oh, if isn't Hetty bloody Wainthrop herself.'

'Sorry, Mum,' I mutter. There doesn't seem much point in saying anything else.

'Sit down,' she instructs. I obediently find a chair and catch Dave's eye. He doesn't look any closer to putting the incident behind him.

'Can I point out,' she continues tersely, 'that this is the first sniff of a good job I've had since . . . well, ever.'

'We know,' Dave and I mutter.

'Can I also point out how unhelpful it was for you two to march in and have a go at my new boss?'

'We know.'

'And then there's the fact that Jasper Paige – while charming, attractive and immaculately dressed – is happily married,' she continues, '*to another man.*'

'I know,' I say, shamefaced. Dave looks shocked.

'So what did you think you were doing?'

I bite my lip. Dave looks out of the window.

'You could have told us,' I say weakly. 'About your new job, I mean.'

'It was only confirmed on Friday.' Mum crosses her arms. 'I didn't want to say anything before then, in case it didn't come off.'

'Well, don't blame me,' Dave adds. 'I said you'd never cheat on Dad. Lucy was convinced you were swanning round like Lady Chatterley. This is your dopey daughter's fault – not mine.'

'Cheers, Dave. That's really big of you.' I know he's feeling delicate after being dumped by Cheryl, but I'm not going to take this abuse without a fight.

'Big? You were the one who—'

'ENOUGH!' bellows Mum, like Boudicca silencing two insubordinate soldiers. 'Promise me you will never do anything like that again,' she adds.

'Course, Mum,' says Dave angelically.

I give him a filthy look, then realize Mum is waiting for me to respond.

'Of course,' I mumble.

'Now, bugger off the both of you and let me do Your Lordship's tea.' She opens the oven and pulls out a tray, smoke billowing around her head. 'Oh God,' she coughs, glaring at the blackened chips, which have clearly been overcooked by about an hour and a half. 'You could arm a Trident Submarine with these.'

Dave leaps up and pushes past me, as eager to escape this bollocking as the ones we got twenty years ago. When I try to leave, Mum touches my arm.

'Hang on a minute.' She puts the tray on the hob.

'Yes, Mum?'

She pauses. 'Is something the matter, Lucy?'

'What do you mean?'

She leans on the work surface and removes her oven glove.

'Why would you think I was having an affair?' she asks softly. 'Have I ever done *anything* like that?'

'Oh, I don't know.' I sit down again. 'I put two and two together and made five, that's all. I'd also just seen Dominique's boyfriend cheating on her. It probably put ideas in my head.'

'There's a difference between Dominique and her fella and me and your dad,' Mum laughs. 'Thirty-odd years, for a start.'

'I know.' I feel silly now. 'I suppose . . . maybe I wish Dad didn't take you for granted so much.'

'Take me for granted?' She raises an eyebrow. 'Love, we've been together *for ever*. All couples take each other for granted after that time. It doesn't sound romantic, but that's reality.'

I frown. 'But he's never even bought you an anniversary card.'

'So what?' she says. 'It doesn't mean we don't love each other.'

'Really?'

'Of course.'

She looks at my expression and sits down. 'Your father was a real catch when we were young, you know.'

'What – Dad?'

'Yep. Good-looking *and* charming. Honestly, he had half the girls in Liverpool after him. If you think it's bad with our Dave now, you should have seen your father.'

'Well, I bet you were a catch too,' I tell her. 'I've seen your old pictures – you were really glam.'

'Maybe,' she shrugs. 'I never thought so in those days, though.'

'Why?'

She ponders. 'I don't know, really – I just didn't. If I'm honest, I used to try to make out I was better than I really was. I used to be a terrible one for exaggeration, Lucy.'

'Oh, what did you say?'

'I'd tell people all sorts of nonsense. You saw how difficult it was to drag me to salsa? I'm not one of life's natural dancers. But when I met your dad, I managed to convince him I was on the brink of being signed by Pan's People.'

'The dance troupe?' I giggle.

She chuckles. 'I was always at it – pretending I was more talented or glamorous than I was. Fortunately, your dad worked out I was boring old Carolyn Gates and decided he liked me anyway.' She gives a sigh. 'Be glad it hasn't run in the family.'

I stop laughing and something strikes me.

'Why are you blushing?' Mum asks.

'Am I? Oh, no reason,' I say.

'The point is, your dad and I have always loved each other, warts and all. The fact that we don't run down the streets shouting it every other day doesn't make it any less true.'

I'm sure she's right, that after thirty-one years together that's normal. I can't help preferring the Hollywood version of true love though.

353

'Lucy,' she says again, her tone quite gentle for a change, 'is that the only thing that's the matter?'

'Yes, of course. Why do you ask?'

'Look, I may have got the wrong end of the stick, so by all means tell me to butt out.'

'What are you on about?' I ask, bewildered.

'Ever since this makeover business, I've sensed you've been a bit . . . funny. I don't mean to pry, love, but do you have feelings for Henry?'

I bite one of my nails. 'Of course. He's my best friend.'

'That's not what I mean and you know it.'

As I meet her eye, something inside me seems to break. Tears well up and my lips start wobbling uncontrollably.

'You can tell me, love. I'm your mother.'

I take a shuddering breath and attempt to compose myself. I fail. Instead, I collapse into a heap of tears.

'I'm in love with him, Mum,' I sob. 'Only, so is one of my best friends.'

Chapter 77

Mum and I were never big on heart-to-hearts. I knew a girl at university who was happy to discuss with her mother the finer details of everything from contraception preferences to inverted nipples. Not Mum and I. We stuck to whether I'd stocked up on baked beans, and that was how I preferred it.

Today though, I'm discovering that she's not a bad shoulder to cry on. And cry I have.

'I think it's too late, Mum,' I weep, as she puts her arm around me.

'It's never too late,' she promises.

'But it's not like he's going out with just anyone now. He's going out with Erin. Worse than that, she loves him. And he thinks she's "sexy in an understated sort of way". Oh God!'

Mum frowns. 'I'm not saying it's not complicated. I know you have your loyalty to Erin. But I stand by my guns. You've got to tell him.'

'But, Mum, I tried to tell him before I found out he was seeing Erin and it was hard enough then. Now it's impossible.'

Mum leans back in her seat. 'Can I tell you something, Lucy? I've always thought there was something special between you and Henry.'

'Have you?' I feel a flicker of hope.

'What you've got – what you've always had – goes beyond friendship. Even when you were twelve, it was as if you really loved each other.'

I smile shakily. 'I suppose we did, in a way.'

'I never thought anything would happen because I assumed there was no attraction there.'

'That was *then* – I fancy the pants off him now. Only now he can have anyone he chooses.'

Mum hesitates. 'So you keep saying. But I can't help but think, Lucy, that given the choice . . .'

'What?'

'He'd choose you.'

As I close the door and walk to my car, Dad is on his way in.

'All right, love?' he says, taking his keys out of his back pocket.

'Hi, Dad,' I mutter, wanting to get to the car before he notices I've been crying.

Something makes me pause. 'Hey – Dad?'

He turns round. 'Yeah, love?'

'When was the last time you bought Mum flowers?'

He looks at me as if I'm speaking an obscure dialect of Swahili. 'Flowers?'

I nod. 'Yeah. Even from the garage. Or supermarket. Anything.'

'Your mum and I don't go in for that sort of thing,' he laughs, shaking his head as he puts his key in the door.

'Dad,' I say, before he can get inside the house, 'you should. You really should. When was the last time you did something really special for her?'

'I'm always doing special things for her. I got Sky Plus for her, didn't I? And I've got something coming in a bit that she'll love.'

'Oh?'

'A Jacuzzi,' he tells me proudly.

'A Jacuzzi?' I repeat in disbelief. 'Where the hell are you going to put one of those?'

'We've got plenty of room since you and Dave moved out,' he says casually. 'It'll be great. Millsy's coming over to plumb it in, in a couple of weeks' time.'

Giving up, I open my car door and toss my handbag on the passenger seat. 'You really are the last of the romantics, aren't you?'

He narrows his eyes. 'D'you know what, Lucy? You sound more like your mother every day.'

Chapter 78

The last time I watched Henry playing rugby he was sixteen. I've never seen him play in adulthood and can't help thinking that if I had, I'd have realized long ago how attractive he is.

He's sensational on the pitch, tackling fearlessly, scoring effortlessly, playing faster and harder than anyone else. As he celebrates another try – his third of the match – I squeal with pride as his team-mates dive on top of him.

Then I remember he's not mine. His rippling, muddied biceps aren't mine. The toned torso under his gloriously sweaty shirt isn't mine. The long, muscular legs aren't mine. They're Erin's.

Along with the gorgeous smile and gentle personality that makes him unconcerned about what anyone thinks as he waves to me energetically at the sidelines.

'What a fantastic surprise,' he says, running over as soon as the whistle blows. 'I didn't think you were interested in rugby.'

'I hadn't realized I was. I was really getting into it then!'

'Glad to hear it,' he grins. 'We'll make a fan of you yet.'

'Er . . . I wouldn't go that far.'

He laughs. 'Can you give me ten minutes to shower and change? I'm in a real state.'

When Henry emerges, he looks just as sensational, his hair wet from the shower and his clean jeans and T-shirt clinging to his body. Today he smells of fabric conditioner and deodorant, and this makes my pulse flutter uncontrollably.

Mum's words flash into my head again. *Given the choice, he'd choose you.*

I have no idea whether it's true, but I do know one thing: this time I'm telling him. It might destroy everything – but I've got to tell him.

'Good match, Henry.' The voice belongs to one of his team-mates, a tall, Afro-Caribbean scrum-half. 'Catch you later,' he adds, slapping him on the back.

Henry raises his hand. 'See you, Carl.'

When we're alone again, I take my courage in both hands. 'Do you want a drink?' I ask him. 'There's something I need to talk to you about. Something I've *got* to talk about.'

He slows down and looks at me. 'Is everything all right?'

'Yes, of course,' I reply hastily. 'Let's get out of here, shall we?'

The beer garden of the Black Lion is relatively quiet – probably because it's unseasonably chilly for the start of July. I head for our favourite spot, under the jasmine in the cobblestoned patio. I pull the arms of my jumper over my hands and shove them between my legs as Henry returns from the bar.

'Are you not too cold?' he asks, putting down the drinks and rubbing my back. As his hand makes contact with my body – even through two layers of clothes – warmth radiates through me.

'I'm fine – are you?'

'You know me: I'm used to a bit of cold. We needed to be suffering frostbite before Dad would put on the central heating when I was growing up.'

There's a silence. I can see he's expecting me to say something.

'How's work?' I decide I need a warm-up to the grand declaration.

'Brilliant, actually. The clinical trials in Tanzania that some of the team are involved in are really promising.'

'Hey, that's great.'

He nods. 'It's complicated though because malaria isn't like polio or measles where there's one vaccine – you need lots of different ones to fight it. But we seem to be going in the right direction.'

'How exciting to be involved in something like that.' I put my elbows on the table.

'You're right, it *is* exciting. It's going to be difficult to leave . . .'

He stops mid-flow, giving me a stricken look. As his words sink in, my brain starts whirring. Was he about to say what I thought?

'To leave?' I repeat.

He takes a ponderous mouthful of beer, lowering his eyes. 'I suppose I needed to tell you at some point.'

'Tell me what?'

'I've been dreading it because I feel awful about the flat and—'

'Tell me *what*, Henry?' My voice is wobbly.

'Though I'm sure it's silly. I know you'll be happy for me, because that's the way you are.'

'Henry!' I snap. 'Tell me what you're talking about?' My heart is thumping as I stare at him in a befuddled daze.

He swallows. 'You know how Erin's been talking about going travelling?'

'Yes.' I suddenly feel numb.

'Well, she's finally decided to go ahead.'

'Oh.' For a tiny, split second, my heart surges with joy at the thought of Erin being off the scene. I know it doesn't make me a nice person, but I can't help it.

'When she suggested that I should go with her, at first I dismissed it. Then, after a while, the idea seemed more appealing. An opportunity that was too good to miss.'

I look up at him again, realizing what he's trying to tell me. My stomach turns inside out and my chest feels as though someone's tightening a belt round it.

'I never took a gap year before university and that's probably one of the few things I regret in my life,' he continues. 'I guess I didn't have the confidence then. But that's changed now.'

I get a waft of jasmine and the intense sweetness I usually adore makes me want to regurgitate my lunch.

'So,' he smiles, 'I've made a decision.'

'Oh?'

'I'm going with her.'

His face is filled with excitement and happiness. As I lift my wine glass to my lips I can hear it chattering against my teeth.

'You're not annoyed, are you?' he asks quickly. 'Over the flat, I mean? I figured you'd easily get another flatmate and, if not, there are lots of one-bedroom places available. If you couldn't sort yourself out, I'd continue paying rent while I'm away. The last thing I want is to cause you any trouble.'

I gulp in an attempt to hide my emotions.

'It's no trouble, Henry,' I manage.

'Honestly, Lucy,' he continues, 'there's no way I'm going to leave you in the lurch. You can take as long as you want.'

'I – I know. It's fine.' I force a smile.

'I knew you'd understand.'

He leans over and hugs me. As his arms envelop my shoulders I fight tears and try to pull myself together. When he finally releases me, he brushes a strand of hair from my face and looks into my eyes.

'Hey,' he says softly. 'You're not upset, are you?'

I go to shake my head. Then I nod instead.

'Oh, Lucy,' he tuts, putting his arm around me again. 'You've got Dominique to look after you while I'm away. You'll be fine.'

'How long are you going for?'

'A year.'

Two simple words. Yet they punch me twice in the stomach.

'Perhaps longer,' he goes on. 'We'll play it by ear.'

'A year?' I reply hoarsely.

'It's you I've got to thank for this,' he whispers, stroking my hair again.

I look up, the pain in my chest worsening. 'Me?'

He nods.

'I could never have done this if you hadn't given me the confidence. Honestly, Lucy Tyler – you're the best friend in the world.'

Chapter 79

I've never had a little black book. I've had a little purple book, covered in silk with a picture of an oriental bird on the front. I got it on a fifth-year excursion to a Wildlife and Wetlands Trust Centre, and buying it was the highlight of the trip. That might make me sound like a philistine, but after six cold hours observing three ducks and a temperamental Whooper Swan, I'm unapologetic. At least they had a shop. I went home with a china tea-cup, a tin pencil-case, several new rubbers and my little purple book. I was happy.

In the ten years after I bought it, the book was gradually filled with the names and numbers of men I went out with. *Briefly and unsuccessfully* went out with.

I sit on the edge of my bed, alone while Henry and Erin shop for new rucksacks, and silently flick through its pages.

I dug it out because in films, when the heroine has a romantic crisis, she reaches for her address book and conjures up a stream of hunky specimens from her past. My expectations are significantly lower – but surely there must be *someone* I could ask out without risking a restraining order.

I open the first page, where there are seven entries. I can't believe I'm only on A and there are that many.

Right . . .

Chris Austen. He was ages ago – just after university. As I remember, he had the bum of a sprinter and a smile that could melt icecaps. But that's about all I can remember. I put a star next to his name. Promising.

Next . . .

Ben Ainsley. He must have been three years later. A trainee property surveyor with whom I went to see *Minority Report*. Not bad-looking as I recall, although slightly tight-fisted (I bought the popcorn), with a funny lisp that . . . oh no. I can't phone him. He was the one whose car I directed into a ditch the size of the Panama Canal. He was *so* unreasonable about that.

Next . . .

Marc Abbott. No, no, no. Shattering his mum's patio window with my red patent leather stiletto is not my proud-est moment – particularly since my version of the 'Time Warp' song from *The Rocky Horror Show* wasn't even the most animated at the party. God, that was unfair. As I watched the shoe hurtle off my foot, through the air and straight through his mother's window, there was only one thought in my head. *Why* has this happened to me and not Caroline Decker, when I'm sober (relatively) and she's drunk a bottle of Malibu and has danced as if she's being electrocuted all evening?

By the time I've got through the book an hour and a half later, I'm even more depressed. Is my adult life really little more than a series of disastrous dates?

I sit up straight and force myself to think positively. Besides, I've got stars next to eleven men who I think it's worth another shot with. It's not that I remember them as being spectacular examples of manhood, or even that we hit it off especially. These are the ones with whom I didn't make a complete fool of myself. At least, I think not.

I pick up the phone, my heart pounding, and dial Chris Austen's number. I'm looking forward to speaking to him again, and not least because it's making me think of that bum. It's years since I've seen him so he's probably got a new number, but—

'Hello?'

I don't recognize the voice immediately.

'Hi,' I say nervously. 'Is Chris there?'

'Speaking.'

My heart skips a beat.

'Oh. Chris. Right. Well. You might not remember me after all these years. In fact, I'm sure you don't remember me because it's been ages. But my name is Lucy Tyler and—'

'Lucy Tyler?' he interrupts.

'Yes, and—'

'Of course I remember you.'

'Oh,' I reply, pleasantly surprised. 'Gosh, that's a turn-up for the books. I assumed because it'd been so long that—'

'Lucy, love, I could never forget you.'

The way he says it makes me feel uneasy.

'Really?'

'I still tell the story of the night we went for a quiet Chinese,' he continues. 'The doctors had me worried at first when they said my sight might not return.'

It comes back to me in a sickening flash.

'They'd never seen anyone stabbed in the eye with a chopstick before.'

Oh *God*. I hold my breath, as the memory unfolds in glorious Technicolor.

'I don't think I quite *stabbed* you, Chris,' I say, hoping my indignation covers my embarrassment. He always was prone to exaggeration, but still. 'I'm not trying to shirk responsibility or anything, but it was more of a . . . poke than anything else. And very easily done.'

'Don't worry, Lucy – I'm not going to sue you. It was fine after a few days. Well, weeks. The blurring went eventually and my sight's as right as rain now. And, to think, you spent all that time in the Far East – I thought you'd have been an expert.'

'Um, yes,' I mutter. 'But I was out of practice with the chopsticks and—'

'That anecdote was one of the first things I told my wife on the night I met her. She says that story was what attracted her to me – she knew immediately I had a blinding sense of humour. Ha! Blinding! Geddit?'

The next few phone calls are even less productive. The guys in question either have a thoroughly Significant Other now or a forgotten tale of horror, or – like Chris Austen – both. Reluctantly, I decide to give up. The men in my past are clearly best left there.

Three days later, I get a phone call.

I'm surprised at how much it brightens my spirits. And, call me a blundering optimist, but an attempt at a relationship – one that *doesn't* involve Henry – could be exactly the tonic I need.

Chapter 80

Paul isn't as good-looking as I remember, but that doesn't put me off: his behaviour this evening is so close to perfect he should write a textbook on dating etiquette. Since we arrived at the comedy club half an hour ago, I can't fault him; he's complimented my dress sense, enquired about my job, leaped to the bar every time I attempted to do so. He's made me feel attractive and clever when I was feeling about as irresistible as a malodorous warthog. For that, I owe him a lot.

With five minutes to go before the first act, he turns and smiles. 'I feel like an idiot, Lucy.'

'Oh. Why?'

'For not phoning you after the Grand National. You must have thought I was a prat.'

'Well . . . yes,' I agree, but without rancour.

He looks embarrassed.

'I've always had this problem with commitment,' he explains. 'Whenever a girl likes me, I feel the need to create some space – to take a breather.'

'Hey, don't worry, Paul.' I laugh gently. 'You didn't break my heart.'

'Of course.' He's unable to hide his disappointment. 'The point is, I'm over it.'

'Over what?'

'My commitment issue.'

'Oh. Well, good for you.' I don't mean to sound sarcastic. 'I mean that,' I add.

He smiles gratefully and something strikes me: Paul hasn't made a single innuendo all night. He really *has* changed. 'I'm so pleased you agreed to come out with me again tonight.'

'Good,' I shrug.

'I'd almost forgotten how stunning you were.'

I smile awkwardly and, as the lights dim, part of me is relieved not to have to think of an answer. I'm not used to men being like this around me. It's hard to put my finger on why it's happening. Could it be that the more nonchalant I am, the more take-him-or-leave-him, the more interested he becomes? Surely not.

As the compère walks on, I feel Paul's eyes on me again. When I look up, he has such a dreamy expression I feel like a Chunky Kit-Kat at a Slimming World meeting.

I turn away hastily.

I haven't been *trying* to play it cool, it's just how I feel. I like Paul – at least I think I do. But after the hoo-ha with Henry, I've struggled to get myself worked up about this date. Hence the absence of fake tan, the presence of last year's jeans with a minor stain on the front thigh, and legs as stubbly as Kurt Russell's chin.

The show ends up being a good one. The compulsory unfunny comic keeps his act mercifully short; the two amusing ones dominate proceedings.

By the time we spill out with the rest of the crowd, for once I can't decide what I want the turn of events to be.

'So,' says Paul, 'what would you like to do now?'

'I don't know. What are the options?'

'Well, we could go for a drink, or to a club – Heebie Jeebies is only down the road and my friends are there.'

He glances at my expression. 'Though, on second thoughts, maybe not.'

I smile.

'Or,' he continues tentatively, 'you'd be welcome to come over to my place. For a nightcap.'

'How about a drink?' I offer diplomatically.

'Oh. Great,' he says.

As we head to a bar, I try to work out my feelings for Paul. When he slips his hand into mine and squeezes it, it gives me a comforting glow. There's no doubt Paul wants me tonight. No doubt at all. When we get to the bar, he insists on buying the drinks again, despite my protestations.

'Do you still go to the Lake District often?' I ask when he returns.

'I do,' he replies. 'Why, would you like to do it again some time?'

I hesitate and think back to the conversation Henry and I had the night he was with Davina – when he implored me to be more honest on my dates. 'I don't think so,' I tell Paul. 'I feel silly saying this, but I may have misled you about the amount of experience I had in fell-walking.'

He smiles. 'I suspected.'

'I'm no expert – at that or anything else. I'm just me. Boring old me.'

'There's nothing boring about you, Lucy,' he says, and

before I get a chance to think, he starts moving towards me. His eyes close and his lips meet mine and I find myself looking at his face at close range as he kisses me, with the fiercest intensity in his expression.

I pull away.

'What's up, Lucy?' he asks.

'I . . .' I begin.

But I haven't got an answer. Not really. I only know that Paul isn't what I want.

Chapter 81

'How's the Jacuzzi?' I am on the phone to Mum the day after the new addition to their spare bedroom has been installed.

'Jacuzzi? That's what he told me it was too.'

'Oh. So Dad hasn't brought home a Jacuzzi?'

'No, Lucy, he hasn't. We have a ten foot by ten foot pool of water in our spare room, but it is *not* a Jacuzzi.'

'I'm confused. What is it then?'

She sighs. 'It's a birthing pool.'

'A birthing pool? As in, a pool you give birth in?'

'Correct. Just when I thought your father's taste in knock-off goods couldn't get more outlandish, he brings this home.' She doesn't sound impressed. 'Apparently they were getting rid of them at the maternity hospital where your dad's mate Robbo works as a porter. Over a thousand babies have been born in that thing. Which is a beautiful statistic – but it does shatter the vision I had of sipping martinis in it like Joan Collins.'

I hear a splash. 'I don't know what your problem is,' Dad shouts. 'It's great in here. And it's been cleaned out. You'd never have known if I hadn't told you.'

'There is a sticker on the side about what to do if your

amniotic sac breaks,' she growls. 'You must think I was born yesterday.'

I decide to change the subject. 'How's your new job going?'

'Absolutely brilliant. I love it.'

I hesitate, trying to work out if she's being sarcastic.

'Honestly,' she continues, sensing my scepticism. 'The team is great and Jasper's a fantastic boss. I can't believe how lucky I am.'

'God, you do sound enthusiastic.'

'For the first time, I feel like I've got a career ahead of me. Anyway, love, are you packed yet?'

'Not really. In fact, I'd better crack on. I'll pop round and see you at the weekend, okay?'

I put down the phone and wander into my bedroom, surveying the chaos.

'Was that your mum?' asks Henry from the hall. 'How's her new job?'

'She's enjoying herself so much I keep expecting her to break into the company song.' I pick up an old set of straighteners and take them to the hall to add to the pile. 'I can't believe how much rubbish we've accrued in four years.'

'Tell me about it,' mutters Henry, adding what appears to be half a scuba-diving kit.

'Where did you get that?' I ask.

'Mum brought it back from a field trip,' he grins. 'It caused quite a stir at Garston Leisure Centre.'

I burst out laughing.

Our charity-shop pile is now so high it resembles the peak of Borneo's Mount Kinabalu, and I'm unconvinced they'll thank us for it. It's difficult to work out which has the least appeal: my CDs – a collection of crap late-1990s albums – or Henry's textbooks.

'I'm amazed you're getting rid of that,' I say, as he adds *A Textbook of Malaria Eradication* by Emilio Pampana.

'I've got two copies.'

'What about your other books?'

'Going to my parents' place,' he shrugs.

'Their spiritual home.' Spontaneously, I feel tears prick the backs of my eyes. All morning I've been more emotional than an *X-Factor* finalist and it had to happen at some point. I studiously return to my packing.

'Feeling all right?' asks Henry softly.

'Yeah,' I sniff. 'My hay fever's playing up.'

I quickly walk to the kitchen, determined that he won't catch me crying, and begin wrapping the crockery in tea-towels.

'Lucy . . .'

Henry is standing in the doorway, his face filled with concern. My lip starts quivering.

'Oh, come here.' He steps forward to hug me. I press my face into his soft, smooth neck as tears stream down my cheeks, stinging my skin. The more I try to stop crying, the harder it is.

'I'm going to miss you, that's all,' I manage to say.

'I'm going to miss you too.' He strokes my hair. 'More than you know.'

His words make me pull back. Could he mean . . .

'But it's not as if we're going to lose touch,' he goes on. 'We'll always be friends.'

A thousand unspoken words stick in my throat and the only thing I manage to mutter is: 'Yup.'

He kisses me on the head and rubs my back. 'Now. Come on, woman, pull yourself together. You've got a beautiful apartment to move into.'

There's a knock on our front door.

'Hey, you two,' calls out Dominique, as she steps over a pile of clutter. 'Don't you have any notion of security? Someone could walk in and steal half the stuff in your flat.'

'I'd leave them a tip for taking it off our hands,' says Henry.

'I've popped over to see how my new flatmate's getting on,' says Dominique. She's looking better than she was a couple of weeks ago – not quite as immaculate as usual, but her skin is so much brighter, her hair shinier.

'Oh, fine,' I tell her. 'I'm not picking up the van until tomorrow morning, so I've still got time to get this stuff packed.'

'And what about you, Henry?' she continues. 'Are you ready for the big trip? I've just been to Erin's place and she can barely contain herself.'

'Yeah, I'm very excited, thanks,' says Henry. 'Only two days to go.'

He looks at me anxiously, to determine whether I'm still weepy. I do my best to look stoic.

'Listen, Gorgeous,' Dominique turns to me. 'I've got the keys to the flat. Do you fancy coming to have a peek? I know we're not meant to move in until tomorrow, but I can't resist.'

Chapter 82

Our new dockside apartment is everything I've ever wanted in a home: it's spacious, tastefully decorated and in a spectacular location. I wander into my bedroom, which is twice the size of my old one and five times as luxurious. It's expensive of course – though everywhere is compared with the flat Henry and I shared. It was a bargain when we found it four years ago – and even more so lately given our rent has hardly increased. As I open the balcony doors, a breeze skips across my bare arms and lifts my spirits. But it's short-lived. Even this isn't enough. I should be fizzing with excitement, but I'm not. Because I won't be living with Henry any longer. It's as simple as that.

When we've finished planning out the furniture, Dominique and I decide to stop for a drink at a bar beside the dock. We find a table from which to watch the setting sun, as concert-goers heading for the nearby arena mingle with art lovers who've come from the Tate Gallery.

'I'm going to enjoy living here,' Dominique says.

'Me too,' I agree decisively. 'How are you feeling?'

She twirls her finger around the stem of her glass. 'I'm okay, Lucy. I've promised myself I'm not going to wallow in it.'

'Good,' I reply. 'You've never struck me as a wallower. I

don't think it'd suit you.' She smiles. 'Are you still determined that you're off men?'

She looks at me and pauses. 'To be honest I haven't the energy at the moment. I'm sick of dating. I want to keep my head down for a while.'

'Justin has a lot to answer for,' I mutter crossly.

At that, her eyes mist over and she stares into her glass. I immediately regret bringing up his name. 'I'm sorry, Dom.'

'It's fine. I'm not the first girl in the world to have her heart broken.'

'I suppose not. Though being the zillionth doesn't make it hurt any less.'

'True. But you know what, Lucy? I'm not going to let this get me down. You and me – we might not have found the right men, but we're doing okay, aren't we? We've got great jobs, a great apartment . . . *and* we've got each other.'

Suddenly, I've never felt more grateful for Dominique's friendship.

'Speaking of which,' she continues, 'are you up to anything tonight?'

'Just packing.' I sigh a little. 'I'll be doing it until midnight at this rate.'

'That's a shame. Erin phoned me earlier asking if I wanted to go for a drink.'

'Oh . . . sorry.' I feel a flash of guilty relief to have an excuse not to go out with Erin.

'It's okay,' continues Dominique. 'She sounded weird anyway. I think she's nervous about leaving everything behind for a year.'

Before I get a chance to answer, a shadow is cast over our table.

'All right, sis?'

Dave is dressed from head to toe in Emporio Armani and appears to have laid off the sunbed. It's an improvement.

'Oh – hi. Have you forgiven me yet?'

He laughs, ruffles my hair and pulls up a seat. ''Course. We need to stick together when Mum's in the sort of mood she was in the other day.'

I shiver. 'She can be scary when she wants to be, can't she?'

'Just a bit. What did she call you . . . Hetty Wainthrop?'

We collapse into giggles, before I say, 'I don't think you've met Dominique. Dom, this is my brother, Dave. Dave, Dominique.'

Dominique holds out her hand and grins. 'You are *nothing* like your sister described.'

Dave shakes her hand. 'Let me guess: terminally lazy wideboy whose only interests are football, women and looking in the mirror.'

'She never mentioned the football,' Dominique replies, deadpan.

Dave chuckles, amused.

'What are you doing here?' I ask.

He gestures to a group of businessmen and women at the other side of the bar. 'I'm hosting a corporate event. We've been to an exhibition at the Tate.'

'You're joking?' I snigger. 'Don't they know the closest you've ever been to modern art was the graffiti you used to carve into your desk at school?'

'Very funny.' He takes a gulp of beer. 'Actually, I enjoyed it. Are you an art fan, Dominique?'

'I could be,' she replies.

I do a double-take at my friend and my brother. A terrible possibility bursts into my head and I almost spit out my wine.

I detect a subtle upward curve in Dominique's lips as she holds his gaze for a fraction too long. Dave's face breaks into an audacious smile as his eyes sparkle.

And I wonder if either of them knows what they're letting themselves in for.

Chapter 83

There are two new starters at work today: Peter, a sweet IT whiz whose fashion hero is Shaggy from *Scooby Doo*, and Stacey, a marketing trainee with legs that don't appear to end. It's no surprise which one Drew decides to take under his wing.

'Come on, Stacey, put me out of my misery,' he smirks. 'I've got two tickets for Kings of Leon and one has your name on it.'

'Oh,' giggles Stacey, obviously flattered. As she's new to the organization – and Drew – I can forgive her. 'I had something else on tonight, sorry.'

'Cancel it,' he instructs her. 'You won't regret it – I guarantee.'

'You *will*,' I mutter under my breath. 'I guarantee.'

I've got loads on today, not least pursuing a new client to replace *Peach Gear*. Although it's sickening that they still think I was the source of their story leak, I've accepted that they're never going to believe me. The only way to move on is to find a replacement client. I'm therefore polishing off a presentation for a meeting tomorrow with a big online fashion firm. I'm determined to make it the most persuasive piece of prose since Barack Obama's final pre-election speech.

Two letters land on my desk and, by the time I look up, Little Lynette is halfway across the office with her back to me. She's been off sick for a week and I've not heard a peep from her since she returned this morning. I'm about to return to my proposal, when Lynette takes a sharp left and sprints to the ladies. I frown, hoping someone will go after her, but quickly realize that the unperceptive buggers haven't even noticed.

Reluctantly closing my presentation, I go to check on her.

'Are you in here, Lynette?' I push open the door and scan the bottom of the cubicles.

I'm greeted by silence, then a sniff that sounds like an industrial sink unblocker.

'Lynette?' I repeat.

The door of the end cubicle creaks open.

I find Lynette sitting on the loo seat in tears. When she looks up, she's rubbing her beautifully made-up eyes so much they look like two great chunks of charcoal.

'Don't tell anyone I'm here, will you, Lucy?' She attempts to wipe away mascara, but succeeds only in disconnecting her false eyelashes.

'Of course not,' I reassure her. 'What's going on?'

She beckons me in and makes me shut the cubicle door. 'You know my new man?' she says huskily.

'Yes?'

'Well, he dumped me.'

I crouch down and hold her hand. 'Oh Lynette, that's awful. I'm so sorry.'

'Worse than that, Lucy, he used me. He thought nothing of me. He used me to his own h-horrible ends.'

I frown. 'I'm sure that's not true.'

'It *is*. Because I'd fancied him for so long, I couldn't see it.

380

Now, not only has he dumped me, but because of me, someone really nice is in trouble. Someone who doesn't deserve to be.'

I try to console her.

'Listen,' I continue softly, 'whatever's happened, I'm sure—'

'It's Drew,' she interrupts.

I stop momentarily to see if I've heard right. 'What's Drew?'

'Drew was my new man.'

'But . . . he's an *arse*.' I spit out the word.

'I know that now,' she whimpers. 'Now he's out there flirting with Stacey.'

'Oh dear.' I'm genuinely shocked by this. Little Lynette has never been the sharpest tool in the box, but I always believed her flirtation with Drew was nothing more than that.

'I thought he really liked me,' she sobs, 'but all he wanted me for was . . .'

'Sex?' I finish for her.

'No, actually,' she says, to my surprise. Then: 'Oh Lucy, I'm so sorry.'

'What on earth for?'

She hides her face with her hand. 'You know that report you asked me to get bound professionally?'

My throat tightens. 'The *Peach Gear* strategy?'

'I didn't think it'd do any harm showing it to him,' she babbles. 'He said he only wanted to take a copy of one of the logos . . . If I'd known the consequences . . . God, Lucy, I feel like killing myself.'

I stand up, jaw clenched. 'Not as much as I feel like killing Drew.'

Drew could tell I knew, the second he saw my face. And despite his denials, now I've got him by myself in a meeting room, his body language couldn't be more of a giveaway if he had big flashing lights.

'Lynette said *what*? I don't know what she's talking about,' he sneers, as if the mere suggestion of impropriety is absurd. 'The little slag's bitter because I dumped her. Now, get out of my way, you silly, stuck-up bitch, and let me get back to work.'

He tries to push past me to get to the door, but I refuse to move.

'There's no point denying it,' I tell him, crossing my arms. 'Lynette told me everything. The only thing I don't know is why. Why did you do it, Drew?'

'You're insane,' he replies. Then he steps back and accidentally bangs his head on one of the framed cuttings on the wall. He's clearly rattled.

I go on. 'Do you despise me so much that you'd try to bring down my career – out of spite?'

'This is a tedious conversation.'

'Or was there another motive?'

'This whole thing is ridiculous and I resent these preposterous allegations.'

'Come on.' I stand my ground. 'Cough up. What possible reason would you have to leak a piece of information like that to the *Gazette* when—'

I'm halfway through my sentence when, for a reason I can't fathom, I find myself scanning the cuttings on the wall: they consist of frame upon frame of Peaman-Brown-generated publicity. The ones Roger considers to be our best. There are loads of examples from Dominique, Stephen, Emma and Douglas and – if I do say so myself – me. Everyone has at least a few articles up there. Everyone except Drew. He has only one: the Ernst Sumner story that appeared in the *Gazette* in the same week as the *Peach Gear* débâcle.

'Oh my God,' I say, beginning to see the light.

'What?' snaps Drew, as his forehead starts to glisten with sweat.

'You did a swap,' I say accusingly. 'You gave them the scoop about *Peach Gear* in return for them printing your crappy story about Ernst Sumner. A story you'd spent months trying to get in print, without success – until it mysteriously appeared in the same week as the *Peach Gear* story, that is.'

He looks out of the window as if he can't hear me.

'Drew, do you know how serious this is?' I continue, exasperated. 'Forget our petty rivalry: you risked the reputation of one of this company's biggest clients to get one poxy story in the paper.'

He glares at me. 'They were going to sack us,' he whines.

'Whose fault was that?' I demand. 'They had no coverage because you didn't manage to get any legitimately. The answer isn't to go trampling on the other clients.'

He says nothing and I wonder for a second if I've finally shamed him.

'I'll never admit it,' he whispers. 'And you'll never prove it.'

'*She doesn't have to.*'

When I spin round, Roger's at the door. The expression on his face is one I've never seen before: it's like thunder, which is quite an achievement for someone who's often mistaken for Bill Oddie.

'Lucy – perhaps you could give Drew and me a couple of minutes.'

I glance at Drew. His jaw is twitching, but he remains defiant.

As I leave the room, I close the door and head to my desk. I reopen my presentation and try to focus on it, but within five minutes, Dominique appears.

'What's going on with you and Drew? I saw you drag him to the meeting room and wondered from the look on your face if he'd make it out of there alive.'

'*I'm* the least of his worries,' I say quietly. 'Roger's in with him now. God knows what he's going to—'

'Lucy, could you pop over here, please?' Roger is heading into his office.

I glance at the meeting room where he was with Drew. The door's open but I can't see if he's still in there.

'Of course,' I say, standing and heading towards him as he emerges from his office with his jacket in his hand. 'Um . . . have you finished with Drew?'

Roger snorts. 'You could say that. Come on, let's go for a coffee. I want to make you an offer. One I should have made a long time ago.'

Chapter 84

Our final night out is a jubilant affair for most of the group. Erin and her friends – Darren, James and Amanda – are bursting with excitement about the start of the trip. Dominique has spent the evening demanding to know *everything* about my brother (so far, I've revealed that his feet smell worse than a recently-deceased bear's bum, but it appears not to have put her off). And Henry, entirely reasonably, is brimming with as much anticipation as the others. If he has second thoughts, he's not showing it.

As for me, I'm making a fair-to-average job of looking happy. Which is an achievement. Because I feel as if I'm having a bad dream and can't wake up. I feel as if I'm in a hang-glider heading for a mountain. I feel . . . like crap. Sorry. It's difficult to be poetic when you're this upset.

'Have some taramasalata, Lucy,' says Darren, as he pushes the bowl towards me. 'You've hardly eaten a thing.'

'Oh, thanks.' I take a scoop of bubblegum-coloured dip and begin picking at it with a pitta bread. Everyone agrees that it's the most delicious dish outside Lesbos. I feel as if I'm forcing cement down my throat.

'Just think,' says Amanda, 'this time next week we'll be in

Budapest, eating goulash and drinking . . . whatever they drink in Hungary.'

'They're big on dessert wine,' Henry tells her. 'I think it's called *Tokay*.'

'I've never liked sweet wine,' Erin frowns. 'I'll stick to the beer.'

'They're good at that too,' Henry adds. He catches my eye for a second and it sends a bolt of lightning through my chest. I look away quickly and try to look like I'm relishing a dollop of tsatziki.

'Make us jealous, why don't you?' Dominique nudges Henry. 'Lucy and I are stuck here while you lot jet off to these exotic places.'

'You're welcome to join us,' grins Darren. 'There's always room for two more ladies.'

'Oh God!' groans Amanda. 'Someone hold him down. He never could resist a blonde, Dominique.'

'My kind of man then,' she winks. 'Thanks for the invitation, but I made a vow years ago never to stay anywhere with less than four stars. Which I believe counts out some of the places on your itinerary. I'd get a nose-bleed on entry.'

The wine flows freely through the night and, the merrier the group becomes, the further into despair I sink. I can barely look at Henry. I convince myself that, unless I keep my head down, he'll guess. About my fierce, brilliant and terrible love for him, a love I fight every day – and lose.

At one point Erin leans over to pick up an olive and Henry smiles tenderly at her. Tears prick into my eyes and I panic that I'll have to leave the room.

'I believe congratulations are in order, Lucy,' says Amanda. 'Erin said you've got a new job.'

Roger promoted me. After the scene he witnessed with Drew, he says he finally realized how much he appreciated me. A few months ago, I'd have been ecstatic about this. Now I can hardly bring myself to care.

'Yes, I'm an Account Director now,' I tell her. 'So I've got a team of my own – and I'll be on the management board.'

'Nice pay rise?' asks Darren.

I nod.

'No one deserves it more than Lucy,' adds Dominique, grabbing another piece of pitta. 'It's about time Roger acknowledged what an asset she is.'

As the waiter comes over to pour some wine, Dominique turns to me and says quietly, 'I can't believe what a conniving little shit Drew was, though. I know you and he were never the best of friends, but to stitch you up like that . . . honestly, I was stunned.'

'Hmmm.'

'It's a shame he got to quit of his own accord and skulk away without any of us noticing,' she muses. 'I'd have liked to see him fired and marched out by security.'

'We don't have security.'

'I know – more's the pity. Still, it amounts to the same thing: he's out of the picture.'

'Hmmm.'

'Well, for goodness sake,' she turns to me, looking exasperated. 'You've been promoted, woman. And you no longer have to sit opposite Drew watching him massage his bits. You should be over the moon.'

I smile. 'I am. Honestly. I've got a headache, that's all.'

Dominique is about to respond, when I realize my phone is ringing. I remove it from my bag and see that it's Dave. Given that he never phones me, my first suspicion is that he's after Dominique's number.

'Hi. Let me guess . . .' I stand and move to the door so I can hear him better.

'Lucy—' He sounds out of breath. 'You're going to have to come.'

'What?'

'It's Mum and Dad. The house is on fire, Lucy. The bloody house is on fire.'

Chapter 85

Henry abandons the car outside Mum and Dad's house and we leap out. The air is thick with smoke and fear as neighbours with grey faces huddle among themselves. There are fire-fighters everywhere, running and shouting. I stand in front of the house and struggle to breathe as flames roar from three windows and smoke billows into the night sky.

'Where are they?'

'Still in there,' Dave croaks, his eyes heavy with tears. 'I tried to go in, but the hall's filled with smoke and . . .'

Instinctively, I rush towards the house, but Henry pulls me back.

'Let the experts do this, Lucy.' He wraps his arms around me tightly as fire-fighters equipped with breathing apparatus head in.

Orders are shouted and soon the house is being doused with foam and water. I feel a rush of hope at the fact that something bold and decisive is being done. But it doesn't matter how much the men attempt to quench the fire – after a few moments the flames continue, taunting us with their unremitting energy.

Time stands still as Henry, Dave and I wait helplessly outside the house with heat stinging our eyes. My panic worsens as the realization that there's nothing I can do about this seeps over me like a dark shadow.

'I can't cope with this, Henry,' I sob as I lean into his chest, desperate for his embrace to somehow make this go away. 'I can't cope.'

Dave stands next to us, his hand over his face.

'They're definitely in there?' I ask for the sixth time.

'I've tried both their mobiles over and over,' he replies. 'There's no answer.'

A figure emerges at the doorway. As it comes closer, barely recognizable through the smoke, I run forward.

'Dad!' I shout in desperation.

But it's not Dad.

It's a fireman, one who went in earlier. He's joined seconds later by his colleague who emerges from the house, blackened and defeated.

'Any luck?' I ask, and he shakes his head.

'Oh God!' I scream.

I turn to Dave and fall into his arms. My brother and I weep like never before as shock envelops us.

'Lucy.' Henry touches my shoulder. But I can't answer him. I can't move or think.

'*Lucy.*' He has hold of my arm, prising me away.

I try to look up, but can't. 'What?' I sob.

'Look.'

I lift my tear-soaked face from my brother's shoulder.

'There.' Henry points to the door.

As we peer through the smoke, I detect movement in the doorway. At first it's impossible to make out; an outline in the distance. It could be nothing.

Only, it's not: it's the shadow of a person . . . no, two people – one carrying the other. As the figure staggers forward, hope rises in my chest. A fire-fighter *might* have saved her. At least then we wouldn't have lost both of them.

Oh, please God, make that be it. Make that be it.

'Jesus Christ,' mutters Dave. 'Is that . . .?'

'It can't be . . .' I add.

Then the blurred outline becomes clear.

Dad has Mum in his arms, her body draped across him lifelessly. We rush forward, beaten by the paramedics as Dad falls to his knees. Mum is conscious, but only just.

'See to Carolyn first,' Dad wheezes as the paramedics get to work. 'Please. See to my wife.'

As Mum is lifted onto a stretcher, Dad leans over and clasps her hand. He bends down and presses his lips against hers.

Mum opens her eyes and coughs painfully. 'Thank you,' she manages.

'What for?' whispers Dad.

'Saving my life,' she croaks.

He smiles, wiping his face with a greasy sleeve. 'I *love* you, Carolyn. I know I don't say it often, but I do.'

She nods and closes her eyes again, looking peaceful. My heart surges. Mum . . . Oh God, Mum . . .

One eye reopens then and she fixes it on Dad. 'You know next time you want to prove it? Try some flowers instead, won't you?'

Chapter 86

Henry has popped out to the newsagent, like he always does on his days off. Except this isn't a normal day off.

His bags are by the door, packed and ready for his departure in an hour. I am supposed to go with him to the airport to see him off, but when I woke this morning I knew I couldn't go through with it. I wouldn't be able to watch him and Erin head off together without bursting into tears and giving the game away.

Taking a notepad and pen from my bag, I start writing as quickly as I can. I haven't got long until he returns.

Henry,

Sorry I didn't get to go with you to the airport, but if I don't make visiting hours at nine-thirty, I won't see Mum – and she needs me more than you after what happened. I know you'll understand, under the circumstances. Have an amazing trip – but don't forget about me, will you? I'll miss you loads – and I wasn't joking about wanting a postcard from every destination. Don't let me down!

Lots of love

Lucy xxx

My Single Friend

I fold the note and place it on the doormat so he'll see it as soon as he walks in. Then, grabbing a sweater, I head out of the door and make straight for my car. I reach for the door handle and glance up – at exactly the moment Henry turns the corner at the end of the road, newspaper in hand.

I look away, pretending not to see him, and leap into my car. Without looking back, I shove the key into the ignition, put the car in gear and hurtle away. Out of Henry's life.

Chapter 87

Considering my mother was staring death in the face eighteen hours ago, she's looking remarkably chipper.

'Typical, isn't it?' She unwraps a chocolate and pops it in her mouth. 'Everyone in *Dynasty* had a Jacuzzi – and none of their houses burned down.'

Dominique smiles and offers me the half-empty tin of Cadbury's Roses.

'No, thanks,' I say quietly.

'I suppose Krystle Carrington wasn't swimming around in a piece of maternity apparatus,' Mum continues.

She must be made of stronger stuff than me. While she's happily stuffing her face with chocolate, I feel as if I've been hit on the head with the plate of a steam iron.

It's not just the aftermath of the fire – though that alone could leave me shell-shocked until 2020. My mind is also spinning with thoughts of Henry, who's now en route to Manchester Airport, filled with hopes and dreams about the next twelve months.

I hope he's not too annoyed with me for sneaking off, but then I did have a good excuse, even though visiting hours don't really start until eleven-thirty. Good job Dominique managed to bribe the nurses with half of Mum's Roses to let us in early.

'There aren't many chocolates left in here,' she grumbles, unwrapping a green triangle. 'Who'd you buy them from – your father?'

I wouldn't be surprised if Henry proposed to Erin while they're away. That's what happens on trips like these, they're life-changing. The thought makes me sick to my stomach.

'I *love* your flowers,' enthuses Dominique. On the table next to Mum's bed is a floral display fit for a royal wedding.

'They're from Jasper. He doesn't do things by halves.'

'I want a boss like that,' says Dominique.

Mum grins. 'After twenty-one years of cleaning toilets, I've earned him.'

'Was it definitely the Jacuzzi that caused the fire?' I ask.

'Looks that way.' Mum bites into a hazelnut whirl. 'It'd been set up wrongly, causing a leak in the corner and they think it got to the electrics in the house. The fire service will do a report but that's the theory so far.'

'You're remarkably chilled out, Mum,' I point out. The doctor told me earlier that he thinks she's still suffering from shock. Even with a medical explanation for her coolness, she's freaking me out.

'I'm alive, aren't I?' she shrugs. 'There's nothing like facing the Grim Reaper and telling him to sling his hook to put things in perspective.'

'But what about the house?' I say tentatively. I don't want to upset her.

'Look, part of me is gutted about the house – we've lived there since we were married. But it was hardly the stuff of *Country Life.*'

'Still. You *are* technically homeless.' I say this gently because Mum's got to come to terms with this sooner or later. She doesn't look any less cheerful.

'Well, you'll put us up for a few months, won't you? I'm sure the insurance would pay for a hotel, but they're so faceless . . .'

My eyes widen. I'm overjoyed my parents are alive, but I'd rather not have them squatting in my living room. 'I'll have to have a chat with Dominique about that. There are only two bedrooms.'

'We'll sort something out,' says Dominique, and I can't help admiring her compassion. Or naivety.

There's a knock on the door and when we turn to look, it's Dad. He's wearing a pair of hospital pyjamas that, uniquely, are an improvement on his own. In his case, there's no doubt that last night's events have sunk in. Although physically the doctors say he'll make a full recovery, he looks grey and drawn. Still, as he walks forward, he produces a bunch of flowers from behind his back. They're a quarter of the size of Jasper's, but it doesn't matter.

'I never thought I'd see the day,' Mum says, taking the bouquet and sticking her nose in a hydrangea.

He pauses, with tears in his eyes. 'I'm so sorry, love.'

'About what?' asks Mum.

'About the birthing pool. It's all my fault. All my bloody fault.'

Mum frowns and I notice her eyes welling up. 'Oh, give us a kiss, you soft sod,' she says, drawing him near. 'You saved my life, didn't you?'

Dom and I exchange a look and decide to back out of the room.

Dad spots us and straightens his back. 'Don't worry, I'm not stopping,' he says. 'I've got my consultant coming over in a couple of minutes so I just popped in to drop off the flowers. I'll see you all properly later.'

And with that, he's off. My dad, the hero. Sort of.

'How long have you been married?' asks Dominique.

'Thirty-one years,' says Mum, propping up one of Dad's wilted flowers.

'You're a good advert for it,' Dominique says, 'and I never thought I'd be saying that. Not that Lucy or I have had much luck with our love-lives lately – eh, Luce?'

Mum peers at me. 'You still haven't told Henry then?'

My face flushes.

'Told Henry what?' asks Dominique.

'Thank you, Mother,' I sigh. 'Very discreet.'

'Discreet? Discretion isn't what you need – it's action. Have you told him or haven't you?'

'Well, I—'

'Told him what?' repeats Dominique.

'I . . . look, nothing.'

'Lucy,' says Mum sternly. 'When does he fly off on his round-the-world trip?'

I look down at my hands. 'Today. Now. He'll be on his way to the airport.'

'What do you need to tell Henry?' Dominique just won't let it go.

'I . . . well—'

'Tell her, Lucy,' says Mum. 'Go on.'

'Tell me *what?*' snaps Dominique, who's had enough of all this.

'She's in love with him.' Mum crosses her arms. 'Our Lucy is in love with Henry.'

Chapter 88

Dominique is shrieking so loudly the patients at the other end of the corridor must think she's undergoing an amputation.

'Why didn't you tell me, for God's sake?'

'I . . . I don't know,' I stutter. 'I didn't want to compromise your friendship with Erin, for a start.'

'How?' she asks, incredulous.

'Erin's in love with Henry, like you said. Even if I was going to be a bitch and try to steal him – which I'm *not* – what good would come of telling you? It'd just lumber you with information you'd be powerless to act on.'

'*Arrrggh!*' Dominique rubs her hands over her face. 'What a mess.'

'I know,' I say.

'I don't mean about you and Henry,' she says impatiently. 'Though I grant you, that is quite a mess.'

'What then?'

She sighs and look out of the window. 'You know when I said I thought Erin was in love with Henry?'

I nod.

'I was wrong.'

It takes a second for her words to sink in. 'What?'

'She *likes* Henry,' she clarifies. 'I mean, everyone likes Henry, but . . .'

'But what?'

Dominique comes right out with it. 'But she's got the hots for Darren.'

'*Darren?*'

Dominique nods. 'You know when we stopped off for a drink after we visited the flat and I said Erin had sounded funny on the phone?'

'You thought it was nerves.'

'It wasn't nerves,' she confesses. 'It was lust. She's been in turmoil about what to do.'

I frown. 'I knew Erin had the hots for Darren while they were at university, but that was ages ago. She told me it was history.'

'Yeah, well, her feelings have been reignited.'

'*But what about Henry?*' I have to stop myself from screaming it. 'He's set off on a round-the-world trip with Erin thinking everything's hunky-dory.'

Dominique makes a tsking sound. 'You're missing something, Lucy.'

'What?'

She looks at me as if it's obvious. 'There is no way Henry would have chosen Erin had he thought there was a chance with you. Erin's always known that. Maybe, subconsciously, that's why she turned her attention to Darren: self-preservation.'

I'm astonished. 'What on earth makes you think that?'

'It's *obvious*,' Dominique sighs. 'Where do I start? The way he looks at you. The way he tries to protect you. The way – just, the way he *is* with you. He's had a twenty-year crush, Lucy.'

I sit down, trying to stop my head spinning. 'You never said this before.'

'I assumed you knew. How can you *not* know?' Dominique looks exasperated.

I shake my head. 'It can't be true. Why would he bugger off round the world if it was?'

'Because he thinks the feeling isn't mutual,' she replies. 'We *all* thought the feeling wasn't mutual.'

'You're wrong, Dominique. You were wrong about Erin being in love with him and you're wrong about this.'

'I admit I was wrong about Erin, but there is no way I've misread Henry's feelings. I've known it for as long as I've known you both. You're the love of his life, Lucy.'

'I've meen trying to dell her,' Mum interjects. She has at least three chocolates in her mouth and looks like a greedy chipmunk.

Then she swallows and goes on: 'Well, haven't I? Lucy, you're the only one who won't believe it.'

I turn to the window, my heart and my mind racing as fast as each other.

Could it be true?

Could Henry really be in love with me?

'Right, Lucy.' Dominique looks at her watch. 'You've got one hour and fifty minutes before Henry's plane takes off. So here's the question. What *exactly* are you going to do about this?'

Chapter 89

I am normally the safest driver I know. In fact, I'm an old woman behind the wheel, resolutely sticking to the speed-limit and, more than often, below it.

But with the needle on my speed-dial touching a perilous 73 m.p.h. – look, I *said* I was no Lewis Hamilton – I belt along the M56, leaving a Nissan Micra, two heavy goods vehicles and a six-berth caravan in the dust.

My heart break-dances against my ribcage as a thousand corny movie scenes flip through my mind. Lovers running with open arms. Floaty-haired women being spun around. Kisses that go on for ever. Cue a Leona Lewis ballad . . .

I flick on my indicator and turn onto a slip-road.

Problem is, this reunion isn't going to be straightforward. First, there's Erin. Whether she fancies Darren or not, there's protocol to consider. Call me old-fashioned, but declaring your love for someone else's boyfriend isn't the done thing. Yet, that's exactly what I'm about to do, with God knows what consequences.

Then there's the man himself. Whatever Mum and Dominique say, whatever I want to believe, the only conclusive proof that Henry loves me would be if he told me so. So far, he's said nothing of the sort – and that doesn't fill me with confidence.

Despite this, there's one thing I can't disagree with: enough is enough. I can procrastinate no longer, hesitate no more. Whatever happens today, Henry *must* be told the truth . . .

'OHMYGOD!' I gasp. 'OHMYGODOHMYGODDD!'

I am sailing past an exit sign marked *Manchester Airport.*

Which means I am sailing past the exit for Manchester Airport.

Which means . . . oh Christ: I'm not going to make it!

Wailing in frustration, I beat the steering-wheel with my fist.

'YOU STUPID WOMAN, LUCY!' I howl as tears of desperation blur my vision. 'YOU STUPID COW!'

I glance through the side window and the passengers in a Fiat Punto are staring at me as if they suspect I've dabbled with psychedelic drugs.

'I'M A STUPID COW!' I yell, trying to explain. They look even more worried.

I spend five minutes shouting obscenities and frantically searching for the next exit. When I reach it, I swerve into it, cut up the driver in front and push my way to the lights at the roundabout.

Panting and sweating, I glance at the clock. One hour to take-off. I can still do this.

The lights change to green and I slam my foot on the accelerator, whizzing round the roundabout until I'm back on the motorway, heading to the airport again.

My brain is on overload, but there is no way I'm going to miss the exit this time. I flick on my indicator and speed along a road signposted *Departures.* I abandon my car outside the doors, leaving on my hazard lights and other passengers tutting in disapproval as they battle with their luggage.

I vault over a crash barrier in the departure lounge, push through a throng of youngsters wearing *Ripley Junior Swimming Team* sweatshirts and elbow through a scrum of people clustered round a flight information board.

The first stop on Henry's trip is Madrid and, as I scan the board, I feel a stab of hope when I see a stack of delays. If Henry's is one of them, I'll be able to get to him. Then I spot the line: *CFKHH to Madrid – go to check-in desk number 32.*

My stomach does a triple somersault with pike: *they're still checking in!*

I race to the desk and am confronted by the sort of queue you'd find outside a bread shop in Bolshevik Russia. I start at the front, scanning faces. But after five minutes of sprinting up and down – and recognizing no one – I am forced to accept that they're not here.

Then I get a brainwave. I dive to the front, ignoring the conspicuous looks of displeasure.

'Sorry,' I plead. 'This is life or death. *Really.*'

'I've heard that before,' says the bloke at the front. 'Go on, get on with it.'

At the check-in desk, I am greeted by a surly bottle-blonde who'd easily fit in as a meeter and greeter on Death Row.

'Passport,' she demands, typing randomly into her computer.

'I haven't got one.'

She reaches up to the desk, refusing to make eye-contact, and feels around with her hand.

She looks up.

'Passport,' she repeats sullenly.

'I haven't got one,' I say again.

She frowns as if I am the worst thing to have happened to her all year. 'What?'

'Well, I do have one but I don't have it with me. The point is—'

'You want to fly to Madrid, but you haven't got your passport?'

'Actually I *don't* want to fly to Madrid, I want to know if my friend has checked i—'

'Where's your ticket?' she interrupts.

'I haven't got one of those either because I don't—'

'E-ticket reference number?'

'No. You see, I don't want to fly.'

'You want to fly to Madrid, but you don't have a passport or ticket or e-ticket reference number?'

'*I don't want to fly to Madrid!*' I shriek.

She looks at me, taken aback. 'If you're going to take that tone, madam, I'll call security. This airport has a strict policy on abuse – verbal and physical – towards its staff. Look.'

She points at a notice above her head that says: *This airport has a strict policy on abuse – verbal and physical – towards its staff.*

'Sorry,' I reply, hiding my frustration. '*I* don't want to fly to Madrid, but the man I'm in love with is about to. All I want to know is whether he's checked in. Because if he has, I'm screwed. But if he hasn't, then I can go and declare my undying love for him.'

She looks lost. 'Let me get this straight. You *don't* want to fly to Madrid?'

I try to stay calm. 'No.'

'All you want is to know whether another passenger has checked in?'

Finally. 'Yes.'

She turns away and starts typing something into her computer again. Eventually, she turns back to me.

'I'm not at liberty to give out that information.'

'What?' I say.

'I'm not at liberty to—'

'I heard you . . . but why?'

'Data protection. Terrorism. You name it.'

'Do I look like a terrorist?' I ask.

'What does a terrorist look like?'

I stand there, wondering what to do next.

'Please,' I whisper. '*Please* let me know. If ever you've been in love with somebody, then you'll understand why I need to know. Please. His name is Henry Fox.'

She looks into my eyes. Then returns to her computer.

She leans towards me, her face hard as nails. 'If you tell anyone . . .' she hisses.

'I *swear*,' I tell her, deciding she's my new best friend.

She goes back to her computer and types something in again.

'He's already gone through,' she says. 'Sorry.'

Chapter 90

I try to think of an ingenious method to get through security, but after an infuriating conversation with another official, I'm forced to accept that the measures to combat global terrorism are also enough to scupper a slightly unfit twenty-eight-year-old PR woman.

With increasing determination, I decide to buy a ticket to Madrid, so I can get through the security gates. But after another episode at the sales desk, the fact that my passport is in a box in south Liverpool is clearly a show-stopper.

I stand in the airport concourse as most of the western world seems to be heading off on holiday and take out my phone. I'd wanted to do this in person, but now I've no choice. Closing my eyes, I wait for it to ring.

It goes straight to voicemail.

'OH GODDD!' I cry, but nobody notices.

Despite it being the last thing I want to do, I pull up Erin's number.

It goes straight to voicemail.

'OH GODDD! I cry. Again, nobody notices.

For forty minutes, I pace up and down, trying to come up with a plan so brilliant it deserves recognition by the

Nobel Prize committee. No matter how hard I try, it doesn't happen.

I look at my watch for what must be the seven-hundredth time today and it is eleven forty-five. Henry's flight has gone and so has he.

My head is fuzzy with disbelief as I slump through the crowd and back through the doors. Numbly, I head to my car with tears biting the skin on my cheeks. I reach the spot where I parked my car in a daze and take out my car keys. Then I realize: my car isn't there.

I look up to see a tow truck pulling it away. And I don't even bother chasing after it.

Chapter 91

By the time I've tracked down the company that towed my car, taken a taxi to the compound, waited in a queue, filled out a rainforest of paperwork, paid the fine and retrieved my car, it is mid-afternoon.

The fine is astronomical: the equivalent of food bills for a month, pension contributions for two months or – most distressingly – a third of a pair of strappy sandals from Gina.

Under normal circumstances, I'd be fizzing with pique about this, but today the thought evaporates from my brain as fast as it appeared. The drive home feels as if I'm in a computer game: a hazy, unreal world that I struggle to focus on. The only issue in my head is Henry – and why I didn't say anything sooner. Why I didn't *do* anything sooner.

I know that, technically, I could phone him in Madrid, but it feels way too late. He's gone. How could I ring him to say, 'Sorry I've not mentioned this in twenty years but I'm in love with you. If it's not too much trouble, could you hop on a plane home and spend the rest of your life with me?'

I pull into the garage beneath our new flat and there is an empty feeling in my stomach telling me that I should eat. But I've never felt less hungry. I traipse up to the apartment, pausing to gaze through the stairwell window. The dock is bustling with people soaking up the sunshine and thoroughly enjoying themselves. It's a concept that feels totally alien today.

I get to the apartment and push in my key, prising open the door.

It's then that I spot the envelope.

Chapter 92

There's one word on the front: 'Lucy'. Seeing my name written in Henry's distinctive handwriting makes me gasp. With my heart racing, I fumble to open it and head for the balcony. I sink into a chair, scanning the letter, unable to devour its contents fast enough.

Dear Lucy,

I've written this letter in my mind more times than I can count. Yet, putting pen to paper is even more difficult than I thought. This is the eighth draft and I'm still not entirely happy. I thought about quoting poetry or literature, but nothing seems to explain the situation, so it's down to me instead. There's one problem: what do you say to a woman you've been in love with your entire life?

From the moment I met you, Lucy, I've felt enriched. Life has been happier, deeper, immeasurably more fun. Quite simply, you are the best person I've ever known. The best.

For a long time, my feelings have gone beyond friendship but I think – or hope – I've done a decent job of keeping them to myself. I've always known the romantic love I felt wasn't

410

reciprocated and I could live with that. Being your friend has been no poor substitute – in fact, it's been a privilege.

It was because of our friendship that I've never dared to reveal how I feel. But there comes a point when you can't pretend any longer. That's why I'm leaving, Lucy. As much as it's torturing me, that's the real reason I'm going on this trip. My hope is that, when I return, enough time will have passed for me to look at you as you look at me: through the eyes of a friend.

That said, if there's one thing Project Henry has taught me, it's to take a few risks. So I couldn't leave without letting you know what I've concealed for my entire adult life.

I love you.

There, it's out: three unspoken words that have been on the tip of my tongue for as long as I can remember. I can't imagine what you'll think when you read them. Will you think I've gone mad? Or just that I'm sad? Or maybe (I hope) you'll be happy that I love you – The Real You.

Sorry to bring up The Real You again. I don't mean to get the last word. But you already know I think you should let her get out more – she's a more amazing person than you'll ever know.

Henry xxx

I read the letter over and over again, unable to catch my breath, my cheeks wet and raw. Finally, I stumble to the bathroom, where I stare into the mirror at my mess of a face.

'God, you've screwed up, Lucy Tyler.' Saying it out loud makes it feel gratifyingly harsh. 'The love of your life has been in front of your nose for twenty years and you've never

411

noticed. Worse than that . . . he loves you! He loves you, but he's buggered off round the world – *to try to get over you*.'

I unravel a piece of loo roll and hold it to my nose, which is so red it looks as if it's been sandpapered. I am mid-blow when I hear something.

Knocking.

I stop and gawp at myself.

Dominique had her keys this morning and the only other people who know my new address are Mum and Dad, who are still in hospital.

Could it be . . .

Of course it couldn't. He's on the plane, the woman at the airport said so. Get a grip on reality, Lucy. Stop fantasizing and act like an adult.

The knocking starts again.

Despite myself, my heart is hammering as I head to the door.

It *cannot* be Henry. It's not possible.

I take a deep breath and open the door.

Chapter 93

The second I see him I am struck by how handsome Henry is, how irresistibly sexy. I'm looking at a man who, thanks to *Project Henry*, is the ultimate manifestation of female desire, who turns heads wherever he goes.

But that's not why I love him. It's not the clothes or haircut, the body or face.

The Henry I love is the funny, clever, loyal and lovely person I met all those years ago. *That's* the Henry I long for; the Henry I can't spend another day without. The trimmings are irrelevant.

'Hello, Lucy.'

He smiles and it sends a surge of hope through my veins, turning my legs to blancmange and killing my ability to speak.

'Are you okay?'

'Yes. I . . . yes.' Emotion rushes through me and my heartbeat gallops in my chest, thundering in my ears. 'Just surprised to see you.'

'And . . . happy?'

I nod, tears clouding my eyes. 'Very happy,' I croak.

He looks at my hands, clutching his letter. 'You got my note then.'

I nod again.

'So, was it a surprise? What I said?'

'Yes. No. I don't know.'

Oh brilliant, Lucy. 'Why are you here?' I manage. 'I thought you'd be on the plane.'

'I'm supposed to be. But I got a phone call after I'd gone through security that put a different take on things.'

'A phone call?'

'From Dominique.'

I swallow.

'She told me a few things that at first I didn't believe. I thought it was her idea of a joke.'

'What did she tell you?'

He looks into my eyes. 'She told me that my feelings, the feelings I explained in my letter . . . She told me that you felt . . .'

'Exactly the same?' I offer.

He breaks into an enormous smile, illuminating his face. 'It took me a while to believe her. In fact, I'm still not sure I believe her. But I couldn't get on the plane without finding out. So – here I am.'

I hear myself giggling with hysteria and sheer, unconditional joy. It feels ridiculous but I can't help it.

'Here you are,' I whisper. 'God, Henry, I'm so glad.'

Unable to hold back, I fling myself towards him and he wraps his arms around me. They are powerful and muscular, pulling my waist into his so our bodies are pressed resolutely together.

We kiss breathlessly as I close my eyes and feel his sumptuous lips melt into mine. His tongue is warm and soft, his breath sweet. As a storm gathers in my insides, I submit to his embrace. We kiss in a way friends aren't supposed to – and we do it for I don't know how long, right here in my new hall. He explores my mouth, kisses the skin behind my ear, caresses the nape of my neck with the smooth pads of his fingertips.

Then he grabs my hand and brings it to his lips, kissing the underside of my wrist. He kisses my palms, my knuckles, the bony bit at the bottom of my arm. Our fingers entwine and he gazes into my eyes. I'm overwhelmed. Then something strikes me. I don't want to ruin the moment by bringing it up, but I have to.

'What about Erin?'

He takes a deep breath. 'Erin and I have had a chat. A brief chat, admittedly – but that was all it took. Erin's going to be fine.'

'Oh?'

'When Dominique spoke to me, she told me to ask Erin about Darren.'

'Ah,' I say.

'It was never serious between Erin and me, Lucy – you know that, surely.'

'I *didn't* know that.'

'I think we've done Erin a favour,' he says. 'I left her and Darren reminiscing about university in the airport bar. I'd put money on them getting together before they finish touring Europe.'

I feel a sudden urge to lean in and kiss him again. As my lips meet his, he takes me by surprise and sweeps me into his arms.

'Henry, what are you doing?' I giggle. 'I must weigh the equivalent of half a blue whale.'

'I promise you, Lucy, you *don't*,' he grins, kicking open the bedroom door. 'A small Orca at most.'

'Oh thank you,' I say in mock indignation. 'And here's me thinking you really *were* in love with me.'

He flings me onto the bed and climbs above me, pinning me down.

'I really *am* in love with you.'

I smile. 'Glad to hear it. Because I'm not sure what I'd have done if you weren't.'

'Does that mean you're willing to make a go of it?' he asks, between kisses. 'With a geek like me?'

I grab his T-shirt and pull him towards me. 'More than willing,' I whisper. 'But what about you? Are you willing to make a go of it with The Real Me?'

He smiles. 'I always said The Real You was my kind of girl.'

Epilogue

If anyone had told me six months ago that Dominique and Dave would become an item I'd have questioned their mental stability. She's sophisticated, intelligent and witty. He farts like a flatulent camel and is as refined as crude oil.

Yet they got together two weeks after the fire, when Dominique expressed a sudden and mysterious desire to join me when I popped round to Dave's to loan him my *Gavin and Stacey* DVDs. I stayed for fifteen minutes. Dominique was there for three days.

Her theory is that I'm blind to Dave's charms because he's my brother. That he's fun, loving, amusing and attentive. She also tried to tell me that he's great in bed but I stuck my fingers in my ears and went 'lalalalalala' until she stopped.

As for Dave, he's smitten. Honestly, she's turned him into a puppy dog – albeit a not very cute one. Despite my reservations, they seem to be enjoying themselves. And for the first time, I *know* Dave's found a girlfriend to keep him on his toes.

Erin and Darren did indeed become a couple before they finished touring Europe. In fact, they were so engrossed in each other at the airport bar they almost missed the plane. Fortunately, the flight was late and they made it to Madrid, where Erin confessed that she'd harboured a crush on Darren since university and he admitted the feeling was mutual. The gang is currently in Thailand, where they've been for over a month, unable to drag themselves away from the beach.

Mum and Dad bunked in with Dominique and me for a month before finding a place to rent while they house-hunt. They were the longest four weeks and five days of my life. I know that isn't a nice thing to say, given that I nearly lost them, and I'd like to stress that I *adore* my parents. But they're significantly more adorable when not cluttering up my living room.

It didn't help that Mum resolved to 'focus on her career' soon after moving in and stop cleaning like a lunatic. I'd have been 100 per cent supportive of this, had she not been living in my flat at the time. Dad also turned over a new leaf and, since the fire, has bought Mum flowers once a week, without fail. He's also bought a home paint-balling kit, a pair of night vision goggles and – my neighbours' favourite – an electronic drum kit. Some things never change.

Henry and I made a big decision after we got together and packed in our jobs. It was risky, irresponsible and the best thing we've ever done.

The shock move (and it shocked *everyone*) came about after Henry was headhunted by an international charity to work in a clinic in Zanzibar. The charity is well-funded, backed by some seriously wealthy philanthropists, and is conducting world-leading research into malaria. Because of this, it was obvious Henry would make his mark here, but I've been surprised at how useful I can be too.

The only thing I thought I knew about is public relations – and there's not much call for that round here. So I've been teaching English to six- and seven-year-olds at a local school. My pupils are bright, full of life, endlessly mischievous and utterly adorable.

I'm in constant touch with the gang at home through Facebook, so I was relieved to discover that things are going well with Dominique's temporary new flatmate – Peter, the new IT guy from work. He's a lot tidier than me (which I'm sure is a relief), and she's apparently taken it upon herself to give him a bit of a makeover.

Life for Henry and me couldn't be more different from back home but we love it. We love our simple but beautiful fisherman's house, minutes from the Indian Ocean. We love playing football on the beach with the local kids, though my goalkeeping skills aren't up to much. We love the random acts of kindness we receive every day, from baskets of fruit delivered to our door, to the simple but lavish dinners our neighbours constantly treat us to.

We've only been here for three months, so it's early days and there's no doubt we'll return to the UK sooner or later. In the meantime, there's nowhere to buy Kurt Geiger shoes and my diet is a distant memory. But, for once, I'm doing something so amazing, I don't need to make it up.

POCKET
BOOKS

Jane Costello
The Nearly-Weds

What's the worst thing that could happen to a blushing bride? To somebody warm, loving, and fun – like Zoe Moore?

After Zoe is jilted by her fiancé Jason, she's unable to face the pitying looks of her friends and family. Fleeing to America, she is employed as a nanny by moody, difficult, but devastatingly sexy single dad Ryan.

Zoe quickly wins over his children, but their father is more of a challenge. Things aren't helped, of course, by her inadvertently displaying her knickers to his colleagues or nearly hospitalising him with a toy bow and arrow.
Thank God she's got her colourful circle of friends to keep her sane: fun-loving Trudie, hippy Amber and chilly, tight-lipped Felicity.

But over time Zoe and Ryan begin to understand each other, and their apparently ill-fated relationship takes on a new dimension. There's just one problem, as Zoe soon discovers: the past isn't always easy to escape, no matter how far away you go.

ISBN 978-1-84739-088-2
PRICE £6.99

POCKET
BOOKS

Jane Costello
Bridesmaids

Four weddings.
Three disgruntled ex-boyfriends.
Two very effective 'chicken fillet' boob-enhancers.
And one gorgeous man . . .

With less than an hour to go before her best friend is due to walk down the aisle, Evie is attempting to fulfill her most important role as bridesmaid: to deposit the bride at the start-line.

Although the odds appear stacked against her, she at least has her new 'chicken fillets' to boost her confidence. Until, that is, they are witnessed popping out of her dress by the dazzlingly handsome Jack.

Evie is 27, a sparkly, down-to-earth journalist who has never been in love and has started to think that she never will be. Small wonder, then, that the prospect of being bridesmaid at so many impending weddings fills her with utter trepidation.

When Jack starts becoming a regular fixture at the nuptials, however, things really start looking up.

Only between her discovery that he's dating the stunning, self-obsessed Valentina, and an unfortunate incident with a 10-inch vibrator, not everything goes quite as Evie might have hoped . . .

ISBN 978-1-84739-087-5
PRICE £6.99

POCKET
BOOKS

This book and other **Pocket Books** titles are available
from your local bookshop or can be ordered direct
from the publisher.

978-1-84739-088-2	The Nearly-Weds	£6.99
978-1-84739-087-5	Bridesmaids	£6.99

Free post and packing within the UK
Overseas customers please add £2 per paperback
Telephone Simon & Schuster Cash Sales at Bookpost
on 01624 677237 with your credit or debit card number
or send a cheque payable to Simon & Schuster Cash Sales to
PO Box 29, Douglas Isle of Man, IM99 1BQ
Fax: 01624 670923
Email: bookshop@enterprise.net
www.bookpost.co.uk

Please allow 14 days for delivery. Prices and availability
are subject to change without notice.